Moon Dark

AURIANO CURSE SERIES
BOOK I

PATRICIA BARLETTA

www.patriciabarletta.com

Published Internationally by Patricia Barletta
Boston, MA
Copyright © 2018 Patricia Barletta

Exclusive cover © 2018 mightyunicorn.ca
Interior design by Tamara Cribley www.deliberatepage.com

PRINT ISBN 978-1-7324769-1-2
EBOOK ISBN 978-1-7324769-0-5

Editor: Joanna D'Angelo

This is a work of fiction. Names, characters, places and incidents are either the
product of the author's imagination or are used fictitiously, and any resemblance
to any person or persons, living or dead, events or locales is entirely coincidental.

Coming Soon

Moon Shadow
AURIANO CURSE SERIES
BOOK 2

Acknowledgments

While this book is my creation and came from my imagination, many people helped nurse it along to this final state. My thanks go to my critique group: Wendy L., Linda, Wendy R., Marcia, and Margaret, who encourage me, help me clear up the confusion in my plots, urge me to add emotion to my characters, and generously fall in love with my heroes; to the faculty and my mentors at the Stonecoast MFA Creative Writing program, Nancy Holder and Jim Kelly, and all my fellow workshoppers, who saw this manuscript in its infancy and guided it into adolescence; to Steven Coppola for a fabulous cover design; and to Joanna D'Angelo, my intrepid editor. Most importantly, my love and gratitude go to my children who support me and cheer me on, and my grandchildren who never fail to bring me joy.

Ken, my love, this one's for you.

Chapter 1

Venice, 1797

Someone—some*thing*—was following her.

Lady Sabrina Barclay hurried between the close-set houses of the humble *sestiere* of Santa Croce. She caught movement from the corner of her eye—down that narrow alley to the right, another to the left, even across the slippery tile rooftops. The motion was too quick, too nimble for a human. A shuddery twinge tiptoed down her back.

The alley opened into the Campo di Rigali, ringed by the plain stucco walls and dark windows of the houses. She halted in the shadows. Her destination was the chapel across the tiny square. Anxiety gripped her as she thought about crossing the open space to get there.

She peered into the deepening twilight. Nothing moved in the dusk. A line of laundry strung between two windows hung motionless. She could see no one lurking in the shadows. Of course she was alone. Everyone was out on the canals or celebrating in the Piazza San Marco. This was the time of the spring *Carnevale*.

Sabrina picked up her satin skirts and hurried across the cobbles, past the carved stone well. At the chapel's wooden door, she glanced over her shoulder. As she did, her half mask caught on the hood of her black wool cape. She wanted to pull off the frippery of green velvet and yellow feathers, but instead, she pushed her hood back. No one went unmasked during *Carnevale*, and she had been told to remain anonymous. If anyone learned her identity or discovered the purpose of her errand, her son's safety, her entire world, would be in peril.

1

Something skittered in a dark corner. Her hand tightened on the door pull of the chapel, the decorative ridges digging into her palm. She peered into the shadows. Only a rat. She grimaced in distaste.

An olive oil lamp flickered on in one of the small windows. Its pale light cast the animal carvings on the stone well into relief and threw the well's shadow across the paving stones. She pressed back against the door and hoped no one could see her. With a click, shutters closed over the light. Stillness. Gloom. Yet she sensed eyes watching. Not from the windows. From somewhere else. She glanced up to the roofline of the houses but saw no silhouette against the dark, ethereal blue of the Venetian sky. An owl winged silently away into the night. The distant snap of a *Carnevale* firecracker startled her, prompting her to move.

Uneasy, she slipped into the chapel and leaned against the plain wood of the closed door. The sense of watching eyes receded, and she forced a breath into her lungs.

The chapel was small and dim and appeared to be deserted. The backless benches marched in formation to the sanctuary, where the carved white marble altar and the altarpiece behind it seemed to be waiting in holy repose. The sanctuary light glowed like a benevolent red eye. But she felt no sense of peace.

Gathering her courage, she pulled up her hood and hastened to a bench halfway down the aisle. Her soft dancing slippers made no noise on the marble floor. The muted swish of her satin skirt and petticoat sounded loud in the quiet. She had dressed as if she were attending a ball. Instead, she was here in this dark chapel on an errand that she had to complete.

The scent of incense and beeswax hung heavy in the air, still chilly despite the warming days of early summer. She shivered and hugged her woolen cloak closer as she sat. Pulling off her gloves, she folded her hands in her lap, bowed her head, and pretended to pray.

Her errand was to be conducted in secret. If someone followed her… No, she would not think of that. She must focus on what she had to do: Retrieve the note. Deliver it.

But first she needed to be sure she was alone. She listened for a footstep, a whisper, a breath—anything that would indicate another's presence in the shadows. She heard nothing.

Sabrina glanced around in the dim light. The chapel was tucked into a quiet, working-class corner of Venice. No songs of gondoliers, no greetings of acquaintances passing on the canals, no shouts of *Carnevale* merrymakers reached her here. The silence was unnerving, but it assured her of solitude. A bank of votive candles cast a soft glow to the left of the altar. Shadows flickered along the frescoed walls and made the saintly figures portrayed there appear to dance. The stained glass windows, which would have sparkled like jewels during the day, were dull and dark, foreboding. Instead of safety and refuge, the dim chapel held an air of menace.

She turned from those unsettling walls and windows to the altar and the crucifix hanging there as if she were beseeching the Almighty, but no prayer formed on her lips. She waited, forcing herself to be patient, her fingers curling into her skirt. She just wanted to be done with her errand. Furtively, she glanced left and right. She saw no one.

She ran her fingers beneath the rough wood of the bench until she touched a small piece of folded parchment affixed to the underside. Prying the small square from the wax, she rolled it into the palm of her hand. Her errand was almost complete. She released a silent breath.

About to bow her head again, she saw the candle flames jump from a draft. The hair on the back of her neck prickled. Someone else was here. She sensed a presence that curled icy tentacles around her heart. A presence that triggered a frail wraith of memory: Evil.

Run. The word exploded in her brain.

She gasped, snapped her head to the right. A shadowy black figure stood beside her. Before she could move or think, it lunged and shoved her off the bench. She cried out as she landed with a teeth-jarring thud on the marble floor. The breath in her lungs whooshed away.

A stiletto skimmed past her ear and thunked into the bench before her. It quivered in the wood, mere inches from her nose. The metal blade gleamed black and menacing. She scuttled back, only to be blocked by the bench behind her.

The dark figure had moved to the aisle and seemed to hover inches above the floor. It was a human-shaped shadow, but more — denser, blacker, canceling all light within its outline. Its eyes glowed like molten gold. They stared directly at her, and for a moment, she could not move. Could not breathe. Those eyes were frightening. Beautiful. Hypnotic.

She tried to suck in enough air to scream. Only a whimper emerged from her throat.

The figure pointed to the door. *Run. There is danger here.* The words growled loudly inside her head.

With a leap, the figure rose into the darkness of the vaulted ceiling and disappeared.

Sabrina gaped up and blinked. Shock froze her. She tried to gather her wits, blinked again. That shadow thing had pushed her aside, saving her from the deadly blade and certain death. Her blood went cold.

Run. The shadow's voice jabbed through her head again.

As she scrambled up, she realized she had dropped the message. Frantically, she searched for the little white square. She had to retrieve it. She shook out her skirts, skimmed her shaking fingers beneath the bench, over the cold marble of the floor.

Nothing. The note was gone.

Abandoning her search, she picked up her skirts and fled to the door. Behind her, she heard a strangled cry and a sickening thud, like a body hitting the floor from a great height. Then silence. The sense of evil snuffed out.

She escaped into the deep twilight of Venice. The sky still glowed cobalt, but the city was dark. The sliver of moon shed little light. Shadows were deeper, blacker. Sabrina rushed back across the square and entered an alley so narrow that the stucco walls of the houses were barely far enough apart to allow two people to pass each other. She checked over her shoulder. Someone could easily trap her. She hurried on, wanting only to reach her gondola.

In this modest part of the city there was little *Carnevale* celebration, so no one strolled the alleys, no old men sat outside to chat. She was alone. The solitary patter of her footsteps seemed much too loud as she hastened to the canal where her gondolier waited. The relative safety felt very far away.

Somehow, someone had learned of her errand. The errand that was to be performed in secret—to collect the note and deliver it to the uncle of her late husband. She had failed him. He would be displeased. Sabrina didn't want to imagine what form that displeasure might take, but she would do everything she could to protect her son from him, the man who allowed her to live beneath his roof.

And she would protect her son from the person — the evil — who had tried to kill her.

But someone — something — had saved her life. A shadow with eyes of molten gold who could speak to her inside her head. The creature intrigued her, awed her, captivated her. Frightened her with its strangeness.

Her stomach lurched. Fear from what was behind her overcame her apprehension of the scalding reprimand that lay ahead. Damning her voluminous skirt and petticoats, she raced the rest of the way to her gondola.

Sabrina arrived safely at the *casa* where she lived. Scrambling out of the gondola, she rushed into the house through the water gate, the canal-side entrance. She did not bother to call any of the servants to take her cloak as she hurried across the rough tiles of the *andron*, the undecorated water-level entry hall. She ran up the stairs to the study. The room, lit brightly by the center wrought iron chandelier, seemed empty. She circled around the massive gum wood desk and went directly to the small table which held several decanters and glasses. Her hand trembled as she poured herself two fingers of brandy. She gulped it down, but even its burn did not stop her shivers. She turned to the fire and its warmth.

"Sabrina."

She jumped. Harold Dunfield, the uncle of her late husband, stared at her in shock from his chair before the blaze. His cool blue eyes pinned her. He was dressed to go out for an evening's entertainment, impeccable in his burgundy velvet coat and yellow silk waistcoat, his silvery hair perfectly tied back with a black satin ribbon. He had obviously been waiting for her. She had not seen him sitting there.

"What is the meaning of this?" he demanded, indicating the empty glass in her hand.

Guiltily, she placed the glass on the mantle. "Someone just tried to kill me." She choked out the words.

His brow furrowed, but he said nothing.

"You never warned me my life could be in danger." Her voice shook, and she took a breath to steady herself.

"Really, Sabrina, I'm sure you are being overly dramatic." Dunfield waved away her reproach.

Of course he would show no sympathy for her ordeal.

"A stiletto missed me by inches," she said.

"You must have been mistaken for someone else. There's no reason why anyone should wish you dead. I'm only selling artwork." Dunfield took a casual sip of his own brandy.

Frustration at his callous reaction to her fright brought tears to her eyes. She blinked them away and tried to make him see the problem—again. "They are Italian masterpieces, and you are selling them to our *English* king. If the Venetians discover their art is leaving the city—"

"They won't." His gaze sharpened. "Did you get the message?"

Sabrina swallowed. She did not want to confess what had occurred in the chapel. She would never reveal to this man that a shadow had saved her life. He would think she had gone mad. Perhaps she had, and the apparition in the chapel had merely been a hallucination. Except she still felt the bruise where she had landed on the hard marble floor. How could she explain something she did not understand herself?

"I lost it." Her admission came out small and quiet.

Anger turned his eyes to ice. "So you thought to cover up your incompetence with some fantasy about an attempt on your life?"

"No! I—"

"Stop." Dunfield gave her a hard stare. "If you cannot perform a simple chore for me, like retrieving a message, then you are of little use. I am disinclined to support a destitute widow with a son if you are unable to give me some recompense."

Her chest muscles constricted, and she had to force air into her lungs. She and Evan had no place else to go. This man, sitting so comfortably before the fire, had been her only recourse when she discovered her late husband had run his estate into huge debt. She had asked — no, begged — Dunfield to take them in. He had readily agreed. So she had moved from England to settle in Venice, where Dunfield had gained some prominence in the English community. When she arrived, she discovered he had other plans for her — delivering his messages to the representative of the English king in return for a roof over their heads. Now, she was trapped in a situation of her own design.

She caught a motion at the window. A pair of molten golden eyes appeared to float in the dark night sky. She stiffened her knees so she wouldn't collapse into a boneless puddle. Dunfield must not learn of her shadowy rescuer. She sidled a tiny step away from the window to keep his attention.

Swallowing her pride, she said, "I am also cataloging your art collection, Uncle. That should count for something."

"Yes, yes." He dismissed her argument with another wave of his hand.

"I'll go back to the chapel now to try to find the note," she said, dreading a return to the place. She cast another glance at the window. Those golden eyes had disappeared.

"It's gone," Dunfield said. "Don't bother." Thoughtfully, he tapped his fingers on the arm of the chair.

Relief flowed through her, but she suspected he was planning some equally odious task for her.

"Tomorrow," he said, "you will take Evan on an outing to the Piazza San Marco, and leave the usual signal that indicates that I must communicate with King George's representative."

Sabrina's insides clenched. Not only would she once again have to play Dunfield's secret messenger, this time he was placing her son in danger. She knew no argument would change his mind.

His gaze pierced her. "The French army is sitting on the border of the Veneto. They're busy with Austria at the moment, but if they turn their attention to Venice, they'll plunder my collection. I need to get it out of the city before then."

Sabrina wondered what the French would do to an English woman with a young son. The thought gave her chills.

"Do not bungle this errand, Sabrina."

Bowing her head, she chafed at his reprimand.

Dunfield abruptly changed the subject. "Is your costume ready for our masquerade ball?"

"Yes, it's ready." Resignation made her sigh. She hated masquerade balls. At the last one, she had spent the evening trying to evade an obnoxious little man who was convinced she was his paramour.

"You know we will be entertaining all of the noble families of Venice. And the Prince of Auriano will be attending." A smug note crept into Dunfield's voice.

"Yes, I know." She clenched her teeth so she wouldn't say anything inadvisable. Getting Auriano to attend the ball was a social coup, but that was not why Dunfield was reminding her. He was putting yet another possible suitor in her path, one more man who would reject her because she was too independent, or too cold, or too intelligent, or too outspoken, or too English. The rejections were embarrassing, despite her relief. When—if—she married again, it would be to someone of her own choosing, someone who would have a care for her, but also for her son.

"He is wealthy and powerful, Sabrina. I wish you to be at your most charming." Dunfield's cool words belied the underlying threat. If she did not perform as he expected, he would be furious.

She tried to find some excuse to avoid the prince. "He is a rogue and a gambler."

Dunfield's blue gaze impaled her. "Auriano wields a great deal of influence. I could use the connection."

That was his true reason for dangling Auriano before her. If she caught the prince, Dunfield would be accepted everywhere in Venetian society, and would not be merely tolerated as an amusing Englishman. The House of Auriano was very old and still possessed their ancestral *castello* in the north. The family was allowed to use the title of "Prince" when no other family in Venice could. None of this swayed Sabrina.

She tried another argument. "He is a rake, Uncle. He has a new lover every week. I refuse to expose Evan to such scandal."

A disapproving frown creased Dunfield's brow. "Your son lives in Venice now, not England. You can't shelter him forever. If you are fortunate enough to catch Auriano's eye, he will set you up in your own rooms."

Sabrina gasped. "Are you saying that I should become his mistress?"

"I am saying to do whatever it takes to get him interested," he snapped. "You may be able to lead him to the altar."

"I've heard tales that he's had men murdered." Her fist clenched in rebellion.

He brushed aside her objection. "What powerful man in Venice is not connected with such idle talk?"

"His family is rumored to be cursed." An absurd argument, but she would try anything to dissuade Dunfield.

He laughed coldly. "Really, Sabrina. The family has more gold than the Vatican. Do you call that being cursed?"

"I'm not looking for a husband, Uncle," she said, and desperately used her last excuse. "I'm still grieving over the death of Richard." Her words were well rehearsed, often repeated.

Dunfield frowned. "Two years is long enough to be in mourning. Your son needs a father. You need a husband. I cannot keep support-ing you and Evan. His tutor is expensive and the boy should be sent to school in England."

"But the sale of the art to King George—"

"—is not enough to sustain all of us forever. When I agreed to take you and Evan into my home, I did not foresee your spending the rest of your life under my roof."

Neither did she, but she refrained from commenting. She wanted more for Evan than being the poor relation of this man. Her husband had been merely a knight, and so her son would never inherit a title. That did not matter. She wanted Evan to grow into a kind, honest person who could hold his head up with self-respect. But for now, living with Dunfield was her only option.

His expression softened. "You should not go through life alone, Sabrina. You need to find a mate, someone to protect you."

Nodding obediently, Sabrina endured another lecture on her duties as a widow with a child to raise. She silently berated herself again for the naiveté that brought her under this man's roof. Dunfield's concern for her was only another form of manipulation. She was not anxious to wed again, despite having to live with this overbearing, hard-hearted man. Although she had been fond of her late husband, he had given more attention to his artifacts and moldy manuscripts than he had to her. With his sudden death, she felt a guilty sense of relief and freedom in taking charge of her life. Somehow, she would keep that freedom and make her own decisions. She just had to figure out how to do that and take care of her son as well.

Evan would be sleeping now, put to bed by his nurse. Sabrina wanted to go to him, check to be sure he was safe. But she could not escape until Dunfield dismissed her. He took great delight in lecturing her. She reminded herself again that she was under his control in order to keep Evan secure, but the situation still chafed.

As Dunfield droned on about the advantages to a connection with Auriano, she wandered closer to the window. Perhaps she could catch another glimpse of that shadow creature. Staring out into the night, she saw nothing unusual. The breeze stirred the shadows, but no eerie figure appeared. She wondered where it had come from.

Shivering, she rubbed her arms as she gazed down to the canal. She thought she saw something move. No, nothing was there. She was seeing specters where none existed.

Abruptly, the shadow creature appeared before her, just beyond the glass. It balanced lightly on the narrow balustrade that guarded the long window. Sabrina swallowed a gasp and blinked. She shifted to block Dunfield's view. He would call the servants, rouse the authorities to chase it down. It had saved her. She would protect it.

Blacker than the black night, its outline was human. Male. *Naked.* Perfectly proportioned. Its eyes glowed golden, and its gaze swept her from head to toe.

She felt its scrutiny as if it were palpable. The tiny hairs on her arms lifted. A shiver ran through her. She felt a bit faint. Gripping the window frame to keep herself upright, she stared.

Then, just as quickly as it appeared, the figure was gone, stepping back into the night air, dissolving once more into the dark.

"Sabrina, are you listening?" Dunfield's irritated voice dragged her attention back into the room.

Chapter 2

Invisible, just one more shadow among the shadows of night, Sandro crouched on the rooftop high above the quiet, narrow canal. Waiting, watching, he focused on the *casa* across the water, where the woman from the chapel lived. He had retreated to this spot after coming face to face with her through the window. She captivated him. Her face, a pale oval, was framed by dark curls. Heavy lashes shaded her light gray eyes, and delicate dark brows flared above them. Her lips were full and lush.

He needed to touch her. Desperately. That brush against her in the chapel could not have been illusion. Even now, he imagined he could feel her. But that could not be. Not now, not when he was Shadow.

He stared down at his shadowy hand and curled his fingers into his palm. He felt nothing, no pressure of muscle, no sense of skin against skin. But he had been able to touch this woman. More than that, he had been able to sense the power within her, hidden and unused. He wanted to know who — what — this woman was. He needed to discover if he truly could *feel* her.

Whenever he turned to Shadow, the sense of touch was denied him, along with smell and taste. The deprivation wore him down, turned to madness when he craved those senses as he entered the Hunger, transitioning back to flesh and bone. He needed to know if that fleeting sensation of skin against skin was more than his imagination.

Sandro studied the *casa*. The house was moderate in size, but comfortable, its stone façade decorated by tall windows and small balconies. With a bit of snooping, he had learned it belonged to that Englishman, Dunfield, who collected artwork and made a moderate income as a merchant. Now, it seemed, from the bit of parchment he had retrieved from the floor of the chapel, the man was trying to sell a portion of his art collection and was using the woman as his messenger.

Although the Inquisitors, who dealt with threats to state security, might be interested, Sandro had no interest in the clandestine negotiations of a foreigner. But the woman who lived under the man's roof... Ah, *si*.

With the darkness of night surrounding the *casa*, the lit rooms and their inhabitants were visible. He watched her listen to the Englishman. Her head was bowed in acquiescence, but her posture suggested resistance. When she exited the room, he could see her clearly. Her shoulders were stiff; her back was straight; her head was held high. Evidently, her relationship with Dunfield was less than placid. *Bene*.

Slowly, the *casa* went dark as lights were extinguished and the occupants went to bed. He had found the bedchamber where the woman slept. It faced the canal, and a small balcony, a *pergola*, hung suspended three stories above the water. Perfect.

Soon, she would be abed and asleep. He would wait.

Then he would know.

Was this woman his redemption or his destruction?

His impatience gnawed at him.

She was asleep when Sandro slipped into her room. With the moon almost dark, hardly any light came through the window, but the lack of light never hindered his ability to see. The embers on the hearth still glowed and cast a faint sheen on her form beneath the covers. He moved silently to the bedside and watched the rise and fall of her chest as she slept. Her lashes lay in a silky dark crescent on her creamy cheek. Raven tendrils curled at her temple where they had escaped in her sleep. She was exquisite.

He remained unmoving, preparing himself for what he was about to do. Apprehensive that what he sensed in the chapel was his imagination, confused if it was real, he merely observed her. Her dark hair, twined into a single braid, lay across her shoulder. Her hand lay palm up beside her head on the pillow. Desperation brought him here, to touch her, to sense her beneath his fingers.

Hesitantly, he reached out and stroked his fingers across her palm. His skin came alive at the touch. In shock, he jerked back, folding his fingers into a fist. He could feel her! He had *not* imagined it.

He reached out again, skimmed his fingers down her arm. Able to feel her soft skin, he closed his eyes in a rush of sensation. How was it possible that he could feel this woman?

Her quiet breath came and went between parted lips. Tantalized, he brushed them and marked their outline. He needed to feel more. His body cried out for more. He had never before craved anything while Shadow. That came later, during the Hunger. But now, all he wanted was to touch this woman.

Discarding common sense and decorum, he trailed his fingers down her neck, around her shoulder, splayed them across her delicate collarbone. Her skin was like silk. He felt a strange, pleasant tingle at the contact. She shifted beneath his fingers and breathed a gentle moan.

He jerked back in surprise. His fingers closed into a fist he held tight against his chest. He still could not feel his own skin. But he had felt her. And *she* had felt *him*.

He watched her as he thought that over. She was not awake and most likely believed she was dreaming. He decided to make her dream memorable. Playfully, he traced his fingers around the neckline of her nightdress. He wondered how long he would have before she realized she was not dreaming, opened her eyes, saw him, and screamed. Testing, he tickled the valley between her breasts, just visible above her neckline.

Her eyes flew open and she gasped. She opened her mouth to shriek.

Do not scream, he said quickly, silently, as he pulled his hand away.

She froze. Shock registered in her eyes.

Don't be afraid. I won't hurt you, he told her. He held up his empty hand to show her, then dropped it to his side. *Do not scream. Please.*

She released her breath in a huff. Scrambling back, she grasped the covers like a shield, as if they would provide protection. Her eyes were wide, frightened. "Why shouldn't I scream?" she demanded.

Because I asked you not to.

"And if I refuse to comply?"

I will be gone before anyone arrives to help you, and you will look foolish trying to explain my presence.

"Get out."

Amused at her bravado at the same time he was captivated, he said, *You are beautiful.*

He watched a soft blush color her cheeks at his compliment, then disbelief and affront etched itself as a thin line between her brows.

Reaching out to erase that line, he curbed his impulse and let his hand drop. His action frightened her, and he saw her preparing again to cry out to alert the household. Without thinking, he placed his hand across her mouth. He was instantly aware of the feel of her. Her eyes widened, and she choked off her cry. Amazed at her reaction, he wondered what she felt when he touched her.

I will not hurt you, he repeated. *Do you believe me?*

She hesitated a moment, then nodded.

Will you scream if I remove my hand?

Speculatively, she gazed at him. She shook her head. When he released her, she inched farther back against the pillows. "What are you?"

What do I look like? he countered.

"A shadow. A man. A man-shadow."

Si.

Confusion, then fear flickered through her eyes. "What happened to you?"

That's a very long story, he answered wryly, *and one that would bring you nightmares.*

She gave a delicate shiver, then tried to cover it by drawing up her knees. "I can hear you in my head," she said. "How can you do that?"

I've had many years of practice.

Frowning, she said, "Why are you here? What do you want?"

The answer to those questions was easy. *You.*

"You can't have me." She swiped up the candlestick at her bedside and held it like a cudgel.

Chuckling, enjoying the exchange, he said, *Ah, a passionate woman. I wanted to touch you.*

The fingers of her free hand curled into the covers as she yanked them higher. That candlestick waved in threat. "No one touches me unless I allow it, and I'm not giving you permission."

Passionate, but unloved, he sighed in mock regret.

Even in the dark, he could see the flush of anger in her cheeks. "How dare you! You know nothing about me. Get out!"

Reluctant to leave, nonetheless, he backed away. *I know enough,* he flung at her as he moved to the door leading to the *pergola* that looked over the canal.

"Wait," she said, just before he slipped out.

He stopped, curious about what made her change her mind.

"You saved me in the chapel," she said, as she lowered the candlestick.

Si.

"Thank you."

Non c'é di che. He dipped his head in a bow, entertained by the contrast between her courtesy and the defense of her virtue.

"But that doesn't give you the right to touch me without my permission." Her chin rose defiantly.

When will you give me permission? he teased.

Drawing herself up and clutching the bedclothes closer and higher, she declared, "Never."

He laughed. *Never is a very long time. Are you sure you can deny yourself that long?*

Even from where he stood, he saw her eyes snap. She whipped the candlestick at him. "Get out!"

With another laugh, he dodged the missile easily. As he saluted her with an elegant bow, he decided to give her something to ponder. *You are mine,* he whispered, and allowed his words to caress her mind. Then he slipped out the door and blended into the other shadows of the night.

Sabrina felt as if his hand had brushed softly through her hair. The sensation arrowed down through her body to end in a throb deep in her center. She gasped, swallowed, and reminded herself to breathe. She stared at the door to the *pergola*, closed now as if he had never gone through. How had he disappeared so quickly? Her heart raced. Her breathing came fast and shallow. She was furious at that thing toying with her. She was frightened at finding it hovering beside her bed. She was aroused by its delicate touch.

How could that be?

It—he—was a mass of darkness punctuated by those molten eyes. He was perfectly formed, like the negative of Michelangelo's statue of David. She had been able to see the faint definition of muscle and features. Not human, and yet…

His touch was charged with something beyond normal. She felt an odd tingle wherever his fingers had traced. Even now, long enough for the sensation to have faded, she imagined if she looked in the mirror, she would see a sparkling trail where he had touched her. And everywhere he touched glowed with warmth.

Her body wanted more. Her mind told her she was crazy. His last words created heat that flowed through her. Those words echoed over and over in her head.

You are mine.

Flopping back onto her pillow, she squeezed her eyes shut. She had been dreaming. Her mind was playing tricks on her. She'd had a terrifying experience earlier in the evening. With the same shadow. Who had saved her life.

But she knew. It had been no dream.

Chapter 3

Alessandro Mateo Baldassare d'Este, Prince of Auriano, entered his dim bedchamber. The flames on the hearth lit the immediate part of the room with an orange glow, but the rest of the large room dissolved into darkness. He bypassed the small tables, the padded chairs near the fire, the wide bed on its low platform, and headed toward the long dark windows. Across the canals, in another *sestiere* of the city, lay the woman who had aroused his sense of touch. Staring into the night, he pondered this new twist on the curse.

"I see you've been out keeping the city safe."

Alessandro spun toward the voice that came from one of the chairs before the hearth. His twin. Antonio had waited up for him—again. Annoyance rippled through him. Then he remembered why his brother kept watch. The new moon would be dark within twenty-four hours, and Alessandro would begin to transform back to flesh and bone. After that came the Hunger until a sliver of moon shone once again in the sky. And then his twin, Antonio, would become Shadow, his turn in their version of hell, until the moon grew to full when the cycle would start all over They needed to retreat to the Canal of Shadows where they hid during the transformation. But that could wait an hour or two. He wanted to tell his brother about his discovery. Moving to the chair opposite his twin, Alessandro settled himself before replying.

Really, Tonio, Alessandro said silently. *Don't you have better things to do than hover over me like a nervous nonna?*

Antonio grinned, showing his dimple, and continued the silent conversation. *I won tonight playing Basetto, made a small fortune at the game actually, and I made sure that the infamous Prince Alessandro kept his tarnished reputation. You met with a young lady determined to cheat on her possessive husband.*

Shaking his head in dismay, Alessandro said, *One of these days, Tonio, you'll find yourself with a blade in your back and floating face down in a canal.*

Tonio gave a bitter laugh and tipped his head, his gold-streaked chestnut hair catching the light from the fire. *Not me. You. Remember, it's your name I use. No one even knows I exist.* He looked away, suddenly serious. *I can't keep up this charade, Sandro. I'm sick to death of pretending to be you. You have no idea...* His unspoken words revealed his misery.

Sympathy, regret, and anxiety churned through Alessandro. He wanted to alleviate his brother's suffering, but they were desperate to break the curse. He could find no other options. *You can't give up. We agreed this was the only way to find the Sphere of Astarte.*

Antonio's eyes pinned him. *I want to be me. I don't know who I am anymore. Part of the month, I'm you, and then the rest I'm only Shadow.* He gave a resentful shrug. *I might as well not exist.*

Alessandro sucked in a breath at the pain in his brother's words. *Don't say that. You're my brother. We are family.*

With a sigh of frustration, Antonio let his head fall back against his chair. *We've been lucky so far that no one has discovered our game, but how long before one of us slips, or before a servant talks?*

Alessandro heard the undercurrent of resentment and truth in his twin's words. They had been playing this game for years since they came to Venice permanently after the fire in Auriano. Having hinted that only one twin survived, they thought the ruse would cover their terrible curse, and might allow them, when each in turn became Shadow, to search out clues to the location of the pieces of the magical Sphere of Astarte. So far, the deception had accomplished nothing. Except tonight, Alessandro had made a discovery that might end their agony.

His gaze strayed to the window, and his thoughts snagged on the woman he had been able to feel. She could be the key. The vision of her, sleep disheveled and adorable, rose up in his head.

Tonio tossed a letter onto the table beside Alessandro and recaptured his attention. *From our seneschal,* his brother said. *He reports that the east wall of the keep has crumbled again — the third time this year. Half the goats have given birth to dead kids. Much of the seed that has been sown is not germinating, and many of the fields are barren. And the grapevines…* His words trailed off in distress.

The information about their ancestral holding in Auriano stabbed through Alessandro, compounding the pain of Antonio's frustration and torment. The curse, which had been passed through many generations, affected more than his immediate family. It also touched the land and its people.

But they could not give up yet, not with the discovery Alessandro had just made. *I followed a young English woman to a small chapel in Santa Croce,* he said.

Antonio rolled his eyes. *Let me guess. She was beautiful and you could not resist, si?*

Of course. But she was in danger.

Exasperated, Antonio shook his head. *So you saved the young lady.*

What else could I do? Alessandro shrugged fatalistically.

You will be the one to get yourself killed one of these days, Sandro. Young English women should know better than to wander about alone. Tonio took a sip of wine.

Alessandro waited until his brother swallowed before he dropped his bombshell about Nulkana, the evil sorceress who had placed the curse on their family all those years ago. He watched his brother place his glass on the small table beside him, then said, *The bitch sent one of her slaves to kill the woman.*

Antonio choked and coughed. *Nulkana wanted to assassinate her?* he exclaimed when he caught his breath. *Why? Who is this woman?*

She is under the protection of the Englishman, Dunfield. She is acting as a messenger for him. He held out his shadowy hand and floated the bit of white parchment he had collected from the floor of the chapel to his brother.

Tonio plucked it out of the air and read it. *So? The Englishman is selling his art collection. What does this have to do with us?*

The woman has come in contact with a piece of the Sphere of Astarte.

Antonio's brows drew together. *How do you know she has touched a piece of the Sphere?* Sudden understanding and astonishment made him shoot to his feet and speak aloud. "You have touched this woman?"

Si.

"How were you able... ?"

I don't know.

"You could *feel* her?"

Si. Alessandro grinned, enjoying his brother's astonishment.

She must be quite powerful, Antonio surmised.

Alessandro shrugged nonchalantly. He was not about to reveal how much the feel of this woman affected him. *She is quite enchanting.*

You cannot use her like one of your other women, Sandro. Tonio paced. *This Englishman, Dunfield, has many influential connections. If this woman is under his care —*

— he'll be able to do nothing, Sandro finished. *Do you think anyone would take the side of an Englishman over that of the Prince of Auriano? The woman will be mine, and I'll learn her secret. If she knows where the piece of the Sphere of Astarte is, then I will learn that, as well.*

Are we so close then? Antonio's question was charged with hope.

Si.

A sharp pain in Alessandro's arm made him gasp and clap his hand over the spot. He was turning back to flesh and bone — with all the sensations that came rushing back with it.

Antonio grabbed a towel on the washstand next to the door and pressed it against his brother's arm, slowly turning to solid flesh. "You're bleeding, Sandro."

Alessandro hissed in agony. *I think the assassin nicked me in his attempt to get the woman. Call Gasparo.*

"Going soft?" Antonio taunted. "The wound will be healed by morning."

Alessandro shook his head. One benefit of the curse was their ability to heal quickly, but something was different about this wound. *This scratch hurts more than it should,* he said.

"Poison?" Tonio asked as he rang for Gasparo.

Magic. Sandro clenched his jaw against the knives of pain shooting through his muscle.

"Are you sure the assassin wasn't aiming for you?" Tonio's brow creased in concern.

Able now to speak aloud, Alessandro said, "No, the knife was meant for the woman." He gasped a breath. "The Hunger is worse this time."

"And it's several hours early," Antonio observed.

Alessandro's gaze cut to the windows where no hint of dawn appeared, but very faint moonlight rimmed one side of their frames. The moon had not yet gone dark. He should not be transforming yet. Unable to respond as pain whistled through him, he fought to remain in control of his wits and hoped Gasparo would come soon.

As if conjured, Gasparo appeared at the doorway in his night-shirt and soft woolen robe. His dark hair, heavily salted with gray, had been hastily smoothed. "*Sior* Sandro?" Even roused from sleep, the middle-aged man was bright-eyed and vigorous. He had been with them their whole lives. He was one of their gondoliers, but much more. He was their protector, their pseudo-father. Their Guide.

Alessandro forced his voice to be steady. "Ah, Gasparo, come sew me up. It seems I've cut myself."

Gasparo moved to Alessandro's side and gently peeled away the towel against his arm. The wound bled profusely, and its edges had a greenish tinge. "A touch of magic. It can be fixed."

Alessandro shook from the excruciating pain in his arm. The magic would have been painful all on its own, but the Hunger began to consume him and heightened all his senses. Soon, beyond control, he would crave an orgy to fulfill every appetite until he was sated.

Gasparo studied him. "The Hunger is almost upon you, *si*?" he said, as he gathered what he needed to medicate, sew, and bandage Alessandro's arm. "It is bad this time, I think."

"Not so bad," Alessandro ground out, then gritted his teeth as his Guide murmured a charm, applied a balm to the wound, then sewed it.

"Hmph. This is dangerous. A magical knife and the Hunger coming early." Gasparo nodded. "You are getting close to your prize."

Gasparo's insight was as sharp as the needle he used to sew the wound. Alessandro winced and distracted himself by exchanging a glance with his brother. "Perhaps," he murmured.

Antonio planted himself in front of his twin. "Sandro, what are you thinking?"

Alessandro ignored him as the Hunger grew stronger, as he gained more of his body, as his senses began to awaken and demand fulfillment. "Gasparo," he ground out. "The woman in the care of the Englishman, Dunfield. I want her. Bring her to me."

Gasparo's hands stilled in the middle of bandaging his master's arm. "I think, *Sior* Sandro, you are mistaken, and it is not this woman you want. I will bring you others, those who are willing."

"I want *her*, Gasparo." Completely flesh and bone now, the pain in his arm forgotten, Alessandro grabbed his servant by the shirt. "Bring her to me." He could feel the Hunger overcoming him, his control slipping away, the fiend taking over. Jumping from his seat, he dragged Gasparo up with him. "Bring her to me," he growled, showing his teeth.

"Sandro, let him go," Antonio said. "He can't kidnap this woman."

With wild eyes, Alessandro turned on his brother and flung Gasparo away. "I want the English woman. I want her now!"

Antonio gazed at his twin in sympathy. During the Hunger, there was only one way to reason with him. Antonio heaved a sigh. Making a fist, he landed it squarely on his brother's jaw. The blow rocked Alessandro. By the time he hit the floor, he was unconscious.

Antonio and Gasparo lifted the senseless man between them and placed him on the bed. Antonio stared down at his twin as he massaged his sore knuckles. "I've never seen him this bad so early in the Hunger. He's never been so crazed about a specific woman." He turned to his Guide. "Take him to the Canal of Shadows, Gasparo," he said. "Care for him. Get him what he needs. I will see to the English woman. If my brother behaves, perhaps I will convince her to visit him."

Gasparo grunted and shook his head. "Kidnapping this English woman is wrong, *Sior* Tonio."

"I know," Antonio answered on another sigh. "But he's never hurt a woman yet. In fact, they beg to return."

"This is not the way to break the curse, taking this woman by force." Gasparo's tone was funereal.

"If this woman holds the secret to a piece of the Sphere of Astarte, then I would go through Dante's Inferno to bring her to Alessandro," Antonio said coldly.

"The Englishman has much influence," Gasparo argued.

"*Cristo!* You know that if Sandro does not get what he craves during the Hunger, he could remain Shadow for the rest of his life.

I will pay off the Englishman if necessary, and I will worry about the Council of Ten and their Inquisitors and spies. The advisors to the Doge are like a bunch of nervous old women. Do what you are told." Seeing Gasparo's affronted gaze, Antonio added, "Please." Then he turned on his heel, strode out the door, and hoped what he planned to do would not damn him to a lower level of Hell than the one he was already in.

Chapter 4

The next night, when Sabrina stepped into her dark bedchamber, the door closed abruptly behind her. She swung around with a cry. A calloused hand clamped over her mouth and a man's arm closed around her waist.

Panicked, she fought and dug her elbow into the man's ribs. He grunted and tightened his hold. She brought her heel down on his foot. He hissed in pain but held on. She could not get free.

"Stop." The single word snapped out from the far corner of the room.

Sabrina startled into stillness. The light of a candle flared, and another man stepped forward. He was tall with broad shoulders and wore the traditional *bautta* of *Carnevale*, a costume of black cloak with hood, tricorn hat, and full white mask. He placed the candle on a nearby table, then turned back to her. In the dancing candlelight, the white mask against the dark clothing made his face appear to float like some spectral apparition.

She struggled in another useless attempt to escape.

"Stop," the costumed man repeated, this time quietly, gently.

He stepped closer and rested the tip of a rapier against the hollow of Sabrina's throat. The chilly metal point burned like ice against her skin. One small move on her part would send the lethal tip plunging through her. One mistake on his side would do the same.

Sabrina froze, afraid to breathe.

"Please, *Donna* Barclay, do not make this difficult," he said. "I do not wish to hurt you, nor do I wish to have to hurt your servant." He gestured to the opposite corner of the room. Cora, her maid, was gripped tightly by a third hooded man, who held a stiletto pointed at her heart. "You will be safe as long as you cooperate."

Sabrina trembled. The threat of that rapier contradicted his mild words. She dared not resist. And Evan was only a few doors away. She could not allow these men to discover him, for she had no idea what their intentions were. She gave a short nod to indicate her submission.

The speaker flicked his wrist. The hand covering her mouth dropped away, and it was replaced with a silk gag. Her wrists were tied together behind her back with velvet rope, then her ankles. Her captor's hands were respectful, gentle, in opposition to the manner he had held her.

The man in the *bautta* spoke again as he lowered the blade from her throat. "My apologies, *Donna* Barclay, for inconveniencing you in this way."

Sabrina's temper flared. An invasion of her bedchamber and a threatening rapier was more than mere inconvenience, and so was being bound and having her maid terrorized, not to mention the possible danger to Evan. Along with a previous attempt on her life, strangers had entered her bedchamber two nights in a row, although each intrusion had been quite different. She wondered why danger decided to stalk her now.

She had no time to contemplate the answer, for the man behind her tied a silken scarf across her eyes. She felt her cloak placed about her shoulders and the hood pulled over her head. Then one of the men lifted her and carried her across the room. When the door leading to the balcony was opened, the chill nighttime air made her shiver. Behind her, Cora struggled and whimpered.

Sabrina heard the scrape of a boot and the rustle of clothing, the thud of someone landing in a boat below the balcony, the slosh of the canal water against the wall of the *casa*. A short, low command came to her ears, and then the man carrying her let go. She fell. Terror wrenched a cry from her throat, the sound muffled by the gag.

Strong arms caught her, and the man in the mask murmured, "I have you." His grip was steady, even as he swayed with the rocking boat beneath his feet. She was surprised he bothered to reassure her.

He set her down in the bottom of the boat. She heard Cora receiving the same treatment and felt Cora laid next to her. She wriggled her fingers, touching Cora's hand. Her maid gripped her fingers in a terrified vise. Cora's presence confused her, for she could not understand why these men would bother to kidnap her maid. The boat was pushed away from the side of the building, and she felt the rhythmic sway of the gondola propelled through the water.

As they slid through the canals, Sabrina heard *Carnevale* revelers in the distance, and the staccato sound of firecrackers. Dismay ran through her. No one would take notice of a gondola of masked, hooded men who appeared to be joining the celebration. No one would know she had been taken until it was too late, until she had been murdered. Evan would be left alone with only Dunfield to raise him. She was not about to let that happen. Somehow she would escape and get back to him.

Determined despite her trembling, she tried to wriggle out of her bindings, but they were tight around her wrists and ankles. The edge of a rapier tapped on her arm.

"Struggling will do no good, *Ma Donna*," she heard the leader say. "You will only hurt yourself. Please behave."

Sabrina gritted her teeth in frustration, but the man's quiet words confounded her. If they did not want her hurt, perhaps they had no intention to kill her, and had nothing to do with the attack in the chapel the night before, which had been much more direct and lethal. These men did not seem to be violent, only resolved and relentless in their purpose. In fact, they had been respectful, nearly gentle. The contradictions bewildered her.

They traveled for many minutes in silence before Sabrina heard the side of the gondola scrape along steps at the edge of the canal. She was picked up, transferred to another pair of arms, and carried inside a building. Up a set of stairs, sideways through a doorway, she was finally set on her feet. The cloak was pulled from her shoulders. Her hands and feet were untied. The blindfold and gag were removed. Blinking and rubbing her wrists to restore circulation, she saw she was alone with the man in the *bautta*. She backed away a step and gasped a breath.

"Where is my maid?" she demanded. "If you have hurt her — "

"I have not," the costumed man interrupted impatiently.

Sabrina opened her mouth to call for Cora, but her kidnapper said, "You may call for her, but she will not hear you. You may scream if you wish, *Ma Donna*, but no one here will come to your aid, and no one outside these walls will hear you." He motioned to a table near the fire. "There is food and drink for your refreshment. Please, make yourself comfortable." He swept her an elegant bow, then turned and left, taking her cloak and all the scarves and ropes that bound her. The lock snicked in the door.

Sabrina was stunned. The bow had been the act of a gentleman, performed as if it were second nature. He had been polite, had provided refreshments. Who were these kidnappers? What could they possibly want with her? What had they done with Cora? What treachery were they plotting? Her only relief came from the knowledge that Evan was still safely asleep in his own bed.

Sabrina stood in the dim chamber, clasped her hands together to keep them from shaking, and studied her surroundings. Her screams might not be heard by anyone, but she would try to escape. She would find Cora and then run for freedom.

The room was well appointed and comfortable, with several chairs upholstered in green silk, and a thick Persian carpet of intricate design cushioning her feet. A large, elaborately carved bed with sumptuous linens of yellow and gold silk dominated one end of the space. She turned away from that. Dark green brocade covered the walls. Yet, there were no paintings on the walls, no wall hangings that might have made the space personal. Except for the tray of wine, cheese, olives, and bread, all the small tables were bare. The only light came from a fire crackling on the hearth, which helped dispel the damp chill, and a single candle flickering on the mantle. More shadows than light inhabited the room.

The large bed suggested things she did not wish to explore, and the impersonal atmosphere of the room, despite its comfort, made her uneasy. Glancing around, she felt something was not quite right about the space. At first, she could not decide what it was. And then she realized that any plans she might form for escape would be stillborn.

The single door had been locked from the outside.

And the room had no windows.

Alessandro prowled the salon like a caged animal. The worst of the Hunger had passed. He had slaked his appetites, but what he had done was a foggy blur of memory. Later would come a vague sense of guilt and self-disgust. But not yet. Now, there was no guilt, no self-disgust, only need.

He had bathed, but the doeskin breeches and soft boots he wore constricted. His light lawn shirt was open halfway down his chest so he would not feel strangled. He felt nearly human, rational. But the fiend that lived in him during the Hunger still craved one more thing — the English woman.

Want, need.

Touch.

His blood foamed. His brain boiled with desire for her, the feel of her skin beneath his fingers, against his body.

He heard the commotion as they brought in the woman and stashed her away. He stopped pacing and raised his head. Antonio's footsteps echoed in the hallway. It was time.

Antonio, unmasked, still wearing his cape, the hood pushed back, met him as he stepped out into the hall.

"The woman is here, as you asked," his brother said but did not move aside.

"Let me pass, Tonio." Alessandro attempted to push past his brother, but Tonio blocked him. Alessandro had little patience for one of his brother's lectures, but he kept the fiend in tight check.

"She is frightened." Antonio frowned his disapproval.

The woman's presence called to him and he shifted impatiently. "*Bene.* A little fear always heightens passion." Alessandro's attention slipped beyond his brother's shoulder to the stairs leading to where the woman waited for him.

Abruptly, Antonio slammed him against the wall. His brother's arm against Alessandro's throat kept him still. Surprise had given his twin the advantage, and the fiend in Alessandro reared up in fury.

"Let me go." Alessandro gasped past the pressure on his throat and whacked a fist into Antonio's ribs.

Antonio grunted, but barely stirred as he stood nose to nose with him. "I'll forgive your thoughtlessness and what you are about to do because the Hunger is still upon you," he bit out. "Remember

29

who and what you are. Remember you are not an animal, but a man. A *prince*."

Guilt and self-loathing shafted through Alessandro. He knew what he was. And he knew what he was supposed to be. He hated the fiend inside him, especially now when the Hunger began to fade and his reason started to return. But his brother's admonition grated against his need. Antonio was always his conscience.

"If I forget, I know you'll remind me," he jeered.

"Someone has to." Antonio pressed his arm harder against his throat.

Alessandro gasped for air. He was furious at his brother for detaining him, furious at himself for what he needed, furious at the curse and the evil sorceress who had placed it on his family. He clutched Antonio's coat and shoved. "Let me go," he growled, as the fiend's impatience clawed at him.

His twin barely moved. "Discover what the woman knows, what her power is, and then release her," his brother ordered.

Narrowing his eyes, Alessandro snarled, "Would you in my state?"

His brother said nothing, but a muscle jumped in his jaw.

"Are you finished?" Alessandro snapped.

After a moment's hesitation, Antonio dropped his arm and stepped back.

Alessandro exulted in his freedom. The fiend would soon be able to play. He saw that his twin wore a rapier. Quick as a panther, he pulled it from where it hung from Antonio's belt. "I think I'll borrow this."

The fiend chuckled.

Antonio growled a warning. "If you hurt her, there'll be Hell to pay."

The corner of Alessandro's mouth lifted in a bleak smile. "We're already paying Hell, Tonio." Then he stepped around his twin and headed for the room where his salvation waited.

Chapter 5

Alessandro slipped silently into the room. After closing and locking the door behind him, he merely stood and watched her. The English woman. *Donna* Barclay. Her back was to him. She moved along the far wall of the room and pounded on it at intervals. He frowned, puzzled at her actions, then he realized she was looking for a secret door or window, a way to escape. He smiled at her determination. The fiend enjoyed a challenge.

She was more than just a beautiful woman. She was brave, spirited. He had learned that the night before in her bedchamber. And she had a secret, which he was here to discover. But the fiend inside him was impatient. *Touch. Feel.* His fingers itched. That craving consumed him, more than the desire to learn her secret.

He shifted his hold on the rapier, pressed the wire-bound grip with the pads of his fingers to ease the agony. It would not be a weapon, but rather an extension of his arm and a means of controlling the fiend. If he did not have some prop, he might bruise her in his fervor to sense her skin against his. Hurting her was the last thing he wanted to do. He would hate himself even more if he did.

Touch. Feel. Take. The fiend prodded. His need burned. He took a breath. *Patience,* he cautioned the fiend. He would touch her skin, feel her warmth beneath his fingertips. Perhaps she craved his touch as much as he craved hers.

All he wanted was to satisfy the fiend's bizarre need. And then he would let her go. He could not afford entanglements. Especially not with the Englishwoman.

But tonight, he would indulge the fiend.

Sabrina did not hear him enter. One moment she was alone searching for a way out, and the next, she felt eyes on her back. She swung around and gasped when she saw him standing inside the door, watching her.

He was tall and broad-shouldered like the man in the *bautta,* muscular and well formed. He could have been the other man, except she sensed a reined-in tension in this one that the other did not have. Unlike her abductor, this man wore only breeches, boots, and a light shirt open halfway down his chest. She refused to look at that scandalous expanse of skin. A red silk strip covered his face from forehead to nose. With cutouts for his eyes, it was embroidered in gold to represent lines, planes, and hollows of the face. His collar-length hair was tied back severely in a queue, except for an errant curl that dipped across his forehead. He dangled a rapier from his fingers.

"*Ma Donna,*" he said in a whispery murmur and gave a slight bow.

Sabrina's heart rate jumped up a notch. Like the men who had brought her here, the contradiction between the appearance of civility and violence, his courteous bow and the rapier, made her more wary and afraid. But she was not about to let her fear or his courtesy dissuade her from letting him feel her displeasure.

"Why did you bring me here?" she demanded. "What do you want?"

Amusement curved his lips. "All in good time, *Donna.*"

"Where is my maid? What have you done with her?"

"She is safe." He motioned negligently with the rapier toward the table with the refreshments. "Have you eaten? Had some wine, perhaps?"

She sniffed and looked away. "I want nothing."

"Ah, *Ma Donna,* you must at least have some wine." He strolled to the table and poured a glass, then held it out to her. The dark red liquid sparkled in the fine crystal. Despite its beauty, Sabrina was suspicious. It could be poisoned. When she did not move, he brought

32

it to her. When she still did not take the glass, he rested his rapier on her shoulder. "It would please me if you would drink it."

The light weight of the rapier was more threatening than if he had curled his hand into a fist and shook it beneath her nose. Gulping, she said, "You first."

He stared at her a moment, and she braced herself for the pain of the rapier slicing through her. Then she caught a gleam of laughter in those shadowed dark eyes, and he smiled, showing even white teeth. A deep dimple in one cheek added a touch of mischief. Raising the glass to his lips, he took a sip and swallowed. For some reason, she was mesmerized by the contractions of his strong throat muscles. Yet, the weapon resting on her reminded her of his menace. He was stronger than she, and he was armed besides.

Lowering the glass, he said, "There. You see? No poison." He tapped the rapier on her shoulder. "Now, *Donna*, it is your turn."

Fearful of the implied threat, Sabrina reached for the glass. She was shaking so badly she was forced to take it with both hands. Her fingers brushed his. Heat bloomed on her skin and she flinched. Had he flinched as well? Confused, she quickly took a small sip. The wine was rich and smooth on her tongue, and it was an excellent vintage. It hit her stomach like lightning.

The wine gave her enough courage to ask again, "What do you want with me?"

"What I want, *Donna*—" He stopped, took a breath. "What I want is for you to drink your wine, then we shall see." His lips curved in a small smile.

Sabrina wondered what he had been about to say first. That hesitation and that small smile made her think that perhaps he was not as confident as he wanted her to believe. Perhaps she could convince him to let her go. She took another tiny sip of the wine. It helped to steady her.

"I have nothing of value," she said.

His gaze swept from the top of her head to her toes. "Perhaps value is found in the eyes of the beholder," he murmured.

She shivered under his intensity. Raising her chin, she said coolly, "I do not know you, sir. Do not look at me in that way."

33

"What way is that?" His amusement showed in the twitch of his lips.

"Like… like you are about to eat me." Sabrina's cheeks flamed.

At that, he laughed. "I think tasting you might be very pleasant."

"What a ludicrous notion." She sniffed in disdain. Men did not taste women. Her husband would never have wanted to taste her.

"Ludicrous? No." He shook his head. "Tempting. Sensuous. Delicious."

"I am not a bonbon, sir," she snapped.

He laughed again. "Are you sure of that?"

She hissed with annoyance at his silliness while she tried to ignore his laugh, rich and throaty, much too attractive. It reminded her of the shadow man who had invaded her bedchamber. But the man before her was real, not some misty, mythical figure of the dark. He was a man of flesh and bone who held her captive and might, at any moment, plunge a rapier through her heart.

She had to get away. Frantically, she searched for another distraction. If she could keep him talking, she might be able to figure out how to slip around him and escape, or at least put some space between her and that weapon. Finally, her brain started working again. "If you think you can get at Mr. Dunfield through me, you are wrong."

"Believe me, *Ma Donna,* the last person I wish to communicate with right now is *Sior* Dunfield."

She lifted her nose in the air with haughty dismissal. "Then I cannot possibly understand why you have brought me here."

Leaning forward, he whispered in her ear, "Pleasure."

His warm breath sent a quiver through her, and she jerked away. Her reaction frightened her. Her naiveté annoyed her. Of course she had been locked in a bedchamber for his pleasure. Yet, he was being absurd to think he could ruin her. Forcing a laugh despite her fear, she said, "You are a little late if you think you can destroy my virtue. I am a widow."

He cocked his head thoughtfully. "Then we shall call this a test, *si?* To discover how much your late husband taught you."

Despite the heat that flooded her cheeks, she drew herself up in dignified affront. "How dare you! If you think I'll—I'll—"

His laugh cut her off. "I do dare, and you will." Slipping the glass out of her fingers, he tossed it across the room. Before the tinkle of breaking glass faded, he ordered, "Turn around."

Stiffening her spine, she declared, "I will not."

He tapped her shoulder with the rapier. "Turn around, please, *Donna*."

The threat of the weapon made her obey. Slowly, she turned, wondering what torment he might inflict. And then she understood. Deliberately, methodically, he cut the laces on her bodice and her corset beneath. With a flick of the rapier, he opened the back.

"Remove it, please," he said.

That rapier came to rest once more on her shoulder. Sabrina did as she was told. The rapier lifted. She quickly stepped away.

"Stop." His command and the rapier landing on her shoulder again halted her.

She swallowed in a dry throat. Postpone. Delay. Distract him. "Is my maid still alive?"

"What reason would I have to kill her?" His question sounded rational. Perhaps she could bargain with him.

"I want to see her." She blurted her demand, then hoped she had not angered him.

"After." He murmured his single word, like a lover murmuring sweet enticements. Yet he punctuated his answer with a tap of the rapier on her shoulder.

She trembled. She did not want to think about what came before the *after,* so she concentrated on his answer. Did he lie? She needed to know, but she was too nervous to face him. "Do you promise?"

He was silent for a heartbeat. "You are hardly in a position to demand a promise from me, *Ma Donna*." His words held an undertone of humor. "If I promise, will you behave?"

She jerked a nod.

"*Bene,*" he whispered. "Don't move."

Alessandro lifted the rapier from her shoulder, and using the weapon with precision, he cut the ties on her garments. As her skirt and petticoats puddled at her feet, the fiend prodded him on. *Touch, touch.* He forced the fiend down. Concentrating on his task helped. He had been raised as an honorable man, even when the fiend inhabited his brain. But this time, the fiend was more insistent. He told himself he could control it. He told himself he only needed to touch her. Nothing more. Just a simple touch, except the fiend demanded more. But he would not harm her. He would never be able to live with himself if he hurt her in any way. The fiend shifted impatiently and shattered his resolve.

He left her wearing only a chemise, her stockings, and shoes. She shook with fright. Guilt streaked through him, but the fiend smothered it. *Feel, feel.* He gripped the hilt of the rapier tighter. *Not yet,* he told the fiend.

"Turn around," he ordered her.

She primly crossed her arms and turned to face him.

"Shoes." He twirled the point of the sword in the vicinity of her feet.

She stared at him in defiance, shook her head, and refused to move.

Inwardly, he smiled. She was an audacious minx. With an exaggerated sigh of forbearance, he brought up the tip of the rapier and laid it on the neckline of her chemise.

"Please, do not be stubborn, *Donna*," he said. "You know I can slice this garment from you with little trouble, and then you'll be left with no modesty." With the tip of the weapon, he plucked up the ribbon tying her chemise closed as if he would cut it through, although he had no intention of doing so. "Remember your maid."

She gave a jerky nod. He let the point of the rapier dip to the floor. She sent him a hostile glare, bent, and slipped off her shoes.

Her feet in their stockings were delicate. Even without the fiend's prodding, he wanted to run his tongue along the sensitive arch and suck each pink toe. She straightened, and he tore his gaze away from her feet.

"Take the pins from your hair and drop them," he said.

She watched him carefully as, one by one, she pulled out the pins and let them fall to the floor. Her hair was a glorious tumble of dark curls. His fingers itched to bury themselves in its depths. But her chin was raised at a challenging angle. She stood with her fists clenched at her sides. She was hiding something.

"Hold out your hands, please, *Ma Donna*," he said.

Trembling, she showed him her clenched fists.

He shook his head. "You are being quite obstinate. Fortunately, I'm inclined to be patient." He tapped the rapier against her knuckles. "Open your hands, please, palms up."

Reluctantly, she obeyed. He nearly laughed aloud in admiration at her defiance when he saw the hairpin laying in her palm. Instead, he tsked once and with a delicate touch, he flicked the pin away with the point of his weapon.

The fiend churned inside him. Alessandro fought for control. As each garment fell away from her, the burn to touch her grew until he thought he might incinerate. *Touch, touch.* The fiend's urging was a litany in his head. The fire beneath his skin raged.

He took a step toward her and reached out to the heavy mass of hair tumbled around her shoulders. When his fingers curled into its soft depths, the fiend inside him stilled as if poised on a precipice. He clamped down on the desire to take that final step forward and plunge over the edge. *Not yet*, he told the fiend. *But soon.*

"Like satin," he whispered, then he wrapped his hand in the dark tresses and tugged her closer. One step. Two. Close enough that he could feel her warmth. Close enough that he could inhale her enticing scent. Almost touching. *Feel, feel.* The fiend strained against his restraint.

Her lips parted and her eyes went wide. She stopped breathing. The pulse in her throat beat frantically. The color washed from her cheeks. *Christo.* She was about to faint. No, he could not let that happen.

"Breathe, *Donna*," he said. "I will not harm you."

She swayed and stared at him as if she did not understand.

Leaning forward, he murmured again in her ear, "Breathe." This time, he flicked out his tongue to tickle her into a reaction. She tasted delicious. *Madre di Dio*, he wanted more.

More, the fiend demanded.

Startled at his touch, Sabrina sucked in a breath. Her head cleared. She felt better, but not much safer, despite his reassurance. He threatened her with a weapon. He cut her clothes from her. He was too close. She could feel the warmth radiating from him and caught the scent of him — wild thyme, sage, and clean male. His body crowded her, making her feel small, defenseless, overwhelmed. She noticed an incongruous bruise on the left side of his jaw. How had he acquired that?

"*Bella mia*," he whispered, then ducked his head to run his tongue across her lips.

Sabrina was paralyzed. The gentle touch, so in opposition to his implied threat, stunned her. It was unusual, nice. No, more than nice. Her husband had never done anything like that.

His mouth brushed hers, back and forth once, twice, then he caught her bottom lip and gently nipped. Her eyes slipped shut. The touch of his lips was like nothing she had ever experienced — almost like the touch of that shadow man.

She had expected roughness, brutality. Not a delicate touch. When his mouth closed fully over hers, she remained perfectly still, drinking in the sensation. It was so… nice. Soft, warm, gentle… nice. Something shifted and uncurled inside her. Wanting to feel him against her, to soak in his warmth, she leaned into him. His hard chest supported her. The heat of his skin burned through her thin chemise. She wanted more.

His huff of satisfaction brought her to her senses, shocked and shamed that she had allowed his seduction. What was she doing? With a great shove, she pushed him away.

"Stay away from me," she said as she backed away from him.

A flicker of surprise in his eyes was quickly replaced by a dark gleam. "I think not, *Donna*. I think, perhaps, your late husband did not teach you much." Carefully, he placed his rapier on a nearby table and took a step toward her. "I think, *Donna*, that you enjoyed that kiss."

Sabrina shook her head and backed up. "No, I did not." She tried to convince herself as well as him. She could not possibly have enjoyed that kiss. He was a kidnapper. He had stripped her. She had succumbed only because she had been surprised. She would not let him kiss her again.

She backed up another step. She was relieved he put down his weapon, but his overwhelming presence was just as threatening.

He prowled closer. "I think you enjoyed it so much that it frightened you."

"I am not frightened," she lied, raising her chin in defiance, even as she retreated.

"I think you are, *bella mia*," he said as he stalked her. "I think you are frightened of the pleasure."

"Frightened of pleasure?" she scoffed. "How absurd."

"Absurd, indeed," he agreed. "But perhaps it is the unknown you fear."

She clenched her fists to hide the tremor in her fingers and shot back, "I fear men who abduct me and force me to strip at the point of a blade."

He blinked, nearly a flinch, as if her words had been some sort of weapon.

That tiny reaction gave her hope. Perhaps he was not a completely heartless rogue.

He spread open his hands to show her they were empty. "I've put down my blade. You have nothing to fear except your own inexperience."

"I know what men and women do together," she said, taking another step back and coming up hard against the post of the bed. "I told you, I've been married."

His gaze taunted and turned wicked, her verbal barb already dismissed. "But I will show you pleasure that you have never known before."

He sauntered closer, too close

She put up her hand. "Stay back."

He ignored her command and stepped forward, his chest pressed against her palm. She could feel the warm, taut muscles beneath the thin lawn of his shirt. The corners of his mouth tipped up slyly, intimately. He reached out, ran his fingers up her neck, beneath her jaw, barely touching. His eyes closed as if savoring the sensation. His fingers circled beneath her jaw where a pulse throbbed.

Sabrina had a chance to run, but the caress wiped out any intention of escape. Her fingers involuntarily clutched his shirt. His touch against her skin was light as an angel's kiss and just as hypnotizing. She had the fleeting thought that sin should not feel so delicious. And she certainly should not enjoy it so much. What was wrong with her?

When his eyes opened again, his gaze smoldered. "Tell me you are not the tiniest bit curious about what I can show you," he murmured.

She *was* curious. His touch did things to her insides that her husband's touch never had. It made her forget he threatened and enticed instead. She should be screaming, fighting, clawing at him. But something held her immobile—her damnable curiosity, his touch. And something else, something inside her head that calmed and soothed.

He dropped his hand. Sabrina swallowed. That strange calm fled. Her brain started working again. In dismay, she saw her fingers curled into his shirt. She jerked her hand away. Something had just happened in her head. Whatever it was, she would not give in.

She slipped around the bedpost. She wanted to distance herself from the bed, but his large frame blocked her. For every step she took away from him, he was right there, keeping pace. Backing away, she banged into the bedside table, one side blocked by the bed. In desperation, she glanced about for a weapon, anything to keep him at bay. His rapier lay on that table across the room, but she had no hope of reaching it before he did, or before he caught her. And then she found her deliverance. The key was still in the lock on this side of the door. If she could get past him, she might have a chance at escape, but she had to distract him, keep him talking.

Squaring her shoulders, she faced him down. "You think you will show me pleasure I've never known?" she taunted. "You are very sure of yourself to make that claim." She edged to the side.

He chuckled and nodded. "I am."

"How arrogant you are." She turned away in scorn.

Another chuckle. "*Si*, very arrogant."

Taking her chances, she dashed past him. She only took two steps. With a single smooth movement, he caught her around the waist.

"I promised you pleasure," he murmured in her ear as he pressed her against his body.

Sabrina shivered.

Alessandro had her just where he wanted her. The sweet curves fit him perfectly. The feel of her against him was heaven. Her contact with the Sphere of Astarte thrummed with her every heartbeat. It soothed him. He should ask her about it, but her body pressing against him made the thought evaporate. The touch of her skin eased the burn of his craving. The fiend rejoiced. The sane part of him understood that he should let her go, now that his anguish had subsided. But the fiend was stronger than his sanity.

Touch her.

Feel her.

Want her.

Need her.

Sweeping her hair back, he ran his tongue in a circle below her ear. Her taste was intoxicating. *Madre di Dio.* He wanted to taste her all night. Gently, he tugged her earlobe with his teeth.

She responded with a hiss and attempted to wriggle free.

He easily held her. Entertained, he murmured, "You cannot escape me, *bella mia.*" He placed his lips against the graceful curve where her neck met her shoulder. Paradise.

Sabrina melted. His touch felt delicious. She wanted to stay exactly where she was. But she knew she would hate herself later if she did.

His words were a challenge. She would escape.

Sabrina squeezed her eyes shut against the magnetism of his body. Not knowing what he would do made her heart race. He could just as easily kill her as seduce her. His chest rubbed against her. His erection pressed in the hollow of her hip. His scent engulfed her; his words frightened her; his touch aroused her. She had to get away from him or she would lose her mind, lose her soul.

His fingers slid lightly up and down the bare skin of her arms. His touch was mesmerizing. Every brush of his fingers sensitized her skin. She never dreamed something that simple could be so erotic. Despite her resolve to escape, she felt herself go moist. Her breasts puckered and ached. She wanted… No. She did not dare think of what she wanted. That was madness. Without realizing it, she whimpered.

"Ah, *bella mia*, you see? It is pleasure you need." He placed tiny kisses across her shoulder. "When you think of this night, all you will remember is the pleasure. There is no escape from pleasure." His voice held dark promises.

She had to escape. This was a nightmare. This was a dream.

Sabrina looked into his shadowed eyes and knew he spoke the truth. There was no escape. Those wicked eyes were dusky, intense, burning. They were the eyes of a rogue. He would do what he wanted. He would make her want whatever he wanted. And the idea that she wanted him horrified her.

His fingers moved again in small slow circles against her skin, trailed up to the pulse at her throat and stroked softly, soothingly. Calm blanketed her. She felt her heartbeat slow to a more normal rhythm. Her tremors quieted.

"Do not be frightened, *bella mia*. Please," he murmured. "I will not hurt you."

For some utterly illogical reason, she believed him.

He traced down to her collarbone, then lower, to the neckline of her chemise. His touch was intoxicating. Her eyes slipped closed at the sensation. His hand cupped her breast. His thumb played with the tight, hard bud of her nipple. Pleasure knifed through her and ended in a throb of desire. She arched up against his hand.

She gasped at the second reminder of the shadow man in her bedchamber. Her eyes flew open, and she stared at him. Could it be? No. She had felt no odd tingle when he touched her, no trail of sparkling warmth left behind. This was a man, all solid and hard muscle. Yet, he had calmed her with a caress of her pulse. How had he done that? He could not have. She was being foolish, letting her imagination run wild. This was a human male who touched her. Nothing more. That other was… what?

He stopped and frowned. "What is it, *bella mia*? Why do you look at me like that?"

"You remind me of someone."

His eyes behind the mask became shuttered. "Do I? Who is this man? Does he give you pleasure like I do?"

She shook her head. "It's not a man."

"I remind you of a woman?" He chuckled in disbelief.

Recklessly, she blurted, "A shadow." She watched his eyes closely for his reaction.

He stilled and said nothing for a moment. "A shadow. Do you think a shadow can do this?" He kissed her jaw. "Or this?" He ran his tongue across her bottom lip. "Or this?" He took her mouth and plundered until she was dizzy. "Tell me, *bella mia*, can a shadow steal your breath with pleasure?"

Fearful she had made him angry, Sabrina turned her head away as she confessed, "I was mistaken."

He grunted in satisfaction. "I will prove I am better than this silly shadow. You will remember only the pleasure I can give you."

His hand roved over her body. His lips followed. Her muscles quivered where he touched. Her skin ignited where he kissed. How could his touch feel so wonderful? Her husband had never… The thought floated away. A moan escaped her.

His hand stopped. He raised his head. Her thoughts returned to a semblance of sanity, and she opened her eyes.

He was grinning like a pirate. "Better than a shadow, *si*?"

"Yes." She closed her eyes again to blot out his arrogance.

What was she doing? This man had kidnapped her, had made her desire him. She had no idea who or what he was. He might be a thief, a murderer. His touch drove her mad. Right now, she would do anything he wanted. Because she wanted more.

Alessandro knew he'd aroused her, and the fiend rejoiced. But in the part of his brain that was sane, guilt stabbed at him. The fiend dulled it. She was naive. So he would give her time.

She wore a thin gold chain around her neck. The attached pendant rested in the crevice between her breasts, a delectable spot. He pulled the pendant out of her chemise, intending to replace it with a kiss. Instead, the solid blue stone arrested him. It was large and flat with a strange iridescence, almost like that of a full moon.

"What is this?" he asked.

"A moonstone," she said.

He held the pendant in his palm. It fascinated him. It seemed to draw him in. He felt a strange tingling on his skin. It spread up his arm, across his chest. He wanted to drop the stone but found he was unable. A burn flashed through his brain. His fingers convulsed around the stone and he hissed in a breath. Pain zapped through him. Everything blanked out.

Then it was gone.

Calm settled over him. He opened his eyes. And saw *Donna* Barclay in his arms.

"*Madre di Dio!*" The words escaped before he could stop them.

What had he done? What atrocity had he committed this time during the Hunger? He blinked, and the memory of the past hour came rushing back. Guilt and regret swamped him. His jaw tightened against any incriminating words. *Donna* Barclay must not learn his identity. He unclenched his fist, glanced at the pendant with distaste, and dropped it. He released the woman in his embrace and stepped back.

"Our lesson in pleasure is at an end, *Ma Donna*," he said stiffly. "I will send your maid to you, and then you will be taken home. I apologize for any inconvenience. *Grazie, bella mia.*"

He bowed, turned on his heel, and escaped.

Bewildered, Sabrina stared at the closed door as she tried to absorb what had just happened. She clutched her arms about her. His sudden departure was very strange. His reaction to her pendant was stranger still, as if touching the moonstone had triggered something unpleasant, cooling his ardor to a frigid reserve. His absence seemed to make the room feel very empty.

She sucked in a breath. Her emotions were roiling inside her. She was relieved he was gone. She was confused by his sudden change in manner. She was aroused like she had never been before, and so unsatisfied she thought she might scream.

One thing she knew for certain. She would remember his touch and the pleasure he had given her.

And she would remember how she had surrendered.

Chapter 6

Alessandro stood at the edge of the masquerade ball in the *casa* of Harold Dunfield, the Englishman, and watched the masked dancers. The *casa* was not large. Only wall sconces and a single chandelier, simple in its design of gilt wrought iron with a sprinkling of Murano glass flowers, were enough to light the ballroom. The ceiling was coffered rosewood, each of the recessed panels carved with a scroll design and burnished to a high degree. Valuable artwork was displayed on the whitewashed plaster walls. Alessandro idly wondered what impoverished Venetians had been desperate enough to sell such masterpieces to an Englishman.

He shifted away from a couple who danced too near, and bumped the arm of a fantastical rooster beside him. Murmuring a polite apology, he could not help but compare what he was now with what he had been only a few short hours before. The Hunger was gone and the fiend along with it. He was fully human again and had regained his customary rigorous control over his appetites. No one in this crowd would believe that the cool, detached man in the *bautta* had been driven by uncontrollable cravings. It was, after all, *Carnevale*, when sane men dressed themselves in costume and gave free rein to their wildest desires. The irony was not lost on him. A self-mocking smile twitched his lips.

The costumes of the guests reflected their fantasies — elves and fairies, queens and whores, lions and jesters, wolves and kings. He heard snatches of conversation about the latest opera, about the latest loss at the gaming tables, about the silly French fighting the Austrians from the border of the Veneto. He wondered how silly the French would seem if they suddenly decided that Venice might be a delectable morsel they wished to sample. Antonio and he had already made plans for that contingency.

It was Ascensiontide, the ten days of *Carnevale* at the end of spring and much warmer than the longer pre-Lenten time of *Carnevale*. The heat from the crowd was stifling, the mingling of perfumes and body odors was overpowering, and all he wanted was to escape into the fresh air, to strip out of his confining mask and costume. Yet, he refused to leave until he found one costumed character in particular—an English milkmaid. Gasparo had once again performed miracles and discovered what costume the Englishwoman would be wearing. But finding her in this crush of humanity was proving harder than he imagined. Gasparo had also learned the woman's given name—Sabrina. Alessandro rolled the name around in his mind like he would a fine wine across his tongue. The name suited her—complex, naive, alluring.

He was beginning to doubt he would find her when a harlequin stepped up beside him. "I understand you are seeking someone," the harlequin said from behind his black and white mask.

"We are all searching for something, are we not, *Sior* Dunfield?" Alessandro responded.

The Englishman chuckled. "Your informants have done well, Excellency."

Alessandro bowed his acknowledgment. "As have yours."

"You will find Lady Barclay in the garden. She does not enjoy such large gatherings."

"Why would I wish to find *Donna* Barclay? I do not crave the company of dowagers." Feigning indifference, Alessandro turned away to watch the dancers. He was not about to give the Englishman any sort of advantage by showing Dunfield how much he wanted—needed—to find her.

"Nevertheless, she is there, a flower waiting to be plucked. *Casa mia è casa vostra.*" My house is your house. With that expansive invitation hanging in the air, the harlequin melted back into the crowd.

Alessandro frowned at the crassness of the man who would offer a lady like a slice of watermelon on a plate. On the other hand, Dunfield had saved him a considerable amount of time and effort. Anticipation surged through him. Despite the passing of the Hunger, the memory of *Donna* Barclay lingered, unlike the others who satisfied his cravings. It consumed him. The desire to touch her made his fingers itch. He did not understand this strange need that spilled from the Hunger. All he wanted was to quench it.

A painful twist of guilt and self-loathing darkened his thoughts. The Hunger made him less than human. If he were not the head of the House of Auriano with all its responsibilities, he could easily see himself hiding away in wretched solitude in an icy cave until the end of his days.

He should not have forced Antonio to kidnap her. He had taken without asking, going against the code of honor passed through the generations, ingrained in him since childhood. But he had stolen a woman, a woman whose touch called to him like a siren song. He never should have teased her, seduced her, felt her beneath his fingers. But then, if he had not, his craving for her would have driven him mad. And without getting what he needed during the Hunger, he would remain Shadow for the rest of his miserable life.

He bit back a sigh. Feeling sorry for himself never helped. At least he had learned something by kidnapping *Donna* Barclay. If he had not taken her, he might never have touched that moonstone pendant she wore, which somehow curbed the Hunger. The memory of the pain that sizzled through him when he touched it remained with him, and the abrupt clarity of his thoughts amazed him. He should have borrowed it to unravel its mystery, a missed opportunity. He had been so shocked by its power and so appalled at what he had done that all he wanted was to flee. But now was not the time to dwell on that.

Now, he needed to see the charming *Donna* Barclay. She would never learn that he was the rogue who had so boldly seduced her, nor the shadow figure who had saved her. To her, he would be merely the all-too-human Prince of Auriano.

After waiting several moments for Dunfield to involve himself with the other guests, Alessandro edged back through the crowd and went in search of the garden. A servant with a tray of empty glasses directed him to the outside set of stairs that led down into the small retreat. The sound of trickling water reached him as he descended the steps. Torches around the garden's perimeter gave off flickering light. The retreat was not large, but elegantly laid out with several olive trees and flowerbeds enclosed by tightly trimmed boxwood. Beyond the far wall, curtained by climbing vines, was the canal. A small fountain stood in the garden's center.

He stopped on the bottom step. At first, he did not see her and thought perhaps Dunfield had been mistaken, but then a soft rustle drew his attention to a shadowed corner. Silently, he stole closer until he could observe her without being seen.

Although her costume mimicked that of a lowly milkmaid, it was constructed of materials no country lass could ever dream of wearing. Her bodice of black silk was decorated with spangles that accentuated the swell of breast that narrowed to the curve of her small waist. The chemise beneath was of a white lawn so thin and fine that it was nearly transparent and revealed the warm skin of her arms. Her skirt was of dark blue satin, its ankle-length hem purposely cut in uneven lengths to suggest tatters, and a gauzy petticoat, cut in the same fashion, peeked from beneath and dragged behind her. Her half mask was made of brown and gold feathers, the tips flaring up and away from the sides. A lacy kerchief was tied over her rich, dark hair, massed in an intricate knot at the back of her head. He wanted to pull the pins from the knot and feel the silken heaviness as it flowed through his hand.

She was counting as she focused on the steps of the minuet being played by the musicians, the music spilling from the upper story windows. He watched for a moment as she practiced her dance steps.

"One, two. Forward, back," she recited under her breath and moved accordingly with an invisible partner. "Step, step, step, around… and curtsey…" She tripped on her petticoat. "Bloody hell!"

Laughing, surprised at her language, Alessandro bounded forward and steadied her. The warmth of her skin beneath her sleeve and her delicate bone structure reminded him of their encounter the night before. Squashing his guilt, he focused on the pleasure of being near her. He was delighted that he had a perfect opening to speak with her.

Sabrina cried out, startled at the sudden appearance of a man who grabbed her. As soon as she did, the man released her and stepped back. When she saw the *bautta*, her first thought was of the man who had stolen her from her bedchamber the night before. And that other man who had made her feel things she never dreamed possible with such a delicate touch.

She knew, of course, who this was. Dunfield had told her he would send the Prince of Auriano to her, that the prince would be wearing the ubiquitous *bautta*, black coat and hooded cape, tricorn hat, full white mask. Of course, the prince's coat and cape were of the finest, softest wool, his white mask of such expert craftsmanship that it gleamed as if made of porcelain. He towered over her, and his wide shoulders blocked any view she had of the *casa*. Her thoughts turned again to the night before, the tall stranger's hard chest, his enticing touch, his seductively whispered words.

She wrenched her mind from that memory. Stupid to think of the man in the red silk mask. But she could not get the previous night out of her head, despite her appalling response to his touch. She watched Auriano execute a graceful bow, and the image of another doing the same crowded her head with shameful recollections.

"Forgive me, *signorina*," he said, his full mask distorting his voice. "I did not mean to startle you."

Sabrina forced herself to focus on the present and willed her heart to slow. Flipping open her fan, she turned her back on him. "Then you should not jump out at me from the shadows."

"But I prevented you from—"

"Making a fool of myself?" she finished sharply, as she swung back to him.

He chuckled. "I was going to say 'injuring yourself.'"

She snapped her fan shut. "Well, as you can see, I am quite unharmed, except for being scared out of my wits by some knave who leaps at me out of the dark." Picking up her skirts, she took a step around him.

"Perhaps I could aid you in some other way," he said, stepping into her path.

Stopping, she waved her closed fan in dismissal. "I have no need of your aid, sir. I came to the garden for some air and solitude."

"Then you do not enjoy *Sior* Dunfield's assemblies?"

"Mr. Dunfield, sir? Who might that be?" She tipped her head in curiosity. Her feigned ignorance was part of the game of the masquerade. She knew he was aware of her identity as much as she was aware of his. But they each had their parts to play.

"*Sior* Dunfield is the Englishman who owns this *casa*," he said.

Her eyes widened as she played her part. "Oh, my. I think I might have made a terrible mistake. I should not be here. I am merely a milkmaid."

"A milkmaid? Does *Sior* Dunfield keep cows in his garden?" He looked about as if searching for the animals.

"I became lost." Sabrina decided she'd had enough of the game. This was not the man from the night before, only another suitor Dunfield dangled before her. "I should go. My mistress will be looking for me."

She started to move past him once again, but he blocked her flight with his arm. The memory of another arm blocking her, holding a rapier, raised her heartbeat a notch.

"Don't go yet," he said. "I'm sure your mistress is occupied for the next several hours. It would amuse me to teach you to dance."

"Oh, no, I couldn't stay." She tried to move past him once more.

He caught her about the waist. "I insist. Would you truly wish to annoy me?"

Another unmannered bore. "You have annoyed *me*, sir, by not letting me pass." She lightly struck his arm with her fan. "Why should I not wish to annoy you in return?"

"Because you have no idea who I am," he said. "I could be a very powerful man."

She tilted her head up and peeked at him through her half mask. "Or you could be a beggar or thief." She opened her fan and fluttered it coyly. She could not irritate him too much, for he would inform Dunfield of her bad behavior. "All I see is a man wearing the *bautta*. You could be anyone, sir."

"Or I could be someone who has saved your life," he said lightly.

Sabrina felt the blood leave her cheeks. She stared up at him. Could he be the shadow man from the chapel? No, impossible. This man was real. The arm at her waist was solid. Swallowing, she flipped her fan closed. "Saved my life? How could you have done that?"

"I *will* do that—by teaching you to dance. Allow me that one service or I will demand a favor. Perhaps removing your mask, revealing your identity, in the midst of *Carnevale*."

Sabrina thought that over. She was not ready to reveal herself to him. Remaining masked, hiding her identity, even as a pretense, at least gave her the freedom to reject him outright if she so chose. She could always claim ignorance later of who he truly was.

Gently, she pried his arm from about her waist. Feeling his bone and muscle beneath his sleeve reassured her. This was a human man with blood running through his veins. She looked up at him and saw his eyes glitter in amusement. They were very human eyes, golden in color with heavy dark lashes surrounding them. This was not some shadowy creature with molten eyes, nor the rogue from the night before with his wicked eyes. He was the Prince of Auriano, supposedly a gentleman with charm and wit. Perhaps they had begun badly. Perhaps she would not discourage him immediately. Besides, she had never been properly instructed in the dance. Her father had been too busy with his scholarly pursuits to find her a dance instructor, and her husband just did not care for dancing. To finally learn the steps would be a relief so she would not step on any future partner's toes.

She nodded regally. "You may teach me to dance, but I must warn you that I am a danger to anyone who attempts to partner me."

He chuckled. "I will take my chances. Now, come, give me your hand and we will begin." He held out his hand.

Sabrina gazed at his strong, well-formed hand. It was merely a hand with long fingers, the palm lightly calloused from practice with a blade, not the soft hand of a pleasure seeker. She was reluctant to touch it. The memory of other hands, of other fingers and the sensations they evoked made her insides throb.

"Come, come," he urged. "I will not bite. Give me your hand, *dolce mia*."

Lightly, she touched her fingertips to his. As she did, she thought she saw him flinch, but if it happened at all, it was too quick for her to be sure. A curious reaction.

He took all of her fingers and covered them with his other hand. "These will be my captives until I have taught you to dance. Only then will I release them."

Ignoring the pleasant warmth of his gentle hands against her skin, Sabrina sighed with resignation. "Then I am afraid I shall lose them forever, for you have taken on an impossible task."

"Nonsense. Now, we shall begin." He took up the opening position of the dance. "One, two, back and forth. And one, two..."

Sabrina concentrated on following his counting and commands. She soon found herself enjoying the rhythm of the steps until she forgot to step right and stepped left instead, trampling on the gentleman's foot, losing her balance, and falling against him. His arm wrapped about her to keep her upright.

"Oh! Please forgive me, sir." Sabrina felt the blush heat her cheeks. Placing her hands on his upper arms to steady herself, she found herself enclosed by his embrace.

"There is nothing to forgive, *cara mia*," he murmured. "The fault was mine."

His close proximity caused the breath to catch in her throat. She tried to push away. It was like shoving against a brick wall. The man was all hard muscle. Another hard male body, one that had trapped her against its length, immediately came to mind. Grabbing her fan, she flicked it open and fluttered it, forcing him to give her some distance. His arms fell away, and she stumbled back a step.

"Perhaps that is enough of a dancing lesson for this evening," he said.

"Yes, perhaps." Even though Sabrina agreed, a stab of disappointment ran through her. She had enjoyed his banter, his tutoring, and his smooth compliments. Despite the fact that he reminded her of the rogue from the night before, despite his reputation, and despite their bad start, Auriano's manners proved he was a gentleman. "I am sure you would much prefer to be dancing with ladies who are adept at the skill." Her head dipped in embarrassment.

"Not at all," he said. "In fact, I find these affairs tedious."

Surprised, Sabrina studied him, although she could see nothing of his face behind the mask. Was he being sincere? This was supposed to be the man who pursued only pleasure, yet his admission indicated otherwise. And why select her, when he could choose among all of the elegant, beautiful women of Venice?

54

But still, she was charmed. She smiled. "And so you came to the garden for some air and solitude," she said, repeating her reason for being there.

"*Si.*" He chuckled. "I understand *Sior* Dunfield owns an extensive art collection," he said. "Would you perhaps have access to it?"

Sabrina fluttered her fan. She suspected he already knew she was cataloging the collection and was merely using the pretense of ignorance to get her to show it to him. She wondered why he had chosen her rather than Dunfield to show him the artwork. Or perhaps Dunfield was behind the request, suggesting, manipulating. She needed to discover the prince's intentions.

Playing the game of the masquerade, she peeked coyly over the top of her fan. "Why would a man of the world, like yourself, be interested in stuffy artwork?" she purred. "Surely, dancing or conversing with a lady is much more entertaining."

"It is discussing the artwork with a beautiful lady that engages me," he said.

That statement surprised her. It indicated the man had an intellectual side that went deeper than his reputation.

Before she could respond, he held out his arm. "Come, *dolce mia,* let us find this collection. It will be like a treasure hunt, *si?* Who knows what else we may discover."

Sabrina felt herself grow warm at his words. His charm was dangerous. His eyes in the expressionless mask seemed to burn her skin. Knowing who he was, she had to tread a fine line between flirtation and insult. Wary of being alone with him any longer, she nevertheless was reluctant to send him on his way. She needed to distract him while she decided what to do. As she cooled herself with her fan, she remembered she had left her shawl on a stone bench in a corner of the garden. "I must get my shawl," she murmured, as she indicated where she had left it.

"Allow me."

With graceful alacrity, he strode into the shadows and reappeared with the filmy blue scarf. He stood behind her, and as he draped it about her shoulders, his fingers moved a hair's breadth above her skin, not touching. A warm tingle erupted along the path of his fingers. A shiver trickled through her. The sensation was similar to what she felt from the shadow man. But that was impossible. This was a real man with her, not some shadow creature. But all she could think of was that shadow's tingly touch.

Getting herself in hand, she reminded herself that this flesh and blood man was the Prince of Auriano. The sensation she had just experienced was only her imagination. Stepping quickly away, she pushed all thoughts of the shadow creature out of her head.

He held out his arm to her. "Shall we explore, *signorina*?"

Sabrina did not miss the double meaning of his question. Keeping up the pretense of being merely a milkmaid, she said, "Since I am a stranger in this house, I'm afraid I might lead you astray."

"I am looking forward to it," he murmured.

Chapter 7

Smiling, Alessandro led her to the stairs. He mused over the odd sensation he felt when he placed her shawl about her shoulders. The feeling was similar to touching her when he had been Shadow, less intense, yet still powerful. Her shivery reaction told him that she had also felt something. This new connection to her was heady and yet disturbing. He craved her more than he should in his rational state. He felt as if the fiend still lived in his brain, and the Hunger had not completely dissipated.

Reining in his passions, putting himself under tight control, he allowed her to lead him through a maze of hallways. He made a game of their journey, opening doors, wondering aloud at each if that were the room with the artwork, and demonstrating disappointment that it was not. She led him finally to a room in a back corner of the *casa*.

As she preceded him through the doorway, he admired the way her skirts swung provocatively. The column of her neck was decorated with wisps of delicate curls. He felt the urge to wrap his hand around the nape of her neck and feel the velvety caress of those curls, the warmth of her silky skin. The idea of skin on skin seemed safer at the moment than that other unnerving sensation. A hint of scent floated back to him — a fragrance he would analyze later. She was enticing and delicious, and the anticipation of discovering more of her secrets fired his blood.

"It appears that we are here," she said, as she lit a taper and held it high. "I imagine the collection would be much more splendid in daylight."

Her candle gently illuminated the walls covered with canvases hung edge-to-edge, top to bottom. Other canvases, stacked four and five deep, leaned against the wall along the floor. The scent of oil paints and varnish filled the air. Alessandro caught his breath in the heavy atmosphere as he glimpsed masterpieces by DaVinci, Boticelli, Titian, and the more contemporary Canaletto, Tiepolo, and many others. The collection was extensive and impressive. If the Council of Ten discovered that Dunfield was sending any of these works out of the city, they would confine the Englishman to the Leads, the prison in the Doge's palace, for the rest of his life. That bit of knowledge might be useful. The lovely *Donna* Barclay could not know that she betrayed Dunfield by bringing him here, for she must have assumed the note she collected in the chapel had been lost.

Mesmerized by the overwhelming beauty of the paintings, he wandered farther into the room. "This is magnificent." He stopped before a Boticelli. "You are quite fortunate to have access to such a collection."

"Oh, I do not have access, sir. I should not even be here." Her words were airy with her false denial and held not a bit of guilt.

He turned to her. "Of course you have access. How else would you have known how to find this room? Despite our game of discovery, you led me here with little trouble."

Her eyes widened, then hanging her head, she sighed. "I must confess, I am a servant in the household."

"*Sior* Dunfield must hold you in very high esteem—for a servant." He used his last words sardonically.

"He is my..." Glancing away, she cleared her throat.

"Your protector?" he prompted.

"Yes. My protector." A blush colored her skin.

Calling her bluff, he stepped very close to her. "Then I think I might ask if he wouldn't mind sharing," he murmured suggestively.

"Sh-Sharing?" she squeaked.

"*Si*. Wouldn't you like two protectors, *signorina*?" Reaching out, he toyed with a curl that fell disarmingly across her shoulder.

"Per-perhaps 'protector' is not quite correct." Her words were breathless.

"What would be the correct word?" He wrapped the curl around his finger and tugged gently.

"He..." She appeared paralyzed as her words died. Her lips parted, and she stared at him.

Remembering her naiveté of the night before, relenting, he finished, "He is your late husband's uncle."

She stiffened, recovering her composure. "I would not presume such a relationship."

Alessandro dropped her curl and smiled behind his mask. "Perhaps not, unless it were the truth."

"Perhaps it is you who presume too much, Excellency." Her tone was tart.

At her use of his title, he laughed and stepped back. "So, shall we stop playing games, *Donna* Barclay? Come, show me this collection. I am fascinated."

She studied him a moment, then she nodded. "No more games. And you must behave yourself."

Spreading his arms in a gesture of surrender, he said, "I will be the epitome of gentlemanly behavior."

With a quelling glance, she led him along one wall and explained random paintings. In the corner, on the floor was a large chest draped by an old shawl. As he approached nearer, a faint thrumming ran through his muscles. Realizing what it signaled, he hid his excitement. That strange sensation could only mean that he was close to the Sphere of Astarte.

"What is this?" he asked, careful to show only mild curiosity. "Some sort of pirate treasure?"

She shook her head. "It is only a dusty old thing. Mr. Dunfield seems to hold it in high regard."

"May I see it?" At her hesitation, he explained, "I have some interest in ancient artifacts."

"Mr. Dunfield has asked that I not show this to anyone."

"Do you believe he would deny my request, *Donna* Barclay?" Shamelessly, he implied his power and position.

She paused, considering him. "I suppose he would not mind if I showed it to you, Excellency."

Noting the pointed emphasis she placed on his title, he merely nodded politely. "*Grazie.*"

He kept a tight hold on himself and watched as she pulled the shawl from the chest, dropped to her knees before it, turned a key, and flung open the top. Reaching inside, she took out a small, ancient casket, covered in strange carvings.

"The piece inside seems unimpressive, but I have been told that it is thousands of years old. There is a legend that it may even have magical qualities," she said.

"Intriguing," he murmured. In order to distract himself from the thrumming through his muscles, he asked, "Do you believe in magic, *Donna* Barclay?"

She gave a little laugh. "Magic is the stuff of fairy tales, Excellency."

"Ah, who's to say that fairy tales do not come true?"

She gave another little laugh and shook her head. He watched her slide decorations on the casket and push various bits and pieces. Finally, the top popped open. As she looked inside, she gasped. "Oh, no," she whispered. "No, it can't be."

"What is it?"

When she glanced up at him, her eyes behind her mask were distressed. "It's gone. The piece is missing."

Disappointment jolted through him. Stepping forward, he peered over her shoulder into the casket. It was empty. Seeing a void where a piece of his salvation should have been was a crushing blow. Yet, even as he hid his disappointment, as he stepped closer, that thrumming became stronger. He labored to breathe and his knees buckled. He concentrated on remaining upright. What was happening to him? Could the absence of this artifact from its casket cause him to transmute to Shadow?

He could not subject the young woman to the transformation. His secret would be revealed. Stepping back quickly, he bowed. "*Mi scusi, Donna* Barclay, but I have just remembered a pressing engagement. Perhaps we shall meet again very soon, *si?*"

Without waiting for her reply, he turned on his heel and strode away.

Startled at his sudden departure, Sabrina watched him go with his black cloak swishing around him. She had no idea what she might have done to send the prince on his way so suddenly. A sigh of regret escaped her lips, for in the end, she had enjoyed his company, a respite from Dunfield's ball.

Alone, she turned to her more immediate problem and stared down into the empty casket. Who had taken the artifact and why? It was an old, dusty thing, carved of amber, seeming to be of little value except for its reputed age. It was not even something one could recognize, but rather appeared to be part of a whole, fitting together with another piece or pieces to create... what?

She had no idea. What she did know was that the piece had been part of her husband's collection, something so old and worthless that she had not been able to sell it. Yet, her husband had seemed to place a high value on it, and Dunfield prized the piece. It was one of the first things he asked about when she had contacted him. She did not look forward to a confession that it was missing. He had entrusted her with cataloging his collection so he would hold her responsible.

As she gazed down into the shadowy casket, she noticed a bit of parchment in one of the corners. Taking it out, she saw that it had been folded many times in order to achieve its tiny size. She worked to unfold it, and a message written in a small but perfect script was revealed: *Il Canale di l'Ombres*. The Canal of Shadows.

She had never heard of such a place. The name sounded ominous. She wondered if it was connected in some way to the strange shadow creature who had saved her life and visited her bedchamber. And then she wondered why the note was in the casket and who had placed it there. Perhaps the note was a clue to where the piece might be found.

Having no answers, she folded up the bit of parchment and pushed it into her pocket. Perhaps in the morning, she would be able to come up with a solution to the mystery. For now, Dunfield would be looking for her, anxious to know how she got along with the enigmatic Prince of Auriano.

For once, Dunfield had chosen someone charming to dangle before her as a possible husband. She smiled at the memory of Auriano's honeyed words and strong arms as he had guided her through the dance. Perhaps, he would come calling in the morning. Then her smile died as reality took over her brain. He would not come calling. His abrupt departure told her that. Somehow, she had discouraged him. Perhaps her comment about her disbelief in magic had disappointed him, or perhaps he had been insulted when she scoffed at the legend of the missing artifact. Venetians lived their lives as if they were fairy tales.

She gave herself a mental shake. She did not need a frivolous, impetuous rogue in her life, no matter how wealthy he was. All that mattered was keeping Evan safe and providing him with a home.

Closing the empty casket, she placed it back inside the chest, shut the cover and locked it, then pulled the shawl back over the top. Everything looked as she had first seen it this evening. No one would ever know that the artifact was missing. She need not tell Dunfield anything. She might even be able to find the piece herself.

And she resolved to discover the location of the Canal of Shadows.

Alessandro stepped into the cool night air and breathed deeply. The disturbing sensations he experienced had dissipated as soon as he moved away from the room where the empty casket was kept. Keen disappointment stabbed through him as he motioned for his gondolier. To have come so close to the missing piece of the Sphere of Astarte and then be thwarted was maddening.

As he waited, he felt a presence watching him. A sense of evil made his skin crawl. Nulkana, the ancient sorceress. Waiting, watching, hoping he would lead her to the Sphere, the magical artifact that would make her immortal. Perhaps also looking for another opportunity to assassinate the lovely *Donna* Barclay.

He would not give Nulkana that chance. Not tonight.

Around him, gondoliers lounged, joked quietly together, flirted with young women who strolled by to catch their fancy. Nothing out of the ordinary. But Nulkana was present and lurking somewhere in the shadows. Before he could move, evil rippled through his soul like acid, burning, blistering. Frozen in pain, he clenched his fist beneath his cloak.

He heard a mocking laugh as the sorceress enjoyed his distress. Then the evil receded. He peered into the dark corners as he tried to see where she was hiding. Everything was the same as it was a moment ago. Nulkana hid herself well.

Staring into the shadows, he sent a mental message: *Show yourself.*

Malevolence trickled through him as if Nulkana were toying with him. He gritted his teeth at the cold ache squeezing his chest.

Not tonight, dear boy. The words of the sorceress pierced his brain like thin blades.

With a final wrench through his heart, the evil was gone. Relief washed over him. He sucked in the cool air. Nulkana's attack had merely been a reminder that she watched him, waiting for him or his brother to lead her to the Sphere of Astarte. *Donna* Barclay would be safe for now. He would not have to confront the sorceress tonight. But the race to discover the pieces of the Sphere was becoming more heated, the enmity from his family's enemy more defined.

He would tell Tonio of this latest attack when he returned to the Ca' D'Este. For now, he wanted—needed—to be just a man, not a cursed being who was forced to fight off evil. He wanted to think on the woman he had just left in the *casa* behind him.

Donna Barclay intrigued him. That sensation he experienced when his hand hovered above her skin fascinated and unnerved him. Never before had anything from his time as Shadow crossed into his time as a man. What had caused it? Despite the unsettling effect *Donna* Barclay had on him, she held something warm and comforting within her that seemed to thaw his soul. She was quite lovely. Even though her dance technique was appalling, she was graceful and alluring. And passionate. He had learned that the night before.

But the empty casket, where a missing piece of the Sphere should have been, disturbed him. Determined to find out more about it, he resolved to call on *Donna* Barclay on the morrow. She might know something even without being aware of it. Besides, mixing business with pleasure was never a hardship.

Chapter 8

Sabrina was busy the next morning writing a description of Canaletto's painting, *Venice: Piazza San Marco,* when a maid announced a visitor, the Prince of Auriano. Her hand froze above the sheet of parchment and a drop of ink fell on it like a malignant raindrop. "Bloody hell," she muttered, as she tried to blot it up. "Show him to the drawing room, Maria," she said, hurrying to straighten her notes.

She was not pleased that he had called unexpectedly, yet she could not deny the tiny leap of anticipation. As a stray curl fell across her cheek, she quickly tucked it back behind her ear and glanced down at herself. Dismay coursed through her. She had dressed that morning prepared to work among Dunfield's mustiest, dustiest artifacts, not to receive the Prince of Auriano, and so she had donned an old brown serge dress. Her apron was smudged and ink stained. Then her thoughts went in another direction, toward reality. Her shabby appearance might discourage him in his futile pursuit of her. She would have to do little to make him lose interest. One less suitor she would have to send on his way, for she had decided he was too much the rogue to be a father to Evan. Or a husband to her.

The maid's quick step and the prince's stronger one announced that he was approaching her workroom. The arrogant scoundrel had opted not to be settled in the drawing room. She smoothed her hair and rose as he filled the doorway. "Excellency," she murmured. She barely caught a glimpse of the man before she dropped into a deep curtsey. She noted he was unmasked, unusual during this time of *Carnevale.* "I am honored." She worked to keep the annoyance out of her tone.

"Ah, no, *Ma Donna,* it is an honor that you receive me," he said as he entered the room. His voice was a rich baritone.

That voice, without the filter of his mask, sounded vaguely familiar, yet not from the night before.

With a hand beneath her elbow, he urged her upright. "Please, let us do away with such ceremony. I'm afraid I insulted you last night with my abrupt departure."

She bit back her agreement. This was the Prince of Auriano. He could do as he wished. His hand on her arm was warm and solid, yet his touch was gentle. She rather liked the feel of that touch. And then she came to her senses, took a step back, and forced him to drop his hand.

He was so tall that all she could immediately see was the expanse of his shoulders covered in the golden russet superfine of his coat with the swath of his bright white shirt and folds of his stock bisecting it. She had to tilt her head up in order to see his face. What she saw intrigued her. Younger than she had thought from her exchange with him the night before, he was perhaps only a year or two older than she, which made him a score and eight or nine. His eyes were the color of aged brandy and surrounded by thick black lashes. His nose was straight, and his lips were full, yet clearly defined. His unbound, collar-length hair was not dark, as she had imagined, but a rich chestnut shot through with gold. Even his skin had a golden cast to it. He was beyond handsome, almost to the point of being beautiful. Incongruously, a bruise discolored his jaw.

Her eyes widened. A memory clicked into place. That jaw. With the bruise. Those sculpted lips. That voice, low and seductive. Rage swept through her as she realized who stood before her. She forgot he was the charming man from the garden the night before. She disregarded his position as the powerful Prince of Auriano. This was the devil who had kidnapped her!

"You!" The word burst out of her. She slapped him across the face. Hard. Then she hit him again. As she wound up for a third blow, he grabbed her wrist.

"Perhaps I deserve to be punished, but three times is a bit much, *Donna* Barclay, and as you can see, my jaw has already been abused." His rebuke was delivered in a cool tone as if he were merely warning her of a puddle in her way.

She jerked out of his grasp, stalked away, swung back to face him. Her anger made her reckless. "How dare you! Do you think because you are the powerful Prince of Auriano that you can do as you wish? Do you have no decency?"

A shadow flitted through his eyes as swiftly as a bird across the sun. "Only sometimes," he said, somewhat ruefully.

"You cannot take what you want whenever you want," she declared with vehemence, shaking in her rage.

Alessandro blinked. Her words pierced him, for that was precisely what he had done. But *Donna* Barclay must never know the reason behind his actions, that it was the Hunger that crazed him and the fiend that lived in him during that time that overpowered him. He knew little about the passionate woman standing before him, except that she was incredible, even in her anger. But he also knew that she had touched a piece of the Sphere of Astarte. Therefore she could be his enemy, working to gain the pieces of the Sphere for her own ends. Since he'd spent years cultivating the persona of a prince who was never denied, he would use that to hide his true nature.

He tipped his head, appearing truly puzzled by the idea of denying himself anything. "Why not?"

"I'm not an object to be stolen and played with." She stood stiffly, her hands clenched at her sides.

"You are definitely not an object, *bella mia*." He curved his lips in a charming smile.

She exploded. "You had me kidnapped! And then you… you…" She waved her hand vaguely as she searched for words. The heat in her cheeks could have warmed a cold room.

"Kissed you," he supplied, not denying what he had done. "A wonderful, glorious experience."

She gaped at him in disbelief.

He paced closer to her. "Did you not enjoy it?"

"No!" She turned her back on him.

He nearly laughed aloud at her denial. Instead, he eased nearer and murmured, "Look at me and tell me you did not enjoy it."

He was so close Sabrina could feel the warmth of his body. Ignoring his magnetism, turning to face him, she said distinctly, "I did not enjoy it."

She lied. She had more than enjoyed it. She could think of nothing else except what he had done to her. At the same time that she was furious at the kidnapping and forced strip, the memory of his seduction and her scandalous reaction heated her cheeks with embarrassment and heated her insides with desire. His body crowded her even now, reminding her of his masculinity, of his tantalizing touch. She wanted more. But she was practical. What she wanted and what she could have were very different things. She stepped back, giving herself some breathing room.

He surprised her by grinning that pirate's smile, showing his dimple, obviously not discouraged in the least. "I will let you pretend that you did not enjoy it. But I plan to remind you of that night every chance I have."

"How will you do that if I refuse to see you again?" She raised her chin.

"I will shower you with gifts, throw flowers at your feet everywhere you walk." With a wave of his arm, he demonstrated.

The idea of the prince wooing her with such passion overwhelmed her, but she could not let him see how he affected her. "And if I remain secluded, will you kidnap me again?" she snapped.

Becoming solemn, he placed his hand over his heart. "Ah, *bella mia*, I meant you no harm. I apologize for frightening you." His grin returned. "But I am not sorry in the least we spent that time together. I intend to spend much more time with you. Each minute will be a reminder of that night. By the time I have finished, you will not be able to wait to have me make love to you."

She suspected he was right, but she would not let on that the mere idea of his touch made her shiver with want. She narrowed her eyes at him. "That's rather arrogant of you."

His grin widened. "*Si*. You have already told me that I am." He stepped back. "But besides calling on the most ravishing lady in Venice, I have come for another purpose."

Her brow crinkled in curiosity.

His lips twitched mischievously. "I have come to see *Sior* Dunfield's collection in the daylight."

The answer surprised her — again. And truthfully, disappointed her. Despite her anger, despite his arrogance, as a woman she had enjoyed being the subject of his ardor. She wanted his touch, his focus on her. What woman would not be flattered to have the Prince of Auriano dance attendance on her? But reality and common sense made her give herself a mental kick. He had kidnapped her, played with her, tricked her. She could not trust him. Why would the powerful, handsome, wealthy Prince of Auriano want her, a poor widow who had nothing to offer him?

Disappointment flickered in her eyes, then she squelched it. Alessandro hid a smile. He wanted her off balance and unsure of him. It was part of the ruthless game he was playing. In the end, he would win, and her secrets would be his. Along with her enchanting self. And his conscience be damned.

He watched her put distance between them as she wandered farther into the room and trailed her fingers along the top of the worktable. She heaved a huge sigh of false regret. "I'm sorry. I can't show you the collection today. Mr. Dunfield wishes me to hurry with the cataloging."

Playing her game, he followed, stopping very close behind her. "Do you think Dunfield would deny my request, *bella mia?*" His breath played with the tendrils of hair that had escaped the bun at the nape of her neck. With difficulty, he controlled the urge to kiss that delectable spot.

Turning to him, stepping back, she rubbed her arms as if she were chilled. "Please, Excellency, do not call me that. I am only a poor widow who is trying to keep a roof over my head and—"

"And what?" He was curious why her words stopped so abruptly.

She lowered her eyes, shook her head. "It is nothing. Only a widow's fears."

"Do you fear me, *bella mia?*" He spoke softly, seductively.

She glanced at him sharply. Apprehension flashed in her eyes. The tip of her tongue wet her lips. Ah, so she did want him, despite her denial or misgivings. Hiding his pleasure, he waited for her answer.

She uttered a false, ironic little laugh. "Why would I fear you, Excellency? You have only kidnapped me."

"Did I hurt you in any way?" he demanded. Then he softened his tone. "I would never hurt a woman, and especially not you, *Donna* Barclay."

Before she could reply, a child's voice echoed in the hallway. "Mama! Mama!" A little boy, about six or seven, barreled through the doorway and slid to a stop inside the room. "Mama, I did all my sums correctly!"

Alessandro was surprised she had a son. How had he missed that bit of information? The child's hair was lighter than his mother's, but his wide eyes were a duplicate of her gray ones, and the determined tilt of his chin was the same. Alessandro saw dismay flicker across her face before she exclaimed with a smile, "That's wonderful, Evan! But I have a visitor and you mustn't interrupt."

The child's eyes grew wide when he realized his mother was not alone. "I'm sorry, Mama."

She made the introductions.

Evan performed a formal bow. "How do you do, Excellency?"

Solemnly, Alessandro nodded with the perfect amount of formality as if he were greeting an adult. "Master Evan," he said.

He sensed her approval at his reaction as she went to the boy, put her arm protectively around his shoulders, and murmured to him. With another bow, the child turned and scampered away.

"He is a charming child," he observed.

"He is—" Once again, her words died, but the love for her child was written plainly on her face. Quietly, she said, "Thank you."

He admired her obvious pride in her son and her fierce protectiveness of the boy. Yet, the child's interruption had broken the tension between them. He wanted to keep her distracted, unsure of him.

As he took her elbow, he said, "Now, *Donna*, you must explain this painting of the Grand Canal to me. I see there is another, the same scene yet somehow different."

She pulled from his grasp and put several steps between them. "Why have you truly come here, Excellency?"

"Why?" He frowned, puzzled at her question. "Why would I not pay a visit to a charming lady who has access to an extensive art collection?"

She stepped away again, putting more space between them. "A lady who has nothing to offer you, Excellency. I am penniless. I can bring you no fortune, no great estate, no family connections. I have a son. Worst of all and most damning: I am English. While you, Excellency, are wealthy and powerful and could have your pick of the many lovely young Venetian ladies, more suited to your position. So, I ask again: why have you come?"

He prowled closer to her, determined to wipe out her list of deficiencies. "Those Venetian ladies who, you say, would be more suited to my position are flighty and frivolous. They care only for their cards or their flirtations — their goal, the next conquest of a heart. They are giddy and empty, turning their attentions from the swain who brings them roses to the one who brings them pearls or the next who writes a love poem. While you, *Donna* Barclay, I find intriguing, delightful, and lovely. Intelligent and well versed in matters beyond the foolish." He had meant only to compliment. Instead, he surprised himself with the truth behind his words.

She circled away from him. "You are very adept at flattery, Excellency, and skillful at misdirection. I know what I am."

"Do you?" he murmured. "I wonder."

"What do you mean by that?" She gave him a startled glance. "Of course I know who I am."

Her surprise might have been genuine, or she might have used it to cover the power deep within her. Perhaps it was time to poke at that cover. He leaned back against her worktable and crossed his arms as he gave her a thoughtful look. "But do you know *what* you are?"

71

She scowled at him. Exasperation colored her answer. "I am a widow in the employ of her late husband's uncle who must finish cataloging his art collection before he becomes annoyed with me. So, if you don't mind, Excellency, either state your true reason for being here or leave. I don't have time for this nonsense."

He was unused to a woman being so forthright and rejecting him so bluntly. He narrowed his eyes in irritation. She was being very obstinate, but he decided to humor her. Besides, her rejection challenged him. "I thought I had already stated why I am here. I find you delightful. Perhaps I will have to kidnap you again to convince you."

His taunt and the implication of further seduction colored her cheeks with a soft blush, and she glanced away. Gratified, he waited to see what she would say next.

"You take what you want like any ruthless pirate," she said.

"I believe there are several among my ancestors," he admitted with a wry smile.

"After you kidnap your victims," she asked, "do you make them walk the plank if they don't please you, Excellency?"

He chuckled. "It depends on how naughty they are—or not." Watching the uncertainty in her eyes, he let her stew for a moment, then he relented. "But come, *Donna* Barclay, that is for another time." He straightened and held out his arm to her. "Now, I would like you to explain these paintings to me."

Sabrina hesitated as she considered his request. She was still furious at his kidnapping, but he was a powerful man who had influence everywhere. An accusation against him of kidnapping would be laughed at by the Doge's Council of Ten. She had already courted his displeasure by insulting him with her slap and then her words. Having such a powerful man displeased with her would be dangerous. Yet, he had kept his temper in check and had continued to taunt and flirt. If she did not want to annoy him further, she needed to be polite. Reaching out, she placed her hand on his arm and was rewarded with a smile that fogged her brain.

As she turned away from that disarming smile and led him to the paintings, she rationalized that she was safe in Dunfield's house. Too many servants were about for Auriano to attempt another seduction. And he certainly would not attempt another kidnapping in broad daylight. Rather, she felt he would use outrageous flattery to entice. She found nothing wrong with indulging herself and spending some time with an elegant, handsome man, even if he did have a hidden motive. A very long time had elapsed since anyone had paid court to her.

She explained the two views of Canaletto's paintings of the Grand Canal and moved on to *The Piazzetta San Basso* by Marieschi and *The Dance in the Campiello* by Gabriel Bella. In doing so, they moved halfway around the room and were near the chest which had held the missing artifact. Auriano stopped abruptly several paces away and gestured at the chest.

"This object that you wished to show me last evening," he said. "Tell me about it."

"I know very little. It is a piece from my late husband's collection. When he died, Mr. Dunfield requested it because he is also interested in oddities and ancient artifacts."

"Can you describe it to me?"

"It looks like it might be part of a sphere, made of amber, carved in an intricate design I have never seen before." Sabrina watched interest light in the prince's eyes. Oddly, when her husband had spoken of the piece, he had the same look.

"Ah, *si*. I think I know what it is."

When Auriano uttered those words, he glanced away as if he had lost all interest. Sabrina suspected otherwise. He was too casual.

"What is it? I would like to know so that I may catalog it correctly for Mr. Dunfield." She gave an excuse that hid her curiosity about the piece and its strange disappearance.

"Is that the only reason you wish to know?" he asked.

"Of course. What other reason could I have?"

"Exactly. What other reason?" he said, baiting her.

Sabrina stared at him as her mind raced. Both her husband and Dunfield valued the piece. Now the prince seemed very interested in it. She wondered if it might be quite a bit more valuable than it appeared. Yet, if it was, then why had neither her husband nor Dunfield sold it? And why had no one wished to purchase it when she offered it for sale? Something about the piece was strange, and she meant to discover what it was. "I don't know what you mean," she said, feigning ignorance.

The prince gave her an enigmatic smile. "We should stop playing games here, *si*?"

"Like last evening, Excellency?" She gazed innocently at him.

"*Si*. Like last evening." His tone was flat and serious.

Sabrina suspected that he was playing a far more intricate game than her little charade. She shrugged. "I am merely curious, Excellency."

The prince's eyes turned fierce. "Do not toy with me, *Donna* Barclay. You are more than merely curious."

"I—" she began, but he cut her off with a sharp wave of his hand.

"This artifact is far more precious than a musty piece of rubble that has gone missing." He took a threatening step toward her. "What do you know about it?"

Alarm coursed through her. This was not the urbane, charming suitor who had danced with her the previous evening and showered her with flattery, nor the rogue who had seduced her, nor the gentleman who had allowed her to insult him only a few moments ago. This was a cold, dangerous man who looked as if he might, at any moment, do her harm.

Swallowing in a dry throat, Sabrina said, "Please, Excellency, I know nothing about the piece except what I have told you. It was my late husband's. When he died, Mr. Dunfield took it. And now it is missing."

The prince stared at her a moment, then stepped back and gave a little bow. "My apologies, *cara mia*. I did not mean to frighten you. I am only concerned for your safety. There could be danger connected to the piece."

Sabrina felt that the only danger at that moment was coming from him.

"You look at me as if I am a monster," the prince observed sadly. "Please, I do not mean you any harm."

Lowering her eyes, she said, "I was surprised, Excellency. I truly know nothing about the missing artifact, and I am curious, that is all."

"Then perhaps I should satisfy that curiosity." The prince smiled, and his fierceness was erased.

Thrown off-balance by his swift change of manner, Sabrina was dazzled by that smile. This man could charm the clouds from the sky. Without even knowing why, she smiled back.

"Let me tell you a story," he said. "Come, sit with me while I entertain you."

Taking her hand, he led her to a window seat half-hidden behind draperies and then sat facing her. The spot was intimate and cozy with a view into the courtyard below and the sun slanting down across the roof opposite. He seemed the perfect gentleman once again, but her experience with him thus far warned her to beware.

Watching her perch on the edge of the window seat, Alessandro realized he had frightened her with his intensity. Now, he had to allay those fears and get her to trust him, not an easy task considering he had begun this relationship with a kidnapping and attempted seduction. But he had not come this far in his life to give up now. Smiling, he hid his desperate desire to regain the missing artifact, and his suspicion that this beautiful woman knew more than she was telling.

"You see," he began, "the missing artifact is, I believe, a piece of the Sphere of Astarte."

"What is — ?"

"Shh." He placed a finger across her lips. They were very tantalizing lips, and the urge to replace his finger with his own lips distracted him for a moment. He reluctantly dropped his finger. "Please, *Donna* Barclay, let me tell my tale.

"The Sphere is ancient and was created in Phoenicia," he said. "It was made by a wizard who wished to live forever. The wizard has been long forgotten, but the Sphere eventually wound up in the hands of one of my ancestors. It was in my family for centuries, until it was stolen and taken apart. It was the symbol of the land my family ruled. Now, obviously, I would like to recover the pieces and restore it to its rightful place for my family, but also for the people of Auriano." Half-truths, he decided, were better than lies, and he could not bear to tell this woman the truth about his curse.

"Who stole it from your family?"

"That is unimportant." He waved away her question. "But what is significant is that a piece of the Sphere is very close."

"What makes the piece so dangerous?" she asked.

He easily constructed more half-truths. "Because of its age, it is very valuable, and as you mentioned last evening, there is the legend that it is magical. There are others who are desperate to possess it." He raised her hand to his lips and placed a gentle kiss on her skin. "Please, *Donna* Barclay, *cara mia*, will you help me recover a part of my family's history and return it to the land where it belongs?"

The touch of his lips sent a thrill up her arm. His steady, intent gaze pleaded with her. But she was wary of his charm. Cocking her head, Sabrina studied him. He was on a quest, like one of King Arthur's knights in search of the Holy Grail. Yet, unlike that noble knight, this man before her was seductive, ruthless, and more than a little dangerous. She could not afford to offend him again, for she feared what he might tell Dunfield. Auriano was the most powerful man Dunfield had dangled before her as a suitor. She had to be careful in her discouragement of his suit.

On the other hand, she was inclined to help him. His story seemed genuine. It would explain why her husband and Dunfield were so interested in the piece. She felt sure Auriano would pay an exorbitant sum to retrieve it. If she found the piece herself, she might be able to sell it to Auriano and completely free herself and Evan from Dunfield's control. The thought was as seductive as the man sitting across from her.

Since she had no idea what had happened to the piece, she felt she could afford to be generous to this charming, handsome rogue. Yet, she was also committed to help Dunfield sell his collection to the English king, and this was part of his collection. If he discovered she went against his wishes or betrayed him, she might find herself without a roof over her head. But if she helped the prince, he might be inclined to help her out of the situation with Dunfield.

Following rules had put her into this tenuous situation in Venice. She decided it was time to be reckless. She smiled. "I would be delighted to help you find this artifact, Excellency."

Relief softened his eyes, and he opened his mouth to speak.

"Wait," she said, "before you thank me. I'm not sure I can be of much help to you. After all, I am only a simple woman who is here in Venice to help Mr. Dunfield catalog his collection." And that was only half a lie.

"Knowing you will help is enough, *Donna*." His thumb stroked the back of her hand. "I have one other tiny request. You must keep this a secret, just between us, *si?* The piece does have some value beyond what it means to my family, and those who would like to possess it will sometimes go to extreme measures to get what they want."

"Of course," she agreed. Whoever these other people might be, she was not in any hurry to help them. Her first priority had to be the welfare of her son, whatever route that took.

"Now, let us make a plan." Smiling, he raised her hand to his lips and kissed her fingers.

Sabrina was charmed, but she refused to be bewitched by the force of his seduction. Yet, when he smiled, she felt as if the air had been sucked from the room. Warning bells rang distantly in her brain, but for now, she would ignore them.

Chapter 9

In a chamber deep beneath the lagoon that separated the city from the mainland, the young woman cowered in the center of the vast black floor. A single torch in a wall sconce was the only light. Around her, columns of black marble marched away into the empty dark space.

Nulkana watched the young woman and allowed the silence to stretch. Dressed in a floor-length, black cape and cowl, she knew her appearance frightened the girl. As a sorceress, ancient, with knowledge gleaned over the centuries, she had learned the importance of intimidation.

The young woman lifted her head, stealing a peek. "I am sorry, Mistress," she sobbed. "I don't know where the piece is. The boy — "

"Excuses!" Nulkana made herself appear to grow larger, then returned to normal size. "I gave you a simple task, and all you bring me are excuses."

"But the boy –"

"Silence!" Nulkana floated toward the woman. "Since you cannot control the boy, I will have to find a solution."

The woman whimpered as Nulkana's delicate and graceful hand reached out from the cape and caressed the woman's cheek.

"There, there, Letitia, do not fret. You know I will find an answer to our problem," Nulkana soothed, like a mother comforting her child. "You say the boy has power? He is able to hide his thoughts from you?"

"*Si*, Mistress." Letitia nodded eagerly.

"That is an interesting twist. I have not sensed such an ability from the mother, but her powers are unused and undiscovered." Nulkana absently stroked Letitia's cheek as her thoughts jumped from one possibility to another. Two innocents with such tremendous power could be a boon. No, her first plan, to destroy the mother, was the only safe route. Then the child could easily be persuaded to help find the piece of the Sphere of Astarte. She knew it was close. She could sense it. If only she could get her hands on it, she would be so much more powerful than she was now. And those Auriano whelps would never be able to wrest it from her grasp again.

"I can test the mother, Mistress," Letitia ventured, pulling Nulkana's thoughts back to the present.

"Ah, you are a good slave, my Letitia," Nulkana purred, patting her on the shoulder. "Yes, perhaps, but not now. You must work on finding the missing piece of the Sphere. Bring it to me, and perhaps I will free you."

"Oh, thank you, Mistress." Letitia would have fallen to her knees in gratitude if Nulkana had not tightened a hand around her neck.

"You may thank me after I have punished you for losing the piece in the first place," the sorceress said.

Letitia's eyes widened and she cried out in fear. Nulkana's fingers at her neck elongated and slid up the back of her head. She pressed her other hand against Letitia's chest. With a whispered word, her hand passed through skin, muscle, and bone, and then was inside, cupping the young woman's heart, massaging, petting it. Letitia's terror made the organ's rhythm race. Nulkana felt the current of energy, absorbed it.

Slowly, the warmth of the heart began to pulse with its rhythm, alternating with cold as the energy, the young woman's life force, eased through Nulkana's fingers and up her arm. *Ah, yes.* The girl's energy was sweet, young, intoxicating. Like a fine wine. Like the erotic touch of a lover. Nulkana sucked it in. Ate it. Devoured it. The heat and cold pulsed, throbbed, ebbed, and flowed. Still Nulkana dragged it in, energy seeping out of the young woman and into Nulkana's hands, filling her, feeding her.

Letitia screamed, a single, high, drawn-out note, the sound reverberating in the empty space. The pain that created it excited Nulkana, caused a shudder to ripple through her. Oh, yes. Pleasure. Ecstasy. Rapture.

When Letitia was nearly spent, when her life force was almost gone, Nulkana reluctantly withdrew her hand from the young woman's chest. Letitia still had some use, so she would not take all her life. Holding the young woman by the back of her head, Nulkana looked into her eyes. They were glazed, but deep within them the sorceress could see her reflection. She smiled coldly. The young woman was hers completely.

Satisfied, Nulkana let her drop to the floor, a mound of sobbing waste. Letitia's energy flowed through her and filled her with glee. Alive, rejuvenated, she laughed, wildly, evilly, madly.

Soon, she would have the Sphere of Astarte. Soon, her enemies would be dead. Soon, she would be able to live forever.

Sabrina flitted about her bedchamber as she searched for her glove. The Prince of Auriano would arrive soon to take her on an afternoon stroll through the Piazza San Marco. She was not concerned about keeping him waiting, for that was a woman's prerogative, but she needed to look her best for her own self-confidence. He could unbalance her composure as easily as breathing.

She had sent a grumbling Cora to look in the rest of the *casa* for the glove. Cora was appalled at the idea of Sabrina going anywhere with the prince, for she had voiced her suspicions about his being the instigator of their kidnapping. Sabrina had laughed at her maid's comments, but she knew Cora wasn't fooled.

Sabrina opened wardrobe doors, rummaged in drawers, and generally turned her belongings upside down.

"I can't imagine what could have happened to it," she said.

A giggle came from the middle of her bed, where Evan sat watching her. Turning to him with her hands on her hips, she scowled with mock severity. "All right," she said, "where did you hide it this time?" He made a game of hiding things on her and then pretending to "find" the items when she was nearly at her wits' end.

Evan grinned, his gray eyes twinkling. "I'm not going to tell you. You'll have to guess."

"Hmm, let me think." She drew her brows together and pursed her lips. Pretending to concentrate very hard for a moment, she brightened as if she suddenly had an idea. "I know! It's under the bed!" She bent to look.

"No." Evan giggled. "Guess again."

Just as Sabrina was about to make another guess, a scream echoed through the *casa*. Yelling and running footsteps followed.

"Mama, what is it?" Evan sat frozen in the middle of the bed. His little face paled. "I didn't do anything, Mama. Really, I didn't."

Sabrina went to him and drew him into the comforting protection of her arms. "It's probably nothing. Maybe one of the gondoliers fell into the canal."

Evan hiccupped a chuckle.

Rapid steps sounded in the hallway, a knock came at the door, then Cora swept into the room. "Oh, my lady! Come quickly! There's been an accident!"

Sabrina smiled calmly at Evan while anxiety rushed through her. "There, you see? It was only one of the gondoliers getting himself wet," she assured him. "Wait here with Cora, and I'll go find out what is happening."

At Evan's nod, she kissed the top of his head, gave Cora a warning to keep the door locked, and stepped out into the hall. The scream and the commotion that followed sounded more ominous than a mere accident. Sabrina waited until she heard the key turn in the lock, then hurried down to the ground floor.

On the *fondamenta*, the small quay beside the canal, a group of servants gathered around a wet heap of cloth. The servants parted, allowing her a glimpse. Alarm coursed through her when she saw the wet heap was Letitia, Evan's nurse.

"What has happened here?" Sabrina demanded.

Letitia moaned and her head flopped to the side. Sabrina gasped.

"*Madre di Dio!*" one of the servants exclaimed.

Letitia's face, youthful when Sabrina had last seen her in the morning, was now the visage of an old woman, with wrinkles around the eyes and mouth. A streak of white ran through her hair, which once had been a rich, dark brunette. Sabrina could think of nothing that would cause such a radical change.

One of the gondoliers muttered, "The plague."

As everyone instinctively stepped back, another figure, masked and cloaked, stepped onto the *fondamenta* from a gondola. "No, not the plague."

Sabrina recognized the voice. Auriano. She had not seen his gondola arrive, but now that he was here, she felt oddly relieved. She stood to face him.

"If not the plague, what then?" Her tone was sharper than she had intended, but the condition of the woman lying at her feet unnerved her.

The prince shrugged. "She has obviously had some sort of fright. Her clothes are wet. Perhaps she fell from one of the bridges."

Sabrina narrowed her eyes at him. Her relief at his presence turned to annoyance. He could not possibly be so witless. Anyone could see that what had happened to Letitia went beyond merely falling into a canal. But then, he was the Prince of Auriano, womanizer, gambler, rogue. Perhaps he was too shallow to understand the gravity of the situation.

Dismissing his suggestion, she gave directions to the servants to take Letitia to her room, call for the surgeon, and watch over her. Then she ordered everyone else back to their duties.

When they were alone on the quay, Auriano spoke quietly. "What do you know of the woman?"

Sabrina turned to him. "She is my son's nurse. I hired her when I came to Venice. She has been dutiful. I believe she has come to care for Evan."

"Do you know anything of her background or her family?" His question was uttered with more than curiosity.

"I believe she has no family, but she came well recommended." She frowned. "Why are you so interested in a servant?"

Auriano glanced about. "Is there somewhere we may speak more privately?"

"What do you know of her condition?" Suspicious, Sabrina did not move.

"Please." He gestured toward the interior of the *casa.*

Sabrina turned on her heel. She led him through the water gate, across the *andron,* the large entry space beyond, to a small room Dunfield sometimes used for conducting business with those he considered unworthy to receive in the upper salon. It had originally been used as a storeroom, so the walls and floor were bare of decoration. The furnishings were spare and roughly made, consisting of two chairs, a table, and a single lamp. She left the door ajar after they were inside.

"We are quite private here," she said.

Looking around, his voice pitched low, he said, "I will have to remember this spot in the future."

"I prefer to be seduced in much more comfortable surroundings," Sabrina stated acerbically.

"I would not have it any other way," he murmured.

Sabrina sent him a warning glance. "About my servant, Excellency, what can you tell me?"

After wandering around the tiny space, he came to a stop before her. "You know she did not fall from a bridge."

"I had come to that conclusion." Her tone was dry.

"I don't know her, but I presume her appearance was quite different the last time you saw her?"

Surprised at his correct assumption, Sabrina nodded. "She is — or was — rather younger than myself. A fairly attractive girl."

The prince sighed. "It is as I thought. She has been the victim of a sorceress."

A laugh bubbled forth before Sabrina could suppress it. "A sorceress? Do you expect me to believe that some witch did this to her?" She laughed again and shook her head. "Excellency –"

"Alessandro," he prompted.

"Excellency," she repeated. "I don't know what caused Letitia's condition, but I rather doubt it was some mythical fiend."

He stilled at her last word, then seemed to collect himself. "*Donna* Barclay… Sabrina…" He swept off his tricorn hat and white mask. "You must believe me. If this terrible thing has befallen your son's nurse, then the whole household may be in danger." He stepped closer.

That small step brought him near enough that his scent of wild thyme and sage teased her nose. It reminded her of that night of seduction and reminded her that he was also a danger. She took a step back, putting a safe distance between them.

His dark brows drew together in consternation. "You and your son could be in great peril."

His statement sent an arrow of ice through her.

"Sabrina…"

His soft entreaty forced her mind back to practicality. No sorceress was after either her or Evan. "What would you suggest, Excellency?" she snapped, annoyed that she had succumbed to his ridiculous fairy tale. "That I call for the prelates of the Church to come and stand guard? Or perhaps I should ask them to hold an exorcism?"

The prince sighed. "No, I'm not saying that. Do you not believe that there are beings who have powers beyond the ordinary?"

"I believe what I can see, Excellency. Anything beyond that, I leave to the mystics." Sabrina gave an airy wave of her hand, belying the apprehension that still clutched at her middle.

"Ah, the mystics. And who might these mystics be?" A dark brow arched upward.

She frowned. "Do not mock me. I have a right to my opinion."

"*Si*, you do. But can you tell me that what befell your son's nursemaid was ordinary?" As she started to protest once more, he placed his finger across her lips with gentle pressure. "No, do not say it. You are in danger. Whether you believe it is from some otherworldly being or from some human monster makes no difference."

An odd urge to kiss the finger across her lips took hold of her. Fortunately, he dropped his hand before she acted on the impulse, and her sanity returned. "What do you suggest?"

"I will protect you and your son," he stated as if the answer were obvious.

She gave a short laugh. "How will you do that? You cannot be with me or Evan every hour of every day."

"No, I cannot." He drew out the words, let them hang for a moment. "I will provide a trustworthy nursemaid for your son, one who will be able to protect him."

"That won't be necessary," she said, uncomfortable with his generosity. "I can find another nurse."

"Would you deny me the privilege of helping you, *Donna* Barclay?" He raised an arrogant, princely brow.

Understanding that she would insult him if she argued, she bowed her head in gratitude. "Thank you."

"And for you..." He allowed his words to hang a moment. "For you, I will do the next best thing. I will become your *cicisbeo*, your *cavaliere sirvente*."

Sabrina gaped at him. A *cicisbeo* was a gentleman companion, an escort, one who attended upon a woman's every whim and her every waking hour. He was her confidante, her protector. He flattered and entertained her; he counseled her and scolded. In return, he was allowed into her chamber upon her waking in the morning, as she was abed at night, in her morning gown, as she dressed for the day, or undressed at night. He might fasten a necklace at her throat, tighten the ribbons on her corset, tie her garter at her thigh. She shared all her secrets and confidences with him. The association was, in theory, platonic.

The idea of Auriano as her *cicisbeo* scared her to death.

"No," she said. "You will not become my *cicisbeo*."

Glancing beyond her shoulder through the open door, he said, "Ah, I see Dunfield. I will make arrangements with him. When I am finished, we will stroll through the Piazza San Marco as we had planned." He took a step around her.

Riled that he completely ignored her, she placed herself in his path. "I do not wish to have you as my *cicisbeo*," she said emphatically.

He smiled that pirate's smile. "Does the thought frighten you, *cara mia*?"

Sabrina raised her chin. "Absolutely not. Why should I be frightened?"

He chuckled. "Why indeed?"

Chapter 10

Sabrina held on to the bedpost as Cora tightened the ribbons on her corset. Across the room, Auriano lounged in a chair and watched through hooded eyes. With his black velvet coat and breeches, his black silk waistcoat trimmed in silver, he looked like a panther waiting for its prey to wander past.

This was the second day he had been her *cicisbeo*, and she was slowly going mad. When he left her in the evening, she could not wait for him to return the next day, for he charmed and entertained her. When he returned, his attraction was so strong that she wanted to hide. He was with her everywhere she went, always ready to serve her with whatever she needed, from fetching a shawl, to stirring her morning chocolate, to sharpening her quills, to rearranging a curl of hair, to gently attaching earrings. Now, she could feel his gaze on her like a caress. It made her skin prickle.

"Perhaps I should help with those ribbons," he suggested lazily.

Sabrina felt Cora's fingers still. Cora had voiced her disapproval of the arrangement the prince had made, but Dunfield had agreed to it, had encouraged it, had forced Sabrina to accept it. Because Cora suspected the prince might be the man who abducted them, she made Cora swear not to reveal anything about that night, not even to speak to her in private about it. No one else in the household was aware of the kidnapping, for she and Cora were returned well before dawn. She intended for it to remain that way to protect her reputation and Cora's position in the household.

"Cora is perfectly capable of tying my stays," Sabrina said, attempting to keep him across the room.

"It would please me to help." He spoke from immediately behind her. His ability to move so silently amazed and unnerved her.

Cora sniffed in disapproval. Then a different set of fingers began pulling on her ribbons. They were firm, yet gentle, and left her room to breathe.

"This is a silly garment for you to wear, *bella mia*," he said. "You have no need for such as this."

Cora gave a second sniff. "Why would you be knowing such a thing? Excellency." Her tone was barely respectful, and she spoke his title as an afterthought.

"One would have to be blind not to see that *Donna* Barclay has no need," he said mildly, a hint of steel beneath the velvet. "As her maid, I should think you would advise her against wearing such a thing."

Before Cora could say something else that would make the man angry, Sabrina said, "Cora, I think I left my shawl in Evan's room. Would you fetch it, please?"

As soon as she left, the prince tied off the ribbons at Sabrina's back. As always, every time he did her a service, his fingers caressed the air a minuscule space above her skin. A tingly warm current radiated across her back. She shivered. The sensation reminded her of the feeling she had experienced when that shadow man had touched her. This was only her imagination, of course, caused by Auriano's allure. The prince was completely flesh and bone. He had proven that when he'd had her abducted. When he actually did touch her, she felt only the contact of skin on skin, although each touch was performed with a sensuousness that made her body throb.

The tingly current ran down her spine again, and she knew his hand hovered a mere breath from her skin.

"Stop that," she snapped.

"Stop what?" His tone was faintly puzzled.

"That thing you do with your fingers." When she tried to explain it, she felt foolish.

"But I have not even touched you yet this evening," he protested. "When I do, you will know." As he murmured, his hand curled over the slope of her shoulder, and his thumb caressed the nape of her neck. Her knees went weak. She gripped the bedpost with white knuckles for support.

Forcing herself to speak, she began, "I sent my maid away—"

"Thank you, *cara mia*, for that," he interrupted.

Sabrina knew his gratitude was in return for giving him the chance to turn her once again into a mindless fool. She rallied her scattered thoughts and started again. "I did not send her away to give you an opportunity for seduction, Excellency. I sent her away so she would not gouge out your eyes with a hairpin, and you would not stab her with that stiletto you are wearing up your sleeve."

He chuckled and dropped a light kiss on her shoulder. "The knife is for your protection, *carissima*."

Slipping away from him, ignoring the fires he ignited with his touch and his kiss, she walked to where her dress lay on a chair. "Who will protect me from you, Excellency?"

Feigning shock, he said, "*Ma Donna!* You wound me. I would never harm you."

As she turned to him with the dress dangling in her hand, her eyes narrowed. "Truly, Excellency? What would you call my abduction?"

Exasperation crossed his face. "Did I harm you, *Donna* Barclay?" Before she could answer, he went on, "I did not." He took a step closer. "In fact, you enjoyed my touch." His hand, hovering above her skin, moved down and then up her arm. His fingers skimmed up the side of her neck, traced around her ear, then his hand came to rest on her shoulder. "You will have to admit it sooner or later."

She tried desperately to put a coherent thought together, but his intense gaze, his fingers, that thing he had done again with his hand blanked out everything else.

With a crooked smile, he slipped the dress from her grasp. "Come, *bella mia*. Let us get you dressed before your maid returns. Perhaps then she will see I am not a monster."

Not a monster, Sabrina decided, but a man with fiendish hands who could drive her crazy with exquisitely gentle torture.

By the time Cora returned with her shawl, Sabrina was decently though not demurely dressed. The gown she wore, in fact almost everything she had on from the skin out, had been sent to her that morning by the prince. His note had explained that attending the theater required more formal attire than brown serge, a reference to her shabby dress the day he had first called on her. Insulted at his barb, she tried to return the garment, only to have Dunfield intercept the messenger and force her to accept the gift. Annoyed, she had added the stays, an item that had not been included with the other garments.

Despite her irritation, she had to admit that Auriano had an excellent sense of fashion. The gown was of the new style with high waist and floating, straight skirt. It left her shoulders bare and plunged deeply at the neckline. Of palest blue silk, it set off her dark hair and made the gray of her eyes shimmer. The gold chain which held her pendant toyed with the crease between her breasts. The gown made her feel beautiful. The pendant made her feel safe, for she remembered his strange reaction to it when he had abducted her.

And she wanted every advantage when she was dealing with the seductive prince who watched her with those predatory golden eyes.

Alessandro admired the way the silken material of the dress caressed Sabrina's curves. His eyes were drawn to the moonstone pendant, not only because of the tantalizing spot where it lay, but also because of his curiosity. When he had touched it during the Hunger, it had burned away his dark cravings. He dared not touch it again, at least not until he could be sure of his reaction. It obviously had some magical force, but Sabrina seemed to be unaware of its power. He resolved to find out more about it.

Alessandro was forced to delay his inquiry because her maid had returned. He slipped the shawl from Cora's hands and turned to *Donna* Barclay, once again admiring her appearance. He had sent the gown to her on a whim and was exceedingly glad. She was exquisite. As he placed the shawl reverently about Sabrina's shoulders, he was careful to stay away from the infinitesimal space between his fingers and her skin where that odd sensation occurred. Even for him, with his carefully nurtured control, enough was enough. Understanding that Sabrina was relatively naive, he did not want to overwhelm her. Even so, he heard her quick intake of breath, signaling her response to him. *Bene.* He hid his smile of satisfaction. Soon, she would reveal anything — everything — to him, including the power she hid and the whereabouts of the piece of the Sphere of Astarte.

Despite his intention to remain calculating and coldly removed from any feelings for this woman, he found himself drawn to her, to her stubborn rejection of his advances, to her sharp mind and sharper words. To her witchy eyes and her tempting lips. To her lovely body that he wanted writhing beneath his in passion. Ah, *si.* That would be worth the wait. He was looking forward to that with impatience. The pursuit of the piece of the Sphere of Astarte might be his ultimate goal, but the seduction of *Donna* Barclay along the way would be the most pleasure he had experienced in a very long time.

Holding out his hand to her, he smiled and noted the wariness in her eyes. Soon, that wariness would be erased.

"*Bellissima,*" he said.

She placed her fingers in his. Taking advantage, he raised them to his mouth and kissed each one. He kept his eyes on her, saw her parted lips, the racing pulse at her throat. "Now," he said, "we are ready for the theater."

"I must say goodnight to my son," she said a bit breathlessly, taking back her hand.

"By all means, let us wish the child pleasant dreams." He motioned for her to precede him, thoroughly satisfied at the progress of his seduction.

Sabrina knocked on the nursery door, pushed it open, and entered. Letitia, Evan's former nurse, was recovering from her terrible accident in the care of an elderly woman he had found. In her place was Evan's new nurse, the one Alessandro had recommended. He exchanged a quick glance with the woman. She answered with a barely perceptible nod. Everything was as it should be. The child was safe.

The boy stood politely at his nurse's side and performed a formal bow.

Once again, Alessandro greeted him as if he were an adult. He sensed *Donna* Barclay's approval at his reaction. Because of his curse, he made a point to avoid children, but something about this child drew him. He spied an array of toy soldiers set up in a mock battle across the floor. Intrigued at the child's complicated formation, he wandered closer and crouched next to it. After studying the array for a moment, he said, "This brigade will be overrun if you do not move them to the left, like this." He rearranged a few of the men.

Evan hunkered down next to him. "I hadn't thought of that," he said with excitement. "I had planned for them to sweep around and catch this unit from the rear."

Alessandro was impressed with the boy's logic. "An excellent plan," he said. "But you will have to let the middle fall back to lure them in." Once again, he moved a few soldiers around the floor.

"That'll bamboozle 'em!" Evan crowed.

Donna Barclay gasped. "Evan! Your manners!"

The boy blushed and hung his head.

Alessandro stifled a laugh. "It will definitely bamboozle them," he agreed. Then he leaned down and whispered, "If you need any more help bamboozling the enemy, just send word."

"Thank you, Excellency." Evan grinned up at Alessandro and his eyes glowed.

Alessandro felt a pleasant warmth at the boy's smile, a rare feeling, and one he doubted he would feel again soon. Children were not part of his plan, not until the curse was broken.

As the boy focused again on his soldiers and scooted closer to them, he accidently brushed up against Alessandro. The unexpected contact sent a faint surge of energy up Alessandro's arm. He hid his surprise. Sabrina's son had a powerful ability, and like his mother, the boy had touched the Sphere of Astarte. Smiling back at the boy, he was doubly determined to learn all there was to know about the fascinating *Donna* Barclay and her son.

Sabrina watched Auriano give her son a warm, sincere smile. At that moment, she could have hugged the man. Evan had been without a father for two long years. While her husband, Richard, had spent little time with her, he had doted on Evan. Yet, even though Auriano seemed to have a rapport with her son, he was too much the rogue to consider him as a proper father. Despite her attraction to the man.

After wishing Evan goodnight, they descended the stairs to the water gate. "Thank you for being kind to Evan," she said.

"Your son is very special, *Donna* Barclay. You must protect him," he said gravely.

"I will. I do," she answered, but she was puzzled at his comment, for she sensed he meant more than the nursemaid he had recommended or the protection he was providing. But she was unable to ask him more as he guided her quickly down the rest of the stairs.

Before they stepped through the water gate, they both donned the *tabarro*, a long domino. The garments covered them from head to toe and hid their identity, a requisite during *Carnevale*, and especially for the theater. The prince handed her into the *felze* of his gondola and settled next to her. The interior of the *felze* was like a tiny sumptuous room, with black leather upholstered seats, a thick oriental carpet, and a little table. Drawn curtains on either side and behind concealed them completely. An open bottle of wine and two glasses were set out for them.

As the prince poured the wine, Sabrina made a decision. He had been attentive, gracious, and seductive since the evening of the masquerade ball. He had her aroused to the point where she thought she might scream. She suspected he was toying with her, although she did not understand the reason. It was time to beat him at his own game. When he held out her glass, she took it and covered his hand with hers.

"*Grazie*," she murmured as she kept his hand prisoner, brought the glass to her lips, and took a sip. She was rewarded with his brow raised in surprise. She slipped the bottle from his fingers. "Allow me to serve you, Excellency." As she reached across him to pour his glass of wine, her hand landed on his thigh, where she let her fingers caress. A quiver ran through the muscle beneath her hand. Ducking her head, she hid her smile.

She held out his glass. He took it, put it down, and slipped her glass out of her fingers. "I would prefer to sip where your lips have been, *cara mia*." Turning her glass, he sipped from the same spot she had sipped from.

Sabrina took back her glass. Without taking her eyes from him, she did the same thing. She watched him watching her. His eyes darkened.

Reaching up, he brushed back her hood and trailed his fingers down her jaw. "It is a dangerous game you play, *Ma Donna*. Are you sure you know all the rules?"

Sabrina gave a little laugh. "Rules? There are no rules in the game you play, Excellency."

"But there are," he murmured, as he teased a curl that lay against her neck. "You make the rules. I simply follow them. If you raise the stakes, then I must do the same."

"You had no rules the night you kidnapped me," she challenged.

Something sad flitted through his eyes. It was gone so quickly, she wondered if she had actually seen it.

"That was then," he said. "This is now. Now, you see, I am your *cicisbeo*, and I must protect you, even from myself."

"I think I am capable of protecting myself from you, Excellency." Her statement was blatant audacity. And a lie. She knew he was an expert at seduction while she was a novice. If he practiced his wiles on her much longer, she might tear off her clothes and throw herself at him. But she would never admit that.

"Then I applaud you for your bravery. We shall see who wins this battle, *si?*" A teasing brow inched up.

Looking him in the eye, daring him, tossing aside caution, she said, "I want you to kiss me."

He stared at her a moment, his gaze unfathomable, then he smiled. "No, I think not."

His rejection hurt. And angered her. "You decline my challenge." Feigning indifference, she sighed and looked away. "It does not matter."

He took her chin and turned her to face him. "It does matter, *carissima*. I do not want you to hate me."

"How can I hate you for something that I ask for?" She knew as soon as she said the words that she had put herself in jeopardy.

"Perhaps you are unaware of the consequences of your request." His thumb stroked across her cheek and stopped at the corner of her mouth.

94

Sabrina wanted to lick at that thumb. "I told you the night you had me kidnapped that I am a widow, Excellency, not an innocent."

Amusement lit his eyes. "I think you failed that test, *cara mia*. Although you are a widow, I'm afraid your husband left you very much an innocent."

Sabrina felt the blush heat her cheeks. "Perhaps I no longer wish to remain an innocent," she said, shocked at her own boldness.

A tiny line appeared between his brows, but he said nothing as he studied her.

"I plan to win this battle, Excellency." She met those golden eyes directly.

He bared his teeth in that pirate's grin. "*Bene.* My surrender will be sweet."

His hand slipped across her shoulder and splayed across her back. The warmth of his palm spread across her skin. With his other hand, he slipped her glass from her fingers. Slowly, he drew her to him, his intent gaze holding her captive. His lips touched the corner of her mouth, then the other corner. His mouth brushed across hers. Yes, this was what she remembered—the gentle touch, the suggestion of more to come.

"My name is Alessandro," he murmured. The tip of his tongue lightly touched her top lip. "It would please me if you used it."

She conceded only partially. "Alessandro. Excellency."

With a chuckle, he relented and brushed her mouth again. "You smell like jasmine and orange," he whispered against her lips, then ran his tongue across them. "You taste like peaches." He nibbled at her bottom lip. "Ah, *dolce.*"

Sabrina shivered. His kisses were heady, but she wanted more. She wanted him to possess her.

Seeming to sense what she wanted, he covered her mouth with his. Her lips parted, and she invited him to explore. He took full advantage of her invitation, tasting, teasing, arousing until her senses were full of him. She was aware only of his mouth, his body pressed against her. He was her only anchor as the world fell away.

His hand slipped beneath her cloak, and the low décolletage of her dress became an advantage as he touched her breasts. Massaging, he rubbed his thumb across a nipple, bringing it to sensitive attention, and wringing a whimper from her. Heat shot through her.

Sabrina needed to touch him. Unbuttoning his waistcoat, she slid her hands up his chest, the silkiness of his shirt softening the hard muscles beneath. She drew her palms across his nipples and was rewarded with his swift intake of breath. A sense of power swept through her as she realized her touch ignited him as much as his did to her.

His hand left her breast, and she felt his fingers beneath her skirt, tracing up her leg, across her knee to her thigh where her stockings ended. His fingers on her bare skin made her shiver. He inched higher on the outside of her thigh and then his hand spanned across her leg. His thumb dipped down to tease the curls between her legs. She was ready for him, for whatever he wanted to do. She throbbed. She was hot, moist. Her knees fell apart.

Someone knocked on the roof of the *felze*. His hand stilled on her thigh. His gondolier muttered something about arriving. Slowly, the prince retreated.

"You are mine," he whispered against her lips, "but this will have to wait." Then he set her away from him.

Dazed by his kisses, inflamed by his touch, Sabrina forced her brain into coherent thought, not an easy task. His words echoed in her head, the same words that the shadow creature had used. But that creature was mere shadow, and next to her sat a living, breathing man. As he helped her straighten her clothes, she could think of nothing but his tempting mouth and his arousing hands. She remembered the night he had kidnapped her. Her anger and shock turned to pleasure. Her reaction bewildered her at the time, but now, there was no confusion. She wanted him.

His seduction was exquisite.

Her surrender was madness.

Chapter 11

As soon as Sabrina entered the theater called *La Fenice* on Auriano's arm, she heard the whispers erupt from the masked patrons in attendance.

"Who is she?"

"She must be his betrothed."

"No, no, I heard he refuses to marry."

"He must have taken a new mistress."

"I heard she is from an impoverished family from the south."

"No, she is a French courtesan."

"Imbeciles, she is a member of Russian royalty."

"Has anyone seen her face?"

"Another Helen of Troy, no doubt."

"Or a Veronica Franco."

"She must be exquisite."

"I'm sure she's an accomplished lover to snag Auriano."

"Madre di Dio, I'd like to sample her charms."

Sabrina felt the heat climb up her cheeks, and the marvelous sensations she had experienced from the interlude in the gondola shriveled and went cold.

As Auriano led her to his box, he raised her fingers to his lips. "Don't let them distress you. You are under my protection. They are merely jealous because you are beautiful," he murmured.

Her blush deepened at his compliment, and she sent him a halfhearted smile of gratitude. She did not want to be under his protection. If he had not forced himself into the position of her *cicisbeo*, she would not be enduring this embarrassment. She longed for the solitude of her workroom and the peace she only felt with her son.

Resigned to an evening of torture, she was surprised to soon find herself engrossed in the comedy by Goldoni. The play was rich with sharp wit and humorous antics, and she could not help laughing and immersing herself in the spectacle, despite Auriano's proximity. But midway through the production, an odd, barely perceptible sensation tickled her mind. The tickle became a pinch, and then an uncomfortable prod. Something — someone — was trying to probe her mind. By the beginning of the last act, she knew what it was... Evil. It was the same presence she had felt in the chapel. Fearful, she glanced around. They were isolated from the rest of the audience in the prince's box, so no one was close enough to be the obvious source. But she knew the evil was there.

She squirmed under the pressure. The probing increased, and pain began to grow behind her eyes. Auriano's hand covered hers in a comforting gesture.

"*Cara mia*, you are unwell." His words were laced with concern. "Come, let us leave, and I will return you home."

When Sabrina stood, the world tilted wildly. Her knees gave way. She grabbed Auriano for support and was immediately swept up in his arms. Nausea and pounding pain wiped away everything else. She buried her face in his shoulder, fought not to retch, and let him take her wherever he wished.

Fresh air cleared her head, and she realized Auriano had carried her outside. As soon as they stepped through the doors, the probing stopped. Sabrina dragged in huge lungfuls of air. The pain in her head faded and her stomach settled. She found herself placed on the seat of one of the delicate chairs from an alcove in the lobby of the theater. Auriano knelt on one knee before her, held on to her hand, and put a glass to her lips with the other.

"Please, *cara mia*, drink. It will revive you," he urged.

She had no idea how he managed to supply both the chair and the wine so quickly. She sipped and felt better.

"I think I should return you to *Sior* Dunfield's *casa*," he said.

"No, please. I'll be fine in a moment," she said.

She could not return home so early. Dunfield would upbraid her for discouraging Auriano. At the moment, she could not counter Dunfield's accusations, and she certainly could not explain the frightening sensations in her head. Dunfield would think she was mad.

She focused on Auriano's solicitous expression. Something in that golden gaze eased her discomfort, made her feel stronger.

"Please, walk with me," she entreated and smiled, hoping to convince him she was recovered.

With a nod, he stood and supported her as she found her feet. Still a bit weak, she swayed unsteadily.

"*Cara mia*," he said in concern, as his arm slipped around her and supported her against his body.

Sabrina was aware of his hard strength as he pressed her tightly against him. She realized his offer of protection was not a hollow suggestion. But she was not going to be seduced into relying on him.

"Excellency, people are watching," she murmured, aware of the curious stares of onlookers on the *fondamenta*, the walkway along the side of the canal. Despite the late hour, or perhaps because of it since it was *Carnevale*, people strolled past and gondolas floated by.

He gave a chilly, sweeping glance to the curious, forcing them to lower their eyes and move on. Leaning close once more, he said, "If I release you, you might fall into the canal. A great deal more embarrassing than being held up by your *cicisbeo, si?*"

The reminder of their relationship brought her a spurt of annoyance, enough to give her the strength to ease away from him. Standing on her own, she discovered her knees were not quite as steady as she thought. His hand gripped her elbow. She sent him a warning glare.

"We will walk," he acquiesced, "but you will lean on me until you feel stronger. And we will discuss the source of your illness later."

Pulling her hand into the crook of his arm, he led her away from the theater. Sabrina was grateful for his support but exasperated at his domineering attitude. What could she tell him about that frightening probe into her mind? She did not understand it. Could it be sorcery? The idea scared her, but Auriano distracted her with idle chatter and outrageous flattery.

They strolled through side streets, bypassing the *campi* and *piazzi* with their *Carnevale* masked revelers, the acrobats who performed amazing feats of balance, the fire jugglers who took away the breath with their flying flaming torches, and the musicians playing lively tunes. Some of the streets were heavily trafficked and others nearly deserted. They crossed bridges over the canals and watched gondolas float by.

Auriano gave her a running commentary of the places they passed, and Sabrina found herself lulled by his charm. They wandered down the street called *Frezzeria*, which, in medieval times, was where citizens went to purchase arrows. He showed her the fifteenth-century Palazzo Contarini del Bovolo with its beautiful external spiral staircase and explained *bovolo* meant "snail shell," which described the staircase perfectly.

As they were walking down one of the narrow, deserted side streets on their way back to the gondola, a hooded, darkly cloaked figure appeared at the far end of the street. Auriano halted, tensed. Sabrina sensed the evil she had felt earlier. As the figure stepped closer, Sabrina knew it was a woman from the way she moved. Auriano remained perfectly still, his attention focused.

Sabrina felt his arm twitch. The stiletto hidden beneath his sleeve flashed into his hand. In response, the woman laughed, the sound scraping along Sabrina's nerves and sending a chill down her back. Who was this person who could project such evil?

"Go back to the gondola, please," he said quietly. "I will handle this."

Despite the danger, she hesitated.

The woman glided toward them.

Sweeping Sabrina behind him, he commanded, "Go, Sabrina. Run." His tone permitted no disobedience. When she still did not move, he gave her a little push to send her on her way. "Go. Now." He was no longer the smooth seducer, the charming gentleman. He had become the protective male, the warrior.

She was reluctant to leave him, but he seemed familiar with this woman, the evil that she projected, and perfectly capable of defending himself. Sabrina had Evan to consider. Hoping Auriano knew what he was doing, she hurried back in the direction of their waiting gondola. Just before she reached the corner of the street, she stopped. She could not leave him to face the evil alone.

The woman had moved closer, threatening. Auriano stood his ground. The woman raised her arms before her, opened her hands, and displayed her palms. Her focus was not on Auriano, but on Sabrina.

Sabrina felt the menace, cold and heavy, flowing toward her, felt it building around her. Reality disconnected. She was pulled into a place that had no time, no space. Pain ripped through her soul.

As if from very far away, she saw Auriano's stiletto flash through the air. It hit the woman, pushed her back a step. Her darkness seemed to expand, then it absorbed the weapon. For a moment, her malicious attention was on the prince, and Sabrina could take a breath. The woman's hands swung up again. A snap and a flash crackled the air. Energy zapped in Sabrina's direction. She froze, mesmerized by its horrible beauty. Before she could move, Auriano threw himself between her and that flash. It hit him in the chest, and he crumpled to the ground.

Instantly, Sabrina was freed from that frightening void. Auriano lay in a heap on the ground. "No!" she screamed. Ignoring the danger, she ran back to him.

Before she could reach him, the woman floated forward and hovered next to him. Sabrina felt the evil gloating at Auriano's prostrate form. She also sensed the woman's pain. The stiletto had found its mark and was sapping her life. The woman bent over the prince and reached out an elongated hand, delicate, yet deadly, to touch him.

"Get away from him!" Sabrina yelled. She skidded to a stop several feet away.

The evil looked in her direction and froze. Snatching back its hand, it hissed, spun around and hurried away. It seeped into nothing before it reached the end of the street. A trail of black blood was all that remained.

What was that thing? Sabrina had no idea why it retreated from her. But the prince—Alessandro—lay unmoving on the ground. She dropped to her knees beside him. His face was chalky. His eyes were closed. A large hole had been burned into his clothing on one side of his chest. The skin beneath was red and black, blistered, peeling and oozing.

"Oh, God," she gasped, as she fought not to be ill. "Excellency," she entreated, trying to rouse him. "Alessandro." He remained unresponsive, barely breathing. Placing her hand on his chest, she felt the faint flutter of a heartbeat. When she brushed his hair back from his forehead, his skin was clammy.

Gently, she pillowed his head on her knees and looked around desperately. The street was still deserted. No one was near.

"Help!" she yelled. "Please someone, help!"

At the edge of her vision, something moved in the shadows, but no malice emanated from the darkness. Instead, the shadow man emerged from the night. Relief at his appearance washed through her. He had saved her in the chapel. She felt he would help save the prince. He crouched on the other side of the injured man.

"Please, can you get help?" she entreated. "He's badly wounded."

Help is coming, she heard in her head.

After only a few moments, she heard running footsteps. Auriano's gondolier arrived with two other men, carrying a wide plank as a makeshift stretcher. Gently, they lifted the prince onto the plank and swiftly carried him back to the gondola. Sabrina hurried along beside them. The shadow man followed.

In the gondola, she kept watch over the prince and held his hand, limp and cold. She prayed to whoever would listen. *Please, don't let him die.*

We will not let him die, she heard in her head.

The shadow man hunkered down on the other side of Auriano's unconscious form, and his molten gaze was fixed on her. With a nod, he turned back to focus with concern on the prince.

"Who are you?" she asked.

After a pause, he answered in her head, *Tonio.*

The voice was a baritone, like the one she had heard that night in her room. Yet, it sounded a bit different. She decided she was mistaken. Surely, there were not two shadow men.

"Thank you for your help, Tonio," she said.

He seemed surprised, then amused. Nodding graciously, he turned his attention back to the man lying between them.

Despite her concern for the prince, despite the fact that Tonio had come to their aid, she was annoyed with him for having invaded her bedchamber. "I've seen you before," she said.

Tonio shook his head.

"You came to my bedchamber." She lowered her voice to a whisper. "You took liberties."

She heard a chuckle inside her head. *No, Ma Donna, that was not me.*

Frowning, she said, "You really shouldn't lie, you know."

True. I've heard lying is a sin.

He was teasing her. She scowled, irritated that he should be so flippant when Auriano was in such grave danger.

The gondola ride was the fastest she had ever experienced. The boat seemed to skim across the water of the canals. After only a few minutes, they pulled up before the water gate of the Ca' D'Este. The gondolier called out and servants swarmed onto the quay. The prince was gently lifted and carried inside. Since no one said otherwise, Sabrina followed them inside and up the stairs to an upper floor. When they reached the bedchamber, the door was closed in her face with a murmured apology.

She was determined not to leave until she discovered the prince's condition. The prince. Auriano. Alessandro. If he had not put himself between her and the evil, she would probably be dead. He had saved her life. He could be dying right now. Grief twisted in her chest. In the few short days she had known him, he had become part of her existence. If he died, who would tease and torment her with whispered words of seduction? And then, appalled at her frivolous thoughts, she pushed them out of her mind.

She paced. She fretted. She tried to listen at the door. People came and went, sometimes carrying bowls of water, sometimes towels and bandages, sometimes odd smelling things in little pots or bottles. After a time, Tonio emerged from the room and crouched in a dark corner. He did not seem to want to communicate with her, so she left him alone.

Finally, the gondolier, who appeared to have some sort of authority over the household staff, came out of the room and bowed before her. "*Ma Donna*, His Excellency wishes to speak with you." He hesitated, then said, "We are grateful for your aid."

Sabrina nodded her acknowledgment, then asked, "Is he… Will he… ?" Her voice broke, and she could not form the words.

"We have done what we can, *Donna*. We have given him something to ease the pain. The rest is up to him." He bowed again and backed away.

Sabrina hurried to Auriano's bedside. His clothes had been cut from him and lay in a pile of tattered strips on the floor. A blanket had been pulled over him to his waist. Above that, bandages wound around his chest and over one shoulder. His eyes were closed, and his lashes were starkly black against his pale skin.

Quietly, she approached the bed on its low platform, and reaching out, touched his hand. She was surprised when his fingers closed around hers. Turning his head on the pillow, he opened his eyes and smiled.

"*Cara mia*," he said. "Thank you for watching over me." He raised her hand to his lips and kissed it.

She forced a smile. "I couldn't leave you. How would I be able to explain the death of my *cicisbeo*?" she teased, trying to cover her concern.

"So you bravely stayed, and you got help," he said, his statement a compliment.

"If it hadn't been for—" She stopped, not sure how to tell him about the shadow man.

"For—?" he prompted.

"Someone helped me," she said.

"Ah, *si*. Tonio." He gave a little nod.

She started, surprised. "You know him?"

"He and I are... well acquainted." A grimace of pain swept across his face and his fingers tightened around her hand.

She wondered if the shadow man could be the source of the rumor of the curse on the family. Obviously, Auriano was not cursed, for he lay before her and endured very human pain. Wanting to relieve that suffering, she smoothed his brow with her free hand. "You saved my life," she said, as she sank into a chair beside the bed.

"So, I am a hero, *si*?" He chuckled, then winced in pain again.

She smiled at his self-mockery. "*Si*. Thank you."

"I will not be your *cicisbeo* for a few days." He became very serious. "I want you to be very careful, *cara mia*. Do not go anywhere alone, and please do not go out after dark."

"I will be careful," she hedged. She was not going to promise to stay at home, particularly if she had to deliver messages for Dunfield.

"You felt the evil in the theater." His statement, rather than being a question, forced her to acknowledge the truth.

She said nothing.

"It gave you the headache." Another question in the form of a statement.

Again, she said nothing.

He sighed. "Be glad that's all it gave you, *cara mia*." When she still said nothing, he narrowed his eyes at her. "I think, perhaps, there are some things you should tell me."

"I have nothing to tell you, Excellency," she said. "But I think you have things to tell *me*. Who was that woman who attacked you? How could she do that thing with her hands?"

"We will talk when I am well," he said, closing his eyes as if he would rest.

"But—" she began, frustrated.

"In a few days," he murmured.

Sabrina thought he might be delirious. She had seen his wound. His recovery would require more than a few days, if he recovered at all. She did not want to think about that.

Dubious, she said, "All right. In a few days."

His eyes popped open. "You do not believe me." He grinned. "I heal quickly." As if to disprove him, agony crossed his face as another wave of pain shook him. After catching his breath, he repeated firmly, "We will speak again in a few days. About sorcery. And other things."

Sorcery. Magic. Was that what she had witnessed? No, that was impossible. Whatever she had experienced must have a logical explanation. Auriano was speaking gibberish. He was wounded and prostrate, and Sabrina did not believe he could heal from such a deadly injury so quickly, if at all.

Yet, she had felt the evil projected by the woman. The same evil she had felt in the chapel. The same evil that had invaded her head in the theater. Whatever it was, she would protect Evan and pray for Auriano's recovery.

"You should rest," she said, as she smoothed that errant curl back from his forehead.

But he did not answer. He was already asleep.

"Careful, you idiot!" Nulkana raged to her assistant as he prepared to pull the stiletto from her side.

His skeletal fingers hovered above the blade's hilt, and he bent his skull-like head to examine the weapon more closely. "I'm sorry, mistress, but the weapon is deeply embedded. It seems to have developed claws and is holding on. This is powerful magic."

"Of course it's powerful magic." Aggravation and pain flitted across her aging features. "I'm surrounded by fools." She gripped the edge of the table in her workroom and leaned against it. "Do it quickly, Kek."

Kek pulled on a thick glove, took hold of the stiletto's hilt, and yanked out the weapon. Nulkana's howl of pain shook the glass jars and vials spread across the table and echoed in the vast darkness beyond.

Kek held up the stiletto. Tiny, finger-like claws protruded from the blade. They snapped and clutched at the air. "Just as I thought," he observed. "Powerful magic."

"Destroy it," Nulkana growled. Grabbing her side, she watched the black blood ooze between her fingers. "I will kill those interfering Auriano whelps. I will kill them slowly and very painfully."

"Mistress, you need to feed," Kek soothed. "I will bring one of the women from the cells."

Nulkana nodded, then her gaze fell on a black-robed, hooded figure standing in a corner of the room. "No. He will bring a woman for me." Her lips drew back in a cruel smile. "Get a woman for me, worm."

The figure's head turned in Nulkana's direction.

"You hate me, worm, don't you?" she taunted. "You would enjoy my death. Oh, yes, I know you would. And you would like me to kill you to end your agony." She indulged in an evil laugh. "Do not lose hope, worm, because hope only increases your pain. I enjoy seeing your pain and watching you fight against my spell."

The robed figure did not move. It only stared with dead eyes at the sorceress.

"Go!" she screamed. "Do as you are told. Get me a woman so I may feed."

The figure nodded once and silently glided from the room. When he was gone, Nulkana slumped into a chair.

"One of the Auriano whelps has found a powerful woman, Kek," she said. "I have not felt such power since… a very long time."

Kek said nothing as he bent his skeletal frame over the sorceress and pressed a cloth against her wound.

"I have already tried to kill her twice." Nulkana's hand closed into a fist. "She has escaped each time." As Kek pressed harder, she sucked in a breath and roughly pushed him away. "Gently, you fool!" Pain and age contorted her features, quickly turning her face into a mass of wrinkles. "Where is that worm with my meal?" she complained.

"Perhaps he has outlived his usefulness," Kek suggested slyly.

"You would like me to kill him, wouldn't you Kek?" she taunted. "That would make you happy, I think. Then you could have me all to yourself." Her purr was deceptively seductive.

Kek bowed slavishly. "I am happy only if you are happy, mistress."

The sorceress grunted dismissively, then her gaze fell on her pet owl. "Come here, my lovely," she said, holding out her arm. The bird flew silently to her and perched on her arm. "You want to fly, don't you?" The owl blinked at her. "Go out and spy on the whelp's woman. Discover where she goes, what she does." She stroked the bird's head. "I want to know everything about her. Go now." She threw the bird into the air. Silently, it took flight, circled the room once, and then flew out.

When it had gone, she doubled over in pain. "Where is the worm with that woman?" she screeched.

Even as far away as the cells, he could hear the screech of the sorceress. He was her worm, her creature, worse than her slave. With no will of his own, he could not remember a time when he did not belong to her. Yet something, some spark, told him he had not always been like this. Sometime in the past, he had lived a full life. He just could not remember what it was.

Coming to a stone chamber closed off with iron bars, he stood for a moment and gazed at the inhabitants. They were all young women, lovely, some fair, some dark, but all in the prime of their lives. When they saw him, they scrambled away from the bars as they tried to hide. Crying, they clung to one another, for they knew the fate that awaited them.

In the corner were a few who had been taken from the chamber and returned, aged beyond their years, part of them desiccated. They huddled in misery against the cold stone of the wall. He would not take one of those. His mistress needed healing. She needed a fresh one.

Unlocking the gate, he stepped into the chamber. Most of the women tried to avoid him, backing quickly out of his path. One woman stood to the side. As he moved farther into the chamber, she attempted to dash past him. He froze her with a gesture of his hands.

She was beautiful, dark hair and dark eyes. Even frozen as she was, he could see the determined bravery in her eyes. He knew she would not go meekly. A glint of memory flashed through his mind, of something, someone from before, but it was gone before he could catch it. Whatever that glint was, it made him turn away from the woman. He would not take her this time. The pain of not remembering twisted through his heart.

Another woman, pale, weaker, cowered nearby. Catching her by the arm, he dragged her to her feet and out through the gate. As he released the other woman from her frozen state, he gazed upon her once more and wondered why she had triggered that memory.

The woman in his grip struggled, crying, pleading with him. Pulling her along, he ignored her entreaties. His heart was stone in his chest. He was allowed no emotion except hate, and he saved that for the sorceress. She had robbed him of everything. That much he knew.

He was her worm, with no memory, no will of his own. He did as he was told, performed his tasks, no matter how distasteful, how disgusting, how evil they might be. As much as he wished for death, he knew she would never release him. Not until she had gained the pieces of the Sphere of Astarte.

He also wished to find the Sphere of Astarte. The goal of the sorceress was his goal. He just could not remember why. But he knew his reason was different from hers.

When he found the pieces of the Sphere, he would lock them together, regain his life, and then die.

Chapter 12

"I discovered that the artifact I keep in the casket is missing, Sabrina. What do you know of this?" Dunfield asked. Although his words were mild, his chilly blue gaze indicated he was very unhappy.

Sabrina stood before him in his study. As usual, he was impeccably dressed in pale gray coat and breeches, green brocade waistcoat, and pristine white shirt and stock. He had summoned her from the workroom where she had caught her skirt on a corner of one of the paintings. Her skirt now sported a huge tear from knee to hem. Ink smudged her hand. Dunfield's gaze swept over her with disdain as he eyed her work clothes, but she refused to be intimidated.

She blinked innocently. "It's missing, Uncle? How could that be? It was there the other day. I haven't touched it since." And that, she thought, was no lie.

"You know it is part of the collection. How could you be so careless?"

She watched him pace and wondered at his tremendous agitation. Dunfield never paced. Usually in control, unctuous, adroit in negotiations, he was wily enough that he could come up with a plausible excuse for the artifact not being included in the sale of the collection. She suspected that the piece was much more valuable than what he implied or what the prince had told her.

The prince. Auriano. Alessandro. The man who had thrown himself between her and evil. She had not seen him since that attack two nights ago. Her inquiries sent to Ca' D'Este about his health were answered with vague responses. She was worried about him. His wound was serious and like nothing she had ever seen before. She feared for his life. If he died… The thought opened an unexpected hollow place in her heart.

Dunfield stopped before her and waited for an answer. She said, "Anyone could have taken the artifact. Did you ask the servants if they had seen anything suspicious?"

"None of them, Sabrina. I've questioned them all, and I would know if one of them were lying." He stepped toward her, mildly threatening. "You were the last one to see it. Where is it?"

"I told you, Uncle, I don't know. Please, I have a headache." She put her hand to her forehead and winced with imaginary pain.

When he said nothing, she turned to leave. Just as she reached the doorway, his voice reached out to her, quiet, cold. "Why did His Excellency not escort you home the other night?"

She halted and turned. No matter what strange things were going on with Auriano, she was not about to confide in the man before her. "There was an… incident."

He scowled, his eyes darkening with displeasure. "What sort of incident? Why was he not here yesterday? Why is he not here this morning? He requested to be your *cicisbeo* only a few days ago, and now he has not come for two days. Did you insult him, Sabrina, or turn him away?"

"I did not insult him." She shrugged. "He is probably recovering from a night of gambling. He is probably still abed." About that last point, she had no doubt. "Is there something else you require?"

Dunfield paused, then turned to his desk. "I want you to deliver another message. Tonight." He opened a drawer and took out the casket that should have contained the piece of the Sphere of Astarte. "You will take this with you."

"But it's empty," she said, confused.

"The man you are to meet will not know that. And you will not allow him to open it. It is a sign of good faith. Do you understand?" Dunfield gave her a hard stare.

She nodded.

"I will give you the details before you leave." He dismissed her with a wave of his hand.

Sabrina moved to the door of the study.

"And get yourself cleaned up." Dunfield's sharp command reached her just before she closed the study door behind her. Ignoring him, she focused instead on Auriano's words. *Do not go out after dark.* Apprehension slipped through her. She had to go, for that was what Dunfield wanted, and she had to take the casket with her. Disobeying him might result in his banishing her and Evan from his household, and she could not allow that to happen.

But she could not rely on the prince. He was still recovering, if the latest message she had received from Ca' D'Este was accurate, if he had not passed into a fatal fever. No, she couldn't think about that possibility. Instead, she concentrated on what she needed to do. She would deliver Dunfield's message this evening. And somehow, she would try to learn more about the enigmatic prince and the Sphere of Astarte.

The quarter moon cast its light across the lagoon as Sabrina was rowed to the mainland. The pale glow would light her way to one of the outbuildings of a deserted villa so that she might deliver Dunfield's message. He had never made her travel quite so far or so late at night before. Not for the first time, she wondered why he had not made the trip himself. He had seemed very concerned that everything she did and said was perfect, going over and over again all the details. His anxiety made her more nervous than she had ever been. And Auriano's words of caution still echoed in her head. But she was going to be on the mainland, out of the city. Surely that evil she had felt would not follow her here. She dipped her head to allow her hood to conceal her face just to be sure she could not be seen. Dunfield had ordered that she wear no mask.

On her lap, hidden in the woolen folds of her black cloak, was the small casket that should have contained a piece of the Sphere of Astarte. She protected it with her hands. Somehow, the value of the object had risen sharply from the time after her husband's death when no one except Dunfield wanted it. Now, it seemed, just when it had gone missing, everyone wanted it. She was not quite sure who everyone was, besides Dunfield, Auriano, and the man she was to meet, but she sensed an urgency in connection to the piece that she had never felt before.

The boat scraped against the bottom of the lagoon. Her rower jumped out and pulled it ashore. After he helped her onto land, she stood for a moment and looked around. Before her was a line of small brush with an occasional tree jutting up and blocking the stars. Beyond that, she could make out the dark profile of one of the many villas built by Venetians as summer retreats. It matched Dunfield's description — a smallish villa, about the size of an English manor house, with a loggia on columns stretching across the second floor. Now, she had to find the outbuilding where this meeting would take place.

She followed a path that wound through the undergrowth. Tonight, she had worn a dark burgundy gown of superfine instead of the satin and lace confection from her last errand. The gown not only provided warmth in the chilly air, its muted color contributed to her dark profile. As she stepped carefully along the packed earth track, she could hear frogs from nearby ponds and small nocturnal animals foraging for food. Wanting to run, she forced herself to stay calm. Nothing, she reassured herself, was hiding in the brush to jump out at her. No stilettos would whiz through the dark. No evil sorceresses would suddenly appear.

The path finally opened up onto a grassy area before the villa. Early spring plants and bushes in the gardens, silvered in the moonlight, took on the appearance of skeletons and strange creatures. The villa was dark, deserted. The colonnade along its front hid black recesses where anyone or anything could hide. Its desolation made her shiver. No one visited their summer villas at this time of year.

She skirted the house. The black silhouettes of several buildings were scattered a short distance away. One showed a rectangle of pale, flickering light through an open door. Her contact was waiting. A nervous tremor ran through her.

Entering the shed-like structure, she saw a man, cloaked, with a hat pulled low on his brow. He was not masked, but his features were shadowed by the hat brim. On the rough table before him was a single lantern.

"*Madame,*" he said with a slight nod. "You have come far with only the moonlight to guide you."

The man's French accent was unexpected, but he had used the key word: *moonlight.* This was the man she was to meet. "I also had the stars to light my way," she answered, giving him the proper response.

His head tipped, and a shaft of light caught his blade of nose. "So. Shall we get to our business?" He tossed a pouch onto the table. It clinked heavily with coins.

"No." Sabrina shook her head. Dunfield had made no mention of the man wanting to buy the artifact. "What I have is not for sale." She gave the pouch a contemptuous glance. "And certainly not for so little."

He stiffened. "Then perhaps I have made a mistake in coming."

"Perhaps only the intent of your journey was a mistake. I was informed that you would be here only to see proof," she said.

"Then show me this proof." His tone was impatient, annoyed.

Sabrina took the casket from beneath her cloak and placed it on the table between them. His eyes gleamed as soon as he saw it. Not quite trusting the man, she left her hand laying negligently atop it.

"So, all you have to show me is this little box?" His disdainful tone was in sharp contrast to the interest he had shown.

"I think you recognize the casket and know what is inside," Sabrina said.

"I need to see it." The feral glitter of his eyes echoed the greed of his words.

"No, *monsieur.* To open the casket and reveal what is inside is too dangerous, even here in this deserted place." She cocked her head. "If you are aware of what is inside, you should know that." Sabrina was dissembling with every piece of her being and prayed he would not discover her hoax.

"I must at least examine the box." His tempered words were accompanied by a smile that sent a chill through her.

Sabrina needed to make him believe and report back to his superiors — whoever they were — that the piece was indeed in the box. Removing her hand, she nudged the casket several inches closer to him. "You may look, but you may not touch." She hoped he had some honor and would accede to her wishes. With no weapon, she had nothing with which to stop his grabbing the box and stealing away with it. She damned Dunfield for sending her on this errand, and herself for not bringing a knife.

The man bent over the box and examined it from several angles. When he straightened, he laid his hand casually on top of it. "It seems to be authentic. I will relay what I have seen."

"The lady said not to touch," a deep voice spoke from behind her. The edge of a rapier landed lightly on the back of the messenger's hand.

With a gasp, Sabrina swung around and was confronted by a man in the *bautta*. She knew that voice and the deceptively casual air. Auriano. Surprise, coupled with relief at seeing him standing and apparently recovered, surged through her. His eyes never flickered from their concentration on the Frenchman. With a firm but gentle push, he swept her behind him and took a step closer to the table.

She scowled. What was he doing? She did not need Auriano to interfere. She would have found a way to deal with the messenger herself. She craned her neck to peek around him.

He tapped the messenger with the rapier once again and said, "Please remove your hand."

The messenger slowly lifted his hand from the box. Auriano raised his rapier. Sabrina watched, wide-eyed, as the rapier blurred in a flurry of movement, and the prince sent it plunging through the man's heart. The messenger choked, then the light in his eyes faded as he died and dropped to the floor.

Sabrina fought for breath. She stared at the body on the floor. Her throat closed up, blocking the scream that was building in her chest. "You—you—you—k-k-killed h-h-h-him!" she gasped.

"*Si.*"

"But-but-but… Oh, God, oh, dear God… Now what am I going to do?" She grabbed the table for support. Dark spots whirled before her eyes.

"Go home." Auriano's tone was coldly angry.

His wrath was like a bucket of icy water thrown on her panic. Her temper saved her from collapsing. "Why did you kill him?" she demanded.

He took her arm and dragged her to where the man lay. Using his bloody rapier, he pushed aside the man's cloak and showed her. The messenger clutched a dagger in his hidden hand. Its wicked edge gleamed in the dim light.

"I do not know whether that was meant for you or for me," Auriano said. "Either way, *Donna* Barclay, I did not wish to find out."

Sabrina felt the room tilt. Only Auriano's grip on her arm kept her knees from buckling. The dagger had to have been for him. She could not imagine why the messenger would want *her* dead. Unless he would have killed her for the empty casket. That thought turned her blood cold.

The prince nudged her to the table so she could lean on it, then he bent and pushed up the sleeve of the man's coat and shirt. Tattooed on the inside of the man's wrist was the glyph of a frog.

"What is that?" she asked.

"The mark of the Legion of Baal. Have you ever heard of it?"

Sabrina shook her head as she swallowed against a wave of nausea.

"It is a group of men who are searching for the Sphere of Astarte," he said.

"But the Sphere belongs to your family."

"*Si*. But the Sphere is valuable. These men believe the Sphere will bring them incredible riches and unimaginable power, and they are desperate to find it. I asked you not to go out after dark," he said, as he wiped his rapier on the dead man's cloak and cut a button from the man's coat. "You said you would not."

Anger raced through her at his accusatory tone, making her forget her fear. Auriano had just ruthlessly interfered with her errand. When he straightened, Sabrina raised herself to her full height, the top of her head coming only to his nose, and told him distinctly, "I said I would be careful. I never said I would remain at home."

His eyes narrowed behind his mask and he bowed sardonically. "My mistake. My injury must have clouded my understanding."

His recovery from his severe wound was remarkable. Any normal man would have still been languishing on his sickbed. What was this man made of? She poked unsympathetically at his solid chest beneath the soft wool of his cloak. He did not even flinch. "I left you in agony just two days ago," she said.

"*Si.*"

"Your wound looked serious, perhaps fatal."

"*Si.*"

She poked him again. "But you have no pain when I touch you."

"Your compassion and delicate touch are overwhelming, *Donna* Barclay," he said dryly.

She ignored his sarcasm. "What happened to your wound?"

"I heal quickly."

His response bothered her. Two days ago she thought he might be dying, and now he stood whole and miraculously unharmed before her. She frowned. "You're not even bruised."

"No."

"But that bruise on your chin…"

Even with his mask, she sensed his wry amusement. "Some injuries heal quicker than others, depending on who is inflicting them. Is there anything else you would like to know about my well-being, *Donna* Barclay?"

His question was rhetorical. She knew he would reveal nothing more, so she tried a new tack. "What are you doing here, Excellency?"

"Saving you." His words were as immutable as his presence.

Frustrated, she turned and stalked away, relieved that she was steady on her feet. She glanced down at the dead messenger, shuddered, averted her eyes, and turned back to the prince. "Perhaps, I did not need saving and only your presence caused the man to turn violent."

"Perhaps." He shrugged. "We will never know, will we?"

"This is the second time I have failed Mr. Dunfield. He will be very angry." Irritation at how pathetic she sounded made her fist clench.

"Dunfield should not have put you in such a dangerous position." His tone was laced with hostility.

"He couldn't have known this errand would be dangerous." She felt compelled to defend the man who sheltered her and Evan.

"Perhaps. Perhaps not."

Sabrina knew Dunfield kept secrets from her but did not want to accept what Auriano implied. "Mr. Dunfield is an honorable man,

Excellency," she told him coldly. "He took me under his roof when I had nowhere else to go. He provides for me and my son."

"Commendable of him."

Her chin jerked up at his sarcasm. "In return, I do small favors for him, one of which was meeting this man tonight." She indicated the dead man on the floor. "You interfered where you should not have."

"I am your *cicisbeo*," he explained with an edge. "It is my duty to protect you."

"I don't need your protection," she flung at him.

"I saved your life." His words were clipped and vexed.

His bald truth and the implied danger, coupled with fear of Dunfield's displeasure made her lash out. "Don't," she snapped. "Do not interfere. Do not save my life. It doesn't need saving. And I can take care of both myself and my son."

Anger flared in those eyes behind the mask, then it was banked and shuttered. He swept her an elegant bow. "As you wish, *Donna* Barclay. I will call on you in the morning at the usual hour to assist with your toilette."

That was the last thing she wanted, but his steady stare and the barely leashed temper she sensed from him made her hold her tongue. She was surprised that he still wished to be her *cicisbeo*. What did he want from her? Suspicion that his motive was far deeper or darker than being her companion narrowed her eyes. He would do whatever he wanted with or without her consent. Her glance turned to the messenger, dead now because of Auriano's interference. With a hiss of fury, she swept up the casket still lying on the table and left.

Alessandro extinguished the lantern, then stood in the doorway of the shack and watched Sabrina stalk across the open field. The moonlight caressed her small dark shape with pale frosting. She was angry with him for interfering, despite the fact that he had saved her life — again. She would be even angrier when she discovered he had dismissed her boatman and she would be forced to travel back to the city with him. He sighed and rubbed the aching spot on his chest where the wound had been and where Sabrina had applied her not-so-delicate touch. He had not exactly told her the truth that her prodding did not hurt.

She had gone out at night. Alone. Two things he had admonished her not to do. Obviously, she had no idea of the danger she was in. At the time of his warning, he had been concerned only with Nulkana and her attacks. Now, Alessandro felt that another threat came from the French. The menace of the messenger indicated that General Napoleon could have knowledge about the Sphere of Astarte. Another unwanted participant in the race to find the artifact. But the messenger had also been marked with the sign of the Legion of Baal. The explanation Alessandro had given Sabrina had been correct in its brevity, but he failed to mention that the Legion's members had dark magical abilities as well. His jaw clenched.

He regretted killing the messenger, but when he saw the dagger in the man's hand, all he could think of was the danger to Sabrina. He was not about to lose his only connection to the piece of the Sphere. At least, that was the justification of the terrible fear for her that caused him to act so rashly. If he had been thinking clearly, he would have merely disarmed the man and then asked him a few questions—at the point of his rapier, of course. But that opportunity was gone, and he had to focus on keeping the beautiful, clever, secretive, headstrong Sabrina safe from harm.

Alessandro was about to step from the shelter of the shack when he sensed the evil. Peering into the shadows, he couldn't see where it was coming from, then a male shape emerged from the brush. Sabrina's head came up, and she stopped. He started to surge forward to help, then halted. She had told him not to help. He could destroy the attacker with ease, and he was angry enough at her dismissal of his protection to teach her a lesson, to see how long it would take her to start screaming for him.

Her outline began to shimmer, and an odd aura surrounded her. Her arm came up, palm outward, and she pointed it at the man. An arc of light leaped from her hand. It paralyzed the man. Incredulous, Alessandro watched Sabrina halt the evil. But another shape emerged from the shadows and began to close in. She swung around and did the same to him. Two more men slunk out of the brush. She froze those as well. But as soon as her back was turned, the first man began to move again. She could only hold them off as long as she was facing them.

The first two attackers slunk dangerously close to her. Sabrina faced them, and a stream of energy shot from her hand. They were punched back to the ground. Dead or merely unconscious? Alessandro's attention snapped to the other two figures closing in on her. She did not seem to notice them. That aura about her wavered and grew weaker. She sank to her knees.

Alessandro exploded out of the shed. With a twitch of his arm, his stiletto slipped into his hand, and he tossed it on the run. One of the men collapsed, the knife winking obscenely from his back in the moonlight. He ran up behind the other man and plunged in his rapier. As soon as he jerked it out, the man fell. He cast a wary glance at the other two pros-trate forms. Still unmoving. He collected his stiletto, wiped the blood off both weapons with one of the dead men's coats, and sheathed them.

In two strides, he was at Sabrina's side. She was barely conscious. Gently, he swept her up into his arms.

Between her breasts, her moonstone pendant glowed softly. It mesmerized him, and he remembered its zing of pain during the Hunger. Her voice drew him from his contemplation.

"Who were they?" she murmured.

"Slaves of evil," he told her, as her head slumped against his shoulder.

When they arrived at Dunfield's *casa*, Alessandro gave Sabrina over to the care of her maid, then went in search of her uncle. The small casket was clasped lightly in his gloved hand. He could guard against its odd sensations now that he knew what to expect. Dunfield was in his study behind his desk. In no mood to wait on etiquette, Alessandro strode into the room before any of the servants could announce him. Dunfield stood, revealing surprise at seeing him, then quickly shuttered his expression.

Alessandro spoke first. "I have brought *Donna* Barclay home."

"Home from where, Excellency?" the Englishman asked, mildly puzzled. "Was she not asleep in her bed?"

"No, she was not." Alessandro would play the man's game for a while to gain his measure.

A leer crossed Dunfield's face. "Excellency, did you arrange for Sabrina to sneak out to be with you? Have you bedded her?"

Alessandro stiffened at Dunfield's crass inquiry and quashed the memory of the night he had her kidnapped. "When I wish to bed *Donna* Barclay, *Sior* Dunfield, there will be nothing *sneaky* about it." He set the small casket on the desk between them.

The Englishman looked blankly from the box to Alessandro. "What is this?"

"You have placed *Donna* Barclay in danger once too often, *Sior* Dunfield. The messenger she met with tonight is dead."

"Messenger? Sabrina met with a messenger?" Dunfield drew in a breath and sank to his chair, an insult to Alessandro's social position. "Is she trying to sell my artwork behind my back?"

Alessandro narrowed his eyes. The man was despicable. He would lie and toss Sabrina to the wolves rather than admit to anything. "Do not," Alessandro said slowly, showing his teeth, "send *Donna* Barclay on any more errands. I will know if you do. The Inquisitors would be very interested to learn of certain negotiations to smuggle artwork out of the city."

The Englishman's eyes turned cold. "Are you threatening me, Excellency?" He twitched his arm, revealing the dark line of a partial tattoo peeking from beneath his cuff.

With lightning speed, Alessandro palmed his stiletto and stabbed it through the material of the man's sleeve, pinning it to the desk.

In shock, Dunfield stared from the knife holding his arm immobile to the man standing before him. "What is the meaning of this, Excellency?"

"*Mi scusi, Sior* Dunfield," Alessandro murmured with a charming smile, more deadly than a scowl. "My hand must have slipped."

"I do not appreciate being attacked in my own home," the Englishman said coldly.

"Why would I do that, *Sior* Dunfield?" Alessandro raised a cool brow. "I am not some outlaw, merely *Donna* Barclay's *cicisbeo*, and

I expect to resume my duties tomorrow. I came this evening to pay my respects. *Buonanotte.*" After pulling the stiletto from the desk, he nodded, turned, and left. He could feel the knife-like stare of the Englishman on his back.

As he made his way back through the *casa* and out to his gondola, Alessandro wondered at the connection between the Legion of Baal, the messenger, and the Englishman's tattoo. Had the true messenger been replaced by the man who was now lying dead in the shack? Or had the dead man been the true messenger? Harold Dunfield's tattoo announced him as a member of the Legion of Baal. That thought made Alessandro uneasy, for it meant that either Sabrina was in grave danger or she was in league with the notorious group. He did not like either option.

Chapter 13

Late the next afternoon, Alessandro strolled with Sabrina through the Piazza San Marco. The spring sun was warm on his shoulders. Around them, other couples sauntered, men hurried to appointments, gentlemen met and exchanged news, women greeted each other and relayed gossip. Peddlers sold their wares and street entertainers juggled, performed acrobatics, or played instruments. The spicy scent of roasted sausages and the sweet aroma of pastries filled the air. Since this was the time of *Carnevale*, everyone was masked, enjoying the last few days of the celebration.

Beside him, Sabrina was icily silent. He had given her most of the day to recover from the previous evening, and perhaps let her temper cool. She had recovered, but her temper still raged. She had not forgiven him for interfering in her errand and had conveniently forgotten that he had saved her life. He had chosen this outdoor venue because at least there was nothing sharp at hand with which she might skewer him. He had carefully concealed his stiletto.

Her hand on his arm was stiff. Her fingers barely touched him. To anyone observing, they were an affectionate couple out for a promenade, not two people who might explode into angry words at any moment.

But there was another reason why he had brought her to this open space. Here, they were less likely to be overheard, despite the fact that one of the *cappa neri*, the black capes, spies of the Inquisitors, trailed them. He could see the man trying to blend into the shadows beneath the arches of the arcade that bordered the *piazza*. Obviously, someone had become suspicious of his connection to the Englishman and alerted the Council of Ten. Or perhaps the

Council had become curious about *Donna* Barclay. Whatever their interest, their spy could wait. He needed to get some answers from the furious woman beside him. Her lack of acknowledgment of his protection went deeper than mere bad manners. She was afraid, and he meant to discover the source of her fear. He was surprised when she spoke first.

"Mr. Dunfield has told me I will perhaps no longer be needed as a messenger for him," she said.

Alessandro sent up a prayer of thanks. At least his visit to the man the night before had accomplished something. "So, isn't this a good thing?"

"No, it is not a good thing at all." Anger rippled beneath her words.

"But it will keep you out of danger, *cara mia*," he reminded her mildly.

"It will make me less useful to him," she hissed. "And don't call me that."

"As you wish, *Donna* Barclay," he said, putting a sarcastic twist to her name. They strolled a few steps before he spoke again. "You are already cataloging *Sior* Dunfield's art collection. Isn't that being useful to him?"

"When the cataloging is complete…" Her voice broke. "When it is complete, he will no longer need me." She looked away across the *piazza*.

Her last words were spoken in such a low tone that he had to strain to hear them. The implication was that the Englishman would force Sabrina and her son onto the street. Furious, he had to breathe a few times before he trusted himself to speak. "I'm sure he will still provide for you." His words were only a salve for her distress and his guilt for interfering. He did not trust Dunfield, and would not bet his fortune that the man might actually throw her out of his house, unless the Englishman could find another use for her.

"I do not want you as my *cicisbeo* any longer," she said, lifting her chin in pride, but fear vibrated beneath her words.

Although he was prepared for that declaration, it still gave him pause. The thought of not being near this woman sent an unfamiliar pang through him. He allowed her statement to hang between them for a few steps as they passed other couples going in the opposite direction. Able to feel her tension in the hand on his arm, he was very glad he had brought her to this public place. She wouldn't wish to create a scene in the middle of the *piazza*, particularly after what he had to say next. "Do you think I will let you out of my sight after what I saw you do last night?"

She gasped and stumbled. Steadying her, he murmured about taking care on the uneven stones.

Her fingers curled into his sleeve. "I did nothing last night. I don't know what you are talking about."

"You do. We need to discuss this." His tone was steely.

"No." Her denial was adamant.

"Ah, *si*, *Donna* Barclay." He made his words light and playful. "They say confession is good for the soul."

"I have nothing to confess," she said tightly.

"There are two types of confessions," he went on blithely. "Public and private. Public confessions can sometimes be so very messy. All those people wanting to watch your suffering. Quite distasteful. While a private confession is merely between you and your confessor."

"I am not about to confess anything to anyone, especially you." Anger vibrated beneath her words.

"We shall see. I think a private confession is the best thing here." He turned her in the direction of the canal and his waiting gondola. "Come, *Donna* Barclay."

She stopped short, forcing him to stop also. "I will not go anywhere with you."

"*Si*, *Donna* Barclay, you will." He said the words conversationally, but at the same time, he covered her hand that lay on his arm. "I do not believe you wish to create a scene in the middle of the *piazza*."

"I will call on the authorities." Her chin rose defiantly.

"And tell them what? That I was trying to abduct you?" Amusement laced his voice, but he kept one eye on that *cappo nero*, the black cape. "Do you really think they would believe you when I reveal who I am?"

"You are despicable," she snapped.

"*Si*." He sighed. "Occasionally I am."

Furious, Sabrina jerked her hand from his arm and started to flee, despite the scene she would create. Before she could take more than a half step, he flung his arm across her shoulders, enveloped her in his cloak, and pulled her tightly against his side. His speed stunned her.

"Please, *Donna* Barclay, do not force me to do something that will cause difficulties for both of us," he murmured. "We are being watched. I really do not wish to tangle with the authorities, and I'm sure you do not wish to have to tell *Sior* Dunfield you have displeased me."

His words chilled Sabrina. Who was watching them? Crushed against him, she realized she would not be able to escape. She knew his enveloping cloak made her appear as if she were a courtesan, out for a stroll with her protector. Fortunately, because they were masked, their identities were hidden. Still, identities could be surmised from a person's size, shape, and movements. If anyone guessed who she was, her reputation would be destroyed, and Dunfield would throw her out. She could do nothing else except accompany him.

"I will go with you if you release me," she said tightly.

"*Bene.*" The satisfaction in his voice made her cringe.

Sabrina had no idea where he would take her, but she was sure it would be some place very secluded and private. The pair of bronze automata figures atop the *Torre dell'Orogolio* clock tower began to strike their bell. The tolling of the hour, which she usually enjoyed, this time sounded like the call to an execution. Not exactly afraid of Auriano, still, apprehension rippled through her as they skirted one of the columns that marked the entrance to the Piazza San Marco.

After handing her into his gondola, he left the curtains of the *felze* open. Sabrina was relieved, having suspected he would use seduction to get what he wanted. Her resistance to his powerful attraction took all of her concentration, and at the moment, she was more concerned about what Dunfield would do since she had once more bungled an errand for him. Dunfield had been curiously distracted that morning when he questioned her about her errand. She wondered when he would reprimand her for failing once again.

As they floated down the *Canalazzo*, the Grand Canal, Auriano entertained her with stories about the *palazzi* they passed and the families who lived in them. The Palazzo Salviati had originally been the headquarters of the Salviati glass company, so beautiful glass mosaics decorated the facade; the Palazzo Falier had been home to Doge Marin Falier who was beheaded in the fourteenth century for treason. Another *palazzo* had housed a family that had used it as a center for a literary society; later residents had conducted autopsies in its salon; then smugglers had used it as a market for their contraband; now it was owned by a member of the Council of Ten. At *La Volta*, the great bend in the canal, they turned off into a smaller canal, which took them into the *sestiere* of Dorsoduro, where wealthy Venetians, who did not own *palazzi* on the Grand Canal, had their homes. As Auriano played the tour guide, he kept his distance and was his most charming. Sabrina remained silent, determined not to encourage him. He might have saved her life, but she was resolved not to trust him.

She was surprised and relieved when they turned down the canal where his *palazzo* was situated and stopped before its water gate. She had expected some place more secretive. Surrounded by servants, she did not think he could act too outrageously. But they were *his* servants. Who knew what he instructed them to ignore?

After he handed her out of the gondola, they entered the *andron*, the hall behind the water gate. She knew that during the Middle Ages, this area in all the *palazzi* had been used by the merchant families for temporary storage and conducting business. In the Ca' D'Este, it was no longer a drab, utilitarian space. The last time she had been here at night, she had noticed little, focused as she was on the prince and his injury. Now, seeing the room in daylight, she realized just how large this *palazzo* was. The water gate wall and the one opposite that led to the street were all windows. The floor, which stretched at great length before her, was alternating red and white stone squares. Dark paneling covered the walls, and stone benches were spaced between doors leading to kitchens and other workrooms. Hanging from the ceiling, which was open to the mezzanine above, was a huge, intricate, wrought iron light fixture. But what caught her attention more than the overwhelming size of the *palazzo* that the *andron* implied, was what she saw on the walls. Above each of the benches, carved into the paneling and painted, was the strange device of a circle, broken into three arcs, with a lightning bolt slashing through its center from top to bottom. For some reason, the sight of that device raised goose bumps on her skin.

"Come, *Donna* Barclay," the prince urged as he directed her up the stairs.

Sabrina docilely climbed the stairs, but with each step, she felt as if she were heading toward her doom rather than a polite chat. Auriano's hand on her arm guided her. She knew if she balked, that gentle pressure would turn into a vise, and his veneer of courtesy would dissolve.

Whatever this man wanted, she was not ready to give it. He had been kind. He had saved her twice. Although he had requested her help in the search for the Sphere of Astarte, how did she know that once he had what he wanted he would not remove his security and discard her? He had already interfered with Dunfield, and that had put her in jeopardy. She had to protect herself and Evan.

They stopped at the mezzanine and entered one of its small, intimate rooms, instead of proceeding to the more formal rooms above. As soon as they were inside, the man who had been the prince's gondolier the night he had been injured appeared.

"Gasparo," the prince said.

"I will have refreshments sent directly, Excellency," the man said and bowed.

He was perfectly civil, but Sabrina felt him taking her measure. There was something not quite servant-like about him.

They removed their cloaks and masks, and then the prince invited her to sit on a settee before the fire. He sat an arm's length away from her. "So, *Donna* Barclay," he began, "we are here in a private place, with no masks, nothing to hide our expressions. You see me as well as I see you. I think this is the perfect time for a little confession, *si*?"

"I told you I have nothing to confess." Sabrina glanced away from those golden eyes that seemed to see everything.

"Of course," he agreed smoothly, sardonically. "It was nothing that caused you to faint last night."

She gave a little laugh. "Excellency, you had just killed a man. I think I had a right to faint."

"Of course you did," he murmured. "Just as it is your right to have your little secrets. But this secret that you have may draw danger to you."

She was saved from answering by a servant bringing refreshments. With an inward sigh of relief, she allowed the prince to pour wine for her and fill a plate with cheese, ham, bread, and olives. She knew something had happened the night before because she certainly was not prone to fainting. But she had no idea what it was. She could not remember anything from the moment she started across the field until she found herself in her own bed the next morning. That blank in her memory terrified her. She was not certain she wanted to fill it in. What terrified her even more was what he implied — that she had done something extraordinary. Was it something evil or something good?

Alessandro played the attentive courtier to her, all the time damning himself for what he was about to do. They had left the *cappo nero* behind at San Marco, but the man's presence annoyed him. When he had entered the *andron* and seen the shadowy form of Tonio perched above him on the rail of the mezzanine, his irritation boiled over. Tonio knew what he was going to do. With a jerk of his head and a glare, he had warned his brother to keep his distance. But he sensed Tonio's disapproval. Even if he was successful, he knew Tonio would berate him for the means he used. And Sabrina might end up hating him.

He served Sabrina himself, urging her to eat and sample the wine. Although she only nibbled at the food, she finished her glass of wine, so he poured her another. His purpose was to get her to relax. What he had planned for her would not work quite so well if she were agitated. Her anxiety spiked off her, and that puzzled him. If she were as powerful as he suspected, he thought she should have been able to hide her nervousness better. As he related some of the history of his *palazzo*, the stories behind several of the tapestries and frescoes on the walls, he watched the tightly coiled tension in her begin to unwind. Her hand, lying between them on the settee, loosened.

"*Donna* Barclay," he began, covering her hand with his, the first move in his plan.

Without looking at him, Sabrina pulled her hand away and placed it on her lap. She would not encourage him in his seduction. He edged closer, curled his fingers around her wrist, his fingertips against her pulse. His thumb strummed across her knuckles.

"*Cara mia*," he said in a low, intense tone.

"I told you not to call me that," she said, but her words had no force behind them. Her anger seemed to seep away from her.

"Sabrina," he continued as if she had not spoken. "Look at me."

Sabrina turned to look at him. Something in his tone skipped along her skin. It commanded her attention. His fingers around her wrist, his thumb on the back of her hand sent a charge up her arm.

"Are you comfortable?" he asked.

Staring into those golden eyes, she felt compelled to answer. "Yes."

He gave her a little smile. "*Bene.*"

Each time he spoke, she had the strange sense of a warm, comforting presence entering her mind and cradling her gently. One part of her was very aware of where she was, who she was with, and her anger at him. Another part of her wanted to give herself up to that presence and curl up within it.

"Sabrina, I'm here with you. Do you understand?"

Of course she understood. She could feel his thumb on the back of her hand and the light pressure of his fingers on her pulse. He was sitting right in front of her. "Yes." As soon as she answered, a warm sigh seemed to caress her mind.

"Do you remember last night?" he asked quietly.

Her anger flared and she tried to pull her hand out of his grasp. He would not allow it. "You interfered," she snapped. "You killed the man I was to meet. Mr. Dunfield is angry at me."

"Shh," he soothed. "*Si*. I am sorry for that."

He was quiet for a moment, but his thumb never stopped. First, back and forth, and then around in tiny circles. That presence in her mind grew, became softer, more calming, lulling her.

"Sabrina, after that man was killed," he said, "what do you remember?"

She frowned. Afterward, they had argued. She was furious with him for interfering. She had picked up the casket and left. "I came back to the city." But the trip was only an impression in her mind, not a true memory.

"*Si*, but before you returned."

She shook her head in confusion.

"Sabrina, as you crossed the field, what did you see?" he probed.

As she stared into his eyes, she saw the moonlit field before her. She could feel his gaze on her back as she walked away. But she could not remember anything after that. Why couldn't she remember? What was wrong with her? Her heart began to race, and she gasped for breath.

"Sabrina." Her name on his lips soothed.

That presence in her mind comforted her as if a hand were stroking her forehead, brushing her hair back from her face, as if arms were holding her, rocking her. Slowly, she calmed.

"May I show you what happened?" he asked.

What did happen? she wondered. What was it that she could not remember?

"I will be with you," he assured her. "I won't let them hurt you."

Them? Who was he talking about? Once again, that presence enfolded her protectively. She felt safe. And curious. Perhaps he could help her remember what took place in that gap in her memory. She gave a little nod.

In her mind, she saw herself leaving the shed and walking across the field in the moonlight. It was from his perspective, she realized; this was what he saw. Four men emerged from the shadows.

Suddenly, she remembered, and she saw them from her own vantage point. She felt the evil oozing from them, not to the degree she had felt that night at the theater, but she knew what it was, nevertheless. It was cold, malevolent. The men surrounded her, and she stopped.

She saw her arm come up, and she sensed the energy swirling around her, the power flowing down to her fingers. She froze one man, then another, but the other two were closing in. Her brain buzzed. The energy pulsed down her arm. She stopped the last two, but the first pair were moving again. She swung to face them. That buzzing was stronger. It engulfed her, taking over her brain, gathering itself. The power surged down her arm, out of her fingers, and slammed into the two men. They were lifted off their feet, thrown back, and fell to the ground in two limp masses.

Oh, God! What had she *done*?! She had killed them!

She was never supposed to use that power. Never. The buzzing in her brain began to fade. The energy in her arm was only a mild tingle. Her strength leaked away and was gone. She sank to her knees.

And she saw her mother, watched as the power in her faded, as she sank to her knees. She watched as two men stole up behind her mother and stabbed her again and again. No! Her mother had told her to hide, to stay hidden no matter what she saw. But her need to protect her mother was stronger than her fear. She jumped up from where she was hiding in the tall grass. She yelled at those two men. *Get away from her!* The men looked at her, recoiled, backed away, then turned and ran. She felt the buzzing in her brain, the power surging down her arms. The energy flashed out of her fingers, slammed into the men. They exploded. But her mother…

She screamed, screamed, screamed.

Sabrina.

The voice was in her head, a faint echo beneath that scream that would not stop.

Sabrina.

It came again, louder this time, more insistent, overpowering the scream.

Sabrina. Open your eyes. Look at me.

The voice held authority. That presence embraced her, grounded her, comforted her.

The screaming stopped. She opened her eyes. And looked directly into his.

What had just happened? What had she done? What had she just revealed? Horrified, she gasped.

Sabrina. It's all right. You're safe.

She shook her head. No. No. No. No. She was never safe.

That presence surrounded her mind, pillowing it on something soft and cloudlike, soothing it.

You're safe, the voice repeated.

A tear escaped from each eye and rolled down her cheeks. She was not going to cry. She could not give in to tears.

I understand, the voice said. *Sleep then. And remember. You are powerful. Close your eyes, cara mia, and sleep.*

Alessandro watched Sabrina's eyes slip closed, and she became boneless in his arms. Shaken at what he had just witnessed, he held her a moment, savoring the feel of her softness against him. He wondered if this would be the last time he might feel her like this. When she awoke and she remembered everything, particularly the way he had invaded her mind, she might hate him. That thought hurt more than he expected. Drawing a shaky breath, he allowed himself the luxury of her complete trust while she slept.

What she had remembered astounded him. Her power was formidable. Despite that, because of that, he was never going to let her get away. Even if he had to tie her to him through sorcery, he would use her to help him break the curse. And that decision made him damn himself all the more. He had never been squeamish about using anyone who might help him in his quest. But this woman...

Reluctantly, he slipped from the settee and laid her down. In sleep, she appeared so helpless. Her loveliness made him ache. Reaching out, he traced his fingers along her jaw.

"Sleep well, *dolce mia*," he whispered. Then he turned away to go in search of his brother.

Tonio accosted him as soon as he stepped out of the room. *What did you do? Did you use Thought Binding?*

Alessandro gave a curt nod and motioned to the stairs. Although Shadow, his brother looked ready to hit him. The conversation needed to be conducted in private, despite the fact that most of it would be silent. He wanted to be alone and process what he had just learned, so he led the way up to his bedchamber.

After he closed the door, he turned to Tonio and took a breath to give himself a moment. Thought Binding was an intimate process that revealed the essence of a person, laying bare that person's hidden thoughts and desires. It was up to him to decide how deep he wanted to go into that person's mind. He could guide that person's thoughts, or allow the thoughts to guide him. With Sabrina, he found himself wanting to explore every bright, mystical corner of her mind. He had denied himself that pleasure. Even so, what he had just done with her had been incredibly intimate, as intimate as making love to her. The last thing he wanted to do was share that with his brother. He steeled himself against his reluctance.

Antonio read his hesitation as something else. *I heard her screaming. I knew you shouldn't have used Thought Binding. Did you hurt her? Cazzo! Sandro —*

Alessandro held up his hand to halt his brother's tirade. "I didn't hurt her, Tonio," he said quietly.

So what happened? Why did she scream?

She was remembering. Alessandro took another breath and let it out. *She is extremely powerful.* He stripped off his coat and tossed it over the leather chair before the hearth.

Then she can help us.

Alessandro slipped out of his waistcoat and pulled apart his stock, draping them over his coat. *Si, she can. I'm not sure she will.*

We — you — will have to force her.

Alessandro shook his head. If it had been anyone but Sabrina, he would have agreed with Tonio. Instead, he came up with excuses. *She's very fragile right now. She had no idea what she can do or what she is.*

So now she knows.

She doesn't know how to use the power she has. The exhaustion that was a side effect of extended Thought Binding was beginning to hit him. Not bothering with his boots, he sat on the edge of the bed. *She needs someone to Guide her.*

Glancing at Tonio, Alessandro saw his brother have the same idea that was running through his own mind. Golden eyes met golden eyes.

Gasparo, they said together.

Do you think she'll allow Gasparo to Guide her? Tonio asked.

Alessandro shrugged. Swinging his feet up, he lay back on the bed and threw an arm across his eyes. *I don't know. After what I saw, she may hate what she is. Or, she may get angry and want revenge.*

Against whom?

Nulkana, he sent to his brother. More privately he thought, *Or me.*

When Sabrina awoke, she was immediately alert. She knew exactly where she was and what she had experienced. She was in the Ca' D'Este, on the same settee where Alessandro had served her cheese and wine. Her mind urged her to move, yet she was relaxed to the point of apathy, and her limbs were so heavy they seemed part of the cushions beneath her. She felt as if she had just experienced the most glorious sex of her life. But she knew she had not.

Beyond the windows, night had fallen. Someone had lit a taper on the mantle and stoked the fire. Someone had covered her with a blanket.

She had missed Evan's bedtime, and regret flickered through her. She never missed saying goodnight to him, spending time with him, playing with his toy soldiers or reading to him. Yet the regret was a transitory flash of feeling, gone before she could latch onto it. Acting on it seemed to require too much effort.

As she lay there, she wondered where *he* was. That thing he had done to her... The effort to describe what she had experienced was beyond her.

As if her thoughts had conjured him, he appeared in the doorway. He had changed from the dark clothing he had worn beneath his *bautta* that afternoon to a lighter coat of bronze silk and a waistcoat of brown satin. The colors warmed his skin tone and made his eyes appear like topazes. All she wanted was to drink in the beauty of him.

She watched him enter and draw close. He crouched down next to the settee so he was at eye level. The warm scent of him, wild thyme and sage, tickled her nose. She inhaled it, then remembered what he had done.

"You made me remember," she said, a simple statement, neither accusatory nor sad.

"*Si.* I am sorry."

His gaze was soft, sympathetic, and she closed her eyes against the stirring of emotion. She felt the tickle of his fingers along her jaw. A tear slipped out of the corner of her eye. But crying took too much effort.

She opened her eyes. "What did you do to me?"

"It does not matter. A trick of the mind, nothing more." His soft gaze reassured.

She knew it was more than a trick, and it mattered a great deal, but arguing took too much energy. Finally able to move a bit, she raised her hand and looked at it. "I'm a monster."

"No, *carissima.*" He shook his head. "Never that."

Her hand fell back against the blanket, and she looked at him. "I killed those two men. And my mother..." Tears filled her eyes, and she closed them again to shut out the memory. Slowly, her emotions were beginning to awaken.

"Those men were sent by the evil sorceress Nulkana. Your mother was very brave." His pronouncement warmed the chill in her heart.

"She never told me how powerful it was." Regret made her voice tremble. "She forbade me to use it, to forget that I had it."

"She was trying to protect you."

"If I had known, I could have saved her." She opened her eyes and gave him a mournful look.

"Please, *cara mia*, do not blame yourself. You were only a child." He took her hand.

The last time he held her hand, he had forced her to remember. She jerked away. "Don't touch me."

Regret flashed through his eyes, then his mouth twitched wryly. He held up his hands palms out. "No tricks. I promise."

Her gaze went to the night outside the windows. "I need to get home. Mr. Dunfield will be wondering where I am, and my son will miss me."

"I sent a message explaining you had taken ill while visiting here." Ruefully, he added, "I wasn't sure how long you might need to recover."

"How long have I been here?" she asked suspiciously.

"Several hours."

Urgency slipped through her. "I need to leave. I can't stay here any longer. People will think…" She stopped, unwilling to speak the thought aloud.

He smiled. "That your *cicisbeo* is more than a companion? That you are my mistress?"

Glaring at him, fully in control of herself again, she snapped, "I'm not your mistress."

"Not yet." That smile turned into a pirate's grin.

Annoyed at his confidence, she threw back the blanket and sat up. "Take me home, Excellency."

"Of course, *Donna* Barclay." Still grinning, he rose to his full height, bowed, and held out his hand to her.

Ignoring his assistance, she stood and promptly sat back down again. Her legs felt like over-boiled spaghetti, and her knees seemed to be useless. A chill ran through her. He tsked once, retrieved her cloak from where it still lay draped over a chair, and placed it about her shoulders. "Not quite recovered, *Donna* Barclay," he said. "Perhaps you should remain here a bit longer."

She gave him a determined look. "Home, Excellency." Unsure how she would negotiate across the floor and down the stairs to the gondola, still, she was resolved not to spend any more time at the Ca' D'Este.

"As you wish." He sighed.

Before she understood his intent, he bent down and scooped her up in his arms.

His strength made her feel weightless. His proximity made her remember the night he had kidnapped her. "You don't have to carry me," she said with a dry throat.

He turned his head. His eyes were only a few inches away. Staring into those golden depths, she saw unnamed things that made her shiver.

"*Si*, I do," he murmured.

She watched his lips move as he spoke, and the urge to kiss him was overwhelming. Just the memory of his kisses made her moist. Swallowing, she forced herself to look away. She could not do what her body obviously wanted. He had invaded her mind, compelled her to remember things, forced her to see. She could not trust him.

Keeping herself as stiff as possible, she endured his arms supporting her, his hard chest pressed against her, as he carried her down the stairs, across the *andron*, and out into the night where his gondola waited.

Chapter 14

"Morning is upon us, m'lady!" Cora said as she pulled back the drapes.

Sabrina winced from the bright sunlight streaming into the room, groaned, and snuggled deeper into her pillow.

Cora directed the servant girl with her to place the tray of hot chocolate on the table beside the bed. The door closed quietly as the girl left.

Sabrina rubbed her eyes. Then she remembered what had happened the day before. The stroll through the Piazza San Marco. The trip to the Ca' D'Este. The odd sensation of someone in her mind. The enticement. The memories.

Sabrina closed her eyes again, trying to wipe out the recollection. Behind her eyelids, all she saw was *him*, his smile, his golden gaze. Her eyes flew open. What was he doing to her mind? The Prince of Auriano was much more than an influential, wealthy rogue. Power like that was nurtured and passed on from father to son. Whatever he had done to her required some sort of wizardry, power that had to go back many generations.

Her thoughts snagged. *She* had power, inherited from her mother. How many generations of women before her had held the same ability? Where had it come from?

Despite the knowledge she had gained the night before, she was furious with him. He had forced her to remember things she had locked deeply away. He had invaded her mind.

Sabrina sat up and reached for her cup of hot chocolate. The thought of Auriano, her *cicisbeo*, waiting below so he could tease her, annoy her, arouse her, discover more of her secrets, set her teeth on edge. She took a sip from her cup.

"Cora, please inform His Excellency that I am unwell this morning and will not require his attendance," she said.

Cora sniffed and smoothed nonexistent wrinkles from her crisp skirt. "The Prince of Auriano is not waiting below." She pulled a stiff folded parchment from her apron pocket and held it gingerly between her fingers. "He sent this." Cora placed the note on the bed beside Sabrina as if the parchment held some sort of pestilence.

Sabrina was surprised and relieved that Auriano was not waiting below. She hid her smile at Cora's obvious dislike of the prince as she put down her cup and picked up the heavy, expensive paper. Pressed into the wax seal was the device she had noticed on the walls of the *andron* of the Ca' D'Este—a circle broken into three arcs and pierced through the middle with a thunderbolt. It was obviously the arms of the House of Auriano, but it was an odd heraldic device. She wondered what it meant. Breaking the seal, she opened the note and read:

Cara mia,
I await with breathless impatience to read word from your delicate hand when I might attend you.

Your Servant,
A.

Sabrina clenched her teeth. The rogue was too confident. He did not inquire after her health, or *if* he might attend her. No, the implication in the note was that he would arrive at the water gate whether she wanted to see him or not. She was sure that a refusal on her part would be met by a demand that she appear, or a search through the *casa* until he found her.

"Cora," she said, "please fetch my writing desk."

When her maid brought the small desk and placed it on Sabrina's knees, Sabrina opened the top and took out a piece of parchment, not quite the same exceptional quality as what she had just received. After dipping her quill in the inkpot, she wrote, "Tonight. *Spigolo.* Ten of the clock." She did not bother to sign it. Let the prince realize that she was displeased with him.

Spigolo was a fashionable card game played at all the gaming rooms. Dunfield wished her to deliver another message during one of the games. She could accomplish two things that evening. She would act the messenger, play wildly and flirt dangerously, and at the same time, teach the cocksure prince a lesson in humility.

After sanding the ink, she folded the note, sealed it, addressed it, and handed it to Cora. "Please see that this note is delivered to the Ca D'Este, Cora." She put her writing desk aside and threw back the covers. "I will require my brown serge dress today. I am going to work on the oldest of Mr. Dunfield's artifacts."

As Cora set out her clothes, Sabrina mused that the only way to get even with the prince for what he had done to her the day before was to learn some of *his* secrets. He had certainly uncovered some of hers— secrets and memories that she had never wanted to remember.

She sat at her dressing table and began to unbraid her hair. As she did, her gaze fell on the small, stoppered perfume bottle that had been her mother's. It held no perfume, but instead, inside was the tiny bit of parchment she had placed there, the one she had found in the casket that should have contained the piece of the Sphere of Astarte. She felt sure there was some connection between the prince, the piece of the Sphere, and the tiny note that read, *Il Canale di l'Ombres.*

"Cora, have you ever heard of a place called The Canal of Shadows?" she asked casually.

Her maid stopped rummaging through the wardrobe. "No, m'lady. It sounds a frightful place."

Sabrina turned to her with a light laugh. "I'm sure the name is nothing but the Venetians' attempt to be mysterious. I heard the place is quite interesting. Do you think you could discover its whereabouts? I have a desire to see it for myself."

Cora frowned. "I daresay the place is disreputable." She looked closer at Sabrina. "It has something to do with the prince, doesn't it?" she asked flatly.

Sabrina turned back to the mirror and continued to unbraid her hair. "Whatever gave you that idea?"

"Hmph. It sounds like a spot where a kidnapper might hide," Cora said darkly.

"Psst." Sabrina glanced at the door to make sure it was closed tightly. "I told you never to speak of that night. If anyone learns of it, my reputation would be ruined."

Cora's lips thinned.

"Please, Cora," Sabrina said.

"Anything for m'lady's happiness," her maid replied grumpily and returned to her rummaging.

Sabrina smiled. Cora would get the information. And then Sabrina would visit the place and see for herself the meaning behind the note. In the meantime, she had an evening of fiendish flirting to plan, for she intended the Prince of Auriano to suffer mightily for his arrogance.

When Alessandro arrived at the *casa* of the Englishman that night, he was intrigued by the activity taking place in the *andron*. Large shipping crates were being constructed, and several stood, sealed and labeled, near the water gate in preparation for shipment. After inquiring about them with one of the workmen, he discovered that the crates were for some of the Englishman's art collection. He strolled closer to those already nailed shut and read the destination: London.

He frowned. Evidently, Dunfield had come to an arrangement with the English king. Yet, that last messenger Sabrina met had been French. Was the Englishman playing both sides, or had the purpose of Sabrina's last errand only been to meet with a member of the Legion of Baal? Or were the French now involved in the search for the Sphere? He did not like any of the options.

The French, led by General Bonaparte, were still in the northern part of Italy fighting the Austrians and threatening the borders of the Veneto, the land controlled by the Venetian Republic. Venice had pled neutrality in the conflict, but if Bonaparte swung his attention toward Venice and the harbor were blockaded, nothing would be able to leave by land or sea. Dunfield was preparing for the worst and getting his collection out before the city was threatened.

If the collection left Venice, he might never get his hands on the piece of the Sphere of Astarte. He could not let that happen. Involving the Council of Ten or their Inquisitors was not an option. They would interfere, demand information about the Sphere. Reveal his secret. The alternative was to keep a closer watch on Sabrina, definitely not a hardship.

The sound of a musical female voice amidst the hammering and sawing made him turn. Sabrina was just stepping off the stairway and speaking to someone over her shoulder. When she turned to him, his breath caught in his throat at her loveliness. Her mask was silver satin and made her eyes appear the same color. Although she already wore her cloak, it parted down the front and revealed the gown he had sent her to wear to the theater. A triangle of creamy skin gleamed between the neckline and the clasp of her cloak. She moved differently, more fluidly than before. He could not take his eyes from her, and then he realized what made the difference: she wore no stays. *Madre de Dio*. She was magnificent.

As she reached him, she said coyly, "Shall we go, Excellency? I do so look forward to playing *Spigolo*." Her lips tilted teasingly.

Bowing, he offered his arm and bit down on his sigh. She had dressed to torment him. Tonight would be punishment. He had entered her mind, forced her to remember painful things that she had deeply buried. She was angry at his invasion. Guilt tweaked him. But he had learned the source of her power. Now he needed to make her see the danger she was in because of that power. And keep her close, to protect her, discover the reason for the connection between them, and learn the location of the piece of the Sphere. *Dio,* fighting the French single-handedly would be easier.

In the meantime, he had to play her chaste, charming, indulgent *cicisbeo* for the evening. Torture.

As Sabrina placed her hand on his arm, she ducked her head to hide her grin. She had seen the appreciative look in his eyes when she approached. But her victory was tempered by his own defense. He had chosen not to wear the *bautta* this night but had instead dressed according to his wealth and station. His coat and breeches were of the finest wool and of a blue so dark it was nearly black. Thin gold braid decorated the cuffs and lapels of his coat. His shirt and stock were snowy and his waistcoat silver satin with black embroidery. But what gave Sabrina pause was his black velvet half mask decorated with swirls of gilt. In the right corner, just above the outer tip of a golden eyebrow, was the mark of the House of Auriano created out of tiny diamonds. Rather than hiding his identity, he was subtly declaring who he was, and by implication, that she was his. He had anticipated her gambit.

As he handed her into his gondola, she resolved not to let his wily foresight ruin her plan. The evening had not yet begun. She would play the coquette with every male available until her cheeks froze in a smile and her eyelashes wore away from being fluttered — every man except one. She would force him to see that he could not take whatever he wished. Not her body, not her mind. Those were hers to give. If only he understood that. Then perhaps she might trust him.

As she settled herself in the seat, she glanced uneasily out of the *felze*. The last time he had escorted her on an evening out, that evil woman had attacked. Sabrina could see no one lurking beside the canal, nor did she feel any menace pressing into her head. Yet, now, because Auriano had forced her to remember, she realized she had the means to protect herself. She relaxed and focused on the evening ahead.

After they floated out into the middle of the canal, he said, "I see Dunfield is crating up his art."

"He says he has too many pieces to keep in view." She kept her tone light and disinterested.

"It appears he is sending some of the pieces to London. Has he completed negotiations then?" He also used a mildly interested, conversational tone.

Sabrina shrugged. "I don't know. He doesn't confide in me on such matters." She knew he was probing for information, but she was not about to volunteer anything.

"Have you delivered any more messages for him?" His tone was dark and hinted at violence for someone if he did not like the answer.

Annoyed at his implied threat, she glared at him. Evasively, she said, "I told you he had no more need for me to do so."

He seemed to accept her answer, turned and looked out of the *felze*. After a moment, he asked, "Has he sold the piece of the Sphere of Astarte?" Not until he finished speaking did he turn back to her.

There. That was the information he sought. "It is difficult to sell something that has disappeared, Excellency," she told him scathingly. "Perhaps you can find the thief, get into his mind, and force him to tell you where it might be."

As soon as she spoke, she knew she stepped across some invisible boundary. His head snapped up as if she had hit him and his whole body tensed. His voice was dangerously low. "Perhaps, *Donna* Barclay, I should leave you to deal with the evil on your own. How far do you think you would get?" His anger radiated from him.

She refused to be intimidated. "I have my own power," she snapped. "You showed me that."

"But do you know how to use it?" His question was a sharp edge draped in seduction.

"I could learn to use it," she declared rashly. "I don't need you."

He gave a short bark of laughter and turned away to stare out into the night.

His opinion of her ability to learn to use her power grated. They traveled in silence for a few moments, then she said, goaded into annoying him further, "I would not even be here if Dunfield had not encouraged me."

Turning back to her, he observed mildly, "Then perhaps I have been mistaken about him. He has better judgment than I first thought."

Sabrina narrowed her eyes, determined to get him to reveal some of his secrets. "Why *are* you here, Excellency? Why do you pursue so avidly where you are obviously not wanted?"

That dimple appeared in his cheek. He raised her hand to his lips and kissed each finger. "Ah, *Donna* Barclay, you make my life so interesting."

She snatched her hand away and glared at him as she hid the urge to melt toward him. She suspected he was merely using her, for that invasion into her mind revealed as much to him as it had to her. She turned to stare out her side of the *felze*. Furiously, she decided she could make his life extremely interesting.

The *casino* was owned and run by the widow of a merchant. It was a suite of rooms attached to a large *casa*, but which the widow did not use for herself. These small *casini* could be found all over the city. Some were used as places for gambling; others were used as meeting places or hideaways for love trysts. In this *casino*, tables had been set up on all three floors, and the crowd was a mix of men and women. However, with everyone wearing a mask, identities were hidden, so the people at a table might include a member of the wealthy elite, or a thief or a harlot, perhaps a staid matron, or even one of the Council of Ten. With so many people talking, laughing, betting, and arguing in such a confined space, the noise was deafening.

Alessandro played the perfect *cicisbeo*, hanging back and allowing Sabrina free rein to play when and where she chose. He had a double purpose, allowing her to vent some of her anger while carefully observing her. After seeing Dunfield's artwork being crated up, he had the feeling that the man was up to something. He wondered if the Englishman had set Sabrina a task.

He watched her play. She lost heavily. When she ran out of coins, he graciously gave her more, the proper thing to do for a *cicisbeo*. But then she decided to move to another table. And she won. The more she won, the gayer she became. She charmed everyone around her. She flirted outrageously with every man near her, except him.

At first, her coquetry merely amused him, for he recognized it for what it was. She was angry with him and wanted him to know it. But as it continued, as she won more and more ducats, she became freer, less inhibited, and the center of attention for many men. He saw their eyes following her every move. He watched them gaze down over her shoulder to her revealing neckline as they stood behind her.

He knew she was becoming the focus of their fantasies. And anger became an icy lump in his chest.

Yet something about her manner bothered him. This was not the quiet, reserved woman who had retreated from Dunfield's masquerade ball because she was uncomfortable, nor the studious, knowledgeable woman who had shown him the art collection. This was not even the woman who was furious with him, although she was certainly getting her revenge. Her gaiety seemed forced, an artifice to cover something else. So he allowed her more space and watched her from a distance.

Yet, he was not the only one who watched. At the perimeter of the room, he caught sight of a *cappo nero,* one of the spies of the Inquisitors. Surprised the spy concentrated on Sabrina, Alessandro split his attention between the woman who tormented him and the spy who watched her. The spy suddenly appeared at his shoulder.

"A word of caution, Excellency," the black cape murmured. "Be careful of your associations. We are watching the Englishman and anyone connected to him."

Chilled at the man's words, Alessandro forced a calm smile. "The woman's politics are not what interest me, *signore.* Surely you can understand that, *si?*"

"As you say, Excellency. You have been warned." The *cappo nero* gave a small bow and slipped away into the crowd.

Alessandro watched Sabrina more diligently after the spy's warning. She was sitting at a table next to a conservatively dressed man, a foreigner from his accent, although Alessandro could not discern his country of origin. At the end of a game, when Sabrina had lost nearly all her coin, she knocked her fan from the table. The man sitting beside her bent to retrieve it for her.

Alessandro realized her clumsiness had not been accidental. A tiny white bit of parchment rolled from beneath the fan. That icy lump of anger in Alessandro's chest congealed into a hard burning coal. Dunfield was still using Sabrina as a messenger. She had not lied to him, but she had not exactly told him the truth.

The *cappo nero* stood several feet away, watching intently. Had the spy seen the tiny note? The idea of Sabrina being arrested, of spending any length of time confined to the Leads, made Alessandro nauseous. He had seen these chambers just beneath the lead roof of the Doge's palace where the most notorious prisoners were held. They were bare rooms, frigidly cold during the winter and blazingly hot during the summer. He would do his utmost to keep her from that torture.

Standing between Alessandro and the spy was a large woman and her escort. With a quick step to the side, Alessandro jostled the couple, and they in turn bumped the spy, distracting him. Murmuring an apology to the couple, Alessandro glanced back to the table, saw the foreigner scoop up Sabrina's fan and hand it to her with a flourish. The little bit of parchment had disappeared. The *cappo nero* had missed it all.

Alessandro forced his jaw to unclench and focused on the messenger. The *cappo nero* was still watching Sabrina. When the messenger rose from the table, Alessandro followed. He was determined to discover what was written on that bit of parchment. As he stood next to the man, he surreptitiously slipped the tiny roll from the man's pocket. He took it to a quiet corner and read: *Meet Lucia Maria. Midnight. Tomorrow.*

Alessandro had no idea who Lucia Maria was, and the note gave no indication of where this meeting was to take place. Frustrating. But one thing he knew for certain: the lovely, infuriating *Donna* Barclay was not going to be involved. He would ponder the meaning of the note later. After slipping the note back into the man's pocket, he decided he'd had enough of the gaming room and *Donna* Barclay's punishment. It was time to remind Sabrina whom she was with and leave.

Sabrina wandered through the *casino* as she took a break from playing. She was relieved that she had completed her errand for Dunfield without Auriano's interference. The coins she had won hung with a satisfactory weight in a pouch at her waist. Some would have to be returned to Auriano, for when she had lost earlier in the evening, she had borrowed from him. The practice was not unusual between a lady and her *cicisbeo*. She made a little moue of regret. Winning had been fun.

Yet, playing the coquette had been hard work, for she was not a silly woman. And the enjoyment that should have come with the attention of so many men faded quickly, especially after Auriano gave her more and more distance. She had caught glimpses of him as she had gambled. One moment, he would be stoically watching her. The next moment, his head would tip intimately toward a masked woman as they conversed, his lips curving in a smile. Despite the chilly antagonism between them, an unexpected wrench of jealousy twisted through her. She berated herself for being a fool.

He frightened her with his ability to enter her mind and make her remember. He had done it without her knowledge, without her permission. He had seduced both her mind and her body. He was too dangerous. He was something other than what he appeared. She was still angry that he had interfered with her errand for Dunfield. She suspected he was using her. So why did his focus on other women upset her?

As she walked by a small space beneath the stairs, a hand grabbed her and pulled her into the shadowed, secluded alcove. She gasped as she was pushed back against the wall. Arms and legs caged her. A large, hard body blocked her in. As she opened her mouth to scream, her gaze met a pair of golden eyes, seething with anger. Auriano. Her teeth snapped together. Although he did not touch her, the proximity of his body radiated heat, energy. And fury.

"I will not be played for a fool, *Donna* Barclay," he growled. "You will stop this foolishness, or I will pick you up and carry you out of here."

"You wouldn't dare," she hissed, his rage reigniting her own anger.

"I would. Do not tempt me." Each word clipped out tersely.

She pushed against his chest, a useless exercise. "Let me go."

"Not until you come to your senses."

"I know perfectly well what I am doing." Her cool words were an utter lie.

"And what is that?" he drawled, goading.

Refusing to answer, she looked away.

"You have made your point, *Donna* Barclay," he said. "I understand you are angry."

Her gaze swung back to him. "Angry? I am beyond angry, Excellency. You interfered in my errand for Mr. Dunfield."

"I saved your life," he snapped.

"You forced me to remember things I never wanted to remember."

"I helped you see who and what you are."

"You lied to me."

His eyes went cold. "I have never lied to you."

Even that statement, she felt, might be a lie. Her temper was on the verge of exploding, and she contemplated the satisfaction of feeling the palm of her hand landing with a slap against his cheek. "You don't own me."

"Don't I?" His voice was a dangerous purr.

Slipping his hands lazily down her arms, he circled her wrists, then swiftly pinned them against the wall. He leaned into her, making her aware of his size, his strength, and her helplessness if she tried to struggle. His scent, that heady mixture of wild thyme and sage and male, tickled her nose, reminded her of his seduction, her arousal. Ducking his head, he sucked at the spot where her neck met her shoulder. She felt an answering pull deep in her core. He ran the tip of his tongue up her neck and nipped her earlobe. She shivered.

"You are mine, *cara mia*," he whispered. Then he covered her mouth with his and ravaged.

This was no soft caress or gentle seduction. This was a kiss meant to claim her, to mark her as his, the dominant male declaring his power over the female. Forcing her lips apart, he thrust his tongue inside, tasting her, teasing, arousing.

Sabrina's senses were filled with him. He was everywhere. There was no escaping. Her traitorous body responded shamelessly to him. She went moist, and she throbbed where his erection pressed against her. She was pliant beneath him. She wanted him. Ever since that night he had her kidnapped. God help her.

From the first moment they had met, she did not trust him. And yet, he had always been considerate. He had always treated her with respect. Even on the night he had kidnapped her, he had treated her with deference. But now, at this moment, with this kiss, he was taking what he wanted.

Anger and hurt cooled her.

Alessandro drowned in her. He had wanted her ever since he had first touched her, to feel her pressed against him, her softness in his arms. Being her *cicisbeo*, playing the gentleman had been agony. Watching her act the bewitching siren had ignited his blood to boiling. More than being connected to him because of her power, of having touched the piece of the Sphere, she was his, and he needed to make her understand that.

He could tell she was surprised into submitting, pressing against him, willing, soft, yielding. He felt a leap of triumph. But her surrender was fleeting, for she became rigid, withdrawing emotionally. Slowly, he came to his senses. This was Sabrina in his arms, a lady, delicate, sheltered, intelligent, courageous.

Lifting his head, he saw the tears sparkling in her eyes. They were like knives slicing through him. *Cristo!* He was acting as if he were in the height of the Hunger. She drove him to madness. He should have more control. Guilt washed through him. Her lips were swollen from his assault, and there, on her neck was his bruising mark. Closing his eyes, he took several deep breaths while he harnessed his need and his emotions.

Finally, when he felt he could speak normally, he said, "I think, *Donna* Barclay, we have had enough *Spigolo* for one evening."

Stepping back, releasing her, he gave her space. He knew he had just blundered badly. Along with everything else he had done, he could not foresee her forgiving him. That knowledge was painful.

But he was not ready to let her go.

Chapter 15

Mortified, wounded, Sabrina bowed her head as Auriano placed her cloak about her shoulders. She refused to look at him. How could she have been so stupid? She had taunted and goaded him the whole evening with her outrageous behavior. Of course he would take advantage. He was, after all, only human.

"Head up, *Donna* Barclay," he murmured in her ear. "People are watching."

She straightened her spine. Anger coursed through her, more at herself than at him. She would not allow anyone to see how badly he had hurt her, especially not him.

He handed her into his gondola. "Take us out into the lagoon, Piero," he told Gasparo's brother, their gondolier for the evening.

Sabrina crushed her cloak in her fist. "I wish to go home, Excellency."

"In time, *Donna* Barclay. Piero enjoys singing, and if I do not allow him the chance, he becomes very sad. Do you wish to make my gondolier sad?" he asked, playing on her sympathies.

With a vague gesture to do as he wished, she leaned into the corner. She would endure the confinement with him in silence.

As they entered the Grand Canal, Piero began to sing a tune from Mozart's opera, *The Marriage of Figaro*, in a pure tenor. The notes soared. The music calmed her as they slipped from the canal to the lagoon. The quarter moon laid a path of light across the water. Celebration torches and *Carnevale* firecrackers lit the night sky above the Piazza San Marco. The city was as alluring as the man beside her.

She gathered the shreds of her composure and examined her relationship with Auriano. She had never met a man who could so easily charm and seduce one moment, and then infuriate and destroy her the next. She had to get away from him. She could not afford his deadly attraction. It interfered in the tenuous bargain she had with Dunfield.

Piero finished his solo, and she applauded him as another gondolier's song echoed across the water.

Auriano shifted toward her. "*Donna* Barclay, I know you are angry at me."

"I am furious and wounded, Excellency." She cast a glare in his direction.

He nodded an acknowledgment. "I am deeply sorry for the pain I caused you."

"Apologies are only words. You have betrayed my trust." She turned to stare out across the lagoon. "You became my *cicisbeo* to protect me, but I find myself in more danger than before."

"*Si*, I know. I am asking your forgiveness for what I have done." He sounded sincere and penitent.

Could she believe him? She wanted to forgive him. He made her feel alive. But he was too seductive. And he had too many secrets. Refusing to look at him, she said, "I do not want you as my *cicisbeo*."

He paused. His voice was cool as he spoke his next words. "Perhaps you are correct. This relationship is no good."

Sabrina closed her eyes against the pain of hearing him speak so impassively about the time they had spent together. Despite the fact that he was a rogue and a scoundrel, despite his ravaging kiss, most of the time she liked him. If only he were not so overbearing, if only he did not take so ruthlessly what he wanted, she would not mind having him as her companion. She certainly was not going to become his mistress. Knowing she would probably never see him again made her both sad and relieved.

She was not used to the wild emotions she felt when she was with him. He made her feel off-balance, as if she tottered on the edge of a precipice. Her life with her late husband had been peaceful, perhaps even staid. But she had Evan and he brought her joy. She was content. But this man evoked emotions in her that left her breathless and reeling. She needed to find her footing again and regain the calm in her life.

He spoke again. "I will speak to *Sior* Dunfield about a contract of betrothal."

Her head snapped around. "What?!"

"It is an agreement—"

"I know what it is," she cut in.

"Then… ?" He appeared puzzled as if he did not understand her confusion.

"I do not want you as my *cicisbeo*, and I do not wish to be betrothed to you," she said, low, intense.

"There are many advantages to becoming my betrothed." He reached out and toyed with a curl resting against her neck. "For instance, you would not have to rely on Dunfield's generosity or good will."

His statement made perfect sense, and perhaps before he had intruded into her mind she might have considered it. But not now. "Dunfield is neither generous nor good-willed," she said, as she knocked his hand away. "But that has nothing to do with my decision."

"Ah." He nodded sagely. "The idea of marriage frightens you, *si*? Yet, you were already married once, so why should this be so?"

He was taunting her. She wanted to slap him. She was not afraid of marriage. She was afraid of *him*—his allure and his secrets. And she was afraid of the danger that surrounded him, danger that could spill over and affect her son. "I am not marrying you, Excellency."

Is someone getting married? she heard in her head.

Startled, she turned to the front of the gondola. The shadow man perched on the prow.

"Tonio," the prince greeted. "*Donna* Barclay and I were having a private conversation."

Have it later, Tonio said. *It's coming*. He gestured toward the sky.

Craning her neck, Sabrina glanced out of the *felze*. Streaming across the quarter moon were hundreds of birds, looking like a streak of dark, oily smoke in the night sky.

"*Mi Dio!*" Piero exclaimed

Auriano spoke one grim word. "Nulkana." He looked at Tonio and continued the conversation silently. *I've never seen anything like this.*

157

Nor I, Tonio answered. His molten gaze landed on Sabrina, but he said nothing.

Nulkana must still be weak from her wound if she's using birds to attack, Auriano mused.

Tonio turned his attention to the prince. *She must be getting desperate.* His glance focused on Sabrina again.

"Why are you looking at me?" Sabrina demanded. "She has no reason to attack me."

The sound Tonio made in her head was part scoffing laughter and part growl.

Not now, Tonio, the prince intervened. Aloud he said, "Piero, how fast can you get us to the Ca'D'Este?"

"I will do my best, Excellency." Piero's answer was grim.

The gondola shot forward. They sped across the lagoon with Piero laboring to get them to safety. Sabrina watched the flight of birds swarming across the sky. As they reached the Grand Canal, the birds streamed down in a line toward the city. It was terrifyingly beautiful.

We're not going to get there in time, Tonio said. *Maybe I can slow them down.*

"No. Tonio—" Auriano tried to stop him, but Tonio had already disappeared into the darkness.

"How can he slow them down?" Sabrina asked. "There are too many. He'll be hurt."

"*Sì.*" The prince ripped off his mask. His expression was bleak as he stared out into the night where Tonio had gone. Turning to her, he asked, "Can you feel the evil?"

Sabrina removed her own mask, closed her eyes, and concentrated, but she felt nothing like that night at the theater, nor at the villa on the mainland. She shook her head. "I can't sense it," she said.

"Nor can I," the prince concurred.

"Maybe it's too far away," she suggested.

"No. There's some other reason." He glanced thoughtfully up at the sky, then ahead, down the length of the canal. "Take us down the next *rio*, Piero. They're coming."

As Piero propelled their gondola into a smaller canal, Sabrina glanced back. Coming around the turn of the Grand Canal, just below rooftop level, was a blot of darkness, blacker than the night. The birds. Other gondolas on the canal scrambled to get out of the way. Screams resounded off the buildings as people caught sight of the frightening phenomenon.

Sabrina prayed they were not too far from the Ca'D'Este. Only a few more minutes and the flight would be swarming around them. Then as she watched, a dark shadow grew and rose up in front of the mass. Tonio.

"*Stupido*," Auriano muttered, concern weighting his word.

Some of the birds flew into the shadow, and the front part of the mass erupted into confusion. But there were too many birds. The shadow collapsed and fell to the surface of the canal. Tonio! Auriano sucked in a breath. Sabrina's wordless cry echoed off the walls of the narrow canal.

They made another turn, and she lost sight of Tonio's dark form. But she had no time to grieve for him. The birds were almost upon them.

Piero did his best to keep the gondola ahead of the swarm. He turned down one *rio* after another, but the birds always followed. Just as they entered the canal where the Ca'D'Este was located, the birds reached them. And she felt the evil.

It was not a single, independent presence as she had felt before, but a swirling confusion, coming from everywhere. It made her head spin. Chaos. She couldn't get her bearings. All she could feel was fear. Panic. The birds swarmed around her head. They beat their wings against the *felze*, flew into it, through it, pecking at her, trying to grab her with their claws. They became trapped under the little roof. She sensed their terror. It fed her horror. Whimpering, lashing out wildly, she swatted them away. The noise of their wings was deafening. In the midst of the tumult, she heard Piero yell, and then a splash.

Auriano pulled her against him, covered her with his cloak and his body. She grabbed onto him, the only stationary thing she could sense. His voice cut through the confusion.

"Sabrina. Focus. Use your power."

"I can't," she sobbed. The evil attacked from every direction. All she could feel was the chaos. It roiled through her brain. She couldn't tell up from down.

Sabrina. His voice was inside her head. *Focus on me.*

Hearing him was like a shaft of light through blackness. She followed his voice and found a place of calm inside her head. The energy was a tiny spark. All she needed to do was fan it to flame.

Sabrina, he said. *I am here. I'll protect you.*

He continued to speak to her. His voice grounded her, guided her. She used it to brighten that spark of energy. She felt the buzzing in her fingers, fainter than before, but still there. She raised her hand. The energy zapped out. One bird, a tiny wren, fell at her feet. A pigeon dropped next. The birds backed away a bit, then a little farther. Finally, the area around the gondola was free from their wings as if a protective bubble surrounded them.

Somehow, they reached the quay. Auriano leaped onto it, pulled her out of the gondola, and swept her up into his arms. She saw Gasparo and many other servants holding torches and swiping at the swarm as if the birds were oversized moths. An occasional bird would get too close, and there would be a snap and sizzle. Piero climbed out of the canal and joined the others fighting the birds.

Sabrina was dizzy, nauseous. The swirling birds seemed to be in her brain. She wrapped her arms around Auriano's neck and buried her head against his shoulder.

His voice rumbled in her ear. "Tonio needs help, Gasparo."

"*Si, Sior* Sandro," the man answered breathlessly as he swiped at another bird. "I will send someone."

Auriano carried her through the water gate, and peace surrounded her. The noise from the birds seemed far away. The chaos in her mind retreated. She still felt queasy, but at least the whirling in her brain had stopped. Sighing in relief, she lifted her head.

Auriano carried her up the stairs and into the small sitting room where she had been before. "Are you feeling better, *cara mia*?" he murmured.

"Yes, thank you."

He placed her gently on the settee, then turned to pour two glasses of wine. As he handed one to her and sat next to her, she saw he had a deep scratch across one cheek, and another through one eyebrow, across his temple and disappearing into his hair. The backs of his hands showed several more.

"You're hurt," she said.

Shrugging it off, he smiled, flashing his dimple. "As I told you, I heal quickly." He gave her a searching look. "Are you hurt anywhere?"

She shook her head. "No, just feeling a bit dizzy." She took a sip of wine. "I can't hear the birds anymore."

"The *casa* is shielded. The evil cannot get in." He took a sip of his own wine and leaned back. "I think, perhaps, you should tell me what you felt when the birds attacked."

Their argument became secondary to the attempt on their lives. He had saved her life—again. Despite her reluctance to reveal any more of herself to him, she owed him her gratitude.

"It was complete confusion," she said. "I couldn't think. I had no sense of up or down. And fear. I sensed terrible fear. I couldn't feel the evil until the birds were all around us."

"Why didn't you use your power to fight them off?"

"I couldn't." She shook her head in confusion. "I don't know what happened, but I couldn't find it, not until you spoke to me."

He traced his fingers gently across her cheek. "Then perhaps I am of some use, *si*?"

She turned away. "Please, Excellency."

"I think, *Donna* Barclay," he said, "that you need to develop this power of yours."

"No, I—"

He spoke over her refusal. "I think, if you do not, then your life will be in grave danger, more than it is now. I think, that if you do not, Nulkana will kill you, and perhaps your son as well."

Sabrina's heart froze in her chest. "You think my son's life is in danger?"

"It's possible."

"Why?"

He smiled grimly. "That is the question, isn't it? Why does she want you dead?"

"How do you know Nulkana wants me dead?" she argued. "The birds attacked everyone—you and Piero as well."

"I felt the evil, but I did not sense the confusion as you did. The birds were after you. Piero and I just happened to be near you."

Hearing that made her head throb. She rubbed her temples. "I can't think anymore. Please, Excellency, I wish to go home."

"Of course, *cara mia*, as soon as Gasparo thinks it is safe. But I wish you to consider accepting help in developing your power."

Sending him a suspicious glance, she asked, "From you?"

He chuckled. "No, I don't think I could, although I would certainly not consider it a hardship. There is someone here who can help you. Will you think about it?"

"I will think about it," she agreed.

"*Bene*," he said, and grinned.

Sabrina thought he looked much too satisfied.

By the time Sabrina arrived home, it was almost dawn. She went first to Evan's room where he was sleeping peacefully. Relieved he had not been disturbed by Nulkana's attack, she took a moment to watch him. A tiny frown creased his brow, and he clutched his stuffed bunny closer as if he sensed her unease in his dreams. She brushed his hair back from his forehead, and his tension eased. She vowed she would do everything she could to protect him, even giving up her life as her mother had in order to protect her. Reassured that he was safe, she retreated to her own bedchamber, for exhaustion had begun to replace her horror.

She sat at her dressing table and looked in the mirror. A woman she barely recognized stared back. The beautiful dress Auriano had given her was torn and filthy. Her face was pale. Her hair hung in a messy tangle. Terror still lived in her eyes. She never wanted to experience that kind of chaos ever again.

Cora clucked and fussed as she pulled the pins from Sabrina's hair. When she gathered it for brushing, her gaze landed on the bruise where Sabrina's shoulder met her neck. Auriano's mark.

"M'lady," Cora breathed. "You're bruised."

"From the bird attack, Cora." Sabrina sighed. "It's nothing."

"Birds don't make this sort of mark, m'lady." Cora peered at the dark smudge more closely. Her scandalized eyes met Sabrina's in the mirror. "M'lady, he marked you!"

"It was a misunderstanding, Cora, that's all." She wished it truly were that simple.

"A misunderstanding?" Cora shook her head. "This is more than a misunderstanding."

Sabrina scowled at her maid. "It was a mistake."

"A strange mistake," she mumbled, then sniffed. "I know a love mark when I see one."

A *love* mark? If Sabrina had not been so exhausted and terrified, she would have laughed. The prince had been far from loving when he had given it to her.

"I think you need to be careful of him, m'lady," Cora went on. "There's something about him I don't trust."

Sabrina silently agreed. Yet, he had saved her life several times, and he wanted to help her learn how to use this power that she had. For that, she was grateful. Yet, what bothered her was his reason for doing so. She sensed that altruism was not his underlying motivation, nor his obvious physical desire for her. Something else drove him.

As she crawled into bed, her thoughts kept spinning. Perhaps, it was his need to find the piece of the Sphere of Astarte, but she had no idea where that had gone, and his explanation that it was the family symbol seemed much too innocuous for his single-minded pursuit of her. She suspected that the Sphere was much more valuable than he admitted. Could it be connected to the rumor of the family curse? Except for Tonio, she had seen no evidence of any curse in the prince. She wondered who Tonio was, and what his connection was to Auriano. The two obviously knew each other well. Tonio had even warned them of the bird attack.

Sabrina shivered and pulled the covers closer. She never wanted to experience anything like that again. If that attack of the birds had been aimed at her, as the prince had said, then she needed to find a way to protect herself and Evan.

Auriano's offer to help her develop her power might not be selfless, but if it could save her life and Evan's, then perhaps she should accept it. She might even find out more of the prince's secrets in the process.

She drew in a breath. Let it out. Her life, so ordinary, so mundane, had become something fantastical. Like a dream. Or a nightmare.

Secrets. And power. An ancient sorceress. A magical sphere. A prince.

On that thought, she drifted to sleep, where *he* waited for her. Charming. Seductive. And always elusive.

Chapter 16

The next day, when Sabrina finally arose, still exhausted, Dunfield requested her to join him in his study. The only time he called her to his private space was to send her on another errand or to scold her. She did not want to relay another message for him, and she certainly did not want to hear him lecture her for insulting the prince because he had not appeared that day.

Steeling herself, she smoothed her skirt, glad she had dressed in the plum colored mousseline gown, instead of the brown serge work skirt and bodice. She knocked on the door and entered. Dunfield, dressed impeccably as always, his shirt and stock bleached and pressed to perfection, rose from behind his massive gumwood desk with its hutch of small doors and drawers placed at one end. A smile curved his thin lips.

"Sabrina, my dear, come in," he said. "How are you feeling? Have you recovered from that terrible ordeal last night? I heard all about it from the servants this morning."

Immediately suspicious of his solicitous manner, she said, "I'm fine, Uncle."

"You were not injured in any way?" he persisted.

Her fingers went to the ribbon around her throat that Cora had tied there to hide Auriano's mark. "No, I wasn't injured."

"Good, good. Come, sit down. There's something I wish to discuss with you."

She moved to a chair and, feeling uneasy, perched on its edge. Dunfield settled behind his desk. He was looking extremely pleased.

"I received a letter from the Prince of Auriano this morning," he said.

Apprehension became a lump in her stomach.

"It seems," he went on, "that he is quite taken with you. For once, you have done as I asked and been charming to a possible suitor."

Sabrina caught her bottom lip between her teeth to hold in her laughter. *Charming* was not the word she would have used to describe herself. Thank goodness, Dunfield had not witnessed any of the interactions she'd had with Auriano.

Realizing Dunfield was waiting for her to comment, she said, "The prince is a very interesting man." *Interesting* did not even scratch the surface of how she would describe him.

"I'm glad you think so." He nodded and that little smile of satisfaction played around his lips again. "You see, he wrote me this morning to request a meeting. He wishes to discuss terms for a contract of betrothal."

Sabrina fought not to slump in dismay. Auriano wasted no time in getting what he wanted. Evidently, he wanted her, despite the fact that she had told him she would not marry him.

Dunfield, a line of impatience between his brows, watched her closely. "Did you hear what I said, Sabrina? The prince wishes to marry you. I should think a little enthusiasm on your part would be appropriate here."

"I—I am overwhelmed, Uncle." She searched for the right words. "After all, we have only known each other a very short time."

"He is a man of action," he said with approval.

She could not deny that. "When is this meeting supposed to take place?"

He glanced down at the letter before him. "In five days. He says he wishes to give me time to consider his terms."

Five days. Five days to convince Auriano to withdraw his intentions. How was she going to do that?

Then the last part of what Dunfield said caught her attention. "What are his terms?" she asked.

"In return for an enormous sum from him, he is asking that I do not sell any of my collection to a foreign nation."

"But your negotiations with King George…"

With a sly smile, he said, "What the prince doesn't know is that some of the artwork is being shipped to England tonight, which is why I had you deliver that message last evening. He also won't know about a trip you and I are taking to Milan to meet with some other buyers. On the return trip, I plan to meet with this French general, Bonaparte, to see if some arrangement can be made if he decides to attack Venice."

"But that's—"

"Circumventing a disagreeable situation," he finished. His eyes turned cold. "You will tell Auriano nothing. If I suspect he has any knowledge of what I intend, you will find yourself shipped back to England where you may fend for yourself and your son on your own." He paused, then said quietly. "Do you understand, Sabrina?"

She nodded because she had to protect Evan, but Dunfield was planning to cheat the prince. Although she suspected Auriano had a hidden motive for seeking a betrothal with her, he had been forthright about announcing his intentions. She didn't want to marry him, but she wondered if there might be some way she could let him discover what Dunfield intended.

And then she had another thought. "Are you including the ancient artifact in the sale?"

"I can't sell something that I do not have, Sabrina," he said drily.

"Then, if you don't mind, could you return the casket to me?"

He studied her for a moment before he spoke. "Why do you want the dusty old thing? I thought you had no use for it." His blue gaze sharpened. "Have you found the artifact? Do you know where it is?"

"No." She shook her head and tried to look as innocent and sad as she could. "It was Richard's, and I... I have nothing left to remember him. Please, Uncle."

"I do not think Auriano would be pleased to discover you are still holding on to reminders of your dead husband." His cold blue eyes echoed his rebuke.

Sabrina thought the prince might be thrilled to discover she was holding on to this particular reminder. To Dunfield she said, "Evan is Richard's son. I want to keep it for him as well, to remember his late father. Besides, Auriano need not know. I will keep it well hidden."

After a long pause, he finally unlocked a drawer in his desk, took out the casket, and placed it before her. "You may keep it until you are wed to Auriano. Or until the artifact is found. It is an important part of the collection, Sabrina, and I expect you to return it to me."

She hid her surprise at his easy capitulation. Perhaps he needed her more than he let on and the threat to return her to England was an empty one. Whatever his reasons, she was relieved she did not have to bargain or beg. And she did not remind him that she was the one who had given him the casket in the first place.

"Of course. Thank you, Uncle," she said, taking the casket in both hands and standing.

"One more thing." He pushed a small, painted wooden box toward her. "Auriano sent this for you with the letter."

Opening the box, Sabrina was stunned at the flash of gold inside. It was a chain, long enough to wrap around her waist several times, made of delicate links. Each link was a different style of oval or curlicue, but each was exactly the same size. The piece was exquisite.

"It seems," Dunfield said, "that the prince is anxious to bed you."

Sabrina's cheeks flamed. She knew that the gift was a message from Auriano stating his desire for her. The chain was also symbolic, implying a bond to him, something she would never agree to.

If she wore the chain, she would be agreeing to allow his seduction. She knew it would be the most sensuous, erotic experience of her life. The memory of the night he kidnapped her, the memory of the kiss in the gondola made her yearn with desire. He had imprinted himself on her. Despite their strained, complicated relationship, she still wanted him. But she could not give in to him. She could not trust him.

She swallowed, her throat dry. "Please send it back. I cannot accept this."

"Send it back?" Dunfield shot to his feet. "You can't send it back. You will insult him." He took a breath and said more calmly, "You cannot insult this man, Sabrina. You *will not* insult him." He pushed the box toward her. "Keep the chain. Wear it or not as you wish until you are wed to him, but you will wed this man. Or..." He let his word hang in the air a moment. "Or England. Do I make myself clear?"

Sabrina stared at him. She could understand his wanting her wed and out of his house, but she sensed he was desperate to have her marry Auriano, and not only because of the obvious wealth and connections such a marriage would bring to him. Something else was driving him. Until she could discover what it was, she was caught, because she couldn't go back to England. There was nothing there for her or her son.

She glanced down at the box once more, fingered the chain, then placed the cover over it. "You are quite clear, Uncle," she said. Picking up the box, she turned toward the door.

Dunfield's voice reached her just before she could escape. "Auriano wrote that he will be here to collect you this evening. Be charming to him, Sabrina."

Giving a short nod, she slipped out of the study. She wondered if she could avoid the prince by pleading a headache, or a broken limb, or perhaps the plague. She might be able to put him off for a day, but he'd soon be at the water gate demanding to see her. Resigned at the inevitable, she left the two boxes in her bedchamber and then went to spend some time with Evan.

She found him moping in his room.

"Evan? What's wrong?"

He glanced up at her with troubled gray eyes, then he pushed over several of the toy soldiers laid out before him. "My nurse says I mustn't talk about Nurse Letitia again. Nurse Filomena says that Letitia is bad."

Sabrina knelt beside him and pulled him close. "Nurse Letitia isn't bad, Evan, but she's very ill."

"She scares me."

A feeling of dread stole through Sabrina at his tone. "Has Letitia been here?"

Evan nodded. "She tried to get me to go to the Piazza San Marco with her. Nurse Filomena wouldn't allow it."

A sense of relief replaced the dread as she realized the nurse that Auriano had recommended was protecting her son. "Did you want to go to the Piazza San Marco with Letitia?"

"At first I did. She said we could watch the jugglers, and then she would buy me a treat. Then when Nurse Filomena came in, Letitia started to get angry with me. I got scared and didn't want to go anymore." He knocked over a few more of his soldiers. "I used to like Nurse Letitia."

Sabrina said nothing as she hugged her son. Gratitude for Auriano's blanket of security for Evan overcame her apprehension at his motives in sending her the chain and stating his desire for a betrothal contract. She wanted to do something to repay him, something impersonal, something that would not involve her getting anywhere near him. As she tried to think of something, her gaze wandered around Evan's room with its shelf of books, its collection of pretty stones and childish trinkets, and there, on the table beside his bed, the ship model she had bought for him when they first came to Venice. It was a beautiful reproduction of a frigate, with all the correct rigging and sails. It had been made by one of the master shipbuilders within the walls of the Arsenale, the enormous shipyard in the city. The gun ports opened and closed; the wheel turned. It even had a tiny compass on its deck.

An idea came to her. She would go to the Arsenale, to one of the shops just inside its walls where miniature reproductions of the great ships could be found. She would obtain another ship model and have it sent to Auriano. But before it left the shop, she would request that it be renamed: *Lucia Maria* — the name of the ship that would carry some of Dunfield's artwork to England. At least then, someone in Venice would know what he was about, and she would not feel quite so guilty about acting as messenger for Dunfield.

Standing, she pulled her son up by the hand. "Come, Evan, we're going on an adventure, and then I will take you to the Piazza San Marco for a treat."

With a grin, he ran to get his hat.

The night after Nulkana had sent the birds, Alessandro sat next to the fire in the hearth. He slouched in a leather chair, one long leg dangling over its arm, the other stretched out before him. On a table at his elbow was the beautiful model ship that had arrived that afternoon. On its hull was the name *Lucia Maria*. Beside it was a short note from Sabrina thanking him for his protection and expressing a desire "to become more familiar with the art and knowledge of the venerable House of Auriano," code for agreeing to use his help to develop her power. Gratified that she had taken his advice, he relaxed as he munched on olives. His twin, still Shadow but safe and whole, perched in a chair opposite him. Occasionally, he tossed an olive at Tonio, who swiped it into the flames with a flick of his finger. It was a game they had played since their youth to perfect their skills at moving objects with their minds.

After the bird attack, after Alessandro had returned Sabrina to her home, Tonio had appeared at the Ca' D'Este, looking a little ragged, but alive. Alessandro was relieved to see his brother had survived the onslaught of the birds but exasperated that Tonio had put himself in such danger. In fond, brotherly fashion, he had expressed his relief. Then, in detail, he reminded Tonio how sore and bruised he would be when he regained his body and the Hunger began.

They were waiting now while Gasparo spoke with Sabrina and Guided her in learning to use her power.

I can't believe you are set on marrying her, Tonio said silently.

Alessandro shrugged. *It's the only way I know to protect her.*

But marriage? It's so permanent. Tonio's confusion was plainly evident in his tone.

Si. Alessandro munched on another olive.

You said she doesn't even like you.

I said she's annoyed with me. He tossed another olive in his brother's direction.

The word you used was 'furious,' Tonio said, as he swiped the olive into the fire with a tiny movement of his finger.

Alessandro shrugged again and gazed off into space.

You said if she'd had a weapon, she would have skewered you with it, Tonio persisted.

Si. Alessandro hurled an olive directly into the fire with such force that it spattered against the bricks at the back.

Why would you want to marry a woman who obviously has no use for you?

Alessandro grinned and tossed another olive in his brother's direction. *She is very beautiful, si?*

Si. Tonio kept his eyes on Alessandro as he sent the olive flying into the flames. His single word was more than merely a response. He expected some sort of explanation.

Alessandro let his gaze fall to the bowl of olives in his lap. His motives for initiating the betrothal were a muddled mix in his own mind, so how could he hope to explain them to Tonio? He grasped onto the one that made the most sense. *Dunfield is a member of the Legion of Baal. If Sabrina is my betrothed, then I can at least legally protect her.* He locked gazes with his twin. *And she sent me the ship model,* he added, as he turned to look at it sitting on the table beside him.

Why would she tell you about the Englishman's intention to ship out his collection? Tonio pressed.

Alessandro gave his brother a thoughtful look. *I'm still trying to figure that out. Perhaps she's telling me she has nothing to do with the Legion. But now that we know about Dunfield's plans, I've set Piero the task of raiding the ship with some men to see if the casket with the piece of the Sphere is on board.*

At that moment, Gasparo appeared in the doorway. "*Sior* Sandro," he said, straightening his somber brown and black woolen waistcoat.

Alessandro glanced up in surprise. "Is the lesson over, Gasparo?"

"No." Gasparo shifted his weight.

"Has something happened to *Donna* Barclay?" Alessandro was poised to bound out of his chair and race to her aid.

"No, *Sior* Sandro." Gasparo paused, then said, "But there is a problem."

Alessandro frowned. "A problem?"

"*Si.*" Gasparo appeared even more uncomfortable, the corners of his mouth turning down. He heaved a tremendous sigh and said forlornly, "I am sorry, *Sior* Sandro."

"Sorry? Sorry for what? Gasparo, what has happened?" Alessandro's consternation deepened and he shot to his feet.

"I cannot Guide *Donna* Barclay."

Blinking in surprise and confusion, Alessandro sank back in his chair. Gasparo's family had been Guides for the House of Auriano for generations, helping them use their minds to overcome the obstacles caused by their curse. "Why not?"

"*Donna* Barclay is—I still do not believe it—" He stopped, his dark eyes widening.

"She is what, Gasparo? *Christo*, what are you trying to tell me?" Alessandro sat forward again, perched to jump up and run to her aid.

"*Sior* Sandro, *Donna* Barclay has the mark of Halima."

Stunned silence fell into the room. Tonio was the first to recover. *She has the mark of Nulkana's sister?*

Gasparo nodded. "*Si*." Holding up his open left hand, he indicated the fleshy skin between his thumb and first finger. "Here. It is unmistakable."

That's why Nulkana wants her dead, Tonio observed.

Alessandro acknowledged Tonio's statement with a nod, then turned to Gasparo. "But why should her relationship to Nulkana make a difference with who Guides her?" Alessandro demanded.

"Her power is too strong for me to help her control it." Gasparo bowed his shaggy gray head. "I am sorry."

Scowling, Alessandro said, "There must be something you can do, Gasparo. She needs help."

"*Si*," their Guide agreed. "She should have been Guided by her mother."

"Her mother is dead." Alessandro's words landed with finality.

"*Si*." Gasparo paused again, then said, "She needs someone to Guide her who is close to her."

"Not Dunfield." After seeing the bit of frog glyph on the man's wrist, Alessandro was not about to allow him to have anything to do with Sabrina's power.

"No, he is not an option," his Guide concurred. "And he is only related to her by marriage."

"So, is there no one then who can help her?" Alessandro's tone was bleak.

"*Si*, there is." Gasparo's gaze wandered to a spot above Alessandro's head.

"Well, who is it?" A bit of hope bloomed in his chest.

Gasparo hedged. "It could be dangerous."

"Not any more dangerous than her meeting up with Nulkana and not knowing what to do. Who is it, Gasparo?"

Looking directly at Alessandro, Gasparo said, "You."

At that single word, Alessandro fell back against the chair. "Me?!"

Tonio's laughter erupted in Alessandro's head. He sent his brother an annoyed glance.

"Gasparo, I can't Guide her," Alessandro protested. "I don't know how."

"*Si, Sior* Sandro, you do. You Guided her during the attack of the birds. And you helped her remember."

Alessandro heaved a sigh. "Thought Binding," he said.

"*Si*. It is the only way to help her. She needs someone who knows her intimately, like her mother, or someone who can connect with her mind."

"And become intimate," Alessandro finished.

Isn't that what you wanted? Tonio taunted.

Sending his brother a quelling glance, Alessandro thought about his options. Sabrina would not be pleased to learn that he would be the one helping her. She would be even less pleased to discover the manner in which he would do it. But she needed to protect herself from Nulkana, and her only hope to do that was with him. He would have to try to make her see that.

Bleakly, he said, "Please remove any sharp objects from the room, Gasparo."

Gasparo bowed and left. Tonio continued to chortle.

Standing, Alessandro said, "*Vanffanculo,* Tonio," and tossed the bowl with the olives at his brother. As Alessandro stalked past him, the olives stalled in midflight, and the bowl slowly floated to the floor. One by one, the olives plopped into it.

Tonio's laughter echoed in Alessandro's head until he was half-way up the stairs.

Chapter 17

Sabrina watched as servants cleared away the racks of rapiers, stilettos and other weapons stored around the room. Disappointment descended on her like a heavy cloak. She thought she had found a way to protect Evan through this power she had discovered, but Gasparo had taken one look at her hand and excused himself. Nervously, she toyed with a pale pink rosette sewn at the waist of her gray moire gown. She stood alone now, curious about the servants' actions.

In any other *palazzo*, this enormous room, empty of furniture except for two plain, straight-backed chairs, would have been the *piano nobile*, the ballroom. The only decorations left in this one were the three magnificent chandeliers dripping with icy crystals. She guessed that the prince was more interested in practicing his skill with weapons than in giving balls. In place of tapestries, the walls were hung with padded mats, and other mats were rolled up and stashed around the perimeter of the highly polished terrazzo floor. Wire mesh covered the windows.

The final rack of swords had been removed when she heard Auriano's step. He appeared at the room's entrance, dressed like the first time she'd seen him, after he'd had her kidnapped. Wearing boots, breeches, and a shirt open at the neck, the only piece missing was the red silk mask. Except this time, he appeared grave rather than rakish, but his eyes lit when he met her gaze. An answering awareness of him tingled through her body.

"*Donna* Barclay," he said, as he bowed, then strolled forward. "I am sorry I could not meet you when you arrived, but I want to thank you for your kind gift."

"I hope the ship model pleased you," she said, dipping a quick curtsey.

"It pleased me very much." He circled around her. "But I see you are not wearing my gift."

She ignored the pull of his presence. "I am merely considering your offer, Excellency." She was not considering anything. Auriano's chain would remain in its exquisite little box. She would endure another lifetime of Dunfield's masquerade balls rather than become the prince's mistress — or his wife. She did not trust this prince, no matter how concerned he was for her safety. He had too many secrets.

His smile did not reach his eyes. "Do not consider too long, *Donna* Barclay."

His warning sounded very much like a mild threat. "Why?" she demanded, using anger to cover her apprehension. "Will you have me kidnapped again?"

The smile on his lips flitted away. "Please, we are not here to argue."

"Of course." His entreaty calmed her uneasiness. "I apologize. I came to learn how to use this power I have."

He gave a single nod. "*Si*. But it seems we have run into a small problem."

"Gasparo didn't look happy when he left," she said. "I suppose you are here to tell me that he can't help me."

"I'm afraid so." His tone was apologetic.

She lowered her eyes to hide her disappointment. "I understand. I will not impose on you any longer, Excellency. If I could have my cloak, I will return home."

"You have not allowed me to finish, *Donna* Barclay," he said. "It seems Gasparo was able to find someone who *can* help you."

"I am grateful. Please thank him for me."

Auriano glanced away as if trying to find words. "You may not be so grateful when you discover who it is."

Sabrina's brows drew together in suspicion. "Who is it?"

That dimple appeared in his cheek. "Me."

Anger flashed through her. "You planned this," she hissed. "You had Gasparo pretend to help me just to get me here."

"I did no such thing." A single brow curved up in cool denial.

"I don't believe you."

Auriano sighed. "I assure you, *Donna* Barclay, I had no intention of bringing you here under false pretenses."

"I don't know what you intended, but whatever it was, I'll have none of it." Her hand slashed through the air.

"What I intended was to help you. Nothing more," he said, his gaze steady.

Sabrina stepped away from him. "How can I believe you? You have tried to seduce me several times."

"If I wished to seduce you again, do you think I would have you brought here?" He waved his arm to indicate the barren room.

"You don't seem to be too particular about where you conduct your seductions. Last night you pulled me beneath a set of stairs, and..." She was not quite sure what to call what happened.

"And kissed you?" he finished drily. "That was hardly seduction." His gaze dropped to the ribbon around her neck. "I was proving a point."

Indignant, she stalked back to him. "You made your point, Excellency, and you made it again when you wrote to Mr. Dunfield to arrange a meeting to discuss a contract of betrothal. Did it ever occur to you to discuss the matter with me?"

"I told you last night what I planned to do, so I don't see the problem." A line of confusion appeared between those dark brows.

The breath hissed between her teeth. "Perhaps I would have liked to have been *asked* how I felt about the matter."

His lips twitched. "I don't think I would have liked your answer."

"Exactly. Asking gives the other person a chance to say *no*."

His eyes widened a moment, then she watched an idea click into place. He cocked his head and amusement made that dimple appear. "All right, *Donna* Barclay."

Sabrina held her breath. Was he really going to formally, politely ask for her hand in marriage?

He went on, "I am asking you now... Since I am the only one, it seems, who can help you learn how to use your power, would you honor me by agreeing to let me Guide you?"

Confounded, she stared at him as she tried to find her footing. His question was not what she expected. She couldn't decide whether she was angry or just surprised that he conceded so quickly in asking her anything. Suspicious of his motive, she remained silent. Was he being forthright with her, or was he planning something else? If she agreed to allow him to Guide her, would she be stepping into some sort of trap?

Turning, she walked down the length of the room as she wrestled with her options. Actually, she only had two. She could refuse his guidance and try to learn on her own, or she could accept it. Learning how to use her power on her own might prove to be a problem, especially since she could not practice in Dunfield's *casa*.

Swinging back to him, she asked, "Why do you wish to help me?"

He strolled toward her and stopped several feet away. "I do not wish to see my betrothed killed, nor do I wish to see her son murdered."

Narrowing her eyes, she told him, "I am not your betrothed yet."

He shrugged. "A minor point. Even so, I can't be with you all the time. If you know how to use your power, you can protect both yourself and your son."

She conceded that point. Protecting Evan was her first priority. But then she saw a flaw in his argument. "You told me last night you couldn't help me. What has changed?"

Instead of answering, he held out his hand. "May I see your left hand?"

Instinctively, Sabrina curled her fingers into a fist and did not move.

"Please, *Donna* Barclay. I will not harm you, but I must see for myself." His gaze was forthright and sincere, and perhaps a bit haunted.

Slowly, she stepped toward him and placed her hand in his. With his other hand, he gently flattened her fingers against his palm and spread her thumb, revealing that odd little starburst freckle between her thumb and first finger, the mark her mother had tried to fade with lemon juice and milk soaks.

Tracing his finger across it, he murmured, "*Incredibile.*"

His delicate touch sent a prickle up her arm and ended deep inside her. She must be losing her mind to have such a little thing make her want him. Determined not to succumb to any seduction, no matter how insignificant, she snatched her hand away. "You have not answered my question, Excellency."

"The mark you have indicates you are a descendant of Halima, Nulkana's sister," he said.

An unsettled feeling bloomed in her middle. "Nulkana, who sent the birds to attack?"

"*Si*."

"She is evil."

"*Si*. A sorceress."

"And I am descended from her sister?" Her voice rose as the beginnings of panic set in.

"*Si*."

Sabrina's hands shook. Her whole body shook as the truth of who she was sunk in. "Then I am evil as well."

"No, *cara mia*, you are not evil." Auriano shook his head.

Sabrina stepped back, appalled at what she had just learned. "I am! I killed those men."

"They were trying to kill *you*. You did what you had to do." He stepped forward and reached out to take her hand again. She pulled it back and cradled it with her other hand. "Sabrina, listen to me," he entreated.

Wide-eyed, she stared at him. She suddenly felt very cold.

"Sabrina."

Her murmured name on his lips was warmth and sunshine, touching inside where she had gone dark and frozen.

"*Cara mia*, you are not evil," he said, his voice calm and soothing. "Halima used her sorcery only for good. She was just as powerful as Nulkana is, but she was *good*."

His last word finally made an impact on her shock. "Good?" she echoed, her voice small.

"*Si*. Good." He nodded once to emphasize the point. "Nulkana learned of the Sphere of Astarte and wanted it for herself. She was devious, and she convinced my ancestor to name her as his advisor. When her sister discovered what she had done, Halima went to my ancestor and told him that Nulkana planned to steal the Sphere. Nulkana was furious and *killed her own sister*."

Shocked at the story, Sabrina stared up into his eyes, steady, clear, gorgeous. Perhaps what he said was true. She began to thaw just a tiny bit.

"The power you have is just as strong as theirs, but it is very intense," he said.

"I am powerful?" she asked, needing to get this straight in her head.

He smiled. "*Si*."

She released the breath that had become stuck in her lungs. "Oh."

His gaze softened. "Because your power is so potent, only mothers can pass the knowledge of the power on to their daughters."

Sabrina frowned. "But—"

The prince smiled wryly. "*Si*. I am far from being your mother. Gasparo seems to think that because of my ability, I can Guide you."

"What ability?"

"It is called *Thought Binding*."

Her eyes widened as she understood what he was saying. "What you did when you made me remember."

"*Si*."

"No." Hugging herself defensively, she said, "No. Absolutely not. You're not doing that again." Spinning away, she strode to the huge window overlooking the canal and stared out into the night. He was not going to invade her mind again, no matter whom she was descended from.

"Sabrina."

Hearing him speak her name sent a delicious shiver down her spine. She refused to look at him.

He spoke again. "When I helped you remember, you let me in."

She swung back to face him. "I did not."

"*Si*. You did." His golden gaze was level and steady.

She shook her head vigorously, not believing.

He took a breath and let it out slowly. "Let me explain. I cannot enter anyone's mind unless that person allows me to do so, either consciously or not. It's similar to opening a locked door."

"But I couldn't—I would never—" she protested.

"You wished to remember. I helped you."

"I didn't want to remember. My mother..." Grief overwhelmed her and tears filled her eyes. She turned her face away until she could get her emotions under control.

"I know," he said gently. "It is very sad. But I think you did want to remember. You needed to remember, so you let me in." He paused, then said, "Once I'm in your mind, you can shut me out if you wish."

"How can I do that?"

"Just by wishing me not to be there."

"It's that simple?"

"*Si.*"

Sabrina searched his face, looking for some indication he might be lying. His gaze was level and steady. He told her he'd never lied to her, and she had no evidence that he ever had. He might have kept things from her, but he had never lied. Could he be lying now?

Thought Binding was beyond anything she had ever encountered. Her whole experience since coming into contact with Auriano was beyond belief. The evil Nulkana, the discovery of her own power and who she truly was all made her head spin. Yet, everything he had told her had proven to be true.

He held out his hand. "Will you let me help you?"

Coming to her decision, she placed her hand in his. "Yes."

Relief swept through his eyes as he smiled. "*Bene.*"

They stood side by side at one end of the room. Two chairs were right behind them, in case, Auriano explained, her strength gave out suddenly. At the other end of the room, servants had placed two straw dummies and had raised a padded mat across the window.

Taking a breath, Auriano asked, "Are you ready?"

Too nervous to speak, Sabrina nodded.

She felt him take hold of her wrist and gently press his fingers against her pulse. His thumb caressed the back of her hand, back and forth.

"Look at me," he urged softly.

She turned her head and was caught in that golden gaze. As if from far away, she sensed that warm, comforting presence she had felt the first time.

"Relax, Sabrina," he murmured. "Think of something pleasant."

She searched for a pleasant memory. The first thing that came to mind was the kiss they shared in the gondola.

He chuckled. "We will do that again later, *cara mia.*"

Mortified, she snatched away her arm. "I can't do this." That distant presence disappeared.

"*Si.* You can," he said, serious again. "You can learn to put up blocks. Until you do, I promise not to peek." Amusement brightened his eyes.

"I find nothing funny in having my thoughts read," she snapped.

"You are right. I'm sorry. Shall we try again?" He held out his hand.

After a moment's hesitation, she allowed him to take her wrist again. Once more, that gentle presence entered her mind.

It is a very pleasant memory, cara mia, she heard in her head.

Annoyed at his incorrigible persistence, she tried to pull out of his grasp, but his fingers tightened around her wrist.

Don't run. Enjoy the memory. Relax. Let me Guide you.

She felt the presence in her mind grow.

Before we start, I want to show you how to block me.

Without waiting for his prompt, she thought about pushing him away.

"Ow!" He dropped her wrist, jumped away, and pressed the heel of his hand between his eyes.

Surprised his reaction had been so severe, but pleased all the same, she giggled.

"You don't have to look so amused," he grumbled, as he shook off the last of the effects of her jolt.

"I'm sorry, Excellency," she said, as she tried not to grin.

He smiled back. "Knowing you can do that feels good, *si?*"

She nodded. "*Si.*"

"Your ability is very strong." He held out his hand again. "Gently, please, *Donna* Barclay, if you wish me to stop. I would prefer not to have my mind incinerated. Save your strength for the evil."

Feeling a bit more sure of herself now that she knew she could push him out of her mind if she wished, she allowed him to take hold of her wrist again. As before, she felt the comforting presence build in her head. It seemed to caress her, then it pulled back as if watching.

Find your center, Sabrina, she heard in her head. *Find the thing that can guide you to your energy.*

She searched in her mind for something, but all she found were jumbled thoughts.

Your mother, he prompted.

Her mother? No. She couldn't. She keened silently.

Shush, Sabrina. Use her death to help you.

No. She wouldn't.

That presence grew, became commanding, demanding.

Use it. Use her death. Use your anger.

Sabrina felt her rage building, not at her mother's death, but at the presence that wanted to violate her mother's memory.

Don't. I am not your enemy.

She felt the odd buzzing in her brain, the tingle down her arm.

Sabrina. Not at me. Direct it outward.

No, not at him. She felt the presence in her mind gather itself as if preparing for an attack.

Find the source of your energy.

She searched and followed the buzzing until she arrived at a bright, sparking light.

There. Mark it. Remember it.

As if planting a flag in her brain, she tagged the spot.

Fan the spark. Feed the anger. Make it grow. Direct it.

The buzzing in her brain grew. The tingling down her arm was nearly unbearable. The presence in her brain turned away, retreated. Raising her arm, she let the energy flow, zapping out of her palm and toward one of the straw dummies at the other end of the room. There was a flash, an explosion. The dummy flamed briefly, then disintegrated into a pile of ash.

Her legs suddenly gave out beneath her, and she sank into the waiting chair. Auriano sat in the one next to her.

Bene. You did it, he said. *You found the source of your energy.*

She turned to him with a grin.

He was not grinning back. His gaze was riveted on her moonstone pendant. She could feel its heat against her skin, and when she glanced down, she saw it pulsing softly.

Tell me about the stone, he said, still in her mind.

She shook her head, not to deny him, but to indicate she knew nothing. Raising her eyes, she met his gaze, intent and probing. That presence in her mind pushed and poked gently, then retreated.

You know more than you think, he said silently, *but I can be patient. You have been very brave, cara mia, and I am thankful for your trust in me.*

He raised her hand to his lips and placed a gentle kiss there. *Come. I wish to show you something.*

Sabrina fell into his eyes, golden, infinite. The presence in her head seemed to stretch out, draw away, and take her with it. It beckoned to her, compelling, seductive. She followed.

She found herself inside his mind.

In awe, she examined her surroundings. His was a mind of power and majesty, of strength. Of sadness. Of torturous pain. She wanted to reach out and ease that pain, erase the sadness, and as she felt the desire to do so, she sensed his gratitude.

A road opened before her. Without hesitation, she took it. It led to a *castello* in the mountains. On a pennant flying from one of the turrets was the same device she had seen carved into the panels in his *palazzo*, the circle broken into three arcs with a lightning bolt through its center. This was his ancestral home, Auriano, in the north of Italy in the foothills of the Alps. The road wound through fields of lavender and wildflowers, groves of olive trees, and vineyards planted in terraces down the hillside. But interspersed among the beauty were fallow fields, orchards dead from disease, and withered vines. The drive ended before a carved wooden door in the wall of the *castello*. As she watched, the door opened, and she entered the courtyard. It was deserted, but the double doors into the hall were open. Hearing voices, she investigated. What she saw made her gasp.

Nulkana, robed in red, her hood thrown back, her face ravaged by age, stood at one end of the great hall. She held a beautiful woman by the back of her neck. The woman's eyes and hair were dark and rich, but her sensuous mouth was echoed in the prince's face. His mother. At the other end of the room, was a man, broad shouldered, tall, proud in bearing, and holding a rapier. His golden eyes and chestnut hair shot through with gold marked him as the prince's father.

"Don't you love your wife enough to save her, Excellency?" Nulkana purred.

"You are never getting the piece of the Sphere, witch," the man spat out.

Nulkana tsked. "All you have to do is tell me where the piece is, and I will let her go."

"Don't tell her, Armanno," the prince's mother said. "She'll kill me anyway."

Nulkana did something to the woman to make her cry out in pain.

Armanno started forward, then stopped as Nulkana raised her free arm. "Come any closer and your wife is dead," the sorceress warned.

Sabrina's perspective changed, and she was looking down on the scene from the gallery. She felt rage, fear, and frustration at what was taking place below and realized that this was the prince's perspective. Nulkana looked up in his direction.

"Watch closely, boy," she said. "This is what happens to those who defy me."

"I'll kill you!" he screamed. "Let her go!"

Hands grabbed him and pulled him back through a doorway. Words whispered urgently, spoke in alarm, warned him. Sabrina sensed two others with him, but they were obscured as if in a cloud.

Despite being pulled back, Sabrina could still see what was taking place. She heard the prince's father speak.

"I've sent the piece of the Sphere to a place you'll never find, witch."

Nulkana seemed to grow in size. She placed her hand on the woman's chest, and the hand disappeared inside her body. The prince's mother screamed in agony.

"Tell me where, or your wife dies," the sorceress threatened.

"No, don't tell her!" the prince's mother managed to whisper hoarsely, and she gazed at her husband with desperate love.

Auriano's father started forward, but Nulkana pulled her hand from the woman's chest and her arm shot out, spraying blood. The man froze in midstride. The sorceress turned her attention back to the woman in her grasp. Once again, Nulkana's hand disappeared inside the woman's chest. Sabrina watched in horror as the woman's beautiful face became old, wrinkled, desiccated, and Nulkana glowed with youth. Finally, the prince's mother was only a shell, and Nulkana let her slip to the floor.

A strangled sob came from the prince's father.

Sabrina understood now why the sorceress could live so long. She sucked the life from young women, like Letitia, like the prince's mother, and used it to stay alive.

"I told you that you would pay with your life and that of your family if you defied me," Nulkana said to Armanno. "Feel my wrath, worm."

Raising her arm, she shot a fireball into the ceiling, and then another and another. The room was soon engulfed in flames, and Sabrina heard the evil, wild laugh of the sorceress.

Immediately, the scene changed, and she found herself lying in the middle of a field. Beyond, the *castello* was engulfed in flames, and parts of it were already beginning to crumble as the fire consumed it. Several people stood scattered about, watching the destruction, and she heard crying. Something wet trickled into her eyes. Swiping at it, her fingers came away red, covered in blood. Pain knifed through her hands, and she saw they were burned, blistered, and raw.

And then everything faded to gray.

He would show her no more.

Sabrina felt his slow, sad, gentle withdrawal like the slide of fingers across satin. He still held her wrist. A filament seemed to still connect them. She gazed into the depths of those golden eyes and knew there were many other secrets still hidden behind them. But he had shared with her a memory… It was sharp, painful, indelible. Devastating.

Your parents, she thought.

Sì, she heard in her head.

You watched Nulkana kill them.

Sì.

Like my mother.

Sì.

I am sorry.

Grazie.

Your father had found a piece of the Sphere.

Sì. He sent it away when he learned that Nulkana had discovered he had it.

But he wouldn't tell her where it was, so she killed him and your mother.

Si.

Their gazes locked, silver eyes staring into golden ones. Even without speaking, without thinking, Sabrina felt him, knew him. The rage he felt against Nulkana was the same as hers. She wished there was something she could do to help him. As she had the thought, she heard him inside her head: *Be with me.*

With his free hand, he cupped the back of her head and drew her to him. As if his will were hers, she accepted the inevitable, leaned toward him. His mouth touched hers gently, barely brushing it. His tongue flicked out, tasting. Her lips parted, and the tip of her tongue met his, a tender touch, but he withdrew, merely grazing his lips against hers. It was a kiss of potential desire, not heated passion. It was a kiss of painful memories shared, of gratitude, compassion. It was a kiss of soul touching soul.

His mind spiraled around hers, an invitation to dance. Captivated, she watched. The invitation beckoned, beguilingly seductive. She could have refused it, but after the memory he shared with her, her only desire was to be with him. Slipping inside his spiral, she matched it, twirl for twirl. They twined together, like the twisted threads of a skein of silk. She felt her mind gently caressed, cherished. Stretching out, up, they rose higher, spinning slowly. Colors flashed — gold, silver, red, purple.

Sabrina was awestruck. Mesmerized. Spellbound. Enraptured. Her senses were flooded. Pleasure flowed through her like syrup. Entangled in his spiral, she found their boundaries blurring. And still they flowed upward, up, up, until they reached a ceiling of sorts, and their spiral spread out, enlarged, mushroomed. The sensations were glorious. That spiral caressed, brushed against every sensitive nerve ending. Her sight was filled with magnificent colors. She tasted incredible sweetness. She heard beautiful music. She smelled the incense of a thousand flowers. Across her skin was the sweep of hundreds of his kisses. Her body throbbed.

And she climaxed. Timelessly. Into infinity. Until she was wrung out, inside out, stretched thin. Shattered. And then snapping back to become whole, put back together, the same yet somehow different.

With only their lips touching.

With only his fingers against her pulse.

Carissima, he sighed in her head.

She focused on that single word, his voice, until her brain began working again. Sated, bewildered, she pulled back and stared into his eyes. His hand still cupped her neck. His fingers still pressed against her pulse. They were still connected, but barely.

"That was—what did you do?" she whispered when she could speak again.

"I gave you pleasure, *cara mia*."

Pleasure beyond belief. She closed her eyes and nodded. "Yes. But—"

Her emotions were a jumble. She couldn't think straight. It was an effort to think at all. He had just given her an amazing, dazzling experience, completely unexpected. Not realizing what he would do, she had gone with him, danced with him, allowed him to seduce her. Should she be angry or grateful? Opening her eyes again, she looked at him.

He gave her a tiny smile, a tender smile.

She wanted to smile back, but something scraped at the edges of her contentment. "Please, let me go," she said.

His smile died. "Have I hurt you in some way, *cara mia?*"

"No. I just… Please." Something in her head was not right. She thought it might be because they were still connected.

Hurt flashed through his eyes, but it was quickly quashed. Slowly, he withdrew his hand from her neck. She felt as if her muscles had turned to rubber, and she fought to keep her head up. Deliberately, finger by finger, he released the pressure against her pulse until his fingertips barely touched her skin. As he did, she felt the connection between them grow weaker.

"You will feel ungrounded when I release you," he said.

As he removed his hand from her wrist, she felt as if she had just lost something very precious. There was emptiness where his presence had been, and her mind flailed. Her physical world tilted, and she teetered as if she were about to fall into an abyss. With a cry, she grabbed onto his shoulder. He steadied her with a hand on each of her arms. Dizziness made her gasp. Her head felt like it contained a thousand needles, all pushing outward.

"The feeling will soon pass," he told her.

But it did not. Light splintered. Everything went black.

Alarmed, Alessandro caught her and scooped her up. He had not induced her to sleep. Her fainting was caused by something else, and he feared he might have done something to harm her. *Stupido.* He had allowed his desire for her to overrule his good sense. As he carried her to a sitting room, he yelled for Gasparo. He laid her on a settee, chafed her hand. Her skin was hot, burning to the touch, and tiny shocks came from the tips of her fingers.

"Sabrina," he said. "*Cara mia.* Wake up." Brushing her hair back from her cheek, he realized she was barely breathing. "Gasparo!" he bellowed again, not bothering with the bell pull. Anxiety burned through him. Rolling her onto her side, he yanked at the ties of her stays and muttered oaths against the fashion. Terror made his fingers clumsy. By the time he had finished, running footsteps announced the arrival of Gasparo.

"*Sior* Sandro, why—?" Gasparo rushed to his side and crouched next to him. "What has happened?"

Alessandro explained, leaving out their intimacy.

"This was my fear," Gasparo said. "This is why only mothers teach their daughters."

Alessandro picked up her hand and winced at the shocks that pricked his skin. Turning it over, he saw tiny sparks erupting from the middle of her palm. "What's wrong with her?"

"She hasn't pulled back and banked her power," Gasparo said. "It's consuming her from the inside. Your connection suppressed it. When you broke the connection, her power surged again."

"Is there nothing we can do?" His words were bleak.

Gasparo looked at him. "You must connect with her again and help her pull back."

Fear clutched at him. "I've never connected with anyone who is unconscious."

"*Si*. It will be difficult and dangerous. She may be so confused she may not recognize you." Gasparo paused, then said slowly, "She may consider you an intruder, someone who means to harm her."

Alessandro stared at his Guide. "Are you saying she may attack me?"

"*Si*."

After watching what Sabrina had done to the straw dummy, Alessandro was not particularly anxious to expose himself to her wrath. If she decided to burn him, he was not sure his mind would mend. He turned to look at her. She was worse, her head thrashing from side to side as she murmured incomprehensible words. Delirium was beginning to claim her. Pain was etched on her face. She was slowly incinerating from the inside out. His decision was already made.

"Stay with me, Gasparo, in case I need you," he said, as he took hold of Sabrina's wrist.

At Gasparo's nod, Alessandro bowed his head, closed his eyes, and concentrated. He could feel Sabrina's pulse beneath his fingertips. It was racing, with barely a pause between beats. He needed to time his own heart rate to hers if he was going to connect with her, but to match that runaway rhythm was impossible. They would both die of heart failure. Somehow, he needed to slow hers down.

Confounded, he opened his eyes and took a deep breath to give himself a moment to think. To slow down Sabrina's heart rate, he needed to calm her. The only way to calm her was to connect with her. But he couldn't connect with her if her heart rate was so fast.

Alessandro shook his head. "Her pulse is too fast. I can't match it."

"Use what you know," Gasparo told him. "Use what I have taught you."

Alessandro looked at her. She had begun to pant, her chest rising and falling almost as quickly as her heart was racing. If he did not do something soon, her body would consume itself. Instinctively, he placed his free hand on her chest to calm her. It did not accomplish what he wanted, but it did give him an idea.

Closing his eyes again, he pictured his hands cupping her heart. Holding it was difficult as it raced and jumped and convulsed. He restrained it firmly, forcing it to remain in his hands, and it began to slow. Gently, he caressed it, soothed it. Gradually, its rhythm became more regular, closer to normal. Now, he could catch up with it.

Dissolving the picture of her heart, he shifted his concentration to the pulse beneath his fingertips and matched it. He connected to her mind quickly, as if their previous connection had not been broken. Knives of light and sparks of energy dazed him. He turned away.

Sabrina, he called.

He heard no answer, but the knives of light became brighter, sharper, and more frequent. They stabbed and burned.

Sabrina, he called again. *Cara mia.*

Go away. The voice he heard was barely recognizable as hers. It was deeper, darker.

Sabrina, I've come to help you.

I don't need your help. I can do this on my own. Sparks of energy zapped out at him.

Enduring the pinpricks of pain, he asked, *What can you do on your own?*

Kill Nulkana.

Sabrina, she's not here.

Of course she is. She's hiding. I need to find her.

Alessandro had a moment of panic. What if he had unbalanced her mind?

Sabrina —

Go away!

Sparks erupted around him again, and he flinched away.

I will kill Nulkana, Sabrina announced. *She killed my mother and she killed your parents. I know she's here.*

Alessandro understood. The memory he had shared with her and the memory of her own mother's death had somehow become entangled with her ability to find and use her power. She didn't know how to shut it down, so it fed on the anger caused by the memories. She thought the memories were present reality. He had to make her understand they were from the distant past.

Sabrina, your mother's death and the death of my parents are in the past.

Of course they are. She sounded exasperated.

Their deaths are memories.

Isn't everything a memory except what we are doing right now? Do you think I'm an idiot that I don't know that?

Stifling his amusement, he said, *I think you are the most intelligent, fascinating woman I have ever met.*

The knives of light retreated somewhat. *You do?*

Si.

She said nothing.

Taking advantage of her silence, he said, *Sabrina, your power is consuming you from the inside. Your anger at Nulkana is feeding it. She's not here inside your head.*

But —

Sabrina, we'll find Nulkana and destroy her. Together.

I will make her suffer.

Si. But she's not here.

The knives of light and sparks of energy faltered.

Sabrina, control your anger. Don't let it control you.

I hate Nulkana. Don't you loathe her?

Si. I am very angry.

Once again, she was silent. The light and energy pulsed, but it had retreated.

He pressed his point. *You must close off your anger so it doesn't feed your power. If you don't, it will consume you.*

The knives of light and sparks of energy pulsed for a while, then contracted and faded to a single glowing ember. He sensed a pause as if her mind were taking a breath, trying to decide its next course of action. The anger had been banked and walled away, and he knew something else was coming. The brightness he experienced the first time he connected with her was shadowed. He waited quietly while she sorted herself out. Feeling something build, he braced himself. Then a wave of deep sadness washed over him. Her emotion was so intense, tears came to his eyes. She needed to grieve. But he knew she would be all right.

Hold me, he heard her whisper, both aloud and in his head.

He opened his eyes. She was looking at him. Her eyes were clear. Her breathing was regular. Her pulse beneath his fingers was strong. Tears streamed down her cheeks. Slowly, he broke the connection. Her gaze remained steady. She reached up and gently touched his cheek.

Gasparo's hand squeezed his shoulder, and then his Guide's footsteps retreated.

Alessandro gathered her close. "*Carissima,*" he murmured against her hair.

She dissolved into sobs.

Chapter 18

By the time Sabrina returned to Dunfield's *casa*, the rim of the sun was just peeking above the horizon. She felt washed out, depleted. The last thing she wanted was to run into one of the servants who would report to Dunfield.

She had sobbed on Auriano's shoulder until she was dry. He had taken her onto his lap, held her, rocked her, comforted her until she had stopped. Exhausted, she had fallen asleep in his arms, her head against his chest. When she awoke, still in the same position hours later, he had also been asleep, his head leaning against the back of the settee, his arms still firmly about her. Changing her position had awakened him, and he had smiled sleepily at her. What would it be like to have him wake up beside her every morning with that sleepy, sensuous smile?

Immediately, she squashed that thought. She was confused about how she felt about him. He had helped her learn how to use her power, had saved her when she couldn't control it, had shared a painful memory with her, and had given her the most erotic, intense pleasure she had ever experienced. Yet, there was something he was hiding. She still wasn't sure if she could trust him.

She was not sure she could trust herself, not after learning she was descended from Nulkana's sister and had the same power as the evil sorceress. Perhaps that was why her mother had forbidden her to use the power. Her mother might have been afraid her daughter would turn evil. Sabrina shivered at the thought. She resolved she would only use her power for good.

As she entered the water gate, one of the servants told her that Dunfield wished to see her immediately. She was caught. A frown creased her brow. The urge to harness her gift and turn the man to ash was overwhelming. But no, that was using it wrongly. Taking a breath, she told the servant to let Dunfield know she would attend him presently, and she hurried to her room to fix her hair and change her clothes. But she was not quick enough. Dunfield met her at the top of the stairs.

"Sabrina," he said. "My study. Now, please." Then he turned on his heel and stalked away.

Having no choice, Sabrina followed.

As soon as she entered and closed the door behind her, his gaze raked over her disheveled appearance. "I see you've been entertaining Auriano," he sneered.

Heat erupted in her cheeks. "It's not what it seems, Uncle." She sighed as she tried to come up with a plausible explanation for her long night. "We were—"

"Yes, yes." He waved his hand in dismissal. "I don't care what you were doing. You obviously changed your mind about accepting the prince's advances."

"But—"

"That isn't why I wanted to speak with you." He paced back and forth once in front of his desk. "Last night, the *Lucia Maria*, the ship that was to transport some of the artwork to England, was raided. I lost a Tiepolo, a Raphael, a Titian, and several minor works."

"That's terrible." She tried to inject some concern into her voice. At the same time, she hid her satisfied smile.

"It's more than terrible. It's a disaster. Do you know how much those paintings are worth?" Dunfield stopped before her. Without waiting for her answer, he went on, "You knew I was shipping some of the artwork last night. I told you I would send you back to England if Auriano or anyone else learned what I was doing."

Anxiety burned through her exhaustion. "But I said nothing to him."

"Then how did he learn of the shipment?" he challenged.

"How can you be sure it was Auriano?" she asked, straining to remain calm. "He was with me all night."

"So you say." Dunfield's eyes were cold. He remained silent, waiting.

Sabrina gazed back at him. "You may believe what you wish. I am telling you the truth. If there's nothing else you wish to discuss, Uncle, I would like to go freshen up."

"You will stay here until I am finished with you," he snapped. "I understand you sent Auriano a gift."

She swallowed, determined not to cower. "It seemed the proper thing to do after he recommended another nurse for Evan and sent me the extravagant gold chain."

"It was hardly *proper*," he said sarcastically. "If you wanted to accept his advances, you should have just worn the chain. What did you send him?"

"If you know I sent him a gift, then you know what it was." Sabrina began to lose her temper. "Why are you playing games with me?"

"It is you who is playing games." His eyes narrowed. "You sent him a ship model immediately after I had told you about sending some of the artwork to England."

Sabrina shrugged, weaving the lie as she spoke. "I went to spend time with Evan and saw his ship model. I thought that since Auriano is to be my future husband, he will also be the future stepfather to Evan. The ship was a gift so that he and Evan could sail their models together."

Without warning, Dunfield slapped her across the face. "Stupid woman!" he thundered.

Her hand flew to her cheek and unchecked tears came to her eyes. In shock, she stared at him. She tasted blood. Drawing herself up, she said coldly, "Do not ever strike me again."

"Or what?" he sneered. "You'll run away? To where? England? Where there is nothing left? Or perhaps to Auriano? He certainly will not wed you if I do not offer anything as your dowry." He paused, allowing his words to hang in the air. "You will do as you are told while you are still under my care. You will tell the prince nothing, or you will lie to him, whichever I say to do. Am I clear, Sabrina?"

Her anger seethed. She could feel the warning buzz in her brain, the tingling down her arm. It would be a simple matter to raise her hand and prove to Dunfield that he could not control her. She could easily send him crashing back across his desk — or worse. But then she remembered the lesson of last night when she had almost incinerated from the inside out. She had to restrain her temper. Besides, she was not ready to reveal what she could do. She still needed Dunfield's protection for Evan just a bit longer.

But she must have revealed something in her expression because he frowned in confusion. She lowered her eyes to hide her thoughts. Taking a shaky breath, she nodded her acquiescence.

"You are very clear, Uncle," she said meekly. She was relieved when the buzzing and tingling retreated.

Dunfield heaved a false, sad sigh. "I do not wish to be so harsh with you, Sabrina. Understand that I am only concerned for your welfare."

Raising her head, she snapped, "Don't lie, Uncle. It's not my welfare that concerns you."

His nostrils flared in anger. "You would be wise to hold your tongue, Sabrina. Now get out of my sight. I have work to do. We are leaving in an hour."

"Leaving? To where?"

"To Milan, as I told you. I wish you to come with me. We will be traveling quickly, so your maid will remain behind."

Sabrina did not like the idea of traveling without Cora, but she acquiesced with a nod. "I will go have Evan's nurse pack his trunk."

"The boy will be staying here," Dunfield snapped.

"But –"

"Don't argue." He waved his hand in dismissal. "Go clean yourself up so you don't look like a whore. And no messages to Auriano. I will have them intercepted and burned."

Furious, frustrated, Sabrina spun on her heel and left. She did not begin to calm down until she reached her bedchamber. She could not even ask Auriano to watch over Evan while she was gone. As she sank, exhausted, into the chair before the dressing table, her gaze fell on the two small boxes there, the empty ancient casket and the painted one overflowing with the gold chain. Reaching out, she ran her fingers over both of them. Coming to a decision, she picked up the painted box, rose, and walked across the room to where a trunk lay open, awaiting the rest of her clothing. Carefully, she hid the box beneath a pile of petticoats, then she rang for Cora to help her freshen up before the trip.

Just after sundown, their coach stopped before a villa outside of Milan. They had been traveling the whole day, first being ferried across the lagoon and then boarding the hired coach which took them the rest of the way. Sabrina had slept for most of the trip and had spoken little with Dunfield when she had awakened. She missed Evan, and without Cora, she felt very alone. And for some reason, being cut off from Auriano made apprehension nag at the back of her mind.

When they stepped through the front door of the villa, no host greeted them, and they were directed to their rooms by servants. Sabrina's room was small but comfortable. A fire had been lit and chased away the dampness of the rain which had begun to fall during the afternoon. In contrast to the comfort of the room was the woman who had been assigned to her as her maid. She was dour, grim and spoke gruffly. A large woman, her hair was untidy and she had a faint mustache.

When she helped Sabrina with her toilette, her touch was rough and harsh, a far cry from Cora's capable hands. Her hair was a nightmare and her stays were too tight. Something dug into her spine. Trying to convey her discomfort to the woman was impossible. Either the woman was an imbecile or she chose not to understand her. Sabrina finally gave up and resigned herself to enduring the torment for the evening.

After dismissing the woman, she returned to the main floor to find Dunfield. No one had given her any indication of the schedule of the villa, when the evening meal might be served, or where. The few servants about seemed to avoid her or refrain from eye contact. The atmosphere of the villa was very odd. She finally heard the murmur of voices coming from behind a partially closed door.

"I shipped half of the collection last night," she heard Dunfield say, "but the piece we are searching for still hasn't been found."

"You questioned all of your servants?" another man asked, also English from his accent.

"Of course," Dunfield responded.

"Perhaps not diligently enough," a third man commented. "There are certain methods that will force the truth from the most reluctant servant, *oui?*" He was French.

"I cannot afford to do what you suggest," Dunfield said. "I have to live in Venice and the Inquisitors have spies everywhere. I would be no help to you if I were thrown into one of their cells under the Leads."

"*Per favore, Sior* Dunfield, we are not asking you to sacrifice yourself. Not yet," Sabrina heard another man say, Italian this time. "The piece of the Sphere is still in Venice. I can sense it. I think *Donna* Barclay will help us."

Sabrina held her breath.

"She knows nothing," Dunfield scoffed.

"*Peut-être* she knows more than you think," the Frenchman suggested. "You have already told us she has some power."

How did Dunfield know that? Sabrina wondered.

"It's insignificant," he said dismissively. "She's not even aware she has it."

"Perhaps," the Italian murmured. "We shall find out, *si?*"

Apprehension slipped through her, and she stepped back from the door. These men frightened her. Dunfield was involved in something far more dangerous than attempting to smuggle artwork out of Venice. He was obviously one of those whom Auriano said wished to obtain the Sphere of Astarte for his own gain. She had no idea where the piece of the Sphere of Astarte was. And she had no idea how Dunfield knew she had some power.

"I have heard that she is about to become betrothed to Auriano," the Englishman said.

"How did you hear that?" Dunfield demanded. "There has been no announcement."

The Englishman chuckled. "You live in Venice where trading gossip is an art. How could I not hear?"

"It's a powerful alliance." Dunfield's tone was defensive.

"It is a dangerous one," the Frenchman said.

"I am merely keeping an adversary close."

Why would Dunfield consider the prince an adversary? Sabrina thought he welcomed the connection with the House of Auriano.

Dunfield continued, "If he proves to be difficult, he can be dealt with."

"As you dealt with her first husband?" the Italian asked.

"Making Lady Barclay a widow twice may arouse suspicions," the Englishman said.

Sabrina felt the blood drain from her face. Richard had been murdered! By Dunfield, his own uncle! Reaching out, she leaned on the wall for support.

"It was fortunate that her father contacted the wasting disease when he did," Dunfield added coolly, "or I would have had to dispose of him as well."

Sabrina's knees buckled, and she sank to a small bench against the wall. Terror swept through her. She wanted to run, hide, but she was in an unfamiliar place and far from Venice. She did not even have Cora to help her.

"Her father sympathized with our cause," the Englishman said. "Doing away with him would have displeased certain people."

"He was becoming *troppo inquisitivo*," the cavaliere declared. Too inquisitive.

"As a scholar, he might have been an asset if he had become one of us," the Englishman added mildly.

One of them? Sabrina wondered. One of what? Who were these men?

The door swung open and Dunfield emerged. "Sabrina, my dear," he greeted her warmly. "We've been waiting for you."

Careful to hide her fear, she said coolly," I am here now, Uncle, as you can see. Dealing with an unfamiliar maid takes some time."

Her barb about Cora's absence made him scowl. "Be gracious, Sabrina," he hissed. "These men are important business associates."

She allowed him to take her by the elbow and lead her into the room, but his touch revolted her. He was a murderer. His "business associates" seemed to condone what he had done, so they were just as bad as he was. She resolved to discover what type of "business" they were conducting. If they were searching for the Sphere of Astarte, then she might be able to learn what they knew and pass it along to the prince.

She no longer felt any obligation to Dunfield after what she'd just learned. Auriano should have the piece of the Sphere. Despite his secrets, she felt the need to protect him from these dangerous men. Somehow, she would help him find the artifact that belonged to his family, keep him safe, and prevent that betrothal contract from being signed. If he wed her, she would be signing his death warrant, not a marriage license. The idea of a world without Auriano seemed very bleak and pained her heart. Even if she couldn't have him, she wanted to think of Venice with a soft golden glow because he was there.

Two men stood when she entered. Sabrina glanced around. She was sure she had heard another man's voice, that there should have been three other men besides Dunfield. Not wanting to give away the fact that she had been listening in on their conversation, she merely waited while Dunfield introduced them. The Frenchman was the Marquis de Vernoux, a tall, thin man several years younger than her uncle, with piercing black eyes. He was elegant, handsome, but with a cruel mouth. The other man, the Cavaliere Tenaglia, the Italian and owner of the villa, was older, plumper, with heavy jowls, fleshy lips, and drowsy eyes that undressed her.

Sabrina felt her power stir in response to the vague threat of their presence. Remembering her lesson from the night before, she attempted to close it off. She avoided physical contact with both men, curtsying when she was introduced rather than extending her hand.

After refusing wine, she turned to the Italian. "Your house is quite lovely, Cavaliere," she said, hoping for an opening to discover more about why these men had gathered.

"Ah, *grazie*, my dear. It has been in my family for many generations." He edged closer to her. "Perhaps you would care to see the rest? I understand you are quite interested in artwork."

Sabrina wished she could take back her words. The last thing she wanted to do was tour the house with this man.

Before she could decline, Dunfield spoke up. "By all means, Sabrina. There is a fascinating collection in one of the rooms below."

Why would one keep valuable artwork in a cellar where it might be damaged by mold or dampness?

The Italian noticed her confusion and smiled. "It is a room off the wine cellar, *Donna* Barclay, and quite a safe place for such things. Very dry, and moderate temperatures."

Besides not wanting to be alone with the man, Sabrina was not anxious to follow him into the wine cellar, a place too similar to a dungeon. "I would not want to delay the evening meal," she demurred.

"We have plenty of time. Besides, these gentlemen would not mind waiting on such a lovely creature as yourself." The cavaliere smiled persuasively.

The marquis bowed. "We are at your service, *Madame* Barclay. Please, enjoy yourself."

At her hesitation, Dunfield said, "I have some matters to discuss with Vernoux, Sabrina, so we will be quite occupied until you return."

She had no other choice but to accept the Italian's invitation. With a nod and a tiny smile, she placed her hand on his arm and allowed him to lead her out of the room. She was careful to make sure there were several layers of clothing under her hand, and to remove it as soon as it was polite to do so.

He led her through hallways and doors, and finally down a flight of steps into the cellars. They were a marvel of architecture, with massive stone pillars and high vaulted ceilings. No one could guess from the villa above that such a place existed below it. There was a main room with various side chambers and dark passageways leading deep into the earth. With only a single lantern to light their way, shadows jumped from behind the pillars, stacks of crates, and piles of indistinguishable things. Finally opening a wooden door, the cavaliere revealed the wine cellar, stretching away into blackness, with rack upon rack of bottles, and casks piled floor to ceiling.

Despite Sabrina's deepening apprehension, she could not help but be impressed. "This is incredible," she said.

Tenaglia smiled. "The room I wish to show you is farther in. Come, this way."

She followed as he led her down a passage between the wine racks. Only a few cobwebs draped across their path. People had passed this way quite recently. He finally turned between a break in the racks, and she saw another wooden door with a lock and a large key. As he pulled it open, the hinges were eerily silent.

Sabrina caught glimpses of shelves on two sides of the room with jars holding odd and grotesque things, grinning skulls, crucifixes, small ancient statues, and various other peculiar artifacts. The other two walls contained art masterpieces. Similar to Dunfield's room, they also were stacked several deep against the walls. In the middle of the room stood a small table with a single chair before it. On the table lay an unusual item, a dagger made of crystal, appearing to glow from within. Sabrina was drawn to it as if it called to her. As she drifted toward the table, the cavaliere hung back.

"It is quite beautiful, *si?*" he said.

"Yes." She stared at the dagger, but she sensed another presence in the room. Glancing to her right, she caught the faint outline of a man's shoulder and arm as the light from the lamp reflected off him. His face was obscured by shadow. As soon as she had seen him, he stepped back farther into the dark. So there *had* been another man with Dunfield. How did he get here without her seeing him? Why was he here, hiding in this room, in the shadows?

"Does the dagger not appear to glow all on its own?" the Italian asked, drawing her attention back to the table.

"Yes, it does." The dagger seemed to cast a spell as it emitted a soft glow, first pale yellow, then blue, then red. She reached out to touch it. Something made her hesitate.

"Go ahead," the cavaliere urged. "Pick it up."

Sabrina's hand hovered over the dagger, but she paused. She felt something strange, similar to the awakening of her power, but somehow backward. This was not flowing out of her, but into her. Not right. It was uncomfortable, invasive. That thing that dug into her spine burned. Balling her hand into a fist, she jerked it away and cradled it against her. An odd combination of relief and regret swept through her.

Forcing herself to turn away from the dagger, she said, "It is a very unusual weapon. What would it be used for?"

His smile was placid. "There are many legends about it. Some say it was created for sacrifices to the god Baal. Some say it was created to kill the evil in the world. It is so ancient that no one is sure where it comes from or why it was made."

Somehow she knew he was spinning a tale, that he was aware of the exact purpose of the dagger. Still sensing the strange aura of the weapon, she stepped away. As soon as she did, she felt a blank open in her memory as if she had just entered the room. Aware that something was missing, some span of time, she could not recall what she had just done. Frustrated, she searched her memory, but those moments were gone.

The dagger pulled at her. She was drawn to it, and she reached out. It pulsed more brightly. She stopped. Her hand hovered above its hilt. She wanted to touch it. To pick it up. To feel its power in her hand.

No. Something was awry. The dagger's pull felt wrong, twisted.

She forced herself to step away. Once again, a blank appeared in her memory.

The dagger dragged at her. The colors pulsed. Instinctively, she knew she should not touch it, despite the fact she could not remember what she had just done in the last few moments. With every ounce of will power, she turned away, and nausea washed through her. Blindly, she groped for something to support her, and the cavaliere reached out, taking her hand. His skin was hot and sweaty, his fingers pudgy and soft. His touch revolted her. Fighting her illness and her disgust, she jerked back her hand.

"Please," she choked out, "I am not well. I would like to return upstairs, please."

"Of course, *Donna* Barclay," he said smoothly. "We can explore the wonders of the room tomorrow, perhaps when you are more rested. And certainly you will keep silent about what you have seen." His eyes were like two hard stones, cold with no feeling.

Sabrina shivered. Although his words were mild, that gaze told her she would be in mortal danger if she did not do as he said. She nodded and followed him out.

As she fought her sickness and her fear, she turned once more to look at the dagger. It enticed, beckoned. She forced herself to look away. Why did it call to her? What had happened in those few moments she could not remember? Why had she forgotten them?

As the cavaliere closed the wooden door behind them and the power of the dagger diminished, she vowed she would get some answers.

They were halfway through the evening meal when a servant entered and whispered in the cavaliere's ear. "It seems we have a visitor," he announced with amusement.

Only a moment later, the servant came to the doorway and announced, "The Prince of Auriano."

Sabrina's fork stalled halfway to her mouth. Auriano here? How had he found her? And then he appeared, handsome, suave, smiling, and quite damp from the rain. He had slicked back his hair into a queue, which emphasized the beautiful bones of his face. The shoulders of his pale gray superfine coat were darkly wet. The shine of his boots was dulled by mud.

Sabrina was never so glad to see anyone, and never so frightened. Auriano should not be here, not after what she had learned Dunfield had done, and what these men might do to him.

"*Buona sera, signori*," he greeted everyone with a bow. He spied Sabrina's uncle. "*Sior* Dunfield, this is a surprise." His glance fell on Sabrina. "And *Donna* Barclay!" Striding around the table, he took her hand and raised it to his lips.

Those lips were warm against her cold hand. She wanted to jump up and hug him in her relief at his appearance, and at the same time she wanted to scream at him in warning to run away, go back to Venice. All she did was nod politely and paste a smile on her face.

"Welcome, Excellency," the cavaliere said. "This is an honor."

The prince sat in the chair next to Sabrina. "I apologize for arriving unannounced. I am on my way to Auriano, and my coach lost its wheel. I'm afraid in the rain and the dark, my coachman won't be able to repair it until tomorrow. Thank you for your hospitality, cavaliere."

As Tenaglia bowed graciously, he observed, "This is a rather roundabout route to take to Auriano."

"*Si*," the prince agreed. "I have business in Milano, which I must see to first."

"Lady Barclay said nothing about your plans to travel outside of Venice, Excellency," Dunfield said.

Auriano cast a glance at Sabrina. "Perhaps it slipped her mind in the excitement of the evening. She also did not mention your plans to travel."

Sabrina released a breath. The last thing she needed was to have Dunfield think she had snuck a message to the prince about this trip.

"This is, as you say, a coincidence that we should meet here in this villa so far from Venice," her uncle observed.

"*Si.*" The prince smiled. "A wonderful coincidence." He turned to Sabrina and raised her hand to his lips again. "Now I will have more time to spend with the fascinating *Donna* Barclay."

Frightened at the danger to him, Sabrina did not smile back.

As a place was set before him and food offered, Alessandro took in Sabrina's frightened eyes and her slightly disheveled appearance. She looked tired and drained. Haunted. Something was not right here. He was relieved he had made the extraordinary effort to find her.

A flash of gold at her waist caught his attention. His betrothal gift, the chain. He quashed a leap of exhilaration. She was not accepting his seduction. She was wearing the chain as protection, a symbol she belonged to him, for she was the lone woman in a group of unscrupulous men. She certainly would have no protection from Dunfield.

When Alessandro had inquired after her at Dunfield's *casa* and learned they had left on a trip, he sensed some sinister reason for the Englishman spiriting her out of the city so abruptly. The man was anxious for the match between Sabrina and himself, so there was no obvious reason why Dunfield would want to separate them. His suspicion that the journey had something to do with the Sphere of Astarte compelled him to follow. That, along with his fear for Sabrina's safety. He could tell himself otherwise as much as he wanted, but the reason he had turned the Ca'D'Este into an uproar in order to leave as soon as possible was because of his concern for her.

Since learning Dunfield was a member of the Legion of Baal, he had been uneasy with Sabrina's living in the same house. After seeing her power the night before and discovering her gone that morning, his concern had congealed into a claw of anxiety that clamped around his heart. If any harm came to her, he realized his soul might never recover. Seeing her eased that anxiety, but he would still need to be diligent to keep her safe.

As he made light conversation, he studied the other men at the table. He decided he did not like either of the strangers. The Frenchman, the Marquis de Vernoux, had a cruel look to him. His eyes were as cold as a snake's. Alessandro did not doubt that he could turn violent very quickly.

The cavaliere was more subtle, though no less dangerous, perhaps even more so than Vernoux. Alessandro had heard of him, although had never met him before now. He was a man who controlled and manipulated through suggestion, innuendo, persuasion, both benign and malicious. Violence was not his first course of action, but he did not shy away from it if necessary. Rumors abounded about men disappearing with whom he disagreed.

He forced himself to hide the rage that boiled in him at Dunfield's high-handed use of Sabrina. The man had placed her in the middle of a pack of jackals. He was startled when she rose from the table.

"If you gentlemen will excuse me," she said quietly, "I think I will retire for the evening." She swayed on her feet.

Alessandro quickly reached out to steady her. "I will escort *Donna* Barclay to her room," he announced with a bow to the table. As he offered his arm, Sabrina sent him a glance he could not decipher. Her fingers dug into his muscle.

She was silent as they exited the room and climbed the stairs. When they were in the upstairs corridor and alone, she stopped before a closed door. "Thank you for your kindness, Excellency," she said politely, then whispered, "What are you doing here?"

He smiled and murmured, "Staying out of the rain while my coach gets repaired."

Laughing coyly as if he had made some outrageous comment, she whispered again, "You can't be here."

His smile turned to a grin, and aloud he said, "I look forward to that stroll through the vineyards tomorrow, *Donna* Barclay."

He watched annoyance, relief, and fear battle in her eyes. Without another word, she turned and entered her room. Thoughtfully, he stared at the closed door a moment as he wondered what had caused such fear in her. Whatever it was, he was determined to protect her and get her to safety as soon as possible. Turning, he descended the stairs to play his part as the stranded traveler and the charming, harmless Prince of Auriano.

Chapter 19

The next afternoon, Sabrina strolled side by side through the vineyard with Auriano. The sun was warm. The birds twittered. The breeze was soft. The fresh scent of growing vines filled the air. It was an idyllic setting, and far from the threat of the evil sorceress. Yet, another danger lay in the villa on the small rise at the edge of the vineyard. No matter which way she turned, menace loomed. Even Auriano threatened her sanity and possibly her safety. Her relief at his familiar presence was tempered by her mistrust of him. And fear *for* him. Somehow, she had to get him to leave.

She was not about to allow him to place himself in jeopardy for her, not after hearing the casual way Dunfield spoke of doing away with her father and Richard's murder. Auriano had already saved her several times, and she was grateful for his security. Yet, his motives were what concerned her, for she had no doubt he courted and protected her for his own reasons. He wanted the Sphere, and he felt she could help him find it. But she was tied to Dunfield and his demands.

As they walked, she had not taken Auriano's proffered arm, and she left space between them. The overwhelming attraction she felt toward him alarmed her. Touching him might destroy her restraint.

After walking for several minutes in silence, she felt they were far enough away from the villa that they could converse safely. "I wanted to thank you for helping me the other night with my power," she said.

"It was my pleasure, *Donna* Barclay," he said with a smile.

Impishly, she grinned up at him. "No, it was my pleasure." She blushed furiously at her impudence. The memory of the exquisite sensations he had given her still made her shiver.

His glance was warm. "Ah, *cara mia,* that was only the beginning of what we can have together, if only you'd let me show you."

The temptation to accept that invitation was very strong. She continued to stroll and shook her head. "No."

"Last evening you wore my gift, a sure sign of your affection." His words probed for an admission.

"Last evening, I was in the midst of men I didn't know. I wore it as protection." She refused to succumb.

"I'm glad it has some purpose," he said drily.

Realizing she had insulted him, she said, "Excellency, the chain is a magnificent gift, and I thank you for it, but I will not become your wife."

"I don't believe Dunfield will give you much choice," he said darkly.

Sabrina glanced away, not willing to acknowledge that truth.

In a tone half-serious, half-teasing, he said, "You do know that once we are wed, I can have my way with you."

She knew he could seduce her with very little difficulty. Her resistance to him was as thin as smoke. Firmly, she said, "I am not marrying you, Excellency."

He sighed. "I am wounded, *Donna* Barclay. I would wish my betrothed to be a little more enthusiastic about our coming union."

"I am not your betrothed," she said flatly.

"Not formally, but I feel that *Sior* Dunfield will soon rectify that small detail, *si?*"

The careless words she had heard from her uncle the day before made her shiver. If the prince meddled, then he would be murdered. She could not let this man step into such a trap. Yet, she knew she had little say in the betrothal negotiations, despite the fact that she was a widow and no longer an innocent girl. She had put herself under Dunfield's protection, so she had lost what little freedom she might have had. She had fully expected to be on her own before any mention of betrothal contracts. Silly of her. The prince seemed determined to want her as his bride, and Dunfield was thrilled with the prospect of the financial and influential gain he would receive from such a union. She suspected that Dunfield also had a more sinister reason for wanting this marriage to take place, especially after the chilling conversation she had overheard. Somehow, she had to convince the prince that he was making a mistake in marrying her.

"Mr. Dunfield is merely using you for his own purposes, Excellency," she said.

"How do you know that I am not using him for mine?" he countered.

Sabrina sent him a sharp look. "What are you planning?"

"Ah, *Donna* Barclay, if I tell you that, you will be compelled to tell him, and that would ruin the amusement of the negotiations."

"God forbid that anyone should tell me anything," she said drily. "It's only my life that is being negotiated."

He chuckled grimly. "I came to find you, *cara mia*. That should tell you something."

She sighed in resignation. He would tell her no more. But the fact that he did come after her created a warm feeling inside her, despite his reasons. "How *did* you find me?" she asked.

He looked out over the vines as if contemplating the vista. "It's amazing what the flash of coin will accomplish."

So he had bribed the servants to find her. "You shouldn't have come."

"I couldn't bear to have my soon-to-be betrothed out of my sight." His tone was light and teasing.

Angry at his casual attitude, she stopped, grabbed his arm, and forced him to look at her. "This is not a game, Excellency. These men, Dunfield included, are up to something."

"Then I will stay until we discover what it is," he said.

His casual words sent apprehension thrumming through her. "I thought you were only staying until your coach was repaired."

"Alas," he said dramatically, "Piero informed me this morning that the repairs will take longer than he anticipated."

Her brows rose in surprise. "Piero? Piero, your gondolier? He is also your coachman?"

"*Si.*"

She sent him a suspicious glance.

"Piero and his brother Gasparo are men with many talents," he answered with a wink.

"You have to leave here," she told him. "It's not safe."

His eyes were grave. "I won't leave without you."

"You have to. These men—" She stopped, refusing to reveal her reaction to that strange dagger. The cavaliere had warned her—threatened her.

"What about these men? Have they hurt you?" His gaze sharpened.

She shook her head. "No." They had not hurt her physically, but the dagger had left gaps in her memory.

The prince stopped her with gentle pressure on her arm. "Something happened," he said. "Tell me."

His concerned gaze touched her. She wanted to keep him safe. As safe as he was keeping her. She couldn't tell him about the dagger, but she could warn him. She smiled up at him. "Please look as if you are enjoying yourself, Excellency," she said. "What I have to say next is rather alarming, and I don't wish to let the men in the villa know that we spoke of anything except pleasantries."

He dropped his hand, and a smile curved his lips. "You are in danger," he surmised, the words sounding more ominous because of his pleasant expression.

"*You* are in danger, Excellency." She tipped her head coyly, playing her part. "I overheard Mr. Dunfield say that he was behind the death of my late husband, *his own nephew,* and had considered a plan to do away with my father. But then before Dunfield could act, my father died through natural causes."

Sympathy flashed through Auriano's eyes even as he gave a false chuckle. "Somehow, I'm not surprised."

She placed her hand on his arm and stepped closer as if she were teasing him. "I also heard him say that he would do away with you if you proved to be a problem."

At that, Auriano threw his head back and laughed. Sabrina drank in the sound. She wished that she had truly made him laugh with some witty remark. Instead, they playacted like two schoolchildren.

The prince patted her hand lying on his arm. "We will see who does away with whom, *si?*"

She realized that he truly was amused at Dunfield's desire to murder him. That was the height of idiocy. Snatching back her hand, she said, "I told you so that you would be warned, not so that you could laugh in the devil's face."

Auriano's foolishness angered her. She turned from him and continued the stroll between the vines. Forcing herself to appear at ease, she brushed her hand along the leaves. But her teeth clenched and her uncomfortable stays irritated. Once again, something dug into her spine. She rolled her shoulders and winced.

Auriano caught up with her. "What is it, *cara mia*? What's wrong?" Anxiety furrowed his brows.

"It's nothing." She waved away his concern. "I couldn't bring Cora, and the maid they assigned to me knows nothing about comfort."

He grinned. "Then perhaps you need your *cicisbeo, si?*" Glancing around, he said, "Come, there's a shed."

Alessandro ignored her protests and took her arm. He directed her through the rows of vines to a small outbuilding. Inside were piles of baskets used to collect the grapes and small farm tools. Slices of sunlight came through the gaps in the wooden panels of the walls. Dust motes danced and shimmered in the air. It was a rustic, private place.

Turning her back to him, Alessandro placed her long, silky rope of hair over her shoulder. He itched to comb his fingers through it, but now was not the time. Deftly, he loosened the ribbons of her stays. Her sigh of relief was audible. As he was about to tie them up again, he felt a lump against the middle of her spine. He quickly pulled the ribbons apart, exposing her chemise beneath. A small, hard object, about the size of a marble, fell into his hand.

"*Merda*," he muttered.

"What is it?" She spun to see.

He showed her a tiny stone carving of a frog. "The sign of the Legion of Baal," he said.

The blood drained from her cheeks. "Like that messenger I met." She shivered.

"*Si.*"

"What does it mean?" Her words were breathy with fright.

"I'm not sure, except that I believe all the men present in the villa are members of the Legion." He was furious at the men who were trying to manipulate her. Fear for her ran like a cold thread through his blood. Closing his fist around the stone, he walked to the door and threw it into the vineyard. When he turned back, her eyes were wide and dark, stark in her pale face.

Her lashes swept down, hiding her terror. "Please, lace me up again," she asked, her tone neutral.

She was hiding something more than her fear. Whatever it was, Alessandro resolved she would leave with him. And that would have to be before the full moon, before the curse took hold. In two days.

He reached to tighten her laces, but the tender curve of her neck, her bare shoulder, her vulnerability enticed him. Her bravery captivated and awed him. He slipped his hands around her ribs and cupped her breasts. They were sweet, heavy, rounded perfection. He expected her to push him away. Instead, she stood absolutely still. He dropped a kiss at the curve of her neck.

"*Cara mia,*" he murmured.

Stroking the tight buds of her nipples with his thumbs, he was rewarded with her shuddering sigh. He wanted this woman more than any other he had ever met. His restraint was torture. In two days, he would be Shadow, and after would come the Hunger. He was not sure he could live through it.

Her head dropped back against his shoulder. The surrender inherent in that small gesture made him hate himself for what he was. Although he had not lied to her, he had not told her the complete truth. He would soon be betrothed to her. And marriage? He had thought he might be able to gain the piece of the Sphere of Astarte, somehow make her safe, and then sever their connection before they ever said their vows. Now, he was not sure he could accomplish any of that. He was not sure he wanted to sever any connection with her. The gaping pit of Hell yawned wider before him. How could he reveal his wretched curse to this woman?

Sabrina felt his hands stop at the same time her head fell against his shoulder. What was she doing? She stiffened and stepped away from him. His touch was like some potent enchantment that enticed her to surrender to him. What power did he have that could turn her so quickly into a mindless idiot?

Angry at him, but more angry with herself, she said quietly, "Please lace my stays, Excellency."

Keeping her back turned, she avoided looking at him. She felt vulnerable and exposed and thought she might break apart if he attempted to beguile her any further. She couldn't deal with both Dunfield's treachery and the prince's seduction. After a moment, his fingers slipped away from her breasts. He deftly tightened her stays and tied off the ribbons. The loss of his touch ached.

"Thank you," she said, forcing her voice to stay steady. "I would like to return to the house alone."

She kept her eyes lowered and moved past him into the bright sunshine. She prayed he would not stop her, nor follow. All her will power had been used up. If he made one move, one advance, she would crumble. Submit to him. Reveal everything to him. That was impossible. She had to keep him safe. She had to keep what she had just learned a secret.

As soon as she had seen that tiny stone frog, her world shifted. Because now the words of Dunfield and the mysterious other Englishman made sense. Because now she knew who she truly was. A descendent of Halima, a potent sorceress, and the niece of the evil Nulkana. And the daughter of a man who was associated with the Legion of Baal. For she remembered very clearly the stone frog she had played with as a child, the one that had sat in a prominent position on her father's desk. The stone frog that was a larger replica of the one Auriano had just removed from her stays.

Had her father been a member of the Legion of Baal? Was that why he kept that stone frog on his desk? Did that mean she was also a member of the Legion? If her father had been a member, did that mean he was her mother's enemy? Did he attempt to force her to touch that strange dagger as Cavaliere Tenaglia had done to her? No, her father had loved her mother. After her death, he had retreated further and further into his books and manuscripts. And he had owned the piece of the Sphere of Astarte. If he had truly been a member of the Legion, wouldn't he have turned it over to them?

The questions rolled around in her head, but she had no answers. The only sure thing she knew was that Auriano should have possession of the piece of the Sphere. And that the Legion of Baal were his enemies. How could she keep him safe if she were one of them? How could she keep herself safe, and how could she protect Evan? She should run as far and as fast as she could.

But she was caught. Evan was in Venice. Here, she was watched. She couldn't even rely on Auriano for protection because he was in as much danger as she was. All she could do for now was discourage his pursuit of her. An almost impossible task.

As she moved between the vines, she could feel his eyes on her back. A caress. Possession. A thin line he would unwind only to reel back in when he wished.

Dunfield met Sabrina as she stepped into the house. Glancing beyond her, out to the vineyard, he commented, "A lover's tiff?"

"No, Uncle," she told him, hiding her fear with annoyance at his snide question. "The prince wished to explore the vines while I wished to return indoors out of the sun. Is there something you wanted?"

"Yes. I want you to come with me to the vault room below. I need your opinion on a few pieces I wish to purchase from the cavaliere."

Sabrina had no desire to revisit that room beyond the wine cellars. Something had happened down there with that strange dagger, something that she could not quite remember but had made her feel ill. Besides, she had no wish to be alone with Dunfield after hearing what he had done to Richard.

"I really don't wish to go, Uncle," she said. "There are things down there that make my skin crawl." She shivered.

"Don't be so squeamish," he snapped, then he smiled persuasively. "Come, Sabrina, nothing will jump out at you. I'll be with you, and I promise to vanquish any ghosts we might see."

Ghosts were not what frightened her. She shook her head. "I would rather not go."

"Really, Sabrina, you can be so tiresome." Taking her by the arm, he pulled her in the direction of the cellars. "Come along. This will only take a few moments."

She dug in her heels and refused to move. "No, Uncle, I'm not going to that room again."

He stopped to look at her. "Remember that ship to England, Sabrina. Remember there is nothing for you and Evan at the end of the trip."

Hating him, fearing him, knowing he would do exactly as he said, she bowed her head in submission.

"There, you see?" he said, satisfaction in his voice. "That was not so difficult, was it? Come along now."

He pulled her through the villa, and down the steps into the cellars. Ignorance at what he intended sent a chill through her, but at least she knew what sat in that vault room. She concentrated on the source of her power, stoking it to a white heat. It might be the only thing she could use for protection. The dagger with its pulsing light was menacing, and the memory loss she had experienced the last time was frightening.

They finally stood before the room's stout wooden door. Even through its thick planks, she could feel the pull of the dagger. It had somehow become more powerful since the day before.

Dunfield turned the key, swung the door open, and urged her forward with a hand at her back. Before her on the table, the dagger throbbed with light—yellow, blue, red. It dragged at her, drawing her closer. Without thinking, she moved toward it.

"Isn't it beautiful?" Dunfield asked as he moved around the table to face her.

Sabrina could not take her eyes from the dagger. She reached out. Tremendous energy tingled and danced along her hand. She paused, her hand hovering just above the weapon. This was not right. A vague memory from the day before itched at the edges of her brain.

"Go ahead, Sabrina," Dunfield urged. "Pick it up."

His demand angered her. No, she would not, not until she was ready. He could not tell her what to do. Not here, not with this magnificent piece before her. He controlled too much of her life. He threatened to evict her and Evan. He had murdered Richard.

Her anger grew. She felt her power shift as if restless to be let loose. The dagger seemed to call to it. Something was wrong.

Wrong.

Her moonstone pendant grew warm against her skin. She pulled it from beneath her bodice and clutched it. Calm surged up her arm and spread through her. The flame of her power dwindled to a spark, and the pull of the dagger weakened. Remembering Auriano's lesson, she banked that spark until it was only an ember.

"Pick up the dagger, Sabrina," Dunfield commanded.

She blinked and clutched the moonstone tighter. Serenity washed over her. Understanding flooded her brain, as well as the memory of what had happened the day before when she had stood before the piece. Dunfield wanted her to pick up the dagger because it was somehow connected to her power. He and the others wanted to see what would happen when she touched it. Or perhaps they already knew. But she would not do what they wished. She would not show them what she could do.

The conflict between the pull of the dagger and the control of her power made her dizzy and nauseous. Gasping, she dashed to a corner of the room and retched into a convenient bucket.

When she was spent, Dunfield said, "Really, Sabrina, that was quite disgusting. Please control yourself. Now, let us try once more."

"I'm not going near that thing again." Standing on shaky knees, she glared at Dunfield.

"Of course you are." He waved at the piece throbbing with light. "It's calling to you."

Instinctively, her gaze followed his hand. She was caught in the dagger's magnetism. As she took a step toward the weapon, her moonstone pulsed hotly against her skin and broke her connection with the malignant piece. But she was not about to reveal that to Dunfield. Holding onto her moonstone tightly with one hand, she reached out with the other and held it over the dagger. It dragged at her. Her power responded.

The struggle between her moonstone and the dagger became a swirl of blinding light in her brain. She felt as if her head were being split in two. The pain built until she thought she might die.

And then nothingness swept everything away.

Chapter 20

Later that night, Alessandro awoke suddenly. Remaining still, keeping his eyes closed, he listened. The faint rustle of clothing betrayed the presence of someone else in his room. Carefully, he inched his hand toward the stiletto lying beneath the pillow next to him. The edge of a blade pressed against his throat.

"Please don't move or cry out, Excellency," an unfamiliar English-accented voice said. "I really don't want to have to slit your throat."

Alessandro opened his eyes and peered into the dark shadows. He could see nothing but the outline of a man, blacker than the black of the room. "You'll find coin in my trunk," he said.

The man chuckled. "Thank you, but that's not why I'm here."

"Then why? You have the advantage of me." As the moon came from behind a cloud, it cast its pale light through the window. Alessandro tried to see the man's face, but the rogue remained deep in the shadows.

"I'll explain all in good time," the intruder said, "but first, I'd like you to rise and face the windows."

Puzzled, Alessandro hesitated.

"Please, Excellency, don't make this difficult." The stranger pressed the blade harder against his throat.

With a short nod, Alessandro conceded. Carefully throwing back the covers, he slipped from the bed.

The Englishman stepped back. "I appreciate a man who sleeps naked," he said chuckling, "even when sleeping alone."

Annoyed, Alessandro snapped, "Just get on with it." He caught the flash of a sword as well as the dagger in the intruder's hands as he turned toward the windows. Whoever this was, he was dangerous.

"Of course, Excellency." Amusement still rippled through the stranger's voice. "Please walk to the wall and place your palms flat against it."

"I am not in the mood for games."

"Neither am I." The Englishman's tone went grim. The point of the sword against Alessandro's back emphasized his request.

Alessandro did as he was told. He was curious about the intruder's identity. Was he in Cavaliere Tenaglia's employ? Or someone from outside the household? Either way, he would wait for the chance to overcome the man.

When he felt the cool wall beneath his palms, he said, "I could alert the whole house with a word."

"But you won't do that because you're wondering why I'm here. And I think you understand that I would have few compunctions about killing you to save myself."

Alessandro felt the sword point prick his back again. The arrogance of the man irritated. "So why the games, and why *are* you here?"

"The 'games,' as you call it, are for my protection. I know who you are, Excellency, and I have great respect for your ability with the stiletto and rapier. I do not wish to lose my life. I am here to pass along some information and to warn you."

"Wouldn't it have been easier to write me a letter?"

The Englishman chuckled at his sarcasm, but the answer he gave was deadly serious. "No." He paused a moment, then said, "Have you ever heard of the Crystal Dagger?"

"If I had, do you think I would tell you?"

"Then in case you are unaware of its existence, perhaps I should enlighten you. It was created centuries ago by a group of men who call themselves the Legion of Baal. I assume you have heard of them?"

Alessandro remained stubbornly silent.

"Your silence speaks for you, Excellency. The Crystal Dagger was endowed with magic in the hope that it could be used to kill the sorceress, Nulkana. But the Legion discovered the magic of the Dagger isn't strong enough to destroy her. They discovered that it needs to be energized by draining the power of a descendant of Halima, Nulkana's sister."

Alessandro hid his frown. Sabrina was a descendent of Halima. Feigning boredom, he drawled, "An interesting story, but hardly a reason to hold me at sword point."

"Patience, Excellency. I'm just getting to the pertinent parts." The Englishman cleared his throat as if he were about to continue a scholarly lecture. "The men in this house are all members of the Legion of Baal, but I think you know that. They are trying to see if the Lady Barclay might be a descendant of Halima, to see if the Dagger will drain her power."

Anxiety clutched at him. At dinner that evening, Sabrina looked ill, and she had that haunted, fearful look in her eyes again. He guessed the men had already tried to drain her ability.

Pretending ignorance, Alessandro scoffed, "*Donna* Barclay is merely a widow with a young son. She could not possibly be a descendent of this woman, Halima."

"You are not that naive, nor that stupid, Excellency. Your visit here is not a coincidence. The Lady Barclay is in grave danger. If you wish her to live long enough to become your betrothed and say her marriage vows, then you need to get her out of this villa."

Cristo, how did the man know he planned to make Sabrina his betrothed? Damn the gossips of Venice!

Casually, the Englishman added, "Your life is also in danger, Excellency. After you wed the lovely Lady Barclay, I suggest that you watch your back."

"Who are you?" Alessandro growled.

"A friend. Someone who is trying to save your life."

The tip of the blade lifted from Alessandro's back. Before he could react, something hit him hard on the side of the neck. He saw stars explode, and his knees buckled beneath him. As blackness closed down on his brain, he heard the man say, "Good luck, Excellency."

The next morning, as soon as he was dressed, Alessandro knocked at Sabrina's room. His neck and shoulder were stiff from the encounter

with the intruder the night before, and his nerves were on edge. Waking up on the floor, cold and uncomfortable, did not help his mood. Although the stranger had come with a warning, Alessandro was not pleased that the man had been able to get the upper hand. Yet, he believed what the man had told him, and he planned to get Sabrina away from this place as soon as he could.

Her maid cracked the door open enough to peer out with one eye. "*Donna* Barclay won't be disturbed," she grumbled.

Affronted at the woman's gruffness, Alessandro schooled his features into their haughtiest expression. "Tell *Donna* Barclay that Auriano wishes to speak with her."

He heard Sabrina's voice, and the maid turned to answer her. This was the woman who had placed that menacing image of the frog inside Sabrina's clothing. Alessandro suspected she would keep him away from Sabrina at all costs. Taking advantage of her distraction, he pushed open the door. The maid actually growled at him as she was forced back. "Get out," he barked. "I wish to speak to *Donna* Barclay in private."

"I'm not supposed to leave her." The woman sulked.

"Do you think I am incapable of watching out for her welfare?" he asked disdainfully.

"Please, do as the prince asks," Sabrina said from the bed.

Sullenly, the maid gave a perfunctory curtsey, sent him a glance bordering on insolence, then left.

"Unpleasant creature," he observed, as the door closed. He turned toward the bed. Sabrina, still in her dressing gown, was prone with a cloth across her eyes. "*Cara mia,*" he exclaimed. "You are ill."

She pulled the cloth from her eyes, tossed it aside, and sat up. "Yes. No." She gave a vague wave of her hand. "It's nothing. A headache." She dropped her forehead to her knees. "An excuse to stay out of Dunfield's way."

He strode to the bed and sank down onto the edge. "What has he done?"

"Nothing. It's nothing." She raised her head, but would not meet his gaze.

She still looked too pale and drawn. "Let me help you," he entreated as he started to brush back a curl from her temple.

226

She caught his arm and held it away from her. "Don't. Please don't touch me."

He had come to help her, and her rejection grated against his black mood. "If I wish to touch you, I will," he asserted. "You will soon be my betrothed, and then my wife."

"I am not your betrothed, and I will not be your wife." Her eyes darkened in anger and began to glaze over.

He recognized the building of the energy in her. Something must have happened the day before to put her in such turmoil. He did not wish to be on the receiving end of that power.

"Sabrina." He snapped her name, forcing her to focus on him, then turned her name to a caress. "Sabrina."

Her eyes cleared. The corners of her mouth tightened. "I'm sorry, but it changes nothing."

He was in no mood for an argument. "You are right. It does not." Standing, he said brusquely, "Get dressed, please, and get your trunk packed. I am taking you back to Venice."

She stared up at him. "You can't." Then she set her mouth mulishly. "I won't go with you."

He was determined to protect her, whether she allowed it or not. "You will. You know I have no qualms about carrying you from here if you defy me. I will do it with you dressed or not, with your belongings or without, but you and I are leaving here today."

Her cheeks flushed and she looked like she wanted to throw something at him. Then she swallowed and glanced away. Her voice was low when she finally spoke. "I can't go with you. Dunfield—"

"I am going to make arrangements with Dunfield now." He turned and walked to the door. With his hand on the knob, he said, "Please don't be stubborn, *Donna* Barclay. I am doing this for your safety."

As he closed the door quietly behind him, something thunked against it hard enough to make the wood vibrate. At least she had waited until he was gone before her temper exploded. He went in search of Dunfield.

He found the man in conversation with Cavaliere Tenaglia. Although he had wanted to speak to Dunfield alone, the presence of the Italian saved him from a separate conversation of farewell. After greeting them, he came directly to the point.

"My coachman tells me that repairs have been completed on my coach, and so I am taking my leave this morning," he said.

"We are sorry to see you go, Excellency," the cavaliere answered. "You have enlivened our little gathering."

Alessandro bowed at the flattery, knowing that the man was relieved he was going.

"Will you be traveling on to Auriano?" Dunfield asked.

"Alas, no. I'll be going back to Venice." He paused a moment before he stated his true reason for speaking with the Englishman. "It has come to my attention that *Donna* Barclay has been feeling ill. I wish to take her back to Venice with me."

"That's impossible." Dunfield's words were flatly adamant.

"We can certainly care for her here," Tenaglia interjected mildly. "My staff is very competent."

Although Alessandro heartily disagreed, he was not ready to cause trouble. "I'm sure they are, Cavaliere, but I feel *Donna* Barclay would be more comfortable in familiar surroundings."

Dunfield glanced beyond Alessandro's shoulder and smiled. "Ah, Sabrina, my dear, we were just discussing you."

Alessandro turned and saw her standing in the doorway. She had dressed in record time in a pale yellow morning gown. She held a wide-brimmed straw hat in her hand. As she stepped into the room, he noticed her high color, which could be construed as fever. He knew it to be the result of her anger.

"I'm sorry I'm interrupting," she said. "I feel the need for some air. Would one of you kind gentlemen accompany me outside?" Ignoring him, she directed her request at Dunfield and Tenaglia.

Alessandro silently applauded her tactic. He could not spirit her away if she was with one of the other men. But he had his own gambit to play. Walking to her, he took her hand and led her to a chair.

"*Donna* Barclay," he said solicitously, "you shouldn't be exerting yourself if you are ill."

She glared at him. "I'm fine."

228

He turned to the other men. "It must be the fever. The maid just informed me that she was ill and not to be disturbed. She really needs to be back in Venice, with her own maid who knows her."

"She can't go back to Venice," Dunfield stated. "I need her here."

"I don't believe she'll be much help to you if she is ill." Alessandro smiled down at her, raised her hand, and brought it to his lips. When she tried to jerk away, he clamped down on her fingers and held on to them, only releasing them when he was ready. "Since I am leaving for Venice, it is only logical that *Donna* Barclay travel with me."

"I won't allow it," Dunfield said. "It would be scandalous for the two of you to travel together."

Alessandro scowled. "Are you questioning my honor, *Sior* Dunfield?"

"No. No, of course not, Excellency, but despite the fact that my niece is a widow, she has lived a very sheltered life, while you are a man of the world. Lady Barclay would hardly know what to do if—"

Alessandro took a threatening step forward. "What to do if what, *Sior* Dunfield? If I compromised her? If I took liberties with her?"

"Gentlemen, please," Tenaglia interrupted.

Sabrina stood. "I am right here, and you are talking about me as if I were a piece of furniture." Her cheeks flushed even darker.

"Not now, Sabrina," Dunfield snapped.

"*Si*, now," Alessandro said, as he took Sabrina's hand and pulled her next to him. "Instead of waiting for two more days, I will sign the contract of betrothal with you here, now."

"No—" she began.

Dunfield talked right over her. "You cannot be serious. You can't do that. We need to discuss this. We need witnesses, an official to draw up the document."

"My secretary can write up something," Tenaglia offered, as he sent a glance in Dunfield's direction.

Alessandro smiled when he saw the incredulous look the Englishman gave the cavaliere. "There, you see, *Sior* Dunfield? Cavaliere Tenaglia supports my suggestion. If he would be so kind, he can act as a witness."

Sabrina jerked out of his grasp. "I don't want to marry you," she hissed.

"Ah, *cara mia*," Alessandro said with a sigh. "You will change your mind once the fever is gone and you are feeling more yourself." He turned back to the Englishman. "Well, *Sior* Dunfield? Do you agree?"

"What about terms?" the man asked cagily.

Alessandro took her hand and raised it to his lips. "*Donna* Barclay is worth more to me than any terms." Sabrina jerked her hand away. Without losing a beat of the conversation, he went on, "But if what I stated in my letter is agreeable to you, then it will be done."

After some hesitation, Dunfield gave a jerky nod.

"*Bene.*" Alessandro smiled. "Now, if you gentlemen would excuse me a moment, I would like to have a few words with my betrothed." He took Sabrina firmly by the arm and steered her out of the room, not allowing her any choice in the matter.

As soon as they were out of earshot, she exploded. "How dare you! You never asked me what I wanted. You just made up your mind and decided for me."

"Shush, Sabrina," he murmured. "You can scold me all you wish once we are in my coach and on the road to Venice. Please, go gather your things and have your trunk brought down. I wish to be out of here within the hour."

"I can't leave," she said, her voice pitched low. "Dunfield—"

He noticed a servant hovering near them. Before she could finish, he slipped his hand behind her neck, pulled her close, and kissed her, cutting off her words. He meant merely to stop her words and conceal their argument, but he was very aware of her soft lips beneath his. The thought flitted through his brain that he would like to be able to savor those delicious lips any time he desired and have her respond willingly to his caress. She was stiff beneath his hand. Her willing response would be a long time coming. When he released her, he would feel her wrath. The servant moved away, and he slowly, reluctantly let her go. She stepped back, glared at him, and slapped him across the face. Then she turned and stalked toward the staircase.

"Within the hour, Sabrina," he reminded her. Rubbing his cheek, he watched her retreat. He hoped she would realize she was safer with him than with Dunfield and his pack of jackals.

Turning back into the room where the men waited, knowing the slap had been audible to them, he gave a negligent wave of his hand. "I apologize for that, gentlemen. A minor lovers' spat. It seems *Donna* Barclay's fever has made her cross. Now, Cavaliere, if you could summon your secretary, *Sior* Dunfield and I can complete our business."

Harold Dunfield stood at the window and watched the coach bearing the Prince of Auriano and Sabrina roll away down the drive. He could not decide between fury or satisfaction. On the plus side, he had just signed a contract with one of the most powerful men in Venice, which would forever connect them and transfer a fortune to him as soon as Sabrina spoke her marriage vows. Auriano seemed to be so smitten with the wench that he had only requested a few pieces of artwork in exchange.

On the minus side, however, was the fact that Auriano had outwitted him, and Sabrina was escaping his plans for her, the reason why he had brought her to this meeting at the villa in the first place. The Crystal Dagger would be of no use if the Legion of Baal could not infuse it with more power. They needed that weapon to annihilate Nulkana and leave the way clear in their search for the Sphere of Astarte. Then, their only opponent in that race would be Auriano, who would be contractually connected to him. What was that saying about keeping one's friends close, but one's enemies closer?

"I feel you are disturbed by *Donna* Barclay's betrothal, *Sior* Dunfield."

The cavaliere's words drew his attention from the view beyond the window. "You were very quick to aid Auriano's plans," Dunfield said. "I find your actions suspect, Tenaglia."

The cavaliere sighed and poured himself some wine. "Sometimes the quickest way to one's goal is by an indirect route."

"Not when the goal is immediately within reach." Dunfield turned back to gaze out the window.

"*Donna* Barclay was being very resistant to our solicitation of her power, and I fear Auriano was more than a little suspicious." Tenaglia took a sip of his wine. "It was better to play out the line a bit, rather than attempt to reel them in and lose them completely."

Dunfield shook his head. "We had them both here. We could have used Sabrina's power and done away with Auriano. I would have gladly given up his wealth and the influence of his connections to be rid of him as a rival in the race for the Sphere."

With a moue of distaste, the cavaliere placed his glass on the table next to him. "You have no finesse, *Sior* Dunfield. I have the impression that your desire to arrange Auriano's demise has more to do with personal gratification than as the means to achieving our goal."

Dunfield's gaze was cold. "Our goal is always my main concern."

Tenaglia shrugged. "I am merely giving you a warning. The Messenger leaves today to report back to the Lord High. He heard your suggestion to eliminate Auriano. I do not think you would want him to report that your personal goals are interfering with those of the Legion. The Lord High has little use for those who place themselves and their desires first."

Keeping his expression impassive, Dunfield sat in the chair across from the cavaliere. He disliked the Englishman known only as the Messenger, the man who acted as the eyes and ears of the Lord High, who led the Legion of Baal. The Messenger could disguise himself as anyone, and had learned of indiscretions and treachery within the Legion that had led to the painful deaths of those imprudent members. He was ruthless in reporting the truth, and so the Lord High trusted him implicitly.

Dunfield needed to speak with him to discover how he would report what had occurred at the villa. Although the goal of the Legion of Baal was also his goal, Dunfield felt that doing away with a competitor was only good business. Eliminating Auriano at the proper time would only further the Legion's goal of finding the Sphere, except the Lord High had mandated that Auriano was to be left alone. The Lord High wanted Auriano for himself.

"When is the Messenger leaving?" Dunfield finally asked.

"As soon as you have explained your overwhelming desire to murder the Prince of Auriano, Mr. Dunfield," the Messenger said.

With a start, Dunfield turned toward the door. The Englishman stood there, dark, handsome, impeccably attired in black riding clothes, a hat and gloves in one hand, a quirt dangling negligently in the other. Dunfield realized that one of the reasons he disliked the man was because of his ability to move so silently. The man was alarming.

Forcing a smile to his lips, Dunfield quickly organized his arguments and hoped he would be convincing enough for the Lord High to allow him to live.

Chapter 21

They had been riding in his coach for two hours in total silence. Sabrina was furious with him, had been angry with him off and on, in varying degrees, for almost a week. Alessandro supposed that was a benefit. Her anger kept a barrier between them, one that he was not about to breach. If that barrier ever came down, he was afraid he would reveal things about himself that he never wanted her to know. She had the uncanny effect on him of thawing his soul, that icy spot deep within him. It was where he stored all those things he never wanted to acknowledge about himself. It was where he hid his secret, the curse. It was where he hid the vague memories of his hideous behavior during the Hunger.

Although the curse was difficult to endure with its deprivation of the senses of touch, taste, smell, and the power of speech, at least it allowed him the ability to reason. The Hunger, with its swift return of his senses, turned him mindless for most of its duration, and it was during that period of time that he acted more animal than human. Fortunately, it also blurred his memory. But he remembered enough to know that he never wanted to reveal anything about his time in that pit of Hades.

So he was glad for her anger and had, in fact, purposely provoked it. The one drawback was her unwillingness to surrender to him completely. And he wanted her — desperately. Holding back the intensity of his advances, restraining himself had been the longest, hardest lesson in self-control he had ever endured, harder even than those lessons he had been taught in his youth by Gasparo. When she finally gave herself to him, he wanted it to be glorious and free. Until then, he would grit his teeth. Knowing that the curse would claim him in only a couple of days was nearly a relief. He did not want to conjecture what the Hunger, starved by his restraint, might be like on the other side of it.

His only problem was how to protect her while he was merely Shadow. He did not want any man near her, not even Tonio. But he had no choice. Something had frightened her during that stroll through the vineyards. As soon as she had seen that little stone frog, her defenses went up. Did she know more about the Legion of Baal than she let on? Even if she did, he would not let them harm her.

The one thing that gave him comfort was the parchment inside his coat. The betrothal contract. The lovely *Donna* Barclay was legally bound to him, despite her protests. Although he regretted forcing her to his will, her anger had been a delight to watch. When she had presented herself for their journey back to Venice, he had swallowed his laughter. She had donned his gold chain, wound many times around her throat until it resembled a slave collar, a subtle statement of what she thought of his treatment of her.

Stubborn, brave, and fiery, she was the most intriguing woman he had ever met. She was demure at the same time that she was impetuous. He suspected that once she gave herself to him, their lovemaking would be magnificent. And he did not doubt for a moment that she would finally succumb. He could sense her arousal every time he was near her. He just had to figure out how to cool her anger and get back in her good graces.

Propping his legs on the seat opposite, he closed his eyes and pretended to sleep while he contemplated his options.

Sabrina watched him feigning sleep. She knew he was aware of everything going on around him, from her chilly silence, to the gait of the horses pulling the coach, to the vista passing them beyond the coach window. Although he appeared to be relaxed, she could sense his body was too coiled to be really asleep. His hand was too ready for that stiletto he kept up his sleeve.

Once again, he had outmaneuvered her, and, surprisingly, Dunfield. Imposing his will, invoking his powerful influence, he had forced Dunfield to sign the betrothal contract. She was now, officially, the fiancée of the Prince of Auriano. Frustration poured through her. He was, beyond a doubt, the most infuriating, aggravating man she had ever met. He was also the most intriguing, compelling man she had ever met. Every time she saw him, she wanted to throw herself at him and wind herself around him. Madness. Only anger helped to keep her sane.

She was still feeling a bit ill after her encounter with the Crystal Dagger the day before. After a sleepless night, the confrontation with the prince, watching herself being discussed and bargained for, having to rush to pack her belongings, and now the ride in the coach, all made her head spin and made her feel queasy. The only bright spot in this horrendous day was that she would be reunited with Evan. She could not wait to hug him and reassure herself he was safe.

But uneasiness sat in a lump in her middle. Although Auriano had guaranteed that she would not be tossed out of Dunfield's house, the alternative — being wed to Auriano — did not give her any sense of comfort. He had secrets, and he used his charm to hide them. What would he be like when he no longer felt the need to be charming to her? What kind of secrets was he hiding? And what would happen when he discovered her latest secret about her connection to the Legion of Baal? The answer to that last question was easy. He would break off any connection with her... or worse. The Legion was his enemy, and with her connection to it, she was also his enemy. The thought did nothing to settle her stomach. She had decided that upon reaching Venice, she would find some way to take Evan and disappear.

She glanced at him, at his strong profile, his hair glinting dark and gold in a shaft of sunlight. She wanted to run her fingers through that hair, trail her fingers along that jaw. Until they reached the city, she could pretend that he was hers, and she could forget her fear for a few hours.

His pretense of sleep irritated her, and she used her anger to cover her fear. She had just become his betrothed, and he was ignoring her. Despite the fact that she was furious with him for being so overbearing, she felt he should be demonstrating a little more enthusiasm for finally winning her from Dunfield. She decided she was not going to allow him to be complacent. Perhaps if she provoked him enough, he would decide she was too much trouble to wed.

"Why do you wish to marry me, Excellency?" she asked.

He opened one eye to a slit and regarded her a moment before he answered. "Because you are beautiful. Because you are passionate." He paused. "And because you are fertile."

Astounded, she sputtered, "F-Fertile! Because I'm *fertile*?"

"*Si.*" He turned to her with a puzzled expression. "I need an heir, and since you already have a son, I know you'll be able to produce other children."

"I'm not a broodmare," she snapped. She could feel her power gathering. Maybe if she gave him a little zap, he might change his thinking.

Quick as a panther, he grabbed both her hands and forced them into her lap. "Please, *cara mia*, I know you are angry and would like to singe me, but I paid many ducats for this coach, and I would be very unhappy if you incinerated it."

"God forbid I should harm a possession of the Prince of Auriano. I hope when we are wed, and I, too, am your possession, that you take as much care for me as you do your coach."

"*Carissima.* Is that what you believe? That you are my possession? Is that why you wear my chain like this?" He ran his finger over the chain about her neck and shook his head. "No. Never my possession." His eyes darkened. "But perhaps..." Leaning in, slipping his finger beneath a couple of loose loops, he pulled her to within a breath of his lips. "Perhaps you wish to be possessed, *si*?" he murmured. "Perhaps you wish me to teach you things that your late husband never did."

His sudden seduction distracted her from her anger. She had no idea what kind of "things" he was talking about, but she was sure they would involve incredible pleasure. The mere thought of what he might do made her moist. She gritted her teeth in annoyance. Stupid to be so weak. She turned away from those beguiling golden eyes. "I have no idea what you are talking about, Excellency."

He tugged gently on the chain and forced her to look at him. "You do. And someday soon, I will teach you. Slowly. With great pleasure." Smiling, he added, "But not today." He placed a tender kiss at the corner of her mouth and released her. "Today, you are angry with me."

Sabrina was relieved he had brought the conversation back to a subject she could handle. "Why shouldn't I be angry, Excellency? You have bartered for me with Dunfield as if I had no feelings and no will."

"I am only trying to protect you," he said, his expression innocent. "Would you prefer to remain with the man who is using you for his own ends?"

"Aren't you also using me, Excellency?" she tossed back at him. "You just told me that one of the reasons you wish to marry me is because I have the potential for being an excellent baby producer."

His eyes narrowed and a muscle jumped in his jaw. Sabrina knew she had hit a nerve.

"What will become of Evan if I have your heir?" she pressed.

"Your son will be well provided for," he answered coolly. Dismissing her concern, he turned away to stare out the window.

His quick response told her he was telling the truth, but she was desperate to keep the upper hand in the argument. "There is only one way I know of to make a baby, Excellency. If I deny you access to my bed, I think the chances of your having an heir by me will be very slim."

Slowly, he turned to look at her. His gaze was heated, reminding her of that night at the *casino* when he had pulled her beneath the stairs. "Do you truly believe you can deny me?"

"Yes. Oh, yes."

"I think you underestimate my powers of persuasion." Reaching out, he lightly ran his fingers along her jaw, and then not touching, back up across her cheek, leaving a trail of sensation. It was a subtle threat of seduction.

She remained perfectly still, forcing herself not to lean into him, not to respond to that warm tingle beneath his fingers, and met his gaze with determination. "I have my own ways of persuasion." Holding up her hand, palm out with tiny sparks erupting, she showed him her intent. "We won't be in your coach then, Excellency." She closed her hand into a fist and dropped it into her lap.

"You forget that I heal quickly, *cara mia*." The corner of his mouth twitched, but humor did not reach his eyes.

"That is true, but you still feel pain." She cocked her head coyly. "I don't think you'll be quite so anxious to steal something I'm not prepared to give once you have experienced my anger several times."

His gaze turned thoughtful. "Perhaps, we should discuss this."

"I thought we were."

This time, amusement flashed through his eyes. "I thought we were arguing." Taking her fist, he pried open her fingers. "Come, *carissima*, let us stop fighting. I will think on what you have said, and we will talk, but not now. Now, I think we need to talk about something else because I think something else besides me has upset you." He dropped a kiss onto her open palm. "I think this something has put you in danger. What happened at the cavaliere's villa that I do not know?"

Narrowing her eyes at him, she refused to let him distract her or pry her secret from her. "It is much easier to change the subject than to continue the argument, isn't it, Excellency?"

He smiled. "I enjoy arguing with you, *cara mia*. I find our disagreements stimulating. Did I ever tell you how magnificent you are when you are angry?"

Sabrina huffed and turned away. He was the most frustrating, beguiling rogue she had ever met.

"Sabrina," he said, his tone solemn. "We will argue again later. I promise. Now, I need you to tell me what happened at the villa."

She sighed in resignation. At least he had acknowledged that she had a point and was willing to talk about it. She was determined not to let the matter die, and she would bring it up again. The problem was, she really did not want to argue either. She was feeling ill. But she knew in order to keep her sanity and not succumb to his wiles, she had to keep some distance between them. And she was not about to allow him to come to her rescue yet again.

"I don't know what you mean," she said coolly.

"Come, Sabrina, you know I can find out if I wish." Lightly, he ran his fingers over the pulse in her wrist.

She jerked out of his grasp. "I thought you said you couldn't connect with my mind unless I allowed it."

"Are you so sure you won't?"

Swallowing, she looked away. The last time he had touched her mind, he had given her exquisite pleasure. But she knew him now. She knew what he could do, how powerful he was. She was not going to let him convince her to allow him access to her thoughts again, no matter how pleasurable the experience.

"Tell me about the Crystal Dagger," he said.

She turned to stare at him. How did he know? Did he suspect that she was linked to the Legion of Baal? He had not connected with her mind. She would have known if he had.

"No, I didn't read your thoughts," he said, answering her unspoken question. "I've always known about the piece and why it was created. I've only recently learned about its weakness. I know why Dunfield brought you with him to visit the cavaliere."

"He brought me with him to evaluate some pieces of art," she told him.

"That was not the only reason."

Not willing to concede the point, she shrugged and turned away. She could tell him about the Crystal Dagger, how it seemed to drag at her, how it made her ill when she tried to fight it. How she had fainted. But Dunfield had issued that threat. Despite her anger at the prince's overbearing manipulation of her life, she did not want to see him murdered. She would handle the situation on her own, without him, and protect him.

"Dunfield brought you to use you, to use your power." He stated the truth, and she wondered how much he knew.

Not trusting herself to speak a lie, she shook her head, keeping her gaze on the passing vista.

"I have taken care of that," he said casually. "I stole the Dagger."

She swung to face him. "You stole it?!"

"*Sì.*"

Panic and nausea ripped through her. If Dunfield found out that Auriano had taken it, he would have the prince murdered like he had murdered Richard. He would send her and Evan back to England.

"No! You can't!"

"But I already have."

"You have to take it back!"

"No. It is too late for that."

As she was about to try to convince him otherwise, the little communication door between the interior of the coach and the driver opened.

"Soldiers ahead, *Sior* Sandro," Piero said, interrupting. "I think they're French."

"Will they let us pass?" the prince asked.

"They want us to stop."

He swore under his breath as the coach slowed. His hand curled into a fist and his jaw clenched. Surprised at his reaction, Sabrina gazed at him. Nothing ever seemed to ruffle him, but this interruption in their journey appeared to cause him both anger and anxiety. Wondering at the reason, she turned to look out at the men on horseback beginning to surround the coach.

As she was considering how many soldiers she might be able to stun, he reached over and placed his hand on top of hers. "Don't reveal what you can do, no matter what happens," he said, then he opened the door of the coach and stepped out.

Chapter 22

They were brought to a small villa on the outskirts of a village where General Bonaparte had his headquarters. Alessandro and Sabrina were separated, and he was brought alone to the general. He knew that the only reason the general and not some minor officer was questioning them was out of deference to his title, but he was annoyed that he had not foreseen something like this occurring on their trip back to Venice. He had not realized that the French had taken over so much of the western part of the Venetian Republic. Obviously, his attention had been on other matters, namely his beautiful and maddening betrothed.

Brought before the general, he studied the man. He was short, not much taller than Sabrina, but carried himself with authority and exuded a galvanizing energy. He wore his blue uniform jacket as if it were armor. Alessandro was impressed and wary. This was not a man who would take kindly to insult. And he was also the man who had perhaps sent that messenger to meet Sabrina in the shack on the mainland, the messenger who had tried to kill her.

"I apologize for the inconvenience, Excellency," the French general said, "but you must understand that you were traveling through French-controlled territory. We have experienced some resistance from the villagers in the area, and so my men are under orders to be vigilant."

Alessandro allowed his annoyance to creep into his voice. "My arms are clearly marked on my coach, General Bonaparte. I am a citizen of the Venetian Republic and clearly not one of the 'villagers in the area.' The Venetian Republic is neutral in your dispute with Austria. I demand that you allow me to continue on my journey."

The General's eyes flashed. "The Venetian Republic has been stubbornly defiant to my requests. My officers and men have been harassed, ambushed, and killed, and the Venetian Senate has done nothing to contain this violence. I see no neutrality in a government that allows its citizens to riot against a neighboring state." Bonaparte paused and stepped forward to a table that stood between them. "And I find no neutrality in a man who is carrying a weapon such as this." In dramatic fashion, he pulled back a cloth and revealed the Crystal Dagger. It pulsed dully.

Alessandro hid his dismay in outrage. "You dared to search my belongings, General?" he said in a deadly quiet tone.

"I'm at war, Excellency, and I will dare anything to win."

"Did you also search the belongings of my betrothed, or perhaps you had the audacity to go so far as to search her person?" His question, he knew, was an insult to the man's honor.

"Your betrothed is quite unharmed," Bonaparte answered obliquely.

"I do not find that reassuring. I would like to see her."

"In time, Excellency, after you satisfy my curiosity about this weapon." The general indicated the Dagger laying between them.

"It is merely an artifact I picked up in my travels." Alessandro gave a casual shrug.

"What is its purpose?"

"I really have no idea, General. It is quite beautiful, *si*?"

"I have a feeling its purpose is more than mere beauty. Perhaps your betrothed can explain more about it."

Alessandro forced a laugh. "My betrothed knows nothing more about it than I do." He hoped he would not have to prove that, or that Sabrina would not reveal what she knew of the piece.

"Then you won't mind if I have her brought here so I may question her." Bonaparte motioned to an aide who was standing by the door. The man left quickly to do the general's bidding.

"Really, General," Alessandro protested, "my betrothed has been unwell, which is why we were hurrying back to Venice. I wished to return her home where she would be more comfortable."

Bonaparte gave a slight smile. "Then the quicker my curiosity is satisfied, the quicker you and your betrothed will be able to continue on your journey."

Figlio di putana, Alessandro thought. The man was as tenacious as a rat after cheese.

"While we are waiting," Bonaparte said, "perhaps you could tell me what you were doing in the vicinity of Milan."

"Visiting."

Alessandro knew his short response bordered on insulting, but he was not about to relinquish any ground in the word battle he waged with this man. He would keep the secret of the Crystal Dagger and protect Sabrina at all costs.

"Visiting whom?" Bonaparte demanded.

"Acquaintances of the uncle of my betrothed."

The general stared at him suspiciously, and he could see questions being formed and discarded behind the man's eyes. The arrival of Sabrina distracted him.

When Sabrina entered, her gaze went immediately to the Dagger and her eyes glazed over. Recognizing the gathering of her power, Alessandro stepped between her and the table on which the Dagger lay, which blocked her from both the Dagger and Bonaparte. As soon as he did, he felt something zing through him, nearly at the threshold of pain. Ignoring it, he moved forward to take her hand and distract her.

"*Cara mia,*" he said, raising her hand to his lips. "How are you faring? Are you feeling any better?" He tucked her hand into the crook of his arm and pulled her close.

Looking dazed, she met his eyes. "I—"

He cut her off as he turned to Bonaparte. "As you can see, General, *Donna* Barclay is quite unwell and unable to answer your questions." He remained between Sabrina and the Dagger.

The general studied Sabrina for a moment. Then he looked down at the Dagger, which had begun to pulse more brightly. "I believe that *Madame* Barclay knows quite a bit about this interesting artifact," he said.

Sabrina straightened beside Alessandro, and he sensed the effort it took. The Dagger's pulsing sent an irritating throb through him as it reached out to her. He hoped she could hide the effect it had on her and belay the French general's suspicions. That stiletto was still hidden up his sleeve. He would do anything to protect the woman at his side, but fighting his way out of the camp of the French army might prove a bit difficult.

Sabrina was relieved when Auriano placed himself between her and the Dagger. It still dragged at her, but its force was weaker and she could pretend it meant nothing. She wondered what it was doing to Auriano because she could feel the tautness in his body. The tension between the two men in the room was tangible. She needed to be away from the Dagger as soon as possible. The only way to do that was to defuse the general's suspicions. She squeezed Auriano's arm twice in warning and curtsied to the general. "General Bonaparte," she said quietly. "Thank you for your kind hospitality. Your men have been most gracious."

The general gave her a slight bow. "Thank you, *Madame*. Auriano was concerned for your welfare."

"I'm afraid that he has become a bit overprotective of late." She peeked coyly up at Auriano. "You see, our feelings for each other overcame our good sense, and, well, you see…" Her voice dropped to a whisper. "I am carrying his child."

Auriano choked.

Sabrina patted his arm. "My love," she said. "It's all right. I know General Bonaparte is an honorable man and will keep our secret."

The general gave a short bow. "Of course, *Madame*, and please accept my congratulations. Having just recently wed myself, I hope that someday soon my wife can make such an announcement."

"Congratulations, General," Sabrina gushed. "May you have many long years of happiness together."

Bonaparte bowed his thanks. "Because of your delicate condition, I will not keep you long, but perhaps you could tell me something about this artifact." He gestured to the Dagger. "It seemed to respond to your presence."

Sabrina glanced at the Dagger and forced herself to turn away. Nausea washed through her as she fought the Dagger's pull. Digging her fingers into Auriano's arm, she struggled to suppress her power.

"Well, of course it did, General." She gave a little laugh. "It is an ancient talisman of sorts. From the Druids, I believe. It reveals women who are with child."

Bonaparte narrowed his eyes at Alessandro. "Not quite the same story, Excellency."

Sabrina laughed lightly. "Oh, my goodness. General, did Auriano lead you to believe this is some sort of magic weapon? I'm sure he was only protecting my honor."

The general turned his attention to Sabrina. "I have heard rumors of secret organizations with extraordinary weapons, *Madame*. Now I find this hidden in the trunk of the Prince of Auriano."

Sabrina felt her stomach drop at Bonaparte's reference to the Legion of Baal. Forcing herself not to react, she said, "Really, *Monsieur*, how effective could something be that is made out of crystal?"

The general pulled thoughtfully on his bottom lip, then nodded and smiled. "You are quite correct, *Madame*." He covered the Dagger with the cloth. "Perhaps you would not mind if I borrowed this to discover when my wife conceives."

Something in the general's manner told Sabrina that he saw through her lie, and his mild request revealed that he wanted to investigate the dagger for himself. She remembered that messenger whom Alessandro had killed had been French. She did not care if Napoleon had some connection to the search for the Sphere and wanted the Dagger. All she wanted was to be rid of it.

"Of course, General," she said before Alessandro could respond.

Alessandro bowed to the general as he said graciously, "May it bring you the same luck it has brought me."

He smiled down at Sabrina. She loaded her answering smile with knives.

Then he added, his smile becoming predatory, "Perhaps we will have twins."

It was her turn to choke.

Soon after, they were back on the road to Venice. They had both been silent, lost in their own thoughts, as they traveled through the small village and the army camp beyond. Alessandro knew Sabrina was relieved to have the Dagger out of her presence. After seeing how it had drawn her and seemed to suck her power, he understood why she had been so upset when he told her he had stolen it. But at least that haunted look was gone from her eyes and her color had returned.

Yet, he felt differently about losing it. He was suspicious of Napoleon, especially after seeing the frog glyph on that messenger he had killed, and he wondered if Sabrina had put the dagger back into the hands of the Legion of Baal once again. Knowing that Dunfield was a member of that group made him even more uneasy. But for now, General Bonaparte held the dagger, and Alessandro felt he would keep it close by him.

He glanced over at Sabrina as she stared out the window of the coach. He was amused at her lie to Bonaparte. It had disarmed the French general and worked to get them released. Once again, she had amazed Alessandro with her quick thinking. But he was not about to let her ignore the game she had played.

"You were very brave with General Bonaparte," he began.

Sabrina turned to him with a wary look. "Thank you."

"But, pregnant?" he asked, raising an amused brow.

"Twins?" she shot back. She had wondered how long he would wait to tease her about her ruse.

"*Si*. I have twins in my family going back many generations." The smile he gave her could have melted glass. "Wouldn't it be delightful to try to make twins together?"

Sabrina scowled at him and turned away. His quiet laugh made her clench her teeth. Making twins with him would be more than delightful. She knew, without a doubt, that it would be delirious, staggering, overwhelming, blissful. The vision that crept into her head caused her body to throb. But she would not give in to him. She could not.

He toyed with a lock of her hair. As she brushed him away, he caught her fingers.

"For a widow, *Donna* Barclay, you are very skittish," he said. "As my betrothed, I think you need reminding about the joys of matrimony."

"I do not," she snapped.

"Tsk. Cross and peevish. This is not good." He shook his head sadly, then he brightened. "But fortunately, I know a cure."

"I do not wish to be cured, Excellency," she said, as she tried to pull her hand away.

He refused to let her go. "The patient often refuses treatment." Kissing her palm, he circled it with his tongue.

Sabrina felt the effects all the way up her arm.

"Do you remember, when I was your *cicisbeo*, you asked me to kiss you?" He started to suck on each fingertip.

"That was…" Her concentration wavered as he made love to each finger. The feel of his lips, the touch of his tongue fogged her brain. Forcing herself to focus, she started again. "That was different."

"*Si.* You were playing a game then, a dangerous game, to see how far you could push me." He slipped his hand up her arm, across her shoulder, to cup her neck.

"I…" She swallowed, gathering courage to confess, although she could not understand her need to do so. "I wanted you to kiss me again, because…" Knowing there had been a good reason at the time, she somehow could not remember what it was, except to feel those marvelous sensations he created in her.

"*Si.* I wanted to kiss you again, too, so I let you win that time." His fingers spread up the back of her head and twined in her hair. "This time, *cara mia*, you are playing my game, and I intend to win because this time, you are my betrothed."

He held her head so she was forced to look at him. Her gaze became tangled in those golden eyes. She knew she should hold him off. She was connected to his enemies. She was supposed to be angry with him. He was overbearing. He had manipulated her into becoming his fiancée. She tried to gather her power, but somehow, she couldn't find it. Dear God, she wanted to lose this game.

He framed her face with his other hand, leaned in, and placed a kiss at the corner of her mouth. "You will yield to me, Sabrina," he murmured. "Sometime soon." He kissed the opposite corner of her mouth.

Her eyes slipped closed and she gave a tiny mewl. Of protest or surrender? She wasn't sure. Yet, it was useless to fight when her body craved what he wanted to give. Placing her hands on his thighs, she angled her mouth across his and slid her tongue across his upper lip. His swift intake of breath revealed how hungry he was.

Despite that, perhaps because of that, her determination hardened. She did want him. She wanted him so badly she spent most of her nights tossing and turning in unfulfilled wretchedness. But she would give in to him on her terms. Just this once, because she would be gone from his life soon. And she would make him understand that he could not take, that he had to ask first, and that he had to abide by her answer. She would teach him a lesson in humility.

"I want you to kiss me," she whispered against his mouth, repeating the words she had spoken in the gondola when he was still her *cicisbeo*.

He stared at her. The heat in those golden eyes seared her. "My game, *carissima*," he whispered in warning. "My rules."

Then his arm went about her, and he crushed her to him, firmly claiming her lips, plundering her mouth with his tongue. She submitted, danced with him, a ballet of sensation, exploration. Breathless and dazed when he raised his head, she was aware when his hand traced over her ribs to the laces on her bodice and stays.

She stopped him, pushed him back into the corner of the seat. Surprise was her ally. When he could have easily resisted her, he calmly allowed her to have her way. Amusement rippled through her. Did he truly think this was his game they played this time? His rules?

Not quite sure how to proceed, she took her cues from what he had done to her. She reasoned that her touch could ignite him as much as his touch fired her. Unbuttoning his waistcoat, she skimmed her hands over his silky shirt. His muscles rippled beneath her hands. Deftly, she untied his stock, unbuttoned his shirt, and pulled it from his breeches. She could feel his gaze, curious, wary, heated, as she ran her fingers over his bare chest from his throat to the waistband of his breeches. His skin under her touch was smooth and warm. The short hairs on his chest were soft. Captivated by the sensations beneath her palms, she stroked and tickled, and became fascinated by the tiny twitches of his muscles at her touch.

Not daring to look at him, she circled his nipples with her fingertips. His breathing quickened, and she became bolder. She remembered his response when she barely touched his nipples that time in the gondola. Teasing them between her thumb and forefinger, she heard him draw in a breath. It urged her on. Leaning in, she licked them and sucked. A low rumble vibrated in his throat. His response made her throb.

Pleased at his reaction, she smiled to herself as she ran her tongue along the thin trail of hair that disappeared into his breeches. She slipped her hands down over his hips and placed one on each thigh. What she planned to do next took courage. She had never done anything like this with her husband. But Auriano had touched her like this, had enflamed her. Why wouldn't it do the same to him?

His hooded gaze, the hitch in his breathing seemed to indicate it was working. On both of them.

He allowed her to play, had kept his hands to himself. Yet, now, he took her by the shoulders and pulled her up so their eyes were on a level. When he began to draw her to him for a kiss, she resisted. This was about her control. His gaze narrowed.

She ran her hands up and down his thighs and let her thumbs trace the inside of his thighs. His gaze intensified, darkened. When her thumbs wandered higher to the hollows of his hips, he sucked in a breath. She sensed his coiled tension. Leaning in, she placed her lips against his, and rubbed her thumbs up and down against the bulge in his breeches. She was rewarded with his growl of pleasure. His hands tightened on her shoulders.

He pulled back, frowning suspiciously. "What game do you play, *cara mia*?"

"Why, your game, Excellency." She kept her tone guileless.

"Not my game. Your game. A dangerous game," he said.

She blinked innocently. "I don't know what you mean."

Scowling, his eyes turned dark and threatening. "Did your husband teach you nothing?"

Embarrassed at her lack of knowledge and that she might have done something wrong, she snapped, "My late husband has nothing to do with this."

"*Madre de Dio*," he muttered. "How many times did he lay with you? Once? Twice?"

Heat lit up her cheeks. His question came too close to the truth. "That's none of your business. He was kind and thoughtful," she said, daring him to contradict her.

He glared at her. "Do not defend him. He left you unloved and naive as a virgin."

"What if he did? You seem to be teaching me everything I need to know."

Saying nothing, he stared at her a moment. Then, quietly, he said, "*Si*. Here is another lesson. You are playing with fire with what you do to me. Once you start this, there is no turning back. I may not be able to control myself."

Defensive over her actions, she baited, "Losing control is a humbling experience, is it not, Excellency?" She ran her thumbs down his penis.

He caught her wrists and pulled her hands away. "Is that what this is about? Control?" Anger tightened the muscles of his face. "Do you think so little of me, *Donna* Barclay, that you would taunt me like this? Have I ever treated you with contempt? Do you think I would take you in a coach as if you were nothing but a courtesan?"

"You had me kidnapped, like some plaything," she accused.

"And had you brought to a comfortable room. Tell me you did not enjoy my touch." His darkened eyes dared her to contradict him.

Unable to do so, she shot back, "You would have taken me in your gondola if we had not arrived at the theater."

"I would not have." His words were quietly deadly. His gaze held hers. "I would have given you pleasure and denied myself."

Humbled by his statement, she knew he was telling the truth. Despite his secrets, despite his roguish seduction, he was an honorable man. Confused, ashamed, she stammered, "I—I—"

"Piero!" he bellowed, cutting her off. "Stop the coach!" Flinging away her hands, he ripped off his coat and waistcoat. By the time he had done that, the coach had rolled to a stop.

Sabrina inched back, away from him. His rage was formidable. Not knowing what he planned to do, she regretted pushing him this far. Perhaps this had been the wrong way to go about teaching him that lesson in humility.

He threw open the coach door and stepped out. "Do not move," he snapped at her, then he stalked away, leaving the door wide open.

She watched him disappear into the olive grove that bordered the road. She did not dare go after him, and she was too embarrassed to ask Piero his opinion. So she waited.

Sometime later, she saw him walking back through the trees. He appeared calmer. His gait was steady, and his tightly wound anger seemed to be gone. He had left his shirt open and untucked, and it fluttered about him as he moved. Moving with grace, he looked like some alluring dark angel. He took her breath away.

But she had done something unforgivably stupid. She waited apprehensively.

He stopped outside the coach and stood with his hands on his hips as he gazed thoughtfully at her. She wanted him to say something, anything. Miserably, she glanced down at her fingers twisted together in her lap.

"I'm sorry," she finally said, feeling the blood heat her face. "I didn't mean… I didn't know…" She took a breath and said again, "I'm sorry."

He spoke to Piero, then he climbed into the coach and closed the door. Reaching out, he untangled her fingers and clasped her hand.

"You do not need to be sorry, *cara mia*," he said. "It was my fault. I should have stopped you, but I was enjoying your touch too much." He gave her a tiny smile. "You see, you do have control."

Confounded, speechless, she stared at him.

Raising her hand to his lips, he gave it a chaste kiss. "Perhaps we should call this a lesson in passion for you, and a lesson in humility for me, *si*?"

"I won't do anything like that again," she said, knowing that she spoke the truth, for she would not have the chance.

He chuckled. "Don't say that, *cara mia*. I hope you do that again very soon. But this was not the time or the place." Holding out his arm in invitation, he said, "Come, *carissima*. A truce. It has been an exhausting several days. Rest with me while we finish our journey."

After only a moment's hesitation, she snuggled against him beneath his arm. His solid body supporting her, his arm holding her close made her feel secure, something she had not felt in a long time. Yet, she knew the feeling was only an illusion. This man had too many secrets, secrets that she was not sure she wanted to know. As she watched the scenery slide by, she was determined not to allow herself to be beguiled by his charming seduction. Somehow, she would find a way to break their betrothal and free both herself and Evan.

Chapter 23

The following day, Sabrina found herself sitting in a chair under a pavilion on the sands of the Lido, the spit of land that protected Venice from the Adriatic. It was unseasonably warm. Auriano had come calling with an invitation to Evan to take their model ships sailing, and an invitation to her to join them for a picnic. Her first impulse had been to decline. The embarrassment of her fumbling attempt at seduction still burned, and his manipulation of her life grated. Besides that, she needed to distance herself from him, to plan her escape from Venice.

But Evan had overheard Auriano and had slipped up beside her to hear her answer. Unable to refuse the excitement in her son's eyes, she had agreed. One last time spent in Auriano's company could not hurt, and it would make Evan happy.

They created a small stir as they crossed the lagoon. Two other boats trailed behind them with servants, the folded pavilion, chairs, a table, and, of course, the food. Wearing no masks, with Auriano's heraldic device hung on the side of the gondola, they were easy to identify. As they slipped between the Italian naval vessels, bottled up in the lagoon by the French, the sailors hung over the sides and called down to them. Some even broke into love songs. Auriano exchanged occasional quips with the men, smiled and waved. Sabrina was amazed at his good-natured nonchalance. All she wanted to do was hide.

Eventually, they reached the beach. Out on the Adriatic, the sails of several French ships were outlined against the horizon. They were part of the blockade that General Bonaparte had established. The fragile safety of Venice became quite clear. At any moment, Bonaparte could refuse to negotiate with the Venetians and order an attack on the city. The thought was chilling. Once again, she wondered what the invading French would do to an English woman.

Even though the patrolling French ships were a threat, they made a beautiful picture, their white sails brilliant against the pure blue of the sky. The day was bright, and Evan's excitement was contagious, so Sabrina put aside her fears. The servants set up the pavilion, table, and chairs very quickly. Auriano saw to her comfort, then headed down to the water with Evan. She watched as the two stood at the edge of the surf and played out lines tied to their models.

They wore only shirts and breeches rolled up above their knees. The low surf ebbed and flowed around their bare feet and ankles. They made an engaging portrait.

Despite her complicated relationship with Auriano, Sabrina had to admit that he seemed to enjoy Evan's company. As their small ships caught the wind and bounded over the gentle swells of the sea, she could hear Evan's groans of dismay as his ship floundered and his crow of delight as the wind took it once again, echoed by Auriano when his ship encountered the same conditions. Occasionally, he would glance down at Evan with a grin or listen attentively to what the boy was saying. She could see that Evan admired him and was quickly falling under the influence of his charm. Her son needed a father.

Dismayed, she realized where her thoughts were leading. She couldn't marry Auriano. Once she did, he would become a target for Dunfield and that would put him in deeper danger with the Legion of Baal. She would never be able to live with herself if she were the cause of Auriano's death. He had insinuated himself into her life. She could not contemplate a world without him. If he were no longer around, a huge piece would be ripped from her heart.

And that understanding appalled her, terrified her. It could only mean one thing.

She had fallen in love with him.

How could that have happened? He had secrets that he held close. He was a rogue. He had kidnapped her, seduced her. He had manipulated her into becoming his betrothed. He infuriated her. He taunted and teased her. Lust. It was only lust.

But she knew it was more. He had given her back the memory of her mother's death. He had protected her. He had taught her about her power. He had shared his own dark memory with her. He was spending time with her son. He charmed her. He aroused her.

He engaged her in a way no other man ever had. And when she looked into his eyes she felt something she had never felt before.

She loved him.

She pushed away her rising panic. Revealing how she felt about him would give him a tremendous emotional advantage over her, something she was not about to surrender. She had to discourage him, push him away. Somehow, she had to force him to break off their betrothal. Regret for what she would never have sat like a heavy lump in her chest. She would need to keep searching for another father for Evan.

She would put off that unpleasantness, at least for the day. For now, she would enjoy watching her son and Auriano together.

They were racing their ships. The breeze whipped their hair about their heads — Evan's gleaming darkly and Auriano's shot with gold. Evan's small body was stiff with concentration as he tried to outmaneuver Auriano's ship, which had taken a slight lead. The race was close. With a tiny surreptitious jerk on his line, Auriano made his ship fall back. Evan's ship surged forward and won the race. Seeing the triumph and ecstatic glow on her son's face, Sabrina wanted to hug Auriano in gratitude. She turned away to control the tears that threatened to fall.

Her gaze fell on Gasparo, who stood at the opposite end of the table from her. His expression was rapt, like a father watching a son. Her curiosity about him was piqued.

"Gasparo, how long have you been with Auriano?" she asked.

He sent her a startled glance, then his expression became shuttered, once again the servant. "I have been with the family all my life, *Ma Donna*. I served His Excellency's father before him."

"Then you knew Auriano as a child. What was he like?"

Gasparo's expression softened. "He was much like your son, *Donna*. Inquisitive, playful, but perhaps not so quiet, a bit more mischievous, until—"

"Until what?"

"Until he lost his parents."

Sabrina had the impression that he was about to answer differently, then changed his mind. Not wanting to lose this chance to discover more about the man who was now her betrothed, she said, "How old was he?"

"He was twelve. He grew up very quickly after that, for as the eldest, he was forced to assume the responsibility for the household."

"The eldest?" Sabrina was not sure she had heard correctly.

An odd expression that looked suspiciously like guilt passed through Gasparo's eyes. "*Si*. His Excellency has a younger sister."

Shocked at learning one of Auriano's secrets, she forced her voice to remain level. "He has never spoken of her. Why haven't I met her? Did something happen to her?"

"He sent her away to keep her safe." Pausing, he gazed at her intently. "Please, *Donna* Barclay, you must not blame His Excellency for saying nothing about her. If you must blame anyone, it should be me. I advised him that he not tell anyone about her, not even you. He has been battling Nulkana all of his life, and there are few people he can truly trust."

"When did you decide I was trustworthy, Gasparo?" she asked acerbically.

Sheepishly, he said, "When *Sior* Sandro was injured and you stayed with him, when Nulkana sent the birds to attack you, when I saw the mark of Halima on your hand."

Sabrina remembered that night when Gasparo had seen the mark. He had looked at her with awe as if he knew things about her that she wasn't sure she wanted to know. She was struck suddenly by the very great danger that enveloped this family, as well as the danger that threatened her because of her connection to Nulkana. Yet, the House of Auriano had survived because of men like the one who stood at the opposite end of the table.

"Who are you, Gasparo?" she asked. "What are you?"

He took a deep breath and let it out. "I am a Guide to *Sior* Sandro in his quest to find the pieces of the Sphere of Astarte and in his fight against Nulkana. Members of my family have had this honor and responsibility to the House of Auriano for many generations."

"What does a Guide do? Do you have power of your own?"

"Only a small amount. We are mainly teachers and protectors. "

"I suppose all that business about not being able to help me learn about my power was a sham," she accused.

"No, *Donna* Barclay, truly it was not. If you had been any other besides a descendent of Halima, I could have helped you."

She was unsure whether to believe him or not and astounded at what she had just learned. Her glance fell on Auriano and Evan. Their boat race was over. They were stomping their feet in the shallow surf and trying to get each other wet with the spray. Their unbridled laughter echoed back to her. Despite Gasparo's unsettling revelation, she had to admit that her son felt very comfortable in Auriano's presence.

"Please, *Donna* Barclay," Gasparo said. "Do not spoil *Sior* Sandro's day. I have not seen him this carefree for a very long time. He planned all this for you and your son. He has never done this for another."

Sabrina looked at him. His eyes pleaded with her, and she saw the heart of the man who acted as servant but was so much more. "You care for him a great deal, don't you, Gasparo?"

He nodded once. "He is like a son to me."

Alessandro cast a speculative glance up the beach where Sabrina sat chatting with Gasparo. He wondered what the two of them could be talking about. He would quiz Gasparo later. Now, he wanted only to watch her.

"Maybe Mama would like to come down to the water," Evan suggested, drawing his attention.

Alessandro gazed down at the boy. "Then we should invite her, *si*?"

At Evan's eager nod, Alessandro grinned. He enjoyed being in the boy's company. The child was intelligent and pleasant, with a touch of mischief. He also wondered at the power that the boy had inherited from his mother. The potential to do good.

Picking up his ship model, Alessandro started up the beach. "Come, then," he said. "Bring your ship, Master Evan."

259

The boy scooped up his ship and ran to catch up. "Are you really going to marry my mother?" he asked artlessly.

"Is that what she told you?" Alessandro was not going to reveal anything about that situation.

"She said you and she are betrothed, and that's what two people do when they want to think about living in the same house, and having babies." The boy was breathless by the time he finished speaking.

"*Si*, that is true."

"If you marry my mother, that will make you my father, won't it?"

Alessandro stopped and looked down at the child. "I will never replace your real father, Master Evan."

Evan made a face. "He never spent time with me like you have." The boy's expression became suspicious. "Are you just spending time with me so that Mama will like you better?"

Astounded at the boy's insight, Alessandro had to smile. Although his initial motive had been exactly that, he found himself beguiled by the child. "I am spending time with you because I like you. I hope you like me as well."

With a vigorous nod, Evan said, "I like you very much, Excellency."

"I am glad. Then let us make an agreement. Even if your mother and I do not wed, you and I shall still remain friends, *si*?"

With another nod, the boy stuck out his hand. "Yes. We should shake hands on it."

Solemnly, Alessandro took the child's small hand in his and shook it. He was charmed by the boy's sincerity and self-possession. He hunkered down so he was at eye level with the child. "If we are to be friends, then perhaps you should call me by my name: Alessandro."

The boy cocked his head thoughtfully. "I would much prefer to call you Papa."

Unnerved by the responsibility that title implied, but touched by Evan's affection, Alessandro smiled gently. "Perhaps that could happen sometime in the future, but for now, I will be just Alessandro."

"All right." The boy grinned. "Come on, then. We must tell Mama and then invite her down to the water." He bounded away across the sand.

"Mama! Mama!" Breathless, Evan ran up to Sabrina and stopped short, spraying sand across her shoes. "Alessandro and I are going to be friends!"

"Evan, where are your manners?" she scolded. "You must not call His Excellency by his name."

"I gave Evan permission because that is what friends do," Auriano told her as he came up behind her son and placed his hand on the boy's shoulder. His gaze dared her to counteract his permission.

She couldn't disappoint Evan, so she said nothing. In the silence, her son looked from one adult to the other.

"Aren't you and Alessandro friends?" he asked.

Startled at the question, not quite sure how to answer, she cast a quick glance at Auriano. His brow quirked up and the corner of his mouth twitched in amusement, but he remained silent. She sent him a warning look, then turned to Evan.

"We have a different type of friendship," she told the boy. She felt Auriano's gaze as if it were a caress. She ignored it.

Evan accepted that, then was off on a new topic. "We would like to invite you to walk with us down near the water," he said. "I want to look for shells."

Without a word, Auriano held out his hand to her. Sabrina couldn't refuse the excitement in Evan's eyes. Placing her hand in Auriano's, she allowed him to pull her to her feet. As she reached for her sun hat on the table, he placed his hand over hers, stopping her.

"No, please," he murmured. "I want to look at you in the sunshine."

The heat in his eyes warmed her better than the sun's rays. But she couldn't bask in that warmth. He would have to observe her from a distance.

She sent Evan a mischievous look.

"I'll race you to the water," she said, challenging them both, as she picked up her skirts and ran.

With a whoop, Evan raced after her. She ran just fast enough that she kept ahead of him. She could only hear his small footsteps pounding the sand. A bit disappointed Auriano had not joined in the race, still, she enjoyed playing with Evan. She reached the water's edge first, but Evan was only a half step behind.

"I won," she announced with a laugh.

"But you had a head start," he protested.

No sooner were the words out of his mouth, when she felt herself scooped up into Auriano's arms and carried headlong into the surf up to his knees. With a cry of surprise, she clung to his neck.

Laughing, he turned to Evan. "You are right," he said. "She didn't run a fair race. I think she needs to be punished."

"A forfeit!" Evan cried.

"I am not giving up a forfeit," Sabrina protested. "I won the race, and you two gentlemen will have to allow me my victory."

As if she had not spoken, Auriano asked Evan, "What shall we demand? Perhaps a dunking in the sea?"

He let her slip a few inches before he tightened his grip again. Sabrina squealed and threw her other arm about his neck.

"Don't you dare let me go," she warned.

He turned to her with a challenging grin. "I dare many things, *cara mia*."

"I know what the forfeit can be!" Evan exclaimed. "Mama can marry you!"

Sabrina's wary gaze met Auriano's speculative one.

"Perhaps that is too much for winning a race unfairly," he said. "But I think a kiss would be a fair price. What do you think?" he asked Evan.

Evan's face screwed up into a grimace. "A kiss?" He thought for a moment, then brightened. "Maybe Mama could do my Latin lessons instead."

"Perhaps a young man should do his own lessons so he may grow into a lettered man of the world," Alessandro suggested gently.

Evan's shoulders slumped. "I guess a kiss is fine," he said. Then muttered, "Yuck."

Sabrina hid her smile. "Do I have to?" she asked him.

Evan nodded eagerly. "Yes."

She sighed and pretended to pout. "Well, if you insist." Quickly, before anyone could say anything else, she pecked Auriano on the cheek.

Raising a brow, he asked Evan, "What do you think? Was that acceptable as a forfeit?"

Evan shook his head. "That was not a proper kiss."

"How do you know it was not a proper kiss?" Sabrina demanded. "That is how I kiss you every night."

"But that is not how Cora kisses Uncle Dunfield's gondolier," Evan said.

Sabrina gasped at the boy's revelation. "Evan, you should not be spying on Cora."

Auriano laughed. "I agree with Evan. You haven't given up an acceptable forfeit."

Sabrina looked at him with rebellion in her eyes.

"Quickly, *cara mia*, or I will have to drop you, and then you will get very wet," Auriano teased. He let her slip again.

Sabrina kept one arm tight around his neck, for Auriano was mischievous enough to carry out his threat. She placed her hand on his cheek, kept her eyes open, and touched her lips to his. The feel of his mouth stirred memories, and her body throbbed in response. If she had not been out in the open, in the surf, with Evan only a few feet away, she feared she might have given in to the temptation of Auriano's attraction. But this kiss was only a forfeit, given as a prize in a race.

Auriano also kept his eyes open, his gaze challenging. His tongue arrogantly flicked against her bottom lip, taunting her, reminding her of the debacle in the coach the day before. Embarrassed, annoyed, she pulled back and sent a spark of power through the hand resting around his neck.

He winced, then grinned. "A fine line between pleasure and pain, *si*?" he whispered.

"You will keep your pleasure to yourself, or you will feel pain," she retorted.

"Sometimes pleasure is pain."

Despite his smile, Sabrina saw a bleak shadow in his eyes. Confused by that shadow, not understanding his words, she frowned. But he would not explain.

She turned to Evan. "Was that forfeit enough?"

Evan grinned and nodded, then, bored with the game, he asked, "Can we go look for shells now?"

After Auriano deposited her safely on the sand, they wandered along the water's edge. Evan collected shells and bits of glass. He would run back to them to show them his treasures, then race ahead to find more. The sun was warm and soothing. With her arm hooked through Auriano's, a sense of peace stole over Sabrina, the first she had felt in a very long time. For once, he was not challenging her, nor seducing her, nor teasing or taunting her. He was being kind to Evan, and he seemed to truly like her son. She felt a yearning for something she knew she couldn't have.

He chatted about inconsequential things, like the new play by Goldoni, and a new opera by Piccini. He spoke of the festival on the island of Giudecca, on the third Sunday in July, when people traveled to the garden island in flower-laden boats and remained there until sunrise. Rafts with make-believe gardens would be created, and there was dancing the *tarentella* and eating fried sole. Then he mentioned the fact that one of his merchant ships out of China was due in port soon, and the French blockade would prevent it from entering the lagoon.

That bit of information intrigued her and piqued her curiosity about his family. "Have members of your family always been merchants?"

"*Si*. Merchants, sometimes pirates, sometimes princes. As in all old families, we have rogues and saints."

"Which are you?"

He grinned that pirate's smile. "Whichever you wish me to be, *cara mia*."

Exasperated at his teasing again, she was relieved that the bleak shadow in his eyes was gone.

Sobering again, he said, "Tell me of your father."

Sabrina was a bit disconcerted at his question. Because of his casual arrogance, she had assumed he was uninterested in her family. She began to suspect he was hiding more about himself than dangerous secrets.

"My father was a scholar," she told him. "He was fascinated by the ancient civilizations of Rome and Greece and Egypt."

"Like your late husband."

"Yes. Richard was one of his students. After my mother died, my father retreated more and more into his books. The only time I could get him to speak to me was if I asked him a question about art or history."

"So you learned about the past in order to converse with him."

Sabrina nodded.

"Poor, lonely child," he murmured and covered her hand on his arm.

His sympathy made her eyes sting. She refused to give in to tears. "When he developed the wasting disease and realized he was dying, he arranged to have Richard wed me. He died not long after the wedding took place."

"Did you love your late husband?"

Hearing an odd note in his voice, she glanced at him. His gaze was on Evan, far ahead of them up the beach. "No," she finally said. "I was fond of him, but he kept to his books as much as my father."

He turned and looked at her. "And then he died."

Sabrina nodded. "Murdered. He fell from his horse. The cinch had been cut." She fought to keep her voice level. Knowing of Dunfield's part in his death disconcerted and terrified her.

"An arranged mishap." Auriano's gaze probed. "Was the culprit ever caught?"

"No." She shook her head. "It was thought to be one of the grooms, but he disappeared and the authorities looked no further."

"Another sad, frightening event for one so young," he murmured.

She glanced away from those tender golden eyes. "Everyone has sad events in their lives, Excellency. You yourself have witnessed tragedy."

"*Si.*" He stopped and faced her. "We have much in common, *carissima*. Please, let us be friends."

Uncomfortable with this serious side of him, she smiled nervously. "Like you and Evan?"

He smiled in return. "Not exactly. Unless you like to sail model ships?"

She laughed. "I'll leave that to you two boys."

He nodded. "Then, shall we be friends?"

Turning over the question, she wondered if he had some ulterior motive. Yet, his gaze was steady and sincere. "Friends," she finally said, "trust each other."

"I trust you with my life." A corner of his mouth lifted. "You have already saved me."

Sabrina thought he was referring to the attack by Nulkana, but she also sensed some other meaning to his words.

Before she could respond, he asked, "Do you trust me, Sabrina?"

She took a breath to tell him no, she did not trust him in the least, then realized that was a lie. She knew he would put himself in danger for her. He had already done that several times. Yet, at the same time, she feared he could rip out her heart. "You have too many secrets, Excellency."

"Even friends have secrets from each other," he said. "I don't think you have revealed all of yours, but I am willing to wait until you feel you can tell me."

Comprehension made her blink. Despite his overbearing manipulation, despite his wealth and influence, he was lonely. Her heart opened to him. "Yes," she said. "Friends."

"*Bene.*" He smiled, leaned down, and kissed her gently on the cheek. "If we are to be friends, then you must call me by my name. Those who are close to me call me Sandro."

She opened her mouth to protest, then closed it again. That bleak shadow was in his eyes again. She wanted to make it disappear. "Sandro," she whispered.

"*Grazie, cara mia.*"

He called to Evan and turned them back toward the pavilion, where Gasparo was laying out their meal.

Auriano—Sandro—was charming during lunch. He entertained with stories about Venice: the *Regata Storica*, when gondola races would take place and the gondoliers from the different districts would compete in acrobatic feats; of the visits of kings when the San Benedetto was draped in blue silk; of the pageant of the election of the Doge of Venice, when the Doge in his red velvet cloak and the Dogaressa in her cloak of gold entered the palace.

266

By the time they finished their meal, the sun was sinking in the sky. Gasparo and the servants packed up everything, and they strolled slowly back to the gondola. They were walking a sandy path between low shrubbery when Alessandro gasped and sank to one knee.

"Pain," he ground out and pressed a fist to his chest.

His face was chalky. He clung to Sabrina's hand like a vise.

Up ahead, Evan was chattering with Gasparo. Neither of them had noticed.

"Sandro," she asked, "what is it? Evil?"

"Not my pain," he panted. He raised his head, glanced around, and pointed. "His."

Sabrina looked. At some distance, on a small sand dune, stood a lonely figure in a black robe and hood. She felt no sense of evil, but the figure appeared ominous. Wanting to protect the man beside her, she raised her hand to send a burst of energy at the figure.

"No," Sandro gasped out. "Don't hurt him."

Sabrina called to Gasparo and crouched beside Sandro. "Where does it hurt? What can I do?"

Sandro shook his head mutely.

Gasparo sent Evan on ahead with the servants and hurried back to them. He glanced where Sabrina pointed, drew in a sharp breath, then knelt beside her.

"*Sior* Sandro… ?" Gasparo placed his hand on Alessandro's shoulder. His touch seemed to give the prince strength.

"I feel —" Alessandro stopped, sucked in a breath. "Agony, shame, loss." He forced out the words. "Emptiness —" His last word was spoken in a tone of utter desperation.

Sabrina cast a glance at Gasparo, but the Guide only shook his head in confusion.

"Ah." Alessandro uttered the syllable as half-release, half-exclamation. His head came up, and the death grip he had on her fingers loosened. "It's gone."

When Sabrina glanced over her shoulder, the figure had disappeared, as if it had never been there. Alessandro appeared ravaged as if whatever had caught him had stripped him of all hope. He took several deep breaths and kept his fingers entwined with hers. His expression slowly cleared, but he remained sober and thoughtful, withdrawn.

"Who… what was that, Gasparo?" Sabrina asked.

"I am not sure, *Donna* Barclay," he said.

"I don't ever want to know." Alessandro's tone was desolate.

Standing, Gasparo sent him a sharp look. "You may need to know, *Sior* Sandro."

Alessandro shook his head. "You did not feel what I felt, the void, the nothingness."

"Your life and those around you may depend on your knowing what that was," his Guide said. "Remember who you are."

Alessandro shot to his feet. "Do not presume to tell me my responsibilities, Gasparo. I know perfectly well who I am. Perhaps you should better remember who *you* are."

Sabrina stared at the two men who locked gazes. She had never heard Alessandro speak so imperiously. Finally, Gasparo lowered his eyes and bowed.

"Thank you for your words, Excellency. Please excuse this servant who must attend to his duties." He backed two steps away, then turned and headed in the direction of the gondolas.

"Gasparo," Alessandro called.

The man waved, but did not turn, did not stop.

Watching him a moment, Alessandro cursed under his breath, then turned to Sabrina, who dared not move from her crouch. She recognized royal rage when she saw it. Despite his charm, despite the fact he had no formal principality, the man before her was still a prince, raised as a prince, committed to the responsibilities of a prince, able to have his commands met with a snap. He had just insulted his most trusted advisor. She suspected the experience with the robed figure had unnerved him. When he held out his hand to help her to her feet, his fingers trembled. She did not hesitate to accept his aid but withdrew as soon as she was upright.

"My apologies, *cara mia*," he said on a sigh. "You should not have witnessed that."

"I think you should be apologizing to Gasparo, not me, Excellency."

A frown creased his brow at her use of his title. He cast a glance in the direction of Gasparo's retreating back. "*Si.* I will. Later. When I can better explain to him what just happened."

"What did happen?"

268

He turned back to her with a haunted look. "I wish I knew."

Chapter 24

By the time they reached the Lagoon, only Alessandro's gondola remained with a nervous, young gondolier. Gasparo had returned to the Ca'D'Este with the other two boats. Sabrina sensed Alessandro's regret at his sharp words to his Guide when he made an effort to greet the youth and set him at ease.

"Taddeo," he explained after they were settled in the gondola, "is Gasparo's youngest son."

"I didn't realize Gasparo was married," Sabrina said.

"*Si.* He is a widower and has three other sons, two daughters."

"Will they all follow in their father's footsteps and serve the House of Auriano?" Her question came out sharper than she intended.

Alessandro turned cool eyes on her. "Only if they wish it. I am not some feudal *patron* who forces his will on those beneath him."

"Only on me, is that it, Excellency?" Sabrina smiled thinly as she pointed out the irony of his words.

His level stare indicated his irritation. He turned away as they passed the Arsenale, and explained to Evan that during the sixteenth century, the shipbuilders could construct and equip a war galley in a day.

Alessandro kept his attention on Evan during the entire trip back to Dunfield's *casa.* Sabrina, left out of the conversation, reviewed the day. Each event disturbed her in every way imaginable. The ominous figure that had appeared and Alessandro's reaction to it scared her. The discovery of her feelings for him terrified her. How was she ever going to keep her feelings for him a secret and protect him from Dunfield's murderous intent?

When they finally reached the water gate, Evan bounded out of the gondola to share his adventures with anyone who would listen. Alessandro helped Sabrina to the step and led her away from any listening ears.

"Please, do not condemn me for who I am, Sabrina," he murmured.

She was fully prepared to be angry with him for his peremptory treatment of both Gasparo and herself. Instead, she found herself disarmed. He was who he was, and she had fallen in love with the whole man.

"But you must allow me the freedom to point out your faults," she countered.

"*Si*," he said with a smile, then sobered. "I must go away for a while," he told her. "I have matters that need my attention."

Twilight had descended on the city during their return from the Lido. The dome of San Marco, visible above the rooftops, glowed in the soft light, and the pastels of the buildings appeared luminescent. The moon, nearly full, sat just beyond Alessandro's shoulder. With his face in shadow, she couldn't read his expression clearly. She wondered if his sudden journey had anything to do with the mysterious figure that had appeared that afternoon.

"How long will you be gone?" She hated the forlorn note that crept into her voice. But this would be the perfect time to disappear from his life.

"A fortnight, no longer."

His hand came up and hovered above her cheek. That tingly warmth spread down the side of her face. She exhaled on a sigh. Her eyes slipped closed as she treasured this last touch she would ever feel from him.

His lips touched the corner of her mouth. "I will miss you," he whispered. "If you need anything, send for Gasparo. He will know what to do, how to contact me."

His hand slipped away. By the time she opened her eyes, he was already in the gondola. It floated away from the water gate. Alessandro stood at midsection, his head bowed, keeping his balance as sure as any seasoned gondolier. His head came up as if he sensed her gaze. He glanced back at her with a smile, then turned away. The dusk enveloped him in its shadows. And she steeled herself against the vise that closed around her heart.

The next day, Sabrina learned that Cora had somehow discovered the Canal of Shadows was located in the Ghetto, in the *sestiere* of Cannaregio. Since Dunfield had not yet returned from the cavaliere's villa, Sabrina decided to take the opportunity to investigate. She might even find a place where she and Evan could hide until they could leave Venice. Fog had moved in during the night. It swirled through the canals, distorted sound, and had thickened by late afternoon when Sabrina made her way to Piazza San Marco to hire a gondola. She wouldn't use Dunfield's gondolier and leave a trail. With darkness falling early in the gloom, many of the gondoliers had abandoned their boats and gone home to sit by the warmth of a fire and indulge in a sip of *grappa*, that alcoholic drink made from the seeds and stems of the grape. She finally found a boatman willing to take her to the Ghetto.

They made their way in agonizing slowness through the canals. When they came to intersecting canals, the boatman would sing out as was the custom, but his voice was swallowed up in the fog. Few others were out, so the danger of crashing was slight, but the eerie silence and blanket of fog made her uneasy.

Once in the Ghetto, the houses they passed were dark for the most part and rose up beside the canal in a black wall. This was not the gay, glamorous section of the city, where pleasure seekers roamed and hearts were light. This was where the Jews congregated, ostracized for their religion, but welcomed for their financial knowledge. Since it was after sundown, they were all behind closed doors. The alleys and canals were deserted. Her gondolier complained of not being able to see, of the creepy atmosphere, of meeting up with *i fantasmi* — ghosts. She reminded him of the coins she had promised on reaching their destination.

They finally turned down a narrow, twisting canal, bordered by dark, empty warehouses. Through the gloom, a torch flickered, marking the entrance to a *casa*. As they floated closer, she saw there were only two narrow steps up to the entrance and the familiar pole where a gondola would tie up. After handing the gondolier the ducats she had promised, she stood watching as he quickly made his way back in the direction they had come. No amount of pleading or promise of more payment would entice him to remain. Alone on the quay, she gathered her courage.

The water gate, surprisingly, was wide open. Beyond, dim light illuminated the small *andron*. Bare of decoration, its walls were plainly paneled, the floor paved in uneven, cheap stone. She heard no signs of life, no footsteps, no voices. Despite the few lamps that had been left burning, the place seemed abandoned. Stepping through the water gate, she saw no stairs and crossed the *andron* to the courtyard beyond. There, in the fog, a set of outside stairs led to the floors above.

At the top of the stairs, before her, stretched the *sala del portego*, the central hall. This floor was the *piano nobile*, the grand floor, where visitors were entertained. The floor was constructed of the usual *terrazzo*, but no decorative nuggets of glass or mother-of-pearl were imbedded in it. Oddly, a sumptuous Persian carpet in deep jewel tones ran down its center. Closed doors ran down one side of the gallery, indicating rooms beyond, but with no hint of what type of rooms those might be. No furniture such as small tables or occasional chairs, used to impress visitors, lined the damasked wall. Two brass chandeliers hung from the ceiling, but they were dark. Candles flickered in wall sconces spaced far apart along the walls and lent their dim light, but that was the only sign of life. The place was tomb-like in its silence.

She decided to explore further, and she climbed to the next floor, where traditionally the living quarters would be. Here, once again, the decor was rich, yet simple, with brocade covering the walls and thick carpet beneath her feet. The doors leading to the rooms were closed, with no indication that anyone was behind them. A noise, like the faint scrape of boot against stone, came from below. Peering down over the railing, she saw no one.

She straightened, puzzled at the emptiness and silence. A hand slipped around her throat from behind. Part threat, part caress. Startled, she froze. That hand pulled her back, too fast, too menacing for her to react. She came up against a body. Big. Hard. A man's body. A powerful man. Her heart jumped.

A male voice murmured in her ear, "Ah, *dolce*."

That voice sounded familiar, yet not.

His other hand came around her, undid the clip holding her cloak closed and yanked the garment from her shoulders. "*Bellissima.*" His hand ran over her from breast to crotch, where he forced her back against his hips. His erection, pressed against her backside, announced his intentions.

"Let me go." She tried to wriggle free and pull his hand away from her throat.

"I think not," he purred dangerously.

The hand about her throat tightened and threatened to strangle her. She stopped struggling, afraid. She had been foolish to come alone.

The hand at her crotch slipped away. He ran it down her arm. His fingers wrapped around her wrist. "You have touched the Sphere," he accused. "I can feel it. Where is it?"

"I don't know." Who was this man who could sense such a thing? Could he be connected to Nulkana? Panic fueled her bravery. "Let me go!" She punctuated her demand with a jab into his ribs with her elbow.

He grunted, but his grip on her did not loosen. "So, that is how you wish to play." He chuckled. "I like to play rough."

A door opened farther along the hall, and a man stepped out. Alessandro? What was he doing here?

His eyes raked over her, then he glared at the man holding her. "She's not for you, Tonio," he said. "Let her go."

Tonio? The shadow man? How could that be? The person holding her was very much flesh and bone, not Shadow.

"But she is so delicious," Tonio purred and demonstrated by running his tongue along her jaw.

Alessandro's face darkened. "Tonio, let her go. Gasparo is bringing women for you."

"But this woman is here, now." He released her wrist and pressed her back against his erection. "She has touched the Sphere, and I want to taste her." He nipped her shoulder, hard.

Sabrina winced. His menacing hand at her throat bound her. She dared not move. The tension between the two men was palpable. Alessandro was in a rage. Tonio's violence was a barely restrained beast. One wrong move might cause either man to erupt.

"Tonio!" Alessandro whipped out the name and stepped closer. His hand went to the hilt of a rapier hanging from his belt.

The man behind her stiffened. His grip about her throat tightened. The hand at her crotch pressed harder. Sabrina fought for breath.

"I want this woman," Tonio growled.

Smoothly, Alessandro pulled the rapier, stepped forward, and pressed the weapon's tip against Tonio's shoulder. "Don't make me hurt you," he threatened.

"You don't have the *cogliones*."

Alessandro's eyes flashed. "Don't I?" He pressed harder with the rapier.

Tonio jerked and hissed in pain. "*Cazzo!*" he swore. "You pricked me!"

"You are holding my betrothed," Alessandro seethed. "I'll do more than prick you if you don't release her. I'm not sharing. Let her go."

Growling again, Tonio slipped his hand back up her body. When he reached the neckline of her bodice, his fingers tangled in the chain holding her moonstone pendant. He pulled it from between her breasts and let the pendant rest in his palm. He went still. Slowly, his fingers closed about the moonstone. One heartbeat passed, then two, three. With a yelp, he dropped the pendant and jumped away, releasing her.

Sabrina spun around. An exact replica of Alessandro stood before her. The same chiseled features, the same gold-streaked chestnut hair, the same male dimple. Twins! Only his eyes were different. They were black as pitch, reminding her of Alessandro's eyes the night he had kidnapped her. A trickle of blood dripped down his shoulder.

And he was as naked as the day he was born.

He stared in astonishment at his hand. "*Merda*, what just happened?"

"Whatever it was, it made you see reason," Alessandro said as he sheathed his rapier. "Here, cover up." He tossed Tonio a small red strip of cloth.

What could he cover with something so small? Absolutely nothing about him was small. Tonio caught the cloth, winked at her, smiled the same pirate grin that belonged to Alessandro, then tied the red silk mask across his eyes.

He turned to the door behind him and pushed it open. Dark bruises on his ribs and back testified to his tangle with the birds the night they attacked. Just before he stepped through the doorway, he announced, "I need more wine, Sandro. Vats of it, and I need it now." His tone was stark, in sharp contrast to the brash grin he had given her. He shut the door behind him.

Still in shock, Sabrina turned to Alessandro. "Tonio?"

"*Si.*" His clipped word indicated his anger was still simmering close to the surface.

"Tonio, the shadow man?"

"*Si.*"

"He is your *twin?*"

"*Si.* My brother, Antonio Valerio Cesare D'Este, Duke of Auriano." Alessandro cast a dark glance at the closed door. "I'm afraid you have not met him at his best."

"But…" She struggled to find the right question to ask.

He held out his hand. "Come with me so we may talk. I think you need to explain some things to me."

Sabrina resolutely put her hand behind her back. "I think *you* need to explain some things to *me*, Excellency." For instance, why Alessandro was here, and why his twin brother, suddenly flesh and bone, was running about naked and accosting women.

He let his hand fall to his side. "You know most of the answers, but do not recognize the truth."

"Then perhaps you should help me see it." Meeting his cool gaze with one of her own, she lifted her chin. She would not let him intimidate her, despite the fact that her insides were shaking. This man before her was not the seductive lover nor the charming rogue she had encountered before. He was not even the insulted male who had stormed away from the coach on their journey back to Venice. His presence was formidable, and she sensed a deep-seated, desperate rage in him. Her appearance at the Canal of Shadows seemed to have unleashed that rage, although he had reined it in considerably from when he had first stepped into the hallway. He had always taken care with her, so she was hoping his restraint would hold a bit longer.

His eyes challenged her. "I'm not sure you want to see the truth because I do not think you will like it once you do."

"That is my decision, isn't it, Excellency, to decide if I wish to know the truth or not?" She returned his challenge.

With a curt nod, he held out his hand to her again. "Your decision, *Donna* Barclay. Come."

Sabrina ignored his brusqueness and took his hand. He led her back to the open door. When she stepped across the threshold, she halted. This was the same bedchamber where he had made her strip and seduced her. Where he had first touched her. Where he had opened her eyes to pleasure. So, this was the purpose of the Canal of Shadows. An uneasiness settled in her middle.

She shook her head. "I don't want to be in this room."

From below came the sound of people arriving at the water gate, female giggles, and a male voice answering, directing them.

He closed the door, shutting out the noise, shutting them in. "This is the safest place."

Safest? she wondered. Safest for whom?

Tonelessly, he said, "I just wish to talk." Then with a strained sigh, he added, "Please."

Sabrina had never heard that distressed note in his voice before. She relented. "But we will only talk."

A glint of humor flashed through his eyes. "*Grazie,*" he murmured with a dry twist. Giving a small bow, he excused himself. She heard the snick of the lock turn.

Alarmed, irritated at being locked in, Sabrina paced. What had happened to the carefree man who had accompanied her and Evan to the Lido the day before, the man who had whispered that he would miss her while he was gone? He obviously had not gone far. From the sounds of the women arriving, he would not have time to miss her. Was that why he was so angry, because she had interrupted his plans for seducing another woman? Yet, his reaction to the new arrivals had been odd, not the reaction of a man waiting for a lover. The anger she sensed from him seemed to come from a much deeper place.

She glanced in the direction of the bed. The memories of the last time she had been in this room rose up like ghosts before her. Of his careful seduction of her. Of the weight of his body pressed against her. Of his touch. Of his kisses. Of the pleasure he had given her. Her body throbbed in response to her thoughts.

Annoyed at herself, she turned her back on the bed and plunked into a chair before the fire. She had to figure out what was going on. Something had enraged Alessandro. She did not think it had been merely her interruption of his love tryst. It had to be something else, perhaps connected to his brother's transformation. That was another mystery. The man had so many secrets she doubted she would ever discover them all.

She heard the key in the lock and the door swung open. Alessandro entered, carefully locked the door behind him, and approached. He stopped, looming over her.

"You should not be here," he said.

"I apologize for intruding upon your secret love nest," she snapped.

Annoyance narrowed his eyes. "How did you find this place? Why have you come?"

She stared at him as she tried to decide if she should tell him. He stared back, patient, waiting. The silence stretched out. Realizing he would win the contest, she pulled out the tiny bit of parchment with the words, *Il Canale di l'Ombres* and handed it to him.

She explained, "I found that in the casket where the piece of the Sphere should have been. I found a similar note in one of my late husband's books. I didn't realize it would lead me to discover that my betrothed is as unfaithful as a rabbit."

Glowering at her, he took the parchment. "Not everything is as it appears." When he glanced at the parchment, the blood drained from his face.

"What is it?" she asked, surprised that the cryptic note should cause him such alarm.

"It's written in my father's hand," he said. "When did your husband acquire the piece of the Sphere?"

"I don't know. I never paid much attention to his artifacts." She would not tell him that it originally belonged to her father, who also owned a carved stone frog, symbol of the Legion of Baal. The man before her had his secrets. She would keep some of her own.

He crumpled the bit of parchment in his fist, and his gaze became thoughtful.

"What does it mean?" she asked.

When he focused on her, his lips twisted sardonically. "It means, *cara mia*, that we are connected in many ways."

"What ways?"

"Answer my questions first," he said coolly, "and then I might explain."

He *might* explain? Her temper simmered. "Don't you think, as your betrothed, I have a right to know the man who is claiming my life?"

"As much as I have the right to know the woman whom I am claiming." His words were deadly quiet. Reaching out, he grabbed the chain about her neck. "Tell me about this pendant."

"I told you. It is a moonstone." Her chin rose a notch.

Tugging the chain taut, leaning over her, he said, "You'll have to tell me more than that."

"Or what?" she snapped.

He bared his teeth in a predatory grin. "Or I might be forced to seduce you. You'd be surprised what secrets can be uncovered with the use of pleasure."

Sabrina shivered. She had no doubt he would be able to do exactly as he threatened. And make her want to do exactly as he wished.

She capitulated. "My mother gave it to me."

"And?" he prompted.

"She told me to never take it off," she amplified.

"Is that all?" His eyes bored into her. When she remained silent, he closed his free hand about her wrist. "I can Thought Bind with you. Not quite so enjoyable as seduction, but still effective."

"But I can keep you out of my mind."

"If there is a competition, who do you think would win?"

Sabrina stared into those golden eyes. She couldn't be sure he was telling the truth, but she really didn't wish to find out. His ability had been honed for years. And in the mood he was in, he would be ruthless. Glancing away, she said, "There is a rhyme she taught me:

Feed the hunger;
Feed the pain.
Wear the moonstone;
Lose the shame."

She watched something click into place in his eyes. Running his hand down the chain, he let the pendant sit in his palm. He appeared expectant, as if he were waiting for something to happen. The last time he held the piece, he reacted as if the stone burned him, the same way his brother had just reacted. She saw no sign that the pendant had any effect on him. Slowly, his fingers closed around the stone. He held it for several heartbeats, then let it drop. It still held the warmth from his hand when it landed against her skin.

With a tight, secretive smile, he paced away, then returned. He slipped the chain over her head. "I need to borrow this."

As he headed for the door, she bounded from her chair. "Wait. You can't just take it." When he ignored her, she sent a tiny blast at his back.

Stopping abruptly, he turned back to her. "I said 'borrow.' I'll return it." His eyes narrowed. "Don't you trust me?"

"No."

His chuckle held no humor as he slipped out the door and locked it.

Chapter 25

Sabrina had been dozing in the chair. When she opened her eyes, he was leaning against the door. His face was shadowed so she couldn't read his expression, but he seemed more composed, less angry than when he had left her. As she had waited, some of the pieces of the puzzle had fallen into place.

"The curse," she said. "It's true."

"*Si.*" Pushing away from the door, he approached, unbuckled the belt holding the rapier, set it on the mantle, and sat across from her. "You should not be here," he repeated, but his words this time were spoken gently. "I never meant for you to see this place."

"Yesterday, you asked me to be your friend," she said. "Friends trust each other. How could we be friends if I never learned of this place?"

A muscle worked in his jaw. Leaning forward, he took her hand between both of his. She thought about pulling away, punishment for his abominable behavior, but something in him spoke of tremendous distress. His hands, sandwiching hers, were warm solace, a reprieve from their chilled confrontation.

"I have acted hatefully, and you have been very brave," he said softly. "I cannot ask you to forgive me, but if you could listen to what I have to tell you, I will be grateful."

She was willing to listen. And learn the truth. She gave a nod.

"*Cara mia,*" he began, but his voice broke. Clearing his throat, he started again. "Sabrina, do you remember the story I told you about my family and the Sphere of Astarte?"

She nodded. "It was in your family for centuries, and then it was stolen."

"*Si*. But I did not tell you the whole truth that day."

"Why does that not surprise me?" she asked drily.

He glanced away. "When I told you that story, I didn't know if I could trust you."

"And now you can?" She gave an ironic laugh. "What has changed your mind, Excellency?"

He looked directly at her. Those golden eyes were soft. "I have come to care for you. Very much."

His statement took her breath. It was the last thing she expected him to admit. Yet, if he expected her to admit the same about him, he would be disappointed. She was not about to bare her soul to him, not after the way he had treated her, not until he conceded to more than just sweet feelings for her. How could she tell him that she loved him and then reveal that her father had been connected to his enemies? He would hate her.

She waited silently.

Giving a little laugh and shaking his head, he said, "I am here to…" His words trailed off and he stared down at his hands holding hers. When he spoke again, his voice was low, and his gaze remained averted. "The history I told you of how the Sphere of Astarte came into existence is true. It was created by a wizard for the goddess Astarte, and it is magical. It gives life and prosperity to the land. But it was never stolen from my family. Nulkana was an advisor to my ancestor, and she wanted the power of the Sphere, for it bestows great power, wealth, and immortality on any individual who knows how to use it. When my ancestor discovered her fiendish plot to steal it from beneath the Castello Auriano, where it had remained for centuries, he broke it apart and sent the pieces far away, so Nulkana would never be able to find them, so she would never be able to use its power. When the sorceress discovered what he had done, she killed him and cursed his descendants.

"My ancestors lived with this curse for many generations. Then my father found one of the pieces of the Sphere and kept it hidden for years. It helped to abate some of the effects of the curse, and he and my mother were able to live an almost normal life. But Nulkana had found a way to remain alive all those years through dark magic. When my father realized Nulkana still lived and had discovered he had the piece, he sent it away. I think he must have sent it to your late husband."

Realizing that he was giving her a gift, she interjected with a gift of her own. "He sent it to my father," she said. "It was his before Richard took possession of it."

"Your father." Raising his head, he looked at her with a tiny smile. "A closer connection than I thought."

They were connected in too many ways. Sabrina slipped her hand from his grasp, immediately missing his warmth, but wanting to break the connection. She needed to become used to the lack of his touch, for she would leave with Evan as soon as she returned to Dunfield's *casa*. Alessandro could never know that her presence near him endangered his life. She suspected he would laugh at her fears as he did in the vineyard when she revealed what she had overheard at the cavaliere's villa. Better he should think her heartless than to be killed.

A small line appeared between his brows as he gazed at her hands folded demurely on her knees. To distract him, she continued his story. "So when your father sent the piece of the Sphere away, the curse overcame him again."

"*Si*. You saw what Nulkana did to my parents. After the destruction of our *castello*, my brother and I came to our *casa* in Venice."

"And your sister?"

He sent her a surprised glance, then murmured, "I wondered what you and Gasparo were chatting about yesterday." Taking a breath, he said, "I sent her to Paris, to hide her. When the curse takes hold, Antonio and I come here."

"Explain the curse to me, Excellency."

He was silent for a moment, then, quietly, he said, "You have met my brother in the clutches of the curse. Tonio helped you when Nulkana injured me. He slowed down the birds when they attacked. For a fortnight, half of every month, he is Shadow. When the moon is full again, he becomes human, but that is when the Hunger takes hold of him. His appetites are overwhelming for two days. If he does not feed them, he will revert back to Shadow for the rest of his life."

"The moonstone," she said, suddenly understanding. "It dampens the Hunger."

"*Si*."

Before he glanced away, Sabrina saw the desolation in his eyes, and something else. She needed to know. "The night you had me kidnapped—"

"The curse touches all members of the House of Auriano," he interrupted.

"And the night before the kidnapping, in my bedchamber... ?"

"What happened in your bedchamber, *cara mia*?" His golden gaze landed on her, wryly inquisitive.

Suddenly embarrassed by what had occurred, she shook her head. "Nothing." Perhaps the shadow man had been Tonio, and he had been lying when he denied being there.

Alessandro sat back. He pulled a parchment from his coat and laid it on her lap. "This is yours to do with as you wish. You may destroy it, or keep it."

Puzzled, she unfolded the parchment. "Our betrothal contract." She breathed, something unraveling painfully in her chest. "You are releasing me?"

"If you wish it."

"But why?"

His gaze was shuttered when he answered. "I cannot make you join a family that is cursed. You and your son deserve more than that."

"But Dunfield—"

"I will take care of *Sior* Dunfield," he told her flatly. "You will not have to be concerned with him because of your decision." Leaning forward again, he placed his hand over hers. "I will protect you, Sabrina, from Dunfield, from the Legion of Baal, from Nulkana, no matter what you decide."

Overwhelmed, she stood and wandered to the hearth where she stared down into the flames. Alessandro had just given her the greatest gift he ever could—the ability to choose her own destiny. Glancing back at him, she saw him watching her, waiting for her answer. His face was like stone. She looked down at the parchment in her hand once again. Conflicting emotions ran through her—elation at her freedom, a sense of loss at her release, despair at her choice to leave. And came to a conclusion.

Folding up the parchment, she tossed it onto the chair she had just vacated. "I would like to think about my decision," she said.

"Certainly." His expression turned grim, and he glanced at the contract on the chair as if he wanted it back in his hand.

"It is a very big decision." She circled the back of his chair and stood on his other side.

"A life-changing decision," he agreed solemnly, turning to look at her.

"I do not think that I should make this decision quickly." Circling behind his chair again, she tickled his ear as she passed behind him.

"That is wise," he said. With a confused look, he ducked from her teasing.

"I need a great deal of information," she said gravely as she stood before him.

"What sort of information?" His gaze was suspicious.

Placing her hands on her hips, she gave him a speculative look. "How do I know that you will not come to bed with cold hands and feet?"

Startled at her question, his eyes widened, then his lips twitched. "I promise never to have cold hands or feet."

She nodded once. "I believe that promise should be written into the contract." She studied him intently. "Or perhaps you snore."

"Snore?" His brows went up in disbelief.

"Yes. I certainly would not wish to be awakened by such an ungodly noise." She gave him a severe frown.

"I promise you," he said, placing a hand over his heart, "I have never snored in my life."

"Can you be sure? Have you ever heard that you do not?" At his confused frown, she waved her hand, dismissing the subject. "There are so many other things I need to discover. For instance, do you like strawberries?"

"Very much," he nodded solemnly.

"Would you like to make love to me?"

He froze. She watched him try to absorb her question. His loss of composure was endearing. Taking pity on him, she framed his beautiful face with her hands. He had offered her freedom — freedom from a forced betrothal, freedom to make her own choice. Freedom to run from him and the search for the Sphere and all the danger inherent in that. And for that, she loved him.

"Alessandro," she whispered. "I want you to make love to me." She kissed each corner of his mouth.

"*Carissima*," he murmured. His hand slipped up the back of her head and his fingers tangled in her curls. Using gentle pressure, his other hand at her back, he drew her down until she straddled his lap. His mouth slanted across her lips. His tongue flicked out, tasting.

Sabrina loved kissing this man, having him kiss her back. The feel of his mouth against hers fogged her brain. The touch of his hands created wicked fires all over her. He loosened the ties on her bodice and stays. His hand slipped beneath. He cupped her breast, massaged it, teased her nipple, brought it to attention. Ducking his head, he took it into his mouth and sucked, flicked it with his tongue. Her head fell back as a shot of desire pulsed deep in her center. He gave her other breast the same delicious attention. She purred.

He set her on her feet and stood. Before she realized what he was doing, he had stripped her down to her chemise. She gazed down at her skirt and petticoats puddled at her feet.

"You've had practice," she said dryly.

He grinned sheepishly and shrugged.

"I've had very little practice," she said, as she stepped out of the pool of her clothing. Turning away casually, she grabbed the rapier laying on the mantle and slid it from its sheath. "I've had very little practice with this, too," she said, examining the weapon, "but I understand it can be formidable in the right hands." She waved it experimentally before her.

"Please be careful with that, *cara mia*," he said, alarm running beneath his words. "It is very sharp."

Glancing at him beneath her lashes, she saw wariness in his eyes. A smile curled her lips. "Then it will easily cut the buttons from your waistcoat." She held the point inches from one of those very buttons.

With a finger, he pushed the point of the weapon aside. "If you don't mind, I'd prefer to unbutton them myself."

She grinned. "By all means, please do so."

Quickly, he slipped off his coat and waistcoat and let them drop to the floor.

Letting the rapier rest on his shoulder, she said, "Untie your stock."

She watched as he silently pulled apart the intricate folds and stripped it from around his neck.

"Shirt." She waved the weapon near his chest.

Smoothly, he pulled the garment over his head and let it drop.

Pointing again with the rapier, she said, "Boots. Stockings."

His gaze narrowed. "What if I refuse?"

"Then we can work on the buttons of your breeches." She brought up the point of the rapier and waved it in that general vicinity. Those buttons were already straining.

Alarm flashed through his eyes. Sitting, he quickly removed his footwear.

She rested the rapier once more across his shoulder. "Stand up, please. Breeches next."

He stood, but his eyes were wicked as he slowly undid each button and pushed the breeches from his hips. They slid to the floor, and he stepped out of them. "Now what?" he challenged.

She pursed her lips thoughtfully. "Perhaps you should ask if you may kiss me."

His gaze focused on her mouth so intently she imagined she could feel the pressure of his lips. In a single swift motion, he slipped beneath the weapon, grabbed her about the waist, and disarmed her. Dropping the rapier, he kicked it away with his heel. She found herself crushed against him.

"May I kiss you?" he whispered. Without waiting for her answer, he did just that.

Sabrina invited him in. Wrapping her arms about him, she pressed herself against him, from shoulders to toes. His hardness was a counterpoint to her softness. His erection nestled in the hollow of her hip. They fit together exactly, like pieces of a puzzle.

His tongue slipped inside her mouth and stroked, teased. All rational thought fled her mind. She wanted only this, only him. When he raised his head, all she could see were those glittering golden eyes.

Sweeping her up into his arms, he carried her to the bed. He knelt over her and braced himself above her.

"Will you try to run away?" he asked.

"If I do, will you try to catch me?" Her question was half-teasing, half-serious.

He shook his head. "Your decision, your game this time, *cara mia.*"

"No, I won't run away." Blushing, smiling, she swept her fingers across his cheek and cupped the back of his neck. "Kiss me again."

He did. Stretching out beside her, he kissed every inch of her thoroughly. He started at her jaw and trailed his tongue down the column of her throat. He nipped at her shoulder, then placed light kisses across her collarbone. As he kissed, his fingers roamed across her skin, along her arm, over her ribs. His mouth, his lips, his fingers made her feel worshipped and precious. She spread her arms wide in languorous abandon.

Then his mouth fastened on her breast and he sucked. She felt an arrow of desire spear through her. He cupped her other breast and rolled the nipple between his thumb and finger. She pressed up into his hand with a breathy moan. Her husband had never given her such pleasure.

"More." She sighed. All she wanted was him — touching, kissing, outside, inside.

He chuckled. "*Avida civetta.*" Greedy minx.

His fingers slid across her belly and down between her thighs. He touched her where she most wanted him to be. Desire and need tangled and danced.

"I want to taste you," he murmured.

His words echoed what he had said when he had kidnapped her. At the time, she thought that was a ludicrous, shocking notion. Now, all she could think of was those glorious lips on her. She wanted to feel him kissing her there. She wanted to know the feeling. She wanted to know if it would feel as delicious as his fingers. Her thighs fell apart in mute submission. His mouth tipped up in an intimate, sly grin, and then that mouth was on her. He licked and sucked gently, expertly. She writhed and whimpered, gasped and moaned as sensations she had never experienced swept over her. And then pleasure exploded through her in a shower of stars.

She lay panting in the aftermath. She had not been disappointed.

"That was…" She could find no words.

He laughed. "Sensuous? Delicious?"

She smiled wryly. He had used those exact words when he had kidnapped her. "*Si,*" she said. "*Grazie.*"

He knelt over her and licked one of his fingers. "We're not done, *carissima*."

Sabrina found she *wasn't* done. She thought she could never feel anything more wonderful than what she had just experienced. She was mistaken. He circled one nipple with his wet finger. Need shot through her again and throbbed between her thighs. She wanted more of him. Much more.

She needed to touch him. Her hands roved over his shoulders, down his chest. His skin was warm velvet. As her fingers wandered, his hands glided over her. His mouth and tongue followed. And then, with a mischievous smile, he lifted his hand just the tiniest bit and skimmed it over her hip, into the curve of her waist. Sparkling tingles erupted everywhere his hand roamed. The sensation was potent and magical. It made her gasp in surprise and delight. He continued across her breast, and down to the crux of her thighs. She squirmed and mewled in unrestrained desire. She thought she had experienced ecstasy with his mouth on her. This was so much more. This was beyond what she had experienced when he had connected with her mind, when his mind had spiraled around hers in a myriad of colors and he had asked her to dance with him. This touch-but-not-touch was part of him. It was what made him special. And she knew it was part of what drew her to him.

But thoughts and reasons were too hard to grasp. She clung to his shoulders as she arched up, straining for more. The tingles were exquisite agony. She whimpered and moaned her passion. Her toes curled. Her muscles clenched. And then in a wild eruption, the tempest took her, tossing her into the whirlwind as she flew apart.

She might have lost consciousness for a moment. Her eyes were closed when she became aware of his hand caressing her cheek, of his arm cradling her against his chest. She snuggled against him.

"Mmm," she purred. "You have devilish hands, Excellency."

His chuckle vibrated in her ear. "Because you tempt me like Eve." He nipped her earlobe. "I want to see you come apart again."

Sabrina had never envisioned that being with a man could be so joyous, that a man could be so generous. Alessandro brought her to delicious, mindless, explosive rapture more times than she could count. And he taught her things about her body that she never would have learned in her sterile marriage bed with her late husband.

After one glorious interlude, she was sprawled across him and enjoying the sensation of his skin against hers. Propping herself on her elbows, she gazed down into his eyes.

"I want to kiss you like you have kissed me," she said.

With a seductive smile, he spread his arms wide. "Do whatever you will."

Like a child with a new toy, she set out to explore, first with her fingers, and then with her mouth. When she toyed with his nipples, he sucked in a breath. His response caused the blood to rush through her veins. She licked lower, across his abdomen. He held his breath. His erection brushed her cheek. She ran her tongue up its satiny side. His breath exploded in a rush.

Surprised at the organ's delicate skin, pleased at his reaction, she took it into her mouth. A low rumble sounded deep in his throat. A throb echoed deep inside her. He grabbed her shoulders, pulled her up across his chest, and rolled her to her back.

"I can't hold out much longer," he said. "You are making me insane." His voice was oddly strained.

"I'm sorry. I didn't mean to hurt you."

Humor swept across his face. "You didn't hurt me. Just the opposite."

Confusion made her frown. "Then?"

"We are going to make love, *carissima*."

Without giving her a chance to respond, he kissed her, driving out any doubt about what he had in mind. "Open your eyes," he whispered against her mouth. "I want you to look at me when I give you pleasure."

Dazed with need, she did. And then he was inside her. She took him in, swallowed him into her deepest part, caressed him, met each thrust with one of her own. Her world dissolved down to the single being who connected with her, the man who held her soul in his hands. She clung to him. He was the only solid thing in a cosmos of swirling mist. She thought he had given her pleasure before, but having him inside her took her to heaven.

They exploded at the same time.

She plummeted through miles of nothing.

Until she settled softly, clutching him with her arms and her legs. He was the only real thing in her universe. He had broken apart her world and rearranged it in a new pattern.

Nuzzling her neck, he held her tightly. They dozed, sated, still connected.

She awoke with him throbbing inside her. He trailed kisses up her neck and breathed into her ear, "I want to make love to you again."

He rolled onto his back, taking her with him. She gasped with pleasure at feeling him buried so deeply inside her. Straddling him, she gazed down into those soft golden eyes, at his seductive smile. He was the beginning and ending of her world. How had that happened? He was the here and now. How long could she make that last? She moved on him, and once again the whirlwind of their lovemaking carried her beyond thought.

They rested, and made love again, and again, until exhausted, they collapsed, entangled together, bound by more than limbs clutching limbs.

Just before she slipped into sleep, she thought she heard him whisper, "*Ti amo.*" I love you.

Her heart swelled with joy. Then shriveled as she realized she would never hear those words again.

Sabrina awoke slowly, drifting from sleep to wakefulness. She felt well loved and lethargic, and more alive than she had ever felt before. Smiling, reaching out, she expected to feel Alessandro lying next to her, but the rest of the bed was empty and cold. He had been gone for some time. Disappointment jabbed through her. With a sigh, she flopped onto her back.

Sabrina, she heard in her head.

Confused, she propped herself on her elbow and scanned the room. The fire had died back to embers, and the candle had gone out. With such little light, shadows to hide in were plentiful. One shadow detached itself from the rest and crouched on the footboard of the bed.

"Tonio?" she asked, pulling the covers close. As soon as she spoke, she knew that was not right.

Alessandro. The name whispered in her brain.

She stared at the shadow man as she tried to connect what she was seeing with what she had heard. *Alessandro.* The warm, passionate, flesh and bone man who had made glorious love to her only a few short hours ago had become Shadow, as cursed as his brother.

No, it could not be. It was not true. When he had spoken of the curse, he had told of his brother's torment, not his.

Not his.

Frightened, appalled, she scrambled back against the headboard and pulled the covers up to her chin.

"Alessandro?" Her voice came out tiny, pleading for him to deny it.

Si.

"No," she cried. "It's not true."

Sabrina. He moved closer, perching within reach.

"Don't touch me." She flinched away.

He emanated grim humor. *Are we going to have the same conversation we had in your bedchamber?*

"So that *was* you, not Tonio."

Of course. Do you think if Tonio had taken such liberties, he would still be walking around? I nearly murdered him last night when I saw him touching you.

His statement warmed her. Her sense of betrayal was stronger. "You lied to me."

No, I did not. I have never lied to you.

"When I asked about the curse, you told me about Tonio, not you."

I said that all members of the House of Auriano are affected.

"That told me nothing," she snapped.

I am here, now, before you. Does that say nothing?

She turned away, not wanting to accept his truth. Although he had not lied, he had not been straightforward. He had deceived her. She had been blinded, touched by his gift of the betrothal contract. She had given herself to him, and that had been glorious, but, too late, he had revealed what he was. He became Shadow every month, and then returning to human form again, endured the Hunger. The vision of Tonio the night before, tormented and ravaged, rose up before her. The same thing happened to Alessandro. Every month. How could she expose Evan to that? Frightened, horrified, on the edge of panic, all she wanted to do was flee. A hole had opened in her heart and bled anguish.

"Friends do not keep secrets from each other," she accused, even as guilt at keeping her own secret twisted in her.

We have both kept secrets, he said. *But we are more than friends, cara mia.*

That was one thing he spoke truly, but it was the one truth she could not face, not yet, if at all. "I want to leave," she said.

Whenever you wish.

He reached out to her, and she jerked away.

Sabrina.

Her pendant dangled in the air between them.

It cures the Hunger, he said. *Tonio is grateful that you let him borrow it.*

Now she understood the meaning of that rhyme her mother had taught her. The moonstone must have been charmed centuries ago in order to counteract the effects of the curse. Her possession of it, and its obvious connection to the House of Auriano scared her. She forced the thought away.

She had not believed that he would return the pendant, but her chagrin at his proving her wrong only added to her anger. As she watched, it floated the short distance between them, then slipped over her head and settled around her neck.

"Another trick of the mind?" she bit out.

Once again, grim humor laced his tone. *Si. Useful when one has no solid body or sense of touch.*

Surprised, she stared. "But you can feel me." She remembered the night in her bedchamber when he had admitted to his desire to touch her, when his touch had left a tingling trail of warmth.

You are the only one I can feel when I am Shadow.

The ramifications of that statement made her want to hide beneath the covers.

We are connected, cara mia, whether you wish to believe it or not.

295

"We are not," she denied hotly, even as the lie mocked her. Then the truth of their connection crystalized. "You pursued me because of the piece of the Sphere."

His gaze skittered away. *At first.* Those golden eyes came to rest on her once more, piercing in their directness. *But not now.*

Sabrina wanted to believe him, but his reticence in revealing his curse kept her wary. He had too many secrets. What else might he be hiding? How could she expose Evan to such risk?

Making her decision, she said, "You gave me the betrothal contract to do with as I wish. I am going to tear it up, then burn the pieces."

He turned away, and she thought he was trying to hide his hurt. Instead, when he turned back to her, the parchment floated down onto her lap, his eyes flat. Picking it up, daring him to stop her, she tore it in two.

Would you like me to toss it into the fire for you? he asked with an edge.

"Bastard," she hissed. "You tricked me. You never meant to go through with a marriage at all."

I did. I still do. We might have made twins this night.

Sabrina emitted a strangled cry of rage, but whether it was at him or herself for being a fool, she was not quite sure. She wanted to lash out and searched for something to throw at him. The rapier lay across the room. All other surfaces were bare. She had only pillows as weapons. One after another, she whipped them in his direction.

"Rogue." One pillow. "Devil." Another pillow. "Knave." And another. "Villain. Cad. Rascal."

She heard a snicker of laughter. *Rascal?*

Her pillows were gone. He had easily dodged them all. And now he was cocksure enough to taunt her. Furious, she stared him down.

"I never want to see you again," she spat. Even as she said the words, she knew she was speaking the truth, for she would be gone before he realized it. Despite her rage, her heart shriveled at the thought that she would never see him again.

His humor fled. *Do you really think you can keep me away?* The question was a velvety threat.

He leaped at her. His force pushed her back against the mattress. She was flat on her back with him above her. He pinned both her wrists over her head. She could not feel his weight, but tingly warmth pulsed where his hands wrapped around her wrists and every place where his Shadow covered her body.

Tell me you do not feel me. Tell me you hate my touch.

She opened her mouth to say the words but found she could not form them. She loved his touch. She loved *him*. As flesh and bone, as Shadow. Even now, she throbbed deep in her core. She closed her mouth again, turning away.

I've never made love as Shadow, he said. *The idea intrigues me.*

He was baiting her. The idea intrigued her, too. But she was not going to allow him to follow through on his notion.

"Let me go." She tried to wriggle free, a useless exercise. Even as Shadow, using only his mind, he was much stronger.

Our connection goes beyond betrothal contracts, cara mia. You cannot fight fate.

Despite the truth of his statement, fate or not, she was furious and bruised by his deception. She stayed perfectly still, stared up into his molten eyes, and waited stonily for him to release her.

His edgy chuckle echoed in her head. He traced his lips down her jaw, leaving a heated trail. Then abruptly, she was free. He stood beside the bed.

I will send a maid to attend you, he said, *and Gasparo will take you home.*

She closed her eyes in relief. The battle she waged was not just with him, but with herself. Despite the pain of his deceit, she wanted him. Yet, she had known from their first meeting she could not have him. How could she have forgotten?

By the time she opened her eyes again, he was gone.

Chapter 26

The morning after Sabrina's glorious, devastating night with Alessandro, she watched from the *pergola* outside her bedchamber as Dunfield stepped from the gondola to the steps before the water gate. He had returned from Milan, and she would have to tread carefully as she planned her escape. Wherever she and Evan went, she wanted to be sure he would be safe. Dunfield scowled up at her before he disappeared into the *andron*. With a sigh, she returned inside to await his summons.

She did not have long to wait.

When she entered his study, he was pouring himself a brandy. As he turned to her, she realized that his usual controlled poise had been shaken. Lines about his eyes and mouth had deepened, adding years to his appearance. As one of those men who seemed to be of an indeterminate age, this change in him was startling. Something had happened at the cavaliere's villa that deeply disturbed him.

"Sabrina." Dunfield nodded a greeting. Without offering her a seat, he sat in one of the chairs before the fire. Silent for a moment, he stared at the flames, then turned to her. His eyes ran over her. "I have been informed that you allowed Auriano to bed you."

Sabrina clenched her teeth. He had set his servants to spy on her. Forcing herself to speak mildly, she said, "What I do on my own time does not concern you."

"Everything you do concerns me, Sabrina," he said, the words a threat instead of reassurance.

Angrily, she placed herself in front of him and announced, "Then I will tell you before you learn it from your spies. Auriano and I have decided to dissolve the agreement of betrothal."

His gaze narrowed. "You have no right to dissolve the agreement. It was between Auriano and myself."

Raising her chin, she declared, "Since I am the one who was to marry him, I think I have some say in how I will spend the rest of my life."

"You gave up all rights to your life when you came to live with me." Dismissively, he took a sip of brandy.

Sabrina knew that she had lost control of her world when she had bargained with him for a roof over her head, but she had not realized just how much she had lost. "I am not some piece of artwork that you can auction off to the highest bidder."

His chuckle was cold. "You are quite right. You are more than that, my dear Sabrina. You are a lifelong connection to Auriano, with all its benefits."

Searching for arguments, she said, "Even if I marry him, there is no guarantee that his influence would extend to you."

"You will make sure that it does."

"I'm not marrying him." Mulishly, she crossed her arms.

"Why not? After spending the night in his bed have you discovered that he cannot perform?"

Her cheeks burned. Alessandro had "performed" so well that she knew no other man would ever come close. But he had deceived her. And she was going to leave him.

Casually, without letting on where her thoughts traveled, she said, "Auriano and I have decided that we would not make a good match."

Dunfield's eyes narrowed. "Auriano's decision, or yours, Sabrina?"

She refused to answer.

"It was your decision, wasn't it, Sabrina? I have seen his reaction to you. He is smitten. He requested your hand after knowing you for only a few days."

Sabrina knew Alessandro had not requested her hand in marriage because he was in love with her, but because of her connection to the Sphere of Astarte. "He has changed his mind."

"Why? Did you not perform in his bed as you should have? Were you cold and frigid?"

When she remained silent, he rose and grabbed her arm. "You will rectify this, Sabrina. You will marry Auriano."

"I will not." She tried to pull from his grasp, but he held her tightly.

"You will marry Auriano, or I will put you and your son on the first ship to England."

She would not let him intimidate her. "Let me go. You are hurting me," she said, as she tried to free herself again.

He shook her. "You cannot run from me, Sabrina. I know what you are."

"You know nothing about me." Her brave words hid the fear that he would invoke her connection to the Sphere of Astarte.

"I know what power you have," he said smugly.

She shook her head, denying what he was saying.

"I saw what happened when you went near the Crystal Dagger."

His eyes held no mercy, but she would admit to nothing. "I don't know what you are talking about."

"I know you and Auriano stole the Crystal Dagger." That icy gaze drilled her.

Her first instinct was to protect Alessandro, despite what he had done to her. "He doesn't have it." As soon as she said the words, she knew she had said too much.

Dunfield smiled cruelly. "Then perhaps you could tell me where it is."

It was Sabrina's turn to smile. "You will never get your hands on it."

He shook her again. "Where is it?" His fingers bit into her arm.

Her chin went up. "General Bonaparte, the French general, has it."

With a growl of rage, he pushed her from him. She stumbled and grabbed a chair. Her power began to sizzle down her arm, but she banked it, reserving it for another time. She was safe for now. Dunfield, deep in thought, paced across the room and back. He might be able to withhold his protection from her, but his desire for the connection to Alessandro was stronger than his rage.

Stopping before her, he said, "You will send a message to Auriano. You will apologize for any insult you might have given him. You will ask—no, beg—for his forgiveness. And you will offer him anything if he will mend the breach between you."

She shook her head. "No, I won't."

"You will." He dragged her to the chair behind his desk and forced her into it. "You will write the note, Sabrina," he said quietly, "or I will retract my protection from Evan. And don't think you can spirit him away. If I suspect anything, I will remove him to another location. You will remain here, but I will find another use for the boy."

Her insides turned cold. "What would you do? Please, he is only a child."

"He is a very clever, attractive little boy. A child like that has many uses, and could be worth a fortune."

Horrified, Sabrina's imagination ran wild with the vile possibilities he implied. Evan could be placed on a ship bound for the slave markets in the East, or sold to one of the houses of prostitution, or...

Bending over her, Dunfield whispered, "Perhaps Nulkana would enjoy having such a child as an apprentice."

She gasped. "You wouldn't dare approach her."

"I wouldn't have to. Nulkana would be able to find the child on her own. A descendent of Halima..." He shrugged. "All I would have to do is leave the child some place in the city."

His calculating leer turned Sabrina's stomach.

He tsked and shook his head. "Did you think I was unaware of who you are? Did you think I took you in out of kindness, that I knew nothing about your mother?" He pulled a piece of parchment before her. "Write the note, Sabrina. I will dictate."

Sabrina fought for breath. Grasping at one last argument, she said, "Auriano is away from the city for a fortnight."

"Then explain to me why I passed him on the Grand Canal." The satisfaction at catching her in a lie swirled through his words.

Hope drained from her. Dunfield had seen Antonio, not Alessandro. She couldn't reveal their secret. Defeated, she took up her quill, dipped it in the inkpot, and bowed her head over the parchment.

In the predawn light, a cloaked, muffled figure arrived at the water gate of the Ca' D'Este and debarked from his gondola. Antonio, completely human again after two weeks of being Shadow and the agonizing hours of the Hunger, waited in the depths of the *andron*. Clothed in a blood red brocade dressing gown, a statement that he was not pleased to be roused at such an early hour, he watched the darkly cloaked visitor come through the iron gates that guarded the entrance. The space was lit only by a few sconces along the wall. The huge chandelier hanging from the ceiling two floors above was dark. In the center of the dim space were two finely carved wooden armchairs with a low inlaid table between. Antonio stood beside one of the chairs as the man approached.

The visitor removed his muffler and hat and greeted him with a curt nod. "Excellency."

Antonio returned the greeting. "General Bonaparte." Indicating the chair opposite him, Antonio sat in the other. "Please, General, make yourself comfortable. May I offer you some refreshment? Coffee from Arabia, or oranges from Jerusalem, perhaps?"

The mention of the imported delicacies indicated the complete disregard for the blockade the French general had thrown up around Venice and demonstrated the power of the House of Auriano. Antonio waved his hand, and a servant appeared with a tray laden with fruit, pastries, a silver coffee pot, and porcelain cups and saucers. The two men remained silent as the servant placed the tray on the table, then disappeared.

Bonaparte did not sit. "This is not a social call, Excellency, nor do I appreciate the offer of contraband."

With a slight smile, Antonio said, "You are in Venice, General, and even when we conduct business here, we bow to the social graces and offer our guests the best we have."

Bonaparte frowned. "I am not Venetian, Excellency, and I am waging war, so I have no time for the social graces."

"Then by all means, state your business. I would not want to hold up your war." Antonio tempered his mocking tone with a smile.

The general did not return the smile. "I am not used to such patent deception as you and your betrothed practiced upon me."

Antonio heard his brother's chuckle in his head, but he refrained from glancing up at the mezzanine railing where Alessandro was perched, just another shadow among the shadows. As soon as they had received word that the French general wished to make a clandestine visit to their *palazzo,* Sandro had told Antonio the story of how he and Sabrina had fooled the Frenchman.

Antonio forced himself to keep a straight face as he answered. "What deception is that, General?"

Pulling a wrapped bundle from beneath his cloak, Bonaparte unwound the cloth and revealed the Crystal Dagger. He took it by the hilt and stabbed it into the wood of the table before him. "That," he said, "does not perform as you said it would."

Having never seen it before, Antonio stared at the piece. In the subdued light of the *andron,* the subtle pulsing of the Dagger appeared dull and lifeless. Sandro had told him how it glowed with a multi-hued array in Sabrina's presence. Despite its present drab appearance and its danger, he was fascinated by it.

Raising his eyes to the man across from him, he asked, "Did it not give you the answers you were seeking, General?"

"The purpose for its existence that your betrothed gave me was false. I seek the truth about this artifact, and I believe that you, Excellency, know what that truth is."

Antonio raised a brow. "And if I do not give you this truth you seek, General? What then?"

Bonaparte's eyes narrowed angrily. "My patience with Venice is growing very thin. If I enter the city with my troops, I cannot guarantee that the Ca' d'Este or its inhabitants will escape unscathed from my soldiers' desire for plunder."

With a frown, Antonio asked, "Are you threatening the House of Auriano, General?"

"I am looking for answers, Excellency."

Perhaps we can use him to our advantage, Sandro said silently.

Antonio settled his gaze on the dagger as if he were deep in thought, studying it, as he replied to Sandro, *Another player in the game would muddy the waters.*

But perhaps a new player might keep the Dagger away from Sabrina, Sandro suggested. *Gift him with the piece. Make him take it.*

I'll see what I can do, Antonio agreed. Keeping his eyes on the Dagger, he said aloud to the general, "Have you ever heard the legend of the curse of the House of Auriano, General?"

"Curses are nonsense from fairy tales." Bonaparte dismissed the story with a wave of his hand.

Raising his head, Antonio looked the general in the eye. "I assure you, this curse is not. The artifact before you was created to kill the sorceress who placed the curse on my family."

"A sorceress?" Napoleon scoffed. "Surely, you don't expect me to believe you."

"Believe what you wish," Antonio said with a shrug, "but even you must see that the Dagger pulses."

The general studied the Dagger. Finally, he asked, "Who could create such a thing?"

"A group of men who call themselves the Legion of Baal."

The general's eyes widened.

At the man's reaction, Antonio smiled without humor. "I see you have heard of them."

Bonaparte frowned. "Of course I have. There is a hive of them in Paris. They are insurrectionists. Anarchists. Devil worshippers."

Antonio nodded. "*Si.* They seek power, wealth, and immortality. They feel that if they can kill the sorceress with this weapon, they will gain everything they seek."

That's a new twist on an old story, Sandro remarked wryly.

Ignoring his brother, reaching into the pocket of his dressing gown, Antonio pulled out the button Sandro had cut from the messenger's coat the night Sabrina had first used her power. He tossed it onto the table, where it spun as if creating its own spell before coming to a rolling halt. "A button that belonged to one of your aides, General. The man was a member of the Legion. He was... dispatched."

Anger darkened Bonaparte's face. "You killed my aide."

"He was interfering in something he should not have."

"He was gathering information for me."

"He was a danger to those who met with him, and to you."

"Impossible." Napoleon's hand slashed through the air. "All of my aides are loyal."

"Then perhaps you know more about the Legion of Baal than you are willing to admit," Antonio speculated. "Perhaps you sent your aide to gather more than information."

"The instructions to my aide were confidential, Excellency," Bonaparte said coolly.

Antonio realized there was a very shrewd mind behind the bland gaze. With a shrug, pretending indifference, Antonio said, "As you wish. It is, of course, your army, your war. To prove our good faith, we would like you to have the Crystal Dagger."

The general's gaze was suspicious. "Why wouldn't you want the Dagger yourself?"

"We cannot use it, and the Dagger is harmful in the wrong hands. We believe you would keep it safe."

General Bonaparte was silent as he stared at the Dagger. Finally, he shook his head. "This is trumpery, some sort of sleight of hand. The Legion of Baal is merely a cadre of bored aristocrats seeking excitement. I will wipe them out as soon as I return to Paris." He narrowed his eyes. "And you, Excellency, insult me with your tales of curses and sorcery."

Antonio could not help but admire Bonaparte's guile. The man would be a formidable opponent at the gaming tables. Silently, he told Sandro, *Be prepared to reveal yourself. I think the general needs to be shocked into cooperation.* "Perhaps," he said aloud, "you would like to meet my brother. He might shed some light on your confusion." With a wave of his hand, he indicated the shadows high above near the ceiling.

Bonaparte glanced up. He gaped in astonishment as he saw a shadow figure with eyes of molten gold drift down to land softly beside Antonio. "*Sacré bleu.*" He breathed, falling back a step. His hand went to his sword.

Sandro executed a formal bow. *Buongiorno, General*, he said, allowing the man to hear his words in his mind, then jerked his hand in an upward sweep. The Crystal Dagger slid from where it was stuck in the table and floated before Bonaparte. *We would like you to keep this for us. If you cannot accept it as a gift, consider it a loan.* He completed his demonstration by wrapping the Dagger in the cloth that had covered it. When the Frenchman did not move to take it, he added, *Please.*

Bonaparte stared. "Who—what are you?"

I am the product of the curse. Surely you did not think that my brother was telling an untruth. He floated the Dagger closer to the Frenchman. *Please, General, take the Dagger.*

Nervously, the Frenchman reached out and took hold of the piece. "What am I to do with this?"

Use it or not, as you wish, Sandro told him. *It is a gift.*

Bonaparte glanced suspiciously between the flesh and blood man and the Shadow. "What will you demand in return?"

"Nothing, for now," Antonio said, "except to keep secret what you have learned here this morning. Perhaps later, we might ask a favor."

"And if I decide not to grant it?" Napoleon asked shrewdly.

"That is your decision." Antonio stood, signaling the end of the visit.

The French general tucked the Dagger away beneath his cloak, placed his hat on his head and took his leave. When his gondola had floated away from the water gate, Sandro said, *He is a determined man. I don't think we've seen the last of him.*

Si. Antonio nodded. *We may need him soon.* Dismissing the Frenchman, he said, *While you were watching over Sabrina last evening, we received a letter from our sister.*

What does Allegra have to say?

She sends her love as always but says that she has become fearful of living in Paris.

Why?

Antonio shrugged. *Nothing specific. Perhaps she is merely imagining a threat.*

You do not truly believe that. Sandro moved to stand before his brother.

No. Now that General Bonaparte has confirmed the presence of the Legion in Paris, one of us should go there. Antonio let his gaze wander from his brother's head to his toes and back up again. Then he grinned. "You're in no condition to travel." *Besides*, he added silently, *you need to make amends with Sabrina.*

Sandro jumped up to the mezzanine railing. *Sabrina will never...* His bleak tone and unfinished thought revealed how deeply he suffered. His twin had never been so affected by a woman's rejection.

Surprised and sympathetic to his brother's torment, Antonio gazed at him a moment. Then his attention was drawn to a servant boy climbing out of a gondola. Beyond him, the sun glinted off the water of the canal. During their interview with Bonaparte, the day had begun.

"A message, Excellency," the boy called upon seeing him.

Antonio retrieved it and tossed an orange to the boy before dismissing him. He glanced at the writing on the outside and held it out for his brother. *It seems you were wrong about Donna Barclay,* he said. *She has sent you a letter.* He watched Sandro float slowly down to the floor once more and land before him. Opening the letter for his brother, he placed it on the table, then walked away to allow him some privacy.

Before he reached the stairway, Sandro stopped him. *Tonio. You can't leave for Paris yet. Sabrina has asked me to take her to the opera.*

Antonio's brow lifted in surprise. "But you told me she—"

Si. There is something wrong. This note doesn't sound like her. She does not merely ask. She begs.

"Perhaps she's had a change of mind," Tonio suggested.

Alessandro shook his head. *She made it quite clear she did not wish to see me ever again. And I do not believe she would ever beg for anything. She knows I cannot take her to the opera as Shadow. You will have to go in my place.*

With a grin, Antonio sauntered back to the center of the room and stood across the table from his brother. "I'm not sure I can endure the hardship of taking a charming, beautiful woman to the opera."

Be serious, Alessandro snapped. *She could be in danger.*

Or she could be playing you for a fool, Antonio suggested.

Alessandro stared at his brother, then stared down at the note. *You will have to discover which.*

As I mentioned, a true hardship, Antonio said.

Beware, Tonio. I'll be watching. To underscore his warning, Sandro lifted a sliced peach into the air and squeezed it over his brother's head.

"Why did you do that?" Antonio complained as he wiped the juice from his eyes.

Just to remind you that Sabrina is forbidden territory. Sandro returned to the mezzanine railing.

"Perhaps she prefers me as the more charming and debonair twin," Antonio taunted.

Si, Sandro agreed. *And perhaps you might like to live long enough to see your next birthday.*

Laughing at his brother's threat, Antonio poured himself a cup of coffee.

Chapter 27

When Sabrina entered the small salon, both Dunfield and the Prince of Auriano rose to greet her. At first, she thought Alessandro was standing across the room, that his appearance as a Shadow had been a horrible dream. Then she realized her mistake. This was Antonio who stood before her, just as handsome, just as charismatic. But not Alessandro.

He bowed and greeted her. "*Donna* Barclay."

She curtsied. "Excellency." Raising her head to look at him, she realized something else about this twin. He was not an exact replica of his brother, but a mirror image. That devastating male dimple was in his left cheek, not his right. And on his left thumb, a gold band winked, an item that Alessandro never wore.

He moved forward, took her hand, and raised it to his lips. "You are ravishing this evening, *bella mia*," he murmured.

Sabrina had dressed carefully in an ivory taffeta gown decorated with gold embroidery across the bodice. A small white feather curled down one side of her head and around her ear. She wanted nothing about this evening to alert Dunfield's suspicions. Smiling coolly, she slipped her fingers from Tonio's grasp. "Thank you, Excellency." Uncomfortable seeing him as flesh and bone, particularly after he had accosted her at the Canal of Shadows, she was not quite sure how to proceed. She was, however, grateful that he had agreed to step in and play out this farce for Dunfield's benefit. "I am so glad you are able to accompany me to the opera this evening."

"It is my pleasure, *Donna* Barclay," he murmured.

His seductive smile and warm gaze almost made her forget that it was not Alessandro before her. Almost.

"Sabrina," Dunfield said, capturing her attention, "you will be pleased to learn that His Excellency and I have agreed upon a date for your wedding. It will take place in two weeks."

Sabrina fought for breath. Was this Dunfield's doing, or Alessandro's deceitful maneuvering? Antonio's hand closed around her arm, and he gave it a warning squeeze.

"*Donna* Barclay, are you unwell?" he murmured.

Angry that once again her life was being controlled by others, she pulled from Antonio's grasp. "I am quite well, Excellency. I was merely overcome by surprise and overwhelmed with the preparations that will have to be accomplished in such a short time."

"I think a quiet wedding would be best, *Donna* Barclay, with little fanfare. It will take place at our *castello* in Auriano," Antonio told her.

Furious at Alessandro's gambit, Sabrina had to clench her teeth to keep from screaming. Despite the fact that he had allowed her to do as she wished with the betrothal contract, he was still controlling her life. Whisking her off to Auriano would isolate her and put her at his mercy. It would also bring his enemies closer. But she had to play along if she did not want to see any harm come to Evan. Swallowing her rage, Sabrina bowed her acceptance. "Of course, Excellency. A splendid idea." With a fierce gaze that belied her words, she said, "I can't wait to see your ancestral home."

Sympathy flashed in Antonio's eyes, and he smiled with grim humor at her irony. "You may come to fall in love with Auriano, *Donna* Barclay."

His double meaning was not lost on her. What he did not know was that she already had.

Dunfield interrupted their conversation. "Ah, Evan, my boy. Come in and greet your new papa."

Evan stood in the doorway. Sabrina had no idea that Dunfield had summoned her son. If she had known, she would have prepared Evan, given him some explanation for Antonio's appearance. She prayed that he would not see the tiny difference between the twins, that he would think his friend, Sandro, stood before him.

He started forward with a grin, but then he stopped, frowned, and stared at Antonio. "You're not Alessandro," he stated bluntly.

Everyone froze.

Sabrina was the first to recover. "Evan," she reprimanded.

Dunfield was livid. "Master Evan," he said, "you will return to the nursery immediately. We will discuss your bad behavior in the morning."

Stepping in front of her son, Sabrina lifted her chin in defiance. "I will discipline my own son, Uncle."

Before Dunfield could reply, Antonio spoke. "Please, *Sior* Dunfield, he is only a child. *Donna* Barclay, may I speak with your son?"

After only a moment's hesitation, Sabrina moved aside. Antonio hunkered down before Evan.

"May I tell you a secret?" he asked the boy. At Evan's nod, he whispered something into the boy's ear.

Sabrina watched Evan's eyes grow wide. He nodded several times. Finally, he said, "I promise." With a smile, Antonio stepped back. Evan drew himself up straight, made a perfect, formal bow, and announced, "I am sorry to insult you, Excellency." Then he bowed to Dunfield. "And I am sorry to disappoint you, Uncle Dunfield. Please excuse me." Turning, he walked away like a dignified little man.

Both Sabrina and Dunfield stared at Antonio. He smiled and shrugged at Sabrina. Turning to Dunfield, he said with a chill, "The boy is embarrassed by his mistake. I trust he will not be disciplined."

Anger flashed through Dunfield's eyes before he gave a nod. "Of course not, Excellency. The boy has apologized."

Antonio sent him a dazzling smile. "Then it is time I take the lovely *Donna* Barclay to the opera." Slipping the gold embroidered, black velvet shawl from her fingers, he placed it about her shoulders, nearly bared by the deep décolletage of her gown. He took his leave of Dunfield, then with a hand at Sabrina's elbow, he guided her quickly down the stairs, out the water gate and into the waiting gondola.

Not until Gasparo had pushed the gondola away from the steps and they were floating in the middle of the canal did Sabrina feel safe enough to ask, "What did you tell Evan?"

Antonio turned to her with a smile. "A secret."

Exasperated, she huffed, "You're as much of a knave as your brother."

His smile turned to a grin. "*Si.*" Becoming serious, he said, "I told your son the truth, that Alessandro asked me to take you to the opera, and I asked him to promise not to tell anyone."

Sabrina was appalled. "How could you ask him to keep such a secret? He is only a child!"

"He is a brave boy and stronger than you think, Sabrina—may I call you that?"

She waved her hand in capitulation. No matter what she said or did, he and his brother would have their way.

Antonio continued, "If Dunfield questions your son about me, he will lie and say he made a mistake and he promised to behave."

"Evan has been taught never to lie."

"He will lie to protect his mother."

Sabrina seethed. "You coldhearted cad! You are using him to protect your secret."

"Perhaps, but by protecting our secret, we are protecting you."

"I don't need your protection," she said rashly. She was so angry she could have spit.

"Sandro believes differently. He has been watching over you since he turned to Shadow."

Every night, she had seen Alessandro crouched on the rooftop across the canal, but she had not believed he was there for her protection. She believed he was haunting her.

"I suppose this wedding that is to take place is just one more way to protect me," she accused.

"*Si.*"

"He told me he would not force me to join a cursed family," she said gloomily.

"He will explain when he wishes. I am only doing as he asks."

Frustrated, Sabrina sniped, "Do you always do as Alessandro asks?"

His expression was solemn when he spoke. "He is my brother."

Sabrina lapsed into thwarted, vexed silence. She couldn't argue with fraternal loyalty. Once again, Alessandro had outmaneuvered her. Although he had given her his copy of the betrothal contract, Dunfield still had possession of the other. The contract was still in effect, and she had been forced to capitulate in order to keep Evan out of danger from Dunfield. She had two weeks to figure out a way to stop this wedding and somehow get herself and Evan out of Dunfield's clutches and away from Nulkana's evil.

In another week, Alessandro would be flesh and bone, devastatingly seductive and dangerous. In two weeks, he would be at the altar, waiting for her. In two weeks, she would be expected to sacrifice her freedom to him. Unless she could come up with a plan.

She sat through Mozart's comic opera, the *Marriage of Figaro*, without understanding the plot or appreciating the singers. Although she was annoyed with Antonio for following his brother's instructions, she could not fault him for his kindness, nor his gentle attendance. He attempted to explain what was happening on the stage, but her mind was racing with possible solutions to her problem and she couldn't focus. Finally giving up, he merely sat beside her in companionable silence.

In the middle of the third act, she heard Alessandro in her head. *Tonio, can you sense Nulkana?*

Sabrina glanced around their box, but she couldn't see him. Antonio placed his hand over hers in warning not to give away his brother's presence.

Si, he answered silently. *But it is strange, different.*

Sabrina? Alessandro asked.

Antonio leaned close to whisper, "Don't speak. Just nod yes or no."

Sabrina had not sensed the painful probing of the sorceress, nor the whirling confusion she had experienced before. As she was about to shake her head in the negative, she felt a deep throbbing in the atmosphere beneath the music of the orchestra, more a sensation than a sound. Different from the rhythm of the music, it nonetheless had a controlled cadence. With wide eyes, she nodded to Antonio.

Take Sabrina to the Ca'D'Este, Tonio. Alessandro's words were urgent. *I'll meet you there.*

Even before his brother had finished speaking, Antonio had risen and placed Sabrina's shawl about her shoulders. Without a word, he hurried her out of the theater and to his gondola. Gasparo quickly propelled them out into the center of the canal.

"I can't go to the Ca'D'Este," Sabrina protested. "I have to see to Evan's safety."

"If you go to him now, you may be putting him in danger rather than protecting him," Antonio said. "We have to figure out what Nulkana is doing."

Unable to argue with that logic, nevertheless, Sabrina fretted. Now that she had noticed the throbbing, it seemed to vibrate up her spine and into her head. Occurring at irregular intervals, it put her on edge. She knew it also affected Antonio, for his hand fisted on his knee and his jaw clenched. But others seemed not to notice, for they passed several gondolas whose passengers acted blissfully unaware of the noise.

Finally reaching the Ca'D'Este, Antonio quickly ushered her inside. As soon as she crossed through the water gate, the shield around the *palazzo* blocked the throbbing pulse. Alessandro was waiting for them in the *andron*. Without a word, he turned and led them up the staircase to the drawing room.

Sabrina sank to a chair with relief, and Antonio leaned an elbow on the mantle. Alessandro perched on a chair across from her. *I followed the source of the pulse to its source and discovered where Nulkana has her lair*, he said. *I think you might enjoy the irony of this.* He paused dramatically. *It is in the sestiere of Cannaregio.*

Antonio straightened in stunned silence. Sabrina understood a moment later.

"The Canal of Shadows is in Cannaregio," she said.

Alessandro turned to her. *Si. Perhaps a coincidence. Perhaps not.*

"Where exactly?" Antonio asked.

In the canes, near the lagoon, Alessandro said. *I couldn't get close enough to locate it exactly. The throbbing kept me away.*

Gasparo entered the room, and everyone turned to him. "I've consulted with Piero," he said. "Neither of us has encountered anything like this before, but we have a theory. We believe that Nulkana is casting a spell of summoning, but we have no idea who or what she might be calling."

Sabrina looked from Antonio to Gasparo to Alessandro. "I can't believe that Nulkana can summon a person with a sound."

No one answered, but some communication was going on silently among the three men. Antonio and Gasparo evaded her gaze. At a gesture from Alessandro, the other two men excused themselves and left.

Sabrina bounded from her seat. "What aren't you telling me?"

Alessandro's molten eyes contemplated her a moment before he spoke. *Have you ever believed anything I told you about Nulkana's desire to exterminate you?*

"Yes, of course."

He rose before her. *No, you have not. You believe this is some fairy tale that I have spun for my amusement.*

His irritation reignited her pain at his deception and chafed against her frustration to keep him safe. "All right," she snapped. "Yes. I thought you were trying to frighten me so you could pretend to protect me."

My protection was never a pretense. His voice had an edge to it.

"You never gave me any proof that Nulkana was after me. I only saw that she was after you."

What of those four men in the field on the mainland? They came after you, not me.

"They could have been outlaws, robbers, looking for an easy target."

You know that is not true.

She dismissed his statement with a wave of her hand and walked to the other side of the room.

And the birds. They were attacking you, not me.

"So you say," she snapped.

What of your mother, Sabrina? She tried to protect you by keeping you ignorant of who you are.

Spinning to face him, she said, "Keep my mother out of this."

He continued ruthlessly. *You saw how she died. Do you wish to die, also, and leave your son an orphan?*

The idea of leaving Evan alone in the clutches of Dunfield churned her insides. Weakly, she sank onto a nearby bench. "How can I believe anything you tell me after your deception about the curse?"

He approached and crouched before her. Placing his hand over hers, he said gently, *I am trying to make you see the truth, cara mia.*

Sabrina turned away from those molten eyes, but she could not dismiss the warm tingle where his hand rested on top of hers.

Sabrina, he said, touching her cheek. *I am sorry I misled you, but I have never lied to you. What is happening now has nothing to do with what is between us.*

Refusing to speak to him, ignoring his touch, she kept her gaze averted.

Carissima. We believe Nulkana might be trying to summon you.

Sabrina's gaze swung back to him. "Me? Why me? Why not you or Antonio?"

Because you are the descendant of her sister, and you have touched the Sphere of Astarte.

"But the piece of the Sphere is gone. I have no idea where it is," she said a bit desperately.

Nulkana might think she can make you see where it is, if she can bring you before her.

"Can she do that? Make me see something that I don't know?" Fear made her words unsteady.

She is very powerful. I'm not sure what she is able to do. He paused as if turning something over in his mind. *I would like you and Evan to stay at the Ca' D'Este until we have this figured out.*

His suggestion was impossible with Dunfield's threat of keeping a close watch on Evan and possibly using him in some nefarious manner if she disobeyed, but she couldn't reveal that. If she did, Alessandro would want to storm Dunfield's casa and spirit Evan away, thus placing himself and her son in danger. Instead, she huffed an incredulous little laugh. "So that I might lose my reputation entirely? So that I will be forced to wed you if I wish to raise my head with any dignity?"

So that you and your son will be shielded, he responded flatly.

"No." Her single word hid her desperate fear. She could not surrender to him. She would remain independent and protect her son. Protect *him.*

Rising to his full height, he stared down at her. *Very well. We will try to discover exactly what Nulkana is doing.*

She looked out at the canal below the window, away from those golden eyes gone cold. "I would like to return home now."

With a nod, he moved toward the door. Before he slipped away, he stopped and turned back to her. *Sabrina,* he said, *I will always protect you.*

His words sliced through her like a blade.

Chapter 28

When Sabrina returned home, she learned from Evan's nurse that he had taken ill. He was tossing and turning in his bed. His skin was hot and dry. He awoke at her touch.

"Mama," he said. "My head hurts."

Sabrina sat on the edge of his bed and wrapped her arms around him. "Tell me, Evan. How does it hurt?"

"It pounds," he sobbed. "I hear a gong in my head."

Fear clutched at Sabrina as she held him. If she never believed anything that Alessandro had told her before, she certainly believed him now. If Evan heard the gong like she did, then perhaps Nulkana's summoning spell was affecting her son. She sent a message to Ca'D'Este to let Alessandro know.

She tried to make Evan more comfortable with a cool cloth on his head. She sat by his bed for the rest of the night. In the morning, he was no better. Dunfield summoned his physician, but she refused to let the man near her son. All he wanted to do was bleed Evan. On the third day, a potion arrived from Alessandro with a note that told her it might counteract the effects of the "evil vapors." Yet, even after she had coaxed Evan to drink it, his fever still raged.

Through it all, that dull throbbing continued, sometimes pausing for minutes, sometimes for an hour or two, but always beginning again. Sabrina felt she might go mad if it didn't stop. And still no one else besides Evan, herself, and members of the House of Auriano could hear it.

Through Evan's window, she could see Alessandro crouched on the rooftop across the canal. His shadowy form reassured her. Each night, he slipped into Evan's room. Never speaking, he stood over

Evan's bed and watched him sleep. After a few moments, he turned to her, and with a nod, slipped silently away. Despite their strained relationship, she appreciated his concern.

Each night, Sabrina watched the moon wane. Soon, Alessandro would transform into flesh and bone, and then he would suffer the Hunger. During that time, he would be unable to protect them, as he had promised. If Evan were well enough, that might be the perfect time to slip out of the city. She began to make small preparations.

On the sixth night of Evan's illness, Sabrina, dozing beside her son's bed, awoke to a warm tingly sensation.

Sabrina, she heard in her head.

Alessandro crouched before her. His fingers caressed her temple, and she realized his touch dampened the effects of the summoning spell. Relief from the constant throbbing escaped her lips in a sigh.

Does that help? he asked.

She nodded. The reprieve from the pain brought tears to her eyes.

He reached out and wiped a tear from her cheek. *Gasparo thought our connection and my touch might ease your suffering. I'm sorry we didn't think of this sooner.*

Her gaze traveled beyond his shoulder, to where Evan lay sleeping peacefully, the first time in many nights. "You helped Evan, too. Is the fever gone?" she asked.

No. I couldn't cure it, but I was able to give him some release from the spell.

"Thank you." She placed her fingers on his forehead. His eyes closed as her touch gave him some respite.

Grazie, he whispered. *It has been a long week, si?*

"*Si,*" she answered.

I have to go to the Canal of Shadows by daybreak. If you need anything, if there is any change in Evan's illness, send to the Ca'D'Este. Gasparo will be with me, but Piero will know what to do. His fingers slipped down over her cheek, to her neck, to her shoulder and down her arm. With his touch, the pain of the throbbing in her head seemed to be dragged out of her.

She wanted to do something for him in return for his kindness and his constant watch during her son's illness. Lifting her moonstone pendant over her head, she held it out to him. "Take this," she said. "You told me it cured Antonio's Hunger. It will help you, too."

He slipped the chain from her fingers and let the pendant dangle between them. The stone caught the faint moonlight and glowed with an internal iridescence. He let it fall into her lap.

With a shake of his head, he said, *You may need it more than I do.*

"But—" she began to protest.

He placed a finger across her lips. *Please, do not argue for this one time.* Standing, he whispered, *Stay safe for me, carissima.* He bent and kissed the corner of her mouth.

Sabrina watched him disappear through a window and dissolve into the other shadows of the night. The tingly warmth of his touch remained after he was gone.

Low in the sky, the moon was barely the width of a hair.

When morning came, the deep throbbing had stopped. And Evan was gone.

Sabrina raised the household and had everyone searching, inside the *casa* and out, up and down the canals, in every *sestiere* of the city. She sent a message to the Ca'D'Este, but received no response. Of course. Both Alessandro and Antonio were at the Canal of Shadows, one man turning to Shadow, the other turning to flesh and bone and enduring the effects of the Hunger. But Alessandro had told her Piero would get a message to him. Why hadn't he answered? Even Dunfield added his aid, although Sabrina knew Dunfield offered his assistance because Evan was an important bargaining chip. He knew she would do as he told her as long as he had control of her son, so finding Evan became a priority.

By midday, no one had discovered her son. No one in the city remembered seeing a child fitting his description. Evan had disappeared.

Sabrina sat at her dressing table with her head in her hands. Cora had finally coaxed her into freshening up and changing the clothes she had been wearing for the past several days, but Sabrina could only think of Evan, alone and frightened somewhere in the city.

"Where could he have gone, Cora?" Sabrina asked again. "He was so ill. How could he have risen from his sickbed and disappeared?"

Before Cora could answer, a knock came at the door. The girl went to answer and came back with a bouquet, a single dark red rose surrounded by reeds and tied with a black ribbon. Cora placed it on the dressing table and said, "From an admirer, it seems." She sniffed disdainfully.

Sabrina stared at the odd bouquet. It seemed more a token of mourning rather than an enticement from an admirer. An uneasy sense of foreboding seeped through her when she saw a small card tucked among the stems. Pulling it out, she read, *Come to me.* It was not signed.

From Alessandro? Was he attempting to seduce her as he endured the Hunger? How could he be so cruel? She crumpled the card and swept the bouquet onto the floor.

"I'll accept no further gifts, Cora," she said. "Please dress my hair quickly. I wish to be alone."

As soon as the girl had gone, Sabrina burst into tears. Her son was missing. The man she was in love with was cursed. If she did not marry him, her son would be in danger from Dunfield. If she wed him, she would be putting him in more danger than before. And an evil sorceress was trying to destroy her. She should have disappeared with Evan weeks ago.

Sabrina drew in a shuddery breath. Crying would not help. She wiped the tears from her cheeks and glanced down at the bouquet lying at her feet. Something about it nagged at her. It did not look like something the charming, seductive Prince of Auriano would send her, even if he were enduring the Hunger. Why tie it with a black ribbon? And why include ugly reeds?

And then she understood. It was a message. From Nulkana herself.

Sabrina went cold inside. The cessation of the throbbing and the disappearance of Evan had been no coincidence. Nulkana had been summoning her son.

The reeds indicated where the sorceress had her lair, for Alessandro had mentioned he had discovered it was somewhere among the canes of Cannaregio. The black ribbon could indicate Nulkana or perhaps her threat of what might become of Evan. And the red rose was Sabrina herself, surrounded by the reeds, unable to extricate herself from the trap Nulkana had set.

Come to me. The three words on the card were ominous. Nulkana had timed her trap perfectly. Neither Alessandro nor Antonio could help Sabrina. One was turning to Shadow; the other was enduring the worst of the curse. The sorceress had also used the perfect bait. She knew Sabrina would do anything to save her son's life, even give up her own.

Sabrina had to obey those words. Splashing water on her face, she washed away the remnants of her tears. She pulled a large, black lace mantle over her head and let it cover her face. The serviceable blue and gray muslin dress would help to keep her anonymous. The last thing she did was clasp her moonstone pendant. If it held any magic at all, she would need it.

She glanced down at her left hand and spread her fingers. The odd starburst that marked her as Halima's descendent had become darker and better defined. She curled her fingers into a fist. Her power thrummed down her arm. She told herself she could be as powerful as Nulkana. She would do everything she could to save her son. The sorceress would not get Evan or her without a fight.

Sabrina stood in the canes and stared out at the lagoon. Across the water on the mainland, thousands of men in blue uniforms were amassing along the shore. General Bonaparte had decided to invade Venice. But the threat of the French army seemed minor compared to the one that was emanating from a small, rundown shack in the middle of the canes near the water's edge. Sabrina knew, without a doubt, that Nulkana waited for her inside.

After pushing her way through the reeds, she stood before the door, hanging loosely on its hinges. She wondered why the sorceress would choose such a poor shield to hide behind. When she pushed it open, she saw only a deserted room, filled with cobwebs, dust, and the scattered, broken remains of simple chairs and a table.

She could sense the evil in the place, like a cold, wet mist on her skin. She eased inside. One step, then two. At her third step, she seemed to step through a veil. The room disappeared. Before her stood a pair of huge metal gates guarding a stone staircase which led down into the earth. The shack was only a disguise for Nulkana's lair.

Sabrina took a deep breath, then descended the stairs. At the bottom, she stared in awe. Before her was a cavernous chamber of black marble, lit by torches set into gold brackets. Several archways led to corridors that stretched away beneath the lagoon. Enormous columns held up the ceiling far above her. The space was out of proportion and she wondered how much was real and how much was illusion. She assumed only very powerful magic could have created such a place.

"I see you like my cozy cottage by the sea." Nulkana's voice came out of the deep shadows in one corner of the chamber.

As Sabrina strained to see her, the sorceress stepped into the light. She was tall and coldly, evilly beautiful. Her skin was white and her eyes black as obsidian. Blue-black hair flowed over her shoulders. Wearing a dark red garment reminiscent of ancient Greece or Rome, she moved with sinuous grace. By her side, holding her hand, was Evan, looking passive, pale, but cured of his fever.

"Evan!" Sabrina started forward to take him in her arms, but she bounced off some sort of invisible wall. Her son made no move of recognition.

"Not so fast," Nulkana warned. "Your son and I have not finished our business yet."

"Let him go," Sabrina said. "He is just a child."

"A child, yes, but a very special child." Nulkana smiled. "You see, I believe he will help me gain the piece of the Sphere of Astarte."

"He knows nothing about it." Sabrina groped for a way out of this trap.

"No, but you do."

"The piece of the Sphere has disappeared," Sabrina told her desperately. "No one knows where it is."

Nulkana nodded. "I thought you might say that, so I wished to provide you with a bit more incentive."

The sorceress gestured to one side of the room where a large cubic object about the size of a closet was covered with a cloth. As Sabrina glanced at it, the whole piece shuddered as if something inside had rammed the wall in an attempt at escape. A howl of agony, filled with desperation, brought tears to her eyes and echoed off the marble walls of the chamber.

Nulkana chuckled. "My visitor is not very happy."

With a flick of her hand, the cloth slipped off the object and revealed a glass box. Inside, in a dark corner, a naked man huddled, clutching his knees, his head bowed. He shivered violently as if he were ill. When he raised his head, Sabrina gasped.

"Alessandro!"

Slowly he turned his head. His gaze was blank as if he did not know her. His skin was deathly pale, and his eyes were red-rimmed, his face wracked with pain. As she watched, his form began to flicker. The edges of his body blurred. Suddenly, he was no longer flesh and bone, but Shadow. That molten gaze cleared. He stood, came to the wall of the box, and pressed his hand against it.

Sabrina, she heard in her head.

Once again, his form began to flicker, and seconds later, he was flesh. His body convulsed in pain. His head snapped back, and he howled in agony. He threw himself against one wall of the box, then another, back and forth. The whole cage shuddered. After several terrible moments, he weakened and slid down to huddle, shivering, on the floor.

"He tried to rescue the child." Nulkana chuckled. "He walked right into my trap."

"What have you done to him?" Sabrina demanded.

"I've done nothing to him," the sorceress said with a smirk. "He is enduring the Hunger, but without feeding any of his appetites." She shook her head sadly. "I'm afraid if he does not get what he needs…" Her words trailed off with a shrug.

Alessandro's torment made her heart ache. If only he had taken the moonstone as she had wanted. Somehow, she had to get the pendant to him, but that seemed impossible. The walls of the box appeared to be solid glass, except for a few tiny holes near the top. Perhaps, using her power, she could smash the box. But that still left Evan in Nulkana's clutches.

The sorceress stepped closer, raised her head, and sniffed. "So, the whelp has planted his seed in you." She turned her head and sniffed again. "Twins." Her mouth twisted in distaste.

"You know nothing," Sabrina snapped, hiding her shock at the sorceress's ability. Even she had not been sure if she were carrying Alessandro's child.

Nulkana's eyes flashed in annoyance. "Are you doubting me, slut?"

Sabrina blinked and fell back a step. "No, of course not." Her hand flattened protectively against her belly. Wistfully, her gaze turned to the glass box, where Alessandro was holding his head and rocking in agony. She couldn't let him die. Even if she did not marry him, he had a right to see his children. And she wanted that for him very much.

"You are wondering how to help our tortured prince," Nulkana said. "There is a way, but you will have to be very quick. I'm afraid he does not have much longer."

"What about my son?" Sabrina willed Evan to look at her, show some sign of recognition, but he seemed to look right through her.

"We will see how well you complete your task." As she spoke, the sorceress drew Evan before her and placed her hands on his shoulders. "He is quite an intelligent child. Perhaps I will keep him as an apprentice."

Fear shafted through Sabrina's heart. She would do anything to keep Evan from the sorceress and keep Alessandro alive. "What do you want me to do?"

"I want you to bring me the piece of the Sphere of Astarte."

Chapter 29

With her heart pounding and anxiety ripping through her, Sabrina hurried through the streets and alleys, and across bridges spanning the canals until she came to the street entrance to Dunfield's *casa*. Her steps faltered on the threshold of the wide-open door. In the *andron* beyond, servants were building crates and carrying artwork down the stairs. Boxes were being loaded onto a ship's tender tied to a pole next to the water steps. Evidently, Dunfield considered his artwork more important than searching the city for Evan, despite using her son to force her to wed Alessandro. She had no time to ponder his motives. If she did not return to the lair of the sorceress soon, there would be no Alessandro to wed.

She needed to get in and out of the house without being seen. Nulkana had been very adamant that Sabrina should complete her task alone. Hoping no one would take notice of her, she slipped in through the door and made her way to her bedchamber.

But when she entered, panic shot through her. The ancient, carved box was gone. Sabrina searched the room, but no box. As she turned from clawing through her wardrobe, she was startled to see Dunfield standing in the doorway.

"Sabrina," he snapped, "where have you been?"

Gathering her composure, she said coolly, "Isn't it obvious? I was out searching for Evan." She wondered how soon she could escape from him.

He scowled. "You should not be out wandering the city alone. You should have told me where you were going."

"I thought you were organizing the search from here," she said. "I didn't wish to disturb you, but my concern, it seems, is unfounded. I see you have abandoned the search for Evan."

"Only temporarily." His gaze slid away to the window before he spoke again. "I have learned something that is more alarming."

"More alarming than the disappearance of your bargaining chip?" she scoffed. "It must be frightening, indeed."

"Despite our differences, Sabrina, I do not wish to see any harm come to you," he said, concern wrinkling his brow.

Sabrina noted how easily the lies slipped from his lips. "Of course not. Then you would lose your connection to the House of Auriano."

Anger flashed across his face, but he quelled it quickly. Wandering into the room, he stared down at her dressing table.

"Your son's disappearance is quite odd," he finally said. "How could a child, on a sickbed for six days, suddenly rise and run away?"

Desperate to be rid of him, she fought to keep calm. "Who knows how a child's mind works? But I am sure that Evan is frightened and lonely. I am leaving now to continue my search for him, so if you will excuse me..." She tried to move past him, but he grabbed her arm.

"I'm wondering if you have not secreted the child someplace in the city and are planning to run away," he said, tightening his grip.

She laughed, hiding her alarm that he might have discovered her intent. "Run away to where? I have no place to go, and I have no wealth to get me there. As you can see, the single valuable piece I own is still there, on my dressing table." Gesturing to the table, she indicated Alessandro's gold chain spilling out of its painted box. "I am still very much your chattel, Uncle."

He stared at her a moment, dropped her arm, then smiled coldly. "Yes, you are. But I wonder why you came back when you could have easily escaped."

She frowned but said nothing.

"Perhaps, you came back for this." He placed the ancient carved box on her dressing table.

She had been too naive, and never should have left it in plain view. Staring at the box, she wondered how she could get it away from him.

"Perhaps you have discovered where the piece of the Sphere is hidden," he suggested silkily.

She frowned as if puzzled. "Of course I haven't."

"Then why were you searching so frantically for the box?" His tone was calm, but his gaze froze her with his fury.

Fortifying herself with a breath, she said, "Why do you think I was searching for *that*?" She dismissed the box with a wave of her hand. "I was looking for my parasol."

"Interesting that you should be searching for such an item," he murmured, "when the sun is hidden by rain clouds."

She turned to look out the window. When she did, she saw one of the *cappo neri*, hidden in shadow across the canal and watching the *casa*. Was the spy watching Dunfield or her? She could not spare the time to worry about that now. She gave a false little laugh as she turned back to Dunfield. "Oh, how silly of me. Of course, it is about to rain."

"You are not silly at all and never have been. Do not lie to me, Sabrina." His tone flatly threatened.

When she said nothing, he picked up the box and headed for the door. "Fine. Remain silent. You will stay locked in your room until you decide to tell me the truth." Stopping in the doorway, he turned to her. "And do not think you can escape by the window, for my servants will be watching."

The thought of being locked in, unable to save either Evan or Alessandro, panicked her. She had to return to Nulkana's lair soon. And she had to bring the box to trick Nulkana into believing she had brought the piece of the Sphere. Just before Dunfield closed the door, she called to him.

"Wait."

He pushed the door wide.

Desperate, she realized that her only option was to tell him the truth. "It's Nulkana," she said. "The sorceress has both Evan and Auriano. If I don't bring her the box—" Her voice broke and she was unable to go on.

"Why should I be concerned about either of them? Your son is a nuisance I've had to accommodate, and Auriano…" He shrugged.

Hearing Evan and Alessandro dismissed so brutally angered her, but she needed to keep calm in order to get that box. "I thought you wanted Evan back to keep me here because you craved a connection to the House of Auriano."

"'Craved' is rather too strong a word. If Auriano happens to die at the hands of Nulkana, I would not mourn his loss. I never liked the man. There are other powerful men in Venice who would enjoy access to your charms."

She straightened her spine. "You'll not use me like that."

Dunfield laughed. "No? What will you do, Sabrina? You have no other choices."

Something snapped inside her at his cold dismissal of Evan and Alessandro and his idea to use her so ruthlessly. Recklessly, she said, "Is that how you used my father? By threatening him?"

Surprise lifted his brows. "Your father?" He chuckled, a cold, mean sound. "Your father, my dear Sabrina, was a spy for the House of Auriano. We fed him useless, false information. I would have eliminated him if he had not died on his own."

Sabrina gaped as she tried to absorb his words. "A spy?" she repeated. Relief poured through her. Her father was not a member of the Legion of Baal. He had been working against them. That meant she had no connection to them. Instead, her connection had been to the House of Auriano, to Alessandro. Hysterical laughter bubbled up. She clapped her hand over her mouth to hold it in.

Dunfield looked at her as if she had gone mad. Perhaps she had. Because tears followed on the heels of her laughter, tears of regret that she had not known her father well enough to understand what he was doing, and tears of frustration and fear that she was wasting time while Evan and Alessandro were in such danger. She decided to use those tears to convince Dunfield that she had given up.

"You are very clever, Uncle. I could not possibly outwit you." She sniffed pathetically and wiped away a tear. "Please, let me bring the box to Nulkana. Help me save Auriano. Think of how grateful he would be to you for saving his life. Then, when we are wed, I could be your spy."

His eyes narrowed in crafty contemplation. "You always did have your uses, Sabrina," he said. "Where is the sorceress?"

Sabrina was not about to give away the only bit of information that would guarantee her release from the *casa*. "I have to show you."

Suspicion filled his gaze, then he gave a curt nod. "Very well. Go direct the servants packing up the artwork."

"But—"

"Do as I say, Sabrina. You will take me to Nulkana later. The French are about to invade the city. If I do not move the pieces now, they will plunder everything."

"God forbid you should lose the artwork to the French," she muttered.

"Get downstairs, Sabrina, and make yourself useful," he snapped. "And remember that I am holding this." Showing her the box, he turned on his heel.

Sabrina's mind raced. She had to get back to Nulkana. Alone. And she had to bring that box. Time was running out for both Alessandro and Evan. She could not afford to waste a minute. She had to use her power, she had no choice.

Bringing up her hand, she sent a small blast at Dunfield's back. He grunted and spun to face her.

"Do you really believe you can use your puny power on me?" Arrogant amusement crossed his face.

Sabrina was not about to argue with him. "Give me the box, Uncle, or I will hurt you." She raised her hand in threat.

"Your intimidation won't work, Sabrina. This protects me." Lifting his arm, he pulled back his sleeve to reveal the glyph of a frog tattooed on his wrist.

Hiding her revulsion at seeing the glyph, she scoffed, "How can a picture of a frog protect you?"

"If you don't believe me, use your power," he taunted with a cruel smile.

Unsure of what he might be able to do, she was desperate enough to take up his challenge. She sent a surge of power at him. It bounced off the glyph and shattered a vase.

Dunfield sneered. "You see? Your power is useless. Just like your mother's before you. You are only good for recharging the Crystal Dagger and a means for me to gain a connection to an influential family. I will hold the box until the artwork is crated," he said. "Now get downstairs." He stalked away.

Humiliated and angered by his casual dismissal of her and her mother, frustrated that she was forced to do his bidding, she left her bedchamber and descended the stairs. She hated him, but he held the box, the key to freeing Evan and Alessandro. She hoped the task of crating the artwork would not take long. As she turned to instruct one of the men how to place an ancient Greek statuette in the packing material, she wondered if she could get a message to that *cappo neri* across the canal. She would wager Alessandro's gold chain that the spy would be very interested to learn exactly what Dunfield was attempting to do.

They traveled through the canals in silence. As they left the *casa*, Sabrina was disappointed to see the *cappo neri* had disappeared. She tasted blood from gnawing her bottom lip. Fear that she would be too late, that the sorceress would have already turned her son, that Alessandro would not have survived the Hunger, tightened her muscles, made her hands shake. Dunfield, in possession of the box, kept his cold gaze fixed on her. She wondered if he thought she might jump over the side of the gondola and try to escape.

As soon as the gondola touched land, Sabrina bounded out and ran through the reeds. Dunfield followed more slowly. She entered the shack, walked through the veil, and started down the stairway. When she reached the bottom, the sorceress was nowhere in sight. Evan sat on the floor and played with some vials filled with various colored liquids. He did not even raise his head to look at her. Alessandro sat shivering, head bowed, huddled in a corner of the box. A sheen of sweat covered him, and his breathing was labored. He flickered into Shadow, but his form was paler, misty, less defined.

She had to get Evan away from those vials, and she had to get Alessandro out of that box.

Raising his head, Alessandro stood and placed his hand flat against the glass. *I'm sorry, carissima. I tried to protect Evan.* A weak caress gently trailed through her mind. The sad sweetness of it brought tears to her eyes.

"I know," she whispered. "I'm going to get you out." After learning of her father's connection to the House of Auriano and seeing

Alessandro's suffering, she realized how wrong she had been to reject him. He had always cared for her, protected her. Despite his secrets, she should have trusted her heart. She should have trusted *him,* but instead she had let her fears guide her. She would not let fear cloud her judgment again. She would do everything she could to save him. She pressed her hand opposite his on the glass and sent him an encouraging smile. Then she turned to her son.

She approached Evan cautiously, uncertain how much control Nulkana had over him. He poured a vial of colorless liquid into another. The mixture popped and flashed. A bilious green fog rose before him. It swirled, forming into a serpent with a forked tail and horrid fangs dripping with venom. Evan's eyes widened. His face paled. The serpent hissed and undulated, towering over her small son. He scrambled back and came up hard against one of the pillars.

Sabrina jumped forward to distract the monster. "Here!" she yelled.

It swung its great, triangular head around and fastened its hypnotic, yellow gaze on her. She had never seen anything so hideously evil. In spite of her determination, fear paralyzed her.

A knife rose from the worktable, flew through the air, and sliced through the monster. The apparition disappeared in a puff.

I won't let anything harm Evan, she heard in her head.

When she turned to Alessandro, she saw he had grown paler. A ragged, gray edge surrounded his shadowy form. Those molten eyes did not glow quite so brightly. She sent him a wave and grabbed Evan's hand.

No recognition reached her son's eyes. He looked through her as if focused on someone else.

"Evan," she said quietly and brushed his hair back from his forehead. He still did not respond. Her heart twisted in her chest. "It's Mama. You have been very brave." She kissed his cheek. His skin was icy beneath her lips. She cupped his face in her hands, trying to warm him. "Evan, darling, it's time to go home."

His cheeks began to warm with her touch, and slowly, his eyes cleared. "Mama!" Throwing himself at her, he clung to her and sobbed.

Sabrina had very little time. Nulkana might return at any moment. She hugged her son, calming him. "Evan, you have to be very brave for just a little longer. We have to get Alessandro out of the glass box."

Evan glanced at Alessandro, then said, "The lady said the glass couldn't be broken. It was made with magic. Is Sandro going to die?" Fearful anxiety drew a line between his brows.

Sabrina smiled calmly despite her apprehension. "No," she said, "we're going to save him. I have magic, too."

She turned to the glass box and threw her power to the middle of the sheer side. As it hit, it dissipated in a burst of jagged light but left the glass unharmed. Alessandro motioned for her to try again.

The second attempt accomplished nothing. Neither did the third. Frustration and desperation brought her nearly to tears. She had to get Alessandro free.

Take a breath, carissima, Alessandro said calmly. *You can do this.*

She did as he suggested and tried a fourth time. Finally, on the fifth try, a tiny chink appeared.

Then, from behind her, she heard Nulkana say, "Very impressive, for someone with such weak power."

Swinging about, Sabrina saw the sorceress standing not far away. Beyond her was that robed, hooded figure they had seen on the Lido.

Nulkana chuckled. "Did you really believe that you could break through my magic, girl?"

"Please, let him go," Sabrina begged. Alessandro's periods of human form were getting shorter while his time as Shadow was longer.

"Did you bring me the piece of the Sphere?" Nulkana asked.

"Is this what you want, witch?" Dunfield stepped off the bottom stair and held up the ancient casket.

Hatred twisted Nulkana's face. "Give it to me," she hissed and raised her hand to shoot her power at him.

Laughing, Dunfield pulled back his sleeve to reveal the frog glyph. "I'm protected by Baal."

Nulkana's eyes slitted and she lowered her arm. "What do you want?"

"A bargain. I will not tell the members of the Legion where to find you, and you will help me search for the other pieces of the Sphere." He sauntered closer to the sorceress.

Sabrina pushed Evan behind her and backed away. She doubted Dunfield was powerful enough to defeat Nulkana, or he would have confronted her before now. And the Crystal Dagger was in the hands of the French general.

The sorceress laughed. "Foolish man. Do you think I need your help to hide from the Legion of Baal?"

She shot out a stream of energy. Dunfield threw up his arm. The glyph on his wrist deflected the blast to the wall where a hole exploded.

"You will need my help once I tell the Legion where you are, witch," he said.

"Do you think I cannot create another safe place?"

Nulkana hurled another blast of energy at him. He bounced it away. A chair shattered.

Sabrina eased back farther. Taking advantage of their battle, she threw her own power at Alessandro's glass prison. The tiny chink she had created burst into a spider web of cracks, but the glass did not shatter. Still Shadow, Alessandro had no weight to use against it for pressure. He remained trapped.

Sabrina's use of her power drew Nulkana's attention. The sorceress threw a warning flash of power at her. It hit the floor only a few feet away. Sabrina felt the impact like thousands of needles stabbing her feet and legs. Pulling Evan with her, she ducked behind a massive pillar as another explosion echoed through the chamber.

"You will not defeat me!" Nulkana yelled.

Dunfield laughed.

Cowering behind the pillar, Sabrina huddled Evan close to her, trying to make them as small as possible. The air pulsed with energy as Nulkana threw blast after blast at Dunfield. Dust rained down on them and debris flew. Sabrina flinched at each explosion, but Evan sat quietly, barely reacting to the noise, the danger. Something was wrong about his calm, but another blast of energy, this time brighter than the others, distracted her. The air hissed and prickled along Sabrina's skin. Dunfield cried out. She peeked around the pillar.

He held one arm against his chest, his hand still clutching the wooden box. The sleeve of his coat was blackened and hanging in tatters, and beneath, his skin was raw, blistered, and bleeding. His glance landed on the knife that had killed the serpent, and he scooped it up.

"Bitch!" he shouted and threw the dagger.

Nulkana waved her hand and the weapon disintegrated midair in a burst of metallic dust. She laughed. "You pathetic little man. You and your silly frog can't compete with me." With a casual flick of her wrist, she sent a blinding burst at him.

He threw up his wrist, but the blast cut through his arm, severing it, and hit him squarely in the chest. He sailed backward through the air and landed high against the wall with a sickening crack, then slowly slipped down to the floor, like a puppet cut loose from its strings. His head tilted at an unnatural angle. His eyes stared, unseeing, at the ceiling.

The ancient carved box had come to rest only a few feet away from where Sabrina and Evan hid. She needed to grab that box. But Nulkana was in a rage. And Sabrina had to protect Evan, who huddled, trembling, next to her.

"Come out, little girl," the sorceress called.

An energy blast smacked into the floor inches from where Sabrina and Evan were hiding. A crackle of energy skipped painfully across her skin. Evan clung tighter. Her power was no match for the sorceress, but she had to do something.

From where she crouched, she could see Alessandro in his glass prison. He flickered back to human form, then to Shadow once more. Time was running out for him. She would not—could not—lose him. She had been such a fool. She should have trusted him and gone to stay at Ca' D'Este where Evan would have been safe and protected. Desperate, Sabrina threw her power at his prison once more. The glass exploded. She slipped the moonstone pendant over her head and tossed it to him. As it flew through the air, Nulkana blasted it. The stone exploded into three pieces that skittered in different directions across the floor.

In the confusion, Evan slipped away from her and ran to collect the box.

"No, Evan!" she cried, as she chased after him into the open.

She felt the blast coming at her. Time slowed to a crawl. Each second seemed to last an hour.

Evan picked up the box.

Sabrina grabbed him, covered him with her body.

A shadowy Alessandro floated through the air. He threw himself in front of her.

The blast ripped through Alessandro.

He fell at her feet.

"Alessandro!" she screamed.

Grief and anger washed through Sabrina. She shot upright. She remembered her mother, how she had died protecting her. Now Alessandro lay before her, another victim of Nulkana. She would not let the sorceress win. She would not let Nulkana have her son. Her motherly instinct to protect her child rose through her and filled her up. It thrummed through her.

"You evil bitch!" she shouted. "It ends here!"

She channeled every bit of anger and hatred she felt toward the malevolent sorceress. It filled her like a great fountain of power. She raised her arms and felt the rush beneath her skin. And then she unleashed it. A great blast of energy surged from her palms.

The bolt hit Nulkana squarely in the chest. She howled in agony and doubled over, clutching her middle. Black blood oozed through her fingers.

"This is not finished, little girl," Nulkana snarled.

With a twist of her hand, a dark void opened behind her. She stepped back and disappeared.

Silence enveloped the cavern like a pall. Sabrina stood very still, afraid the sorceress might return. At her feet, Alessandro's shadow lay unmoving, a hole punched through his chest, those golden, molten eyes closed forever. Evan huddled on the floor and clutched the box.

A movement out of the corner of her eye drew her attention. It was that dark robed, hooded figure. It stared at Alessandro's prone figure, and somehow, she sensed it felt great sorrow. It turned in Evan's direction and seemed to communicate with him, for her son gave a nod. Then the figure was jerked back into the void and disappeared. With a pop, the void was gone.

Sabrina collapsed to her knees beside Alessandro. Her heart was breaking. She felt as if Nulkana had ripped a hole in her chest like the one in Alessandro's.

Gently, she touched his cheek. She felt no warm tingle. She felt nothing, as if the vibrant energy of his being was gone. She did not care about his curse. All she cared about was that she had lost him. She had pushed him away, and now he was gone.

"No," she whispered. "Alessandro, please, you can't be dead. Please." She bent over him, wrapped her arms around his ethereal form, even though she felt as if she were hugging air. "Please, Alessandro," she begged, desperate. "I love you."

But she was too late to tell him. He would never hear her.

"Mama." Evan's voice intruded on her pain.

She turned to him, noticing the strange calm in his eyes. Unable to speak, she hugged him with one arm and draped the other across Alessandro's inert form, holding close the two most precious people in her life. One alive and safe. One now dead.

"Mama." Evan tugged on her sleeve.

"What is it, Evan?" She couldn't understand why her son was so calm about losing his friend.

Without a word, the boy opened the box. He held his hand over the empty interior and mumbled a rhyme. Sabrina only caught a few words: "bright… night… show… glow." Something shimmered. Slowly, the missing piece of the Sphere materialized inside the box. It was just as she remembered, made of amber, dusty, dull, and looking as if it should be connected to another piece. Evan held it out to her.

"I'm sorry, Mama," he said, looking guilty. "I made it disappear, and then couldn't remember how to bring it back."

Astonished, she asked, "You made this disappear? How?"

Evan hung his head. "I made up a rhyming spell. I'm sorry."

"How did you remember how to undo it?"

"The man in the black robe helped me," he said.

Astounded that her son had magical power, mystified by the identity of the robed figure, Sabrina sadly took the piece from him. How ironic that now Alessandro was dead, she would be able to give him what he had sought his whole life. At least Antonio would benefit.

"Mama," Evan said, a bit impatiently. He took her hand holding the piece of the Sphere and pushed it down so it rested against Alessandro.

As soon as it touched his body, the piece glowed as if lit from the inside. Tiny lights swirled around her hand. Where the piece of the Sphere touched Alessandro, the faint appearance of skin emerged, replacing Shadow. The whirl of lights grew wider. That spot of skin became clearer and bigger. It reached the hole blasted through him by Nulkana. The lights danced and pulsed inside and around the wound. It closed up, fully healed. The swirling lights surrounded his whole body. They grew brighter, swirled faster. They lifted his shadow from the floor, spinning around him. Slowly, his shadow became fully flesh and bone. His body slowly floated to the floor. The whirling lights faded and died.

The piece of the Sphere had returned him to human form.

He lay before her perfect, beautiful, but cold. No breath. No heartbeat. He was still dead.

Sabrina's heart ached as if a piece had been sliced away. She reached out and touched his cheek. A pulse of energy, like a single heartbeat, radiated from the piece of the Sphere. It shimmered through his body, then was gone.

Alessandro gasped, filling his lungs, breathing.

He opened his eyes.

Sabrina cried out. Hoping, but afraid she was seeing an illusion.

Alessandro's golden gaze landed on her. He smiled.

"*Tesoro mio,*" he said. My treasure.

"Are you real?" she whispered, hugging the piece of the Sphere to her like a lifeline.

He held up his hand and examined it. "I think so." He turned to Evan. "Do I look real to you?"

Evan nodded solemnly.

Unconvinced, not wanting to be deceived by an illusion, Sabrina remained tightly huddled, her hands fisted against her chest.

"Give me your hand, Sabrina," he said.

Hesitantly, she opened one hand and placed it in his. His flesh was warm. He drew her hand to his lips and placed a kiss on her palm. The feel of his lips was warm and delicious. Then he pressed her hand against his chest. The strong rhythm of his heart beat beneath her fingers. Relief, gratitude, and hope filled her. Her emotions welled up inside her and spilled out as tears that streamed down her cheeks. Even if she could never have him, just knowing that Alessandro was alive in the world was enough.

"You saved my life," he said.

"You saved mine and Evan's," she replied. Then the enormity of what he had done hit her in a rush of anger. "Do you think you are invincible, Excellency? Just because you heal quicker and better than most human men does not mean you are immortal. Don't ever do that again."

His eyes widened. A confounded little smile twisted his lips. "I'll try not to."

"Promise me." She scowled at him and tried to look stern.

"Why should I do that?" he taunted.

"Because—" She stopped. She knew the answer to his question. Saying the words aloud meant admitting to him what he had been telling her all along—that they were connected in many, many ways, including the most important one. Heat rose in her cheeks. She took a breath. "Because I love you."

Solemnly, silently, he gazed at her. She thought perhaps she had made a mistake. Embarrassment, disappointment, hurt made her glance away.

"Sabrina." He captured her attention once again. "I would give my life for you a thousand times if I could." His hand pressed hers more firmly against his chest. "You have my heart, *amore*."

Awed by his statement, she drew a shaky breath, unable to do more.

"May I ask you a question?" he said.

Shyly, she looked into those golden eyes. "Yes."

"Will you marry me?"

She gasped at the ramifications of that question.

He had asked her.

To marry him.

Laughing and crying, this time with tears of joy, she gave him her answer. "Yes."

Epilogue

Four weeks later

Alessandro led the way down the narrow old stone steps. He ignored the cobwebs that snagged on his white satin coat embroidered in gold. The torch he held illuminated the passage carved out of solid rock. With his other hand, he guided Sabrina, who clutched the ancient carved casket containing the piece of the Sphere of Astarte. Antonio trailed her and carried a second torch. Ahead of them, beyond the flickering light, was only darkness, but he knew what lay at the end of this descent into the bowels of the earth.

Behind them, the open portal framed bright sunshine. Through the door, he could hear sounds of merrymaking, a celebration of the people of Auriano in honor of his marriage to his new bride, the Lady Sabrina Barclay. She was Sabrina D'Este now, Princess of Auriano. Still a bit befuddled by the whole experience, he glanced at Sabrina. She looked like a beautiful fairy princess out of some fanciful tale in her yellow silk and gauze gown and crown of white lilies and oleander. But he knew she was no illusion. The warmth in her eyes and the teasing smile on her lips convinced him he was not dreaming.

"If the two of you keep staring at each other like lovesick puppies, we're never going to get this done," Tonio complained.

Too happy to be riled, Alessandro grinned at his brother, dressed in a midnight blue velvet coat trimmed in gold braid and matching breeches, then he turned to Sabrina. "Tonio wishes he could find a woman who would make him happy for the rest of his life."

With a sound of annoyance, his twin said, "Tonio wants to sample the wine and investigate the charms of *Signore* Pastore's youngest daughter. She appears to have grown up since the last time I was here."

"Just remember the black eye you received when you dallied with his eldest daughter," Alessandro reminded him.

"How was I to know she had practiced fisticuffs with her brothers?" Tonio grumbled. Laughing, Alessandro continued the descent.

After several minutes, they emerged into a small circular cavern. It lay far below the Castello Auriano. The two men placed their torches into brackets on the wall, then turned to the center of the space. A large, round, flat stone, too large for even twenty men to move, lay in the middle of the floor. The two brothers positioned themselves on opposite sides of the stone.

Alessandro gazed at Antonio. He and his twin had been flesh and bone at the same time during the day since Sabrina had placed the piece of the Sphere against him. Only at night did Alessandro revert back to Shadow as the moon waned. Part of the curse had been broken. They would have to wait to see if finding the piece of the Sphere also affected Antonio.

The only cloud hanging over them was the effect on Evan of having been under Nulkana's influence. Occasionally, his eyes would become unfocused and glazed, and a strange glint would appear in them. He would seem to be in another world. Gasparo was working with him to try to counteract Nulkana's control. Alessandro hoped that what they were about to do would also help.

With a nod at his brother, Alessandro held his hands over the round stone. Antonio mirrored him. Closing his eyes, he concentrated on the rock. He sensed Antonio doing the same. With great mental effort, he lifted, and slowly, the stone shifted, floated up, and then sideways, finally settling with a thud on the cavern floor. The rock beneath where the stone had lain appeared just the same as the rest of the floor, but Alessandro knew it was not. With one hand outstretched over the space, he walked in a counterclockwise circle. A round spot in the paving stones turned, following his movement. With a flick of his hand, he opened a vault carved into the bedrock of the cavern. It was lined in gold, and in its center was an intricately fashioned golden pedestal. It had been created to hold something globular — the assembled Sphere of Astarte.

Sabrina opened the casket holding the piece of the Sphere, took it out, and handed it to Alessandro. Taking it, he knelt on one knee and placed it on the pedestal. Then he stood back and waited.

Nothing happened for a space of five heartbeats, for a space of ten. He sensed Antonio's disappointment, Sabrina's concern. His own hope began to waver. They had all been so sure that returning at least a part of the Sphere to Auriano would have some effect, that once again its heartbeat would be perceived in the land.

He felt Sabrina's hand slip into his. Then she squeezed it in excitement. He saw what she saw. The piece of the Sphere had begun to glow. It was no longer a dusty old thing, but a beautiful, rich, translucent amber, emitting an inner light. Mesmerized, he watched the light grow stronger. The piece pulsed. A single ripple billowed out and away, flowing through them, beyond them, disappearing into the rock around them. The sound of a single heartbeat reverberated in the stone.

Alessandro gasped as he felt the energy trickle through him. Hearing Antonio's echoing gasp, he knew their efforts had been worthwhile. The power of the Sphere of Astarte would begin to heal Auriano, and perhaps, break the curse on all of them.

As Sabrina slipped her arm about his waist and he pulled her close, he met Antonio's gaze.

It's begun, Sandro, Tonio said silently.

Alessandro gave a nod. *Si. Now, it's your turn.*

About Patricia Barletta

Patricia Barletta is an award-winning author of historical and paranormal romance fiction. After a fulfilling career teaching English Literature in high school, she decided to go back to school herself, and obtained a Master of Fine Arts in Creative Writing at Stonecoast (University of Southern Maine). When she's not at a yoga class doing her best downward dog, Patricia is usually tending her hydrangeas or hosting a brunch for her writing group. Patricia loves to travel, and often finds the inspiration for her dark heroes, feisty heroines, and romantic settings while on a research trip. At the end of each journey she loves going home to her cozy, historical old house outside of Boston where she weaves her magical tales.

Find out more about Patricia and her books on her website: patriciabarletta.com and on facebook.

www.ingramcontent.com/pod-product-compliance
Lightning Source LLC
Chambersburg PA
CBHW030404180626
46812CB00005B/1924